THE
AWFUL
TRUTH
Caroline

Book II

I0587026

Gerry & Sam Conrad

Copyright © 2023 Gerry and Sam Conrad

Library of Congress Control Number: 2023918883

ISBN   978-0-9758710-4-1
eBook ISBN   978-0-9758710-5-8

Cover design by Gerry and Sam Conrad
Eve artwork by Gerry Conrad

First Edition

Other books by Gerry and Sam Conrad

The Awful Truth ~ Dawn Book I

The Storm

*W*hen I woke this morning, I knew I had been dreaming, but all that remained were words I repeated to myself in my half-awakened, half-conscious state.

When the storm comes:
  Some will deny its existence and go on with their lives.
  Some will see the storm but decide it's not about them.
  Some will see the storm and believe they can't stop it, so they don't try.
  Some will experience the storm, acknowledge it, and accept it.
  Some will fight the storm and try to defeat it.
  Some people are the storm.

Eve

Chapter 1

My heart pounds faster as if it's about to burst from my chest. I stumble and trip, ripping my white dress on a thorny bush. A young Tommy Miller yells, "Hurry! Caroline, run. Time is running out!" The Tracker is closing in on me, so close his hot breath prickles my neck. He wants my Gift and will kill to get it. I scream but make no sound. I can't tell how far behind he is, but I dare not look back. When he touches my shoulder, I shriek and open my eyes.

It's still dark, but I'm awake now. The rapid pounding in my chest subsides, and I sigh in relief. I'm nestled in my closet-size room at Cavalry, under the protection of the Peace Force, unwitting agents of the Overlords, trapped deep in the confines of my enemy's realm. But safe for the moment. The glimmering red fluorescent numbers on my digital clock display 00:01:59—1/1/ 2100. I swear I just fell asleep. In times like this, I hate sleeping alone.

When I emerged from the cave over ten years ago, I had an oversized white dress and a backpack, but no memory. I had the Knowing and believed, without doubt, that the road heading west would lead to my destiny. What caused my amnesia? Did the Gift hide my past from me, hoping to send me to the Overlords complex, like a lamb to slaughter? I need Caroline's memories now, more than ever. Tommy Miller warned me time is running out.

How long before the Tracker finds me? There must be someone out there to help me, but I can't remember who. Caroline's memories hold the answers, but that period of my life remains locked in my subconscious. The alien bounty hunter is bound to search our bases eventually, so I'm desperate to uncover Caroline's secrets.

My heart rate slows down now, but this latest nightmare prevents me from falling asleep, so instead, I concentrate on visualizing the secluded cabin I rented to sequester myself for my first rebirthing. The only event I recall after my rebirth occurred years later when I encountered Jade and his alliance.

As if it were yesterday, I remember my trip to the cottage where I prepared for rejuvenation, but that memory ended when I curled up on the bed and closed my eyes. My apprehension was not as intense as my determination. The Gift had kept me healthy and strong, but the Knowing gave me the understanding that I had the ability to rejuvenate. I had lived with my false teeth, droopy body parts, and thin gray hair for far too long and welcomed the chance to become young again. It was a gamble, the outcome unpredictable, but I accepted the risk. Fate would decide.

Relaxed, floating on the edge of consciousness, I visualize the bedroom. The faded patchwork quilt draped over an old rocking chair. A quaint four-poster bed was covered with a well-worn cream-colored bedspread, embroidered with ruby-red roses, bluebells, and twisting fern-green vines. Two fluffy pillows with clean white ruffled pillowcases rested against the dark oak headboard flaunting a huge acorn carving in its center. A full-length, free-standing mirror flanked the matching stressed antique oak dresser. Sunshine poured in the modest window, with its tied-back lace curtains and view of glorious fall foliage.

The memory of stirring from a deep sleep floods my mind as if it happened yesterday. I stretched like a lazy cat awakening from her nap, disoriented, but unconcerned. Sunlight flooded the bedroom, warming my naked body, but its brilliance blinded me, so I squeezed my eyelids shut and turned to face the wall. When I reopened them, I studied the pink paisley floral wallpaper while adjusting to the light. I slipped out of bed and stood, a little wobbly at first, but I felt an immense sense of relief that I made it.

As it was my initial rebirthing experience, I didn't know what to expect. The cabin looked unchanged, except for the bedcovers, now damp and musty, peppered with unknown shredded and shriveled matter smeared into the ripped bedspread. A faint odd smell, like decaying leaves, scented the air. I held my breath and rushed to the full-length mirror to see what I'd become.

Thick, dark amber brown hair replaced my thin gray strands and hung almost to my waist. My wrinkles, sagging jowls, and stretch-marked belly rolls vanished and the face staring back at me was similar to my younger self, but different enough. I stood taller, sporting a darker complexion. I don't look like that woman now except for a slight resemblance.

Flecks of the withered substance clung to my smooth, youthful form, and a thin white pasty film covered parts of me. After cleaning myself in the bathroom sink, I stripped the mattress of its soiled bedding and bunched it into a ball.

I wondered how long I slept. Hours, days, or longer? When I arrived at the cabin, the trees displayed bright orange and red hues, but when I awoke, brown leaves blanketed the ground. I left my cell phone behind when I started my travels. It would have shown me the date. I also trashed any traceable form of identification. I retrieved my suitcase, which I had stashed next to the bed. It held a stockpile of cash, hidden in a secret compartment under several changes of clothes.

When I considered a new name, my cherished childhood friend, Caroline, came to mind. Our life journeys took us on deviating paths, and we lost touch as adults. Decades later, I discovered she passed from lung cancer. Pleasant memories of our close teenage friendship stuck with me. We got into mischief together, kept each other's secrets, and pined for the day when we could leave home to follow our dreams. Although troubled, she was tough and fearless, with traits I'd need to survive. So, in her memory....

Regeneration allowed me to alter my appearance—to become this much younger version of myself, providing a perfect disguise for evading the next alien Tracker. He was hunting a shorter, pale-white, gray-haired, wrinkled, eighty-year-old woman. Still, it was risky to appear as a twenty-year-old with the Captors abducting young women.

Before starting the rebirthing process, I avoided the burden of monthly inconvenience by choosing to continue my post-menopausal infertility. If I ever gave birth again, someday I'd outlive my children or need to leave them. I loved my precious offspring, and the thought of losing or leaving another child was unbearable. Protecting them from capture and assimilation would prove challenging. It's difficult enough keeping myself safe and the Gift out of the Overlords' hands.

It was well known my enemies were building detention camps we now refer to as bases, but I hadn't encountered one yet. Television news reported unusual construction sites spotted in several locations, globally. That was before we lost satellite communications.

In 2030, the world in which I grew up was disintegrating before my eyes, with pandemics, wars, famines, droughts, floods, and terrorists threatening democracy. Each year brought more disasters and terror. After warning my family to abandon city life and find refuge wherever they could, I escaped to the mountains, leaving everything I knew behind. I prayed for my loved ones, but I couldn't save them. The powerful Gift had its limitations, and I understood my mission.

The isolated mountain cabin, hidden from the main highway, was located a few miles from a small town where I had stopped for food and supplies. There, an elderly couple kindly leased the hideaway to me for the summer. I was still driving my timeworn Chevy, although it meant taking a chance. Rebecca Daniels held the title, the mature gray-haired woman who rented the lodge, not the young Caroline with no driver's license.

After rejuvenation, I hid in the cabin for a few weeks before I left to start over. I traveled unnoticed by the Overlords by something short of a miracle.

Here I am, seven decades later, still on the run. Except now, I'm trapped behind enemy lines, a defenseless captive for the last ten years, unaware of my exposure and danger, not realizing I almost compromised myself by revealing my special skills. Had a Tracker found me before I started recovering my memories, I wouldn't have understood the disastrous consequences of my capture, not just for me, but for millions of humans.

Time is running out. Tommy Miller warned me, and Caroline knows what I need to remember.

Chapter 2

I overslept, so I'm the only one in the women's showers, and I am going to be late. I should have dressed and eaten breakfast by now. My towel-dried hair remains damp. The bathroom mirror over the sink in my quarters only shows my face and shoulders, but the enormous shower room mirrors in the dressing area show my entire body. I still appreciate my youthful figure, even though it's been several weeks since I woke up knowing who I am, remembering how old age crept up and overtook me. How it laid waste to the best parts of me, leaving me a shell of my former self.

I'm no longer invisible or ignored. Perhaps conforming to the casual sex culture isn't a terrible idea ... although the way men treat women, or I should say, mistreat them, sets the women's movement back two centuries. There's nothing to vote for or against, no concerns over property rights, no troubling morality, religious or political issues. Planned parenthood is the rule, and the Overlords safeguard pregnancy and childcare to the nth degree.

They decoupled moral virtue from sexual behavior. Guilt-free sex is now the norm, where one gender gives and the other takes. No shame unless she refuses to yield to an officer. They've redefined what family means, all ruled by our benefactors and enforced by the Peace Force. Except when it isn't. They protect women and children. Except when they don't. Some things never change, and my life as Zena was unexceptional.

In this brave new world, on these military bases, women have forfeited their dignity and rights, yielding to the fragile male ego, all at a huge personal cost. Their own worst enemies, these females succumb to this toxic male-dominated system.

No liberated women. Well, one. Me, now that I'm awake.

§

My handler, Major Paul Abrams, hails me as I enter the office.

"Zena, let's meet later this morning. Sometime before lunch."

"Yes, sir. Sounds great."

I pour myself a cup of coffee in the break room and wish Cassie a good morning on my way upstairs. We'll never be friends, but that doesn't mean I can't be nice. Someone left me two orange *petit fours* on my worktable, and with delight, I wash them down with my hot drink. I drag out the aliens' Master Plan and set out my writing materials.

With the open Book before me, I pretend I'm reading in case somebody comes upstairs. As I browse through the volume, worry plagues me, but I try to keep panic at bay. Over the last several weeks, I've recalled almost all of Rebecca's stored memories and integrated them with Zena's. But Caroline's story remains elusive. While the Gift allows me to read other people's thoughts when I Pay Attention, I struggle to access my own suppressed memories. My plans are on hold until I uncover her secrets.

What was my destination? After waking in the cave from my second rejuvenation as a child with no memory, I headed west on that dusty dirt road, following the sun. Who will help me out there? Here, I'm an easy target, but lacking Caroline's knowledge, moving forward is impossible. Meanwhile, I must arm myself with allies without revealing the awful truth. I'll need permission to leave Cavalry when the time is right.

The threat of another Tracker hunting me and discovering me here keeps me on my toes. My top priority is to remain safe. I ache for one true friend to confide in, to advise me, to stand by my side, but that's an impossibility on these bases. Somehow, I survived for sixty years living as Caroline, outside in the free world. Everyone here accepts the Overlords as their benefactors, with no inkling of the danger. But for me, they'll always be The Enemy.

Footsteps bounding up the apartment stairs snap me back to the present. Paul and I plan to meet later, so he's too early. I peek through the opening above the countertop to see Commander Pierce climbing the steps. He sits across from me. Commander's kitchen table doubles as my worktable, giving him the right to sit anywhere he wants.

Commander frowns and clears his throat.

"We're having visitors on Wednesday, Zena."

Visitors? Overlords? Not the Tracker. I hold my breath. I'm not prepared. It's way too soon. I need more time to plan, find my safe haven, and figure out how I'll get there.

"The head of Central Intelligence and your liaison, Lieutenant Fischer, will arrive early in the morning. We're meeting in the main conference room."

"Commander Nadler?" I ask.

Commander Pierce raises his eyebrows.

"When Fischer met with me several weeks ago, he informed me Commander Nadler heads Central Intelligence now."

"Right. We'll meet with them first, then you'll join us."

I breathe a sigh of relief. I can handle Nadler and Fischer.

"Commander Nadler will discuss the results of your assignment and your future placement, so prepare yourself ... and bring the Book."

I glance at the Master Plan open before me on my worktable and nod.

"The entire base is gearing up for our visitors, to impress them, with everyone on their best behavior. Understood?"

"Yes, sir. I understand."

He studies me for a moment.

"You will dress and behave in a respectable and professional manner. If you have questions ... concerning how to comport yourself, ask Major Abrams ... or me. I'm sure you know not to speak unless Commander Nadler asks you a question."

Commander takes a deep breath and glowers, adding, "Do not offer your hand."

I laugh to myself, remembering the day I met Commander Pierce and did exactly that. Seems like a lifetime ago. He looked so handsome in his dress uniform. To confirm I'd be safe with him, I flouted the rules to read him better. It shocked poor Major Morgan when I offered Commander my hand, but he was gracious and held it, reassuring me.

Now that I've lived and worked on Cavalry for nine months, I realize how clueless and wrong I was about everything, including who I am. I'm not that misguided young woman who shook Commander's hand. Even with the Knowing, courtesy of the Gift, I never understood the truth of my situation.

"You'll be respectful, honest, and address him properly. Questions?"

"No sir. I'll behave myself."

"Excellent. We seldom have such distinguished guests as head of C. I., and we will make our best impression."

Commander sighs, and his brusque manner softens.

"They'll take you to Central Control to liaise with your former teammates. Then transfer you to Westview for a secondary assignment, along with translating the Book and passing on your knowledge to your colleagues."

My heart sinks. I'm not ready to leave, and I won't return to Central. Colonel Wickmore may be gone, but my former lover, Michael, might be there. I'll never go back. I study Commander's face and read him, but he hides his innermost thoughts, and I can't discern his feelings about me leaving.

"Fischer mentioned that also ... but ..."

"I understand it's short notice, with only two days to prepare. Take time for laundry, packing, bidding the team farewell, or saying goodbye to your friends. If you need anything, see me or Major Abrams."

"Yes, sir. Are you eager for me to leave?"

"What do you mean?"

"Well, sir, I was an inconvenience when I arrived. There were no proper quarters or office space for me," I say with a shrug. "You sacrificed your apartment during the day so I could work. I've been a challenge, sir."

Commander shakes his head.

"No, no, you're fine. We've had some issues, but they were ... personal. It's not unusual for newcomers to experience some adjustment when they transfer to Cavalry. We're strict and disciplined here and some find it difficult. Don't worry about your reputation. I've spoken well of you. I met with Major Morgan last week at Central and ... you're good."

He made a trip to Central? When was this? I've been so consumed with personal problems and recalling memories I haven't been paying attention to anything around me.

Commander nods and stands. I stand, too.

"No, I mean ... do you want me to leave Cavalry? Are you looking forward to having your apartment back and everything returning to normal? Have I been too difficult?"

Please say I'm welcome to stay.

"No, you're fine. Got used to you. We all have. But we always knew your placement was temporary until Michael returned. You've stayed longer than expected."

Panic grips me like a vise. I can't leave, not without more information. They must welcome me here. I always counted on them wanting me to stay. It wasn't part of the equation for them not to.

"I mean ... what if I stayed here? Would that be all right, sir?"

"That would be fine with us, but Central Intelligence made other plans."

"But what if they let me stay?"

"We're not throwing you out," he says with a wink and leaves without another word.

My preliminary report and its supplements reached the hands of Central Intelligence a while ago, so Nadler's visit was foreseeable. Despite Colonel Wickmore's retirement and departure from Central, I refuse to return, but it's Michael's presence I fear the most.

His desire to introduce me to his mother and ferry me off to the Overlords' complex to meet their citizens scares me. It sends shivers throughout my body, now that I know I'd be walking smack into the lion's mouth. Michael would never put me in danger on purpose. I shudder when I consider that had I not remembered who I am, I might have visited an Overlords' base with him, out of curiosity....

I can't return to my initial line of work with Nadler. It wasn't my choice to become the operative he groomed me to be. I had no clue what I was getting into. And I didn't enlist—I was drafted. I must stay here, pretending to finish my assignment while planning my next steps. No base will be safe for me once the Tracker discovers me hiding in plain sight, trapped like a mouse in a maze. I'm stuck here until I remember my original destination and gather enough information to create an escape plan. Every day, I listen to the voices, waiting to hear, yet dreading distressing chatter of the Tracker's plans to visit Cavalry.

After the disturbing news this morning, I've no incentive to work on my reports. My looming meeting with Nadler makes it impossible to concentrate on anything. The Master Plan remains untouched in front of me next to my notepad, and I stashed the computer on its shelf. I stare out the window from my worktable to observe distant tree-studded mountaintops reaching for the clouds, as I try to resurrect more of Caroline's life. She has critical information and I need it now, more than ever.

Major Abrams arrives for our scheduled session.

"Big meeting on Wednesday," says Paul, sitting next to me. "I hear Nadler's taking you to join him at Westview."

"Major Abrams, how do you feel about me leaving?"

"Got kinda used to you and I enjoy working on this project," he says, grinning. I read him and I'm relieved to sense his disappointment.

"I plan to stick around if I can help it. This is a better environment for me to complete my assignment. We work well together."

He nods and shrugs. I need Paul to want me to stay.

My stomach somersaults at the thought of returning to Westview to serve Commander Nadler. He had no right to take advantage of my thirteen-year-old self. It's irrelevant that my actual age was one hundred and forty. He believed I was a child. Everyone did, including me. With my lost memory, the onus belongs to him, but his abusing me as a young teen works to my benefit. I've kept his secret all this time, and if he wishes me to continue, he'll have to concede and allow me to stay. It pains me to use our relationship as a weapon, but I will. I owe him nothing.

Chapter 3

Muffled male voices resonate through the closed conference room door. I must attend this meeting. They're expecting me. I arrive right on time, but my feet are reluctant to move. I haven't seen Nadler in the eight years since I turned fifteen, and I'm waffling somewhere between excitement and dread.

The image of that pivotal day at Westview sears my mind. Miss Elly caught me with my pants down, seated on Nadler's lap. For almost two years, Nadler played an important part in my early life, as my protector, mentor, trainer, handler, and lover. Miss Elly never even allowed me to say goodbye.

The man had unlawful sex with me, but despite our illicit relationship, he looked after me and I was comfortable with him. He was a tough and formidable leader, with a reputation as the most uncompromising officer in the Peace Force, but with me, he was kind and patient. I've changed a lot. Has he? He could have contacted me somehow. He could have found me and explained why I had to leave. I understand now, but I felt abandoned and discarded then. I can't return to Westview with him and Fischer. Too much water under that bridge.

After taking a deep breath, I knock before entering. Commander Pierce and his team, all in formal dress, gather around the conference table, steeped in cordial conversation. I stand a few feet inside the door, drinking in the dignified display.

Everyone looks striking and important in their dazzling military regalia. For a moment, I forget my apprehension and stare in awe at the sea of splendid regimentals, replete with colorful chevrons, glistening badges, and ribbon racks offset by sparkling medals. Compared to this group, I'm underdressed, and I feel insignificant. Fischer catches my eye, nods at me, then moves aside and I see Nadler. He's handsome in his stately military attire, exuding power and authority.

Commander Nadler sees me. He struts over to me, pulls me to him, plants a kiss on my forehead, and whispers in my ear.

"We need to talk," he says, taking my hand. "I've missed you."

I pull away to study his face, which has aged well. His graying hair is new, along with a few wrinkles, and he's thinner but still muscular, still imposing. He projects a daunting presence to others, but when he looks at me, his eyes hold the same gentleness he always reserved for me.

With his arm around my shoulder, Nadler walks me to the colossal conference table and instructs me to sit across from him. The Book, a legal pad, and a pen are laid out on the table next to Major Paul Abrams who sits to my right. Major Daniel Matthews sits to my left. Lieutenant Fischer is Nadler's right-hand man, and Commander Pierce flanks his left, next to Major Tom Williams, who completes the impressive show of masculinity.

"Young lady, you've done an excellent job, and we're all astonished by your amazing accomplishments in translating the symbols. You succeeded where all others failed."

"Thank you, sir. As challenging as it is, I love working on this project."

Fischer also appears pleased, nodding his approval.

"I received plenty of help, sir. Commander Pierce and my handler, Major Abrams, provided a perfect work environment for me and continue to assist in all my needs."

I turn and motion toward Paul. He relaxes. Commander Pierce looked stunned when I joined the table, but now also appears to relax.

"I understand you received punishment," Nadler says with nonchalance as if speaking of the weather. He searches my eyes like he's trying to read me.

"Yes. When Michael showed up here, I became emotional and, in the moment, forgot my training. It won't happen again. Sir."

The look of compassion on Nadler's face almost appears sincere. It would delight him to think I'm ready and willing to join him. He promised never to punish me and never did.

"Well, Miss Roberts, your report includes little-known information, surprising us with a few unexpected facts. A fascinating read. Very detailed. How far along are you in your translation of the Book?"

"I'm about halfway through, but it's getting much more challenging, and I'm having difficulty finding a frame of reference for many symbols."

With the Master Plan opened on the table in front of me, I turn to its first page.

"As mentioned in my report, the Book describes a Master Plan. After deciphering several sections and verifying them against known history or facts, it appears the Plan veered off course early on. The Overlords designed these bases for themselves but changed plans and confined us here instead. I don't believe we're supposed to be here."

I close the Book and hold it to me.

"It'll take more time, but I think the most significant section of the Book lies ahead, and it is imperative we learn their intentions. It's not clear why the Overlords' plan changed course."

"Why is this important?" asks Fischer, crossing his arms.

"I can't explain it yet, but I doubt their primary goal is in our best interest. It's crucial to identify their true intentions. I understand the Overlords provide for and protect us, but I'm interested in their original plan. They may have only taken a detour until they can reach their actual objective. I've seen enough for concern."

I stand, pick up the legal pad, and then draw a large rectangle, adding a few puzzle pieces in the corners.

"Translating their symbols is like putting together a jigsaw puzzle with several pieces missing and no clear idea what the finished picture means."

I draw more puzzle pieces.

"When solving a jigsaw puzzle, you'd start with what you know. In my case, I started with familiar symbols as building blocks. To assemble a puzzle, you might search for corner pieces with two perpendicular straight sides."

I point to the corners of the square and create a few more mock puzzle pieces around them. I hold my drawing up to make sure everyone understands.

"You wouldn't know which corner they belong to, but you'd have a starting point. Then choose pieces containing one straight side, side pieces, and figure out where they fit …"

"You'd select other pieces by choosing ones with similar patterns or colors, which appear to go together," says Nadler, chiming in.

"Right. At some point, once you fill in enough pieces, you can envision the puzzle picture or at least parts of it. It might be scenery or a collection of different shapes."

Major Tom Williams looks puzzled. I focus my attention on him.

"My puzzle indicates a Master Plan. The missing pieces are symbols I'm having difficulty deciphering. Not only must I solve the puzzle, but it's necessary to understand our history to determine what changed and when. I believe it's vital for our collective security to finish translating the text."

These officers might not have solved jigsaw puzzles or ever played such games growing up, but they either comprehend my analogy or feign to. I see several nodding heads and, true to form, Tom smirks. I imagine him fighting the urge to make a joke.

Little do they realize, I've already read the entire Book with minimum effort, but it's fun to watch these alpha males pretend to follow my ridiculous example.

"In our case, picture a puzzle the size of this tabletop, with thousands of inch-sized pieces, with different shapes and colors," I say, pushing it further, "with similar pieces, and no concept of the image it forms. That's my challenge." The conference table is large enough to seat twelve or more.

Tom opens his mouth to say something as Nadler clears his throat. The officers shift in their chairs and exchange concerned glances.

"What do you suspect the Overlords have in store for us?" Nadler asks.

"It's premature to offer my suspicions until I've solved more of the puzzle, in the event I'm wrong. I want to be certain, so I'm convinced it's crucial to finish translating the Book."

It's too soon to alarm them, but they must understand the significance of my findings and allow me to finish my assignment. I need to buy time to develop my defensive strategy. We spend an hour discussing the conclusions outlined in my preliminary report. The conversation slows, and Commander Pierce glances at his watch.

"It's almost lunchtime. Let's break until my dining room's ready. Zena, you'll join us."

I nod and say, "Thank you, sir," before turning to Nadler.

"Maybe we could visit the cafeteria and catch up over a cup of coffee?"

Nadler gives me a cautionary look but appears to enjoy my blunder. I glance at Commander Pierce, remembering his warning.

"Oh, I forgot, you're a Commander now," I say. "I apologize for asking."

"It won't be the first time we shared a table in the cafeteria, would it?"

"No sir, it wouldn't," I say, relieved he's not offended.

There's a stir of uncomfortable shifting in seats, but I focus on Nadler, who rises, circles around to my side of the long table, and drapes his arm over my shoulder. He escorts me out and I guide him to the third-floor cafeteria.

Mary Jo and her friends enter the cafeteria from the far side, but the minute Nadler and I walk in, everyone in the cafeteria stands at attention.

"As you were," Nadler says with a wave of his hand.

Everyone returns to their seats, or gets in line, with most of them staring at us.

Mary Jo and her companions grab trays while I lead Nadler to my usual semi-secluded table across from where they always sit. A beaming Terry appears with a pot of coffee and two cups. She can't keep her eyes off Nadler.

"Sir, can I bring you something to eat?" she asks. Her doe-eyed stare never leaves Nadler, and I assume she's never seen a commander in full dress in her cafeteria.

"No, just coffee," I say. Her gaze remains on Nadler.

He nods, Terry fills our cups and walks away smiling.

"It's good to see you, Angel."

"It's Zena. I've answered to Zena for eight long years now, ever since they exiled me, punished for your sins."

Nadler keeps his composure, as do I. We're both experts at pretending, so we both feign carrying on a casual conversation.

"I've kept tabs on you and your progress, and your work is impressive. A lot has changed since I saw you last. You're aware I'm head of C.I. now."

I nod. He could have tried to contact me at least once in almost a decade.

"I had no choice, with my career and freedom at stake. Elly held our ... indiscretion ... over my head and insisted I let you go."

"Why was it up to her? You were her superior."

"Because, as the Commander's daughter, she wielded a certain amount of power over me. Ignoring her would have ruined both of our futures."

"It doesn't look like your future suffered."

I sip my coffee and glare at my cup instead of him.

"After you left, I married Miss Elly and gave her what she wanted. She lives on Valleyview. I seldom visit, and when I do it's only to give her another child. We have three children. They keep her busy and out of my business. Now that I'm commander, I have more leverage."

"I hope they're all boys."

A pinched expression crosses Nadler's face.

"I loved you. You were important to me, and I took excellent care of you. I protected you from other men and punishment. I gave you special treatment."

"You had sex with me when I was only thirteen," I say, maintaining a low, calm voice, keeping up the charade. "How would the Peace Force punish a female teenager forced to live and work on a military base?"

Nadler doesn't flinch.

"I didn't force you to do anything. We were a team. I was generous and careful with you. You had everything you wanted, and I had your back."

Nadler sips his coffee and scours the cafeteria, making sure nobody is within earshot.

"You never told anyone," Nadler says in a cocky, self-assured tone.

"No, I kept all your secrets, and trust you kept mine."

"Fischer and I alone are aware of your special skills unless you divulged anything."

"No, that would be too dangerous."

Nadler nods. We understand each other.

"We'll return to Westview. Miss Elly won't be a problem. You'll finish your assignment under my direct supervision, and I'll protect you and take care of you."

"I don't need anyone to take care of me. I'm a grown woman and I've been caring for myself ever since you kicked me off the island."

Nadler stares at me in confusion until he grasps my meaning, and I realize I should be more careful with my unusual century-old adages.

"Jim, I'm staying here. I have plenty to figure out and I've changed. So much has happened, and I can't ignore what I've learned. With working all day, I spend my evenings trying to solve my issues, and I want stable surroundings right now. Everything I need is here. I've made friends, I have a pleasant work environment, and I'm safe here. I need time to resolve my concerns before trying to handle more change."

"What's going on?"

"I'm not sure what they told you about Colonel Wickmore, but he assaulted me several times. The bastard broke the law. Nobody believes me or understands how much he hurt me, and they did nothing. I've been dealing with the aftermath of his abuse alone."

"What do you want done?" Nadler lifts his head, sits back, and squints.

"I want to be believed. Every time bad things happened to me, I kept silent. When I finally spoke up, no one investigated. They took the word of the offender instead of the victim. Not one person interviewed me, even with plenty of evidence of his crimes."

"And if you're believed? How would that help you?"

"They can't allow him to hurt another woman. They must punish him."

Nadler nods. He massages his chin as if he's choosing his words.

"You want revenge."

"No. I want justice."

"They forced the colonel to retire. He lost what he cared about most. Isn't that enough?"

"No. He's still able to harm other women. I don't feel safe with him free."

"He denied your allegations. If we present this before the Peace Council, you'll be in the spotlight, exposing everything in your history, including how he assaulted you. You'll have to testify. Your word against his. Think about it. Are you sure that's what you want?"

"No. But something should be done. He can't get away with this."

"Then what do you want?"

What do I want? I crave justice, but that'll never happen. A sudden feeling of defeat swallows me. He got away with assaulting me.

"I wanted someone to stop him. I wanted them to protect me. To believe me. They didn't. For weeks, they did nothing."

"I believe you, Angel."

His words take me by surprise. Tears threaten to fall, but I'm quick to recover because I'd never let Mary Jo and her friends catch me crying. I'm certain they're watching us.

"There's more. I have other reasons to stay."

"Tell me, baby. You can tell me anything."

I appreciate being able to confide in Nadler. He and Fischer are the only ones with knowledge of some of my buried secret past.

"You remember Andrew? He's the man I stayed in the hospital with, for six months. With the broken leg? I slept in his room, and helped him, keeping him company."

He nods, squints, and tilts his head. I read him. He's remembering how

Andrew revealed to him how I alleviated his pain, using my psychic skills. Nadler knew. His interest in me was more than about my ability to recognize when someone was lying or to read their thoughts. So, he knew about my extrasensory powers all along.

"And Dan, the officer who found me and brought me to Westview? You let him stay in the interview room with me because I wouldn't talk without him. He was my guardian for two weeks until he left with his salvage unit."

Nadler looks perplexed but nods.

"He is a major now, and he's here. Major Dan Matthews sat on my left in the meeting upstairs. He's part of Commander Pierce's Inner Circle. Dan doesn't realize I'm Angel."

Nadler's eyes open wide, and his brow wrinkles.

"Andrew served here also, but he died four years ago, and I don't expect you to understand Andrew's importance to me. We bonded, and I cared a lot for him. He put his cross necklace around my neck and promised he would find me. I've been dealing with a cyclone of feelings: guilt over not searching for him, disappointment ... because he never found me, and ... horrible sorrow because I'll never see him again."

I stop short of disclosing my anger over Andrew's suicide when I could have saved him.

Nadler nods. He closes his eyes for a moment.

"I understand, baby. You have deep feelings for people, sometimes to your detriment."

"I can't talk to anyone here about Andrew, or that I knew Dan."

"Why not?" he asks, but I sense his relief.

"I can't discuss it. You wouldn't understand. There's more," I say, unsure I should divulge this part, but grateful to talk about it to someone.

Nadler sighs. He looks at me with compassion, even though I doubt he's capable of it.

"I fell in love, crazy in love, with an officer here, but it ended, and we're no longer together, and we'll never be. It hurts like something I've never known."

His face changes. Do I detect jealousy?

"You've had your first heartbreak. You'll get over it."

What makes him think it's my first?

"Another thing ... I'm remembering."

"What? You mean your past? Where you came from?"

Nadler appears to be on high alert, but what would trouble him?

"Only little bits and pieces. I can't put them together, but with more time, more memories might surface. Nothing makes any sense. I don't know where I was born, who my family was, or who I am. Dan rescued me from the outside world, but what happened? Who did I leave behind?"

"You were a mere child, having suffered through an ordeal so terrible it wiped your memories. Maybe it's better not to remember. You told us your family all died. You arrived at Westview traumatized. Forget the past. Move on. We're your people now."

"I was a child then, but I can handle it now, and it's about time I remember."

It pains me to lie to Nadler. We always enjoyed an honest relationship, in part because he knew I could tell when he lied. He never possessed that advantage, but he's privy to much of my past, and he always had my back.

Nadler reaches for my hand but immediately draws back. Either he remembers I can read him, or he realizes we're in public.

"Jim, I'm clueless about my future. Right now, I want to quit and live on a civilian base. But I won't abandon my assignment. When I'm finished here, and I screw my head on straight, I may decide to join you at Westview. But not as your mistress or your Angel. As your partner. We'll negotiate the terms when that day comes. You wronged me. I haven't forgiven you yet."

Nadler frowns.

"But I will," I say, just as Paul appears at our table.

"Lunch is ready, sir. I'm happy to escort you both."

When we walk into Commander's dining room, I'm taken aback. David stands at the dinner table, looking drop-dead gorgeous in his dress uniform. He and Nadler greet each other with a bear hug. Nadler scrutinizes David, then pats him on the shoulder.

"Well, son, I've received excellent reports about you. Glad you're joining us for lunch."

"Thank you, sir."

David and I exchange bewildered looks, each surprised to see the other. We're instructed to sit across from Nadler and Commander Pierce. Paul flanks my left next to Dan, who sits on the end. Nadler studies Dan, as if he's trying to remember him. Fischer sits to Nadler's right and Tom sits on the other end next to Commander. I slide into my seat next to David and look from Nadler to David and back.

"Son?" I ask. Did he mean that literally?

"David is my firstborn," Nadler says.

It's a good thing I'm sitting.

"How many children do you have?"

My shock almost betrays me. Nadler just disclosed having three youngsters with Miss Elly, but he never mentioned adult offspring. And David, of all the improbable people?

"I knew David's mother early in my service. The three I mentioned earlier ... two boys and a girl ... the oldest boy just turned seven. That's all."

Nadler gives me a quizzical look like he's trying to figure out why it matters to me and gestures toward David with a question. I shake my head. I can't reveal that David is the lover guilty of breaking my heart. It doesn't escape me that should I need to use my past with Nadler to get what I want, it would devastate David. Family is important.

David gives me the same puzzled look, and the resemblance unsettles me. Not his appearance so much, but he has the same cocky self-confidence.

"You must be very proud," I say. "Lieutenant Cross is a well-respected officer, dedicated to his service."

Nadler appears pleased with my praise, but I sense his approval is conditional, something I'm aware David understands. I'm attempting to read the source of conflict between father and son, but I'm distracted by the bustle of servers bringing in tempting plates of appetizers and the first course with its tantalizing aroma rising from crocks of onion soup. A server follows with relish trays. I watch one black olive roll off the serving plate onto the clean white tablecloth, leaving a small wet streak. In a deft move, the embarrassed server places the relish tray over the spot.

Other servers pour iced tea and set out bread platters.

Commander's staff went all out to prepare a fine feast. We eat with minimal conversation until they clear the table and serve coffee. I feel Nadler watching me as I glance from one face to the next to determine the group's mood. I read discomfort and confusion at the table. My previous lunch in the Commander's dining room ended in an unexpected fiasco, so perhaps there's a fear I'll embarrass the team.

David leans closer to me and asks in a whisper, "How do you know my father?"

"He was my first handler. He ... trained me."

Nadler clears his throat. "You've done excellent work and you are always welcome to return to Westview. I'd see to your protection myself, along with any other needs."

"Thank you, sir, but I can't leave here right now."

The dining room falls silent. Everyone stares at me. David squeezes my leg under the table as a warning.

Fischer clears his throat to get my attention.

"Miss Roberts, you'll do as you're told. We're here to bring you back into the fold."

David pats my leg to calm me.

Fischer looks threatening, but he would have been more menacing with his belt coiled on the table before him. Of course, they'd never allow that here in the dining room.

Nadler waves at Fischer to stand down, then he addresses the group.

"As much as I'd like Miss Roberts to return with us ... we've had a fruitful discussion. I've decided it's in the best interest of the project for her to remain here to complete her assignment ... at least for the near future. Commander Pierce?"

Everyone turns their attention to Commander Pierce.

I hold my breath.

"Of course. She's welcome to stay. We're pleased with her work," says Commander Pierce, nodding, appearing relieved but confused by Nadler's reversal.

David and Dan shoot me questioning looks. Fischer pales like someone suggested they poisoned the food. He looks to Nadler for an explanation. Paul beams. I hide my delight, but I know I won.

Chapter 4

When I arrive for work, Commander and Paul are waiting for me, wearing quizzical expressions, and I suspect they're eager to discuss the unexpected outcome of yesterday's luncheon. After lunch yesterday, I made myself scarce, to avoid running into Nadler or Fischer.

Word has it they left midafternoon.

The men sip their coffee and munch on breakfast sweets while I pull out my materials and prepare my workspace. I watch them from the corner of my eye to gauge their mood.

"Did I break any rules yesterday?" I ask.

Commander cocks his head as he cracks a half smile.

"You never cease to amaze me. Commander Nadler was adamant about taking you with him. How did you convince him otherwise?"

I gaze at Paul, sitting in silence with a sly grin. I read them both.

"While we drank our coffee in the cafeteria, I shared my situation with Commander Nadler, and he understood my needs. He wants what's best for the project. So here I am."

"Commander Nadler is the toughest, most unwavering officer in the military. When he wants something, he doesn't play around. He gets it. Why didn't you tell me you worked with him?" asks Commander.

I don't have to read him to recognize his annoyance.

"I assumed you were aware of my history with Nadler. He was a major then and trained me. He was my first handler. Didn't he tell you?"

"No. Neither did Fischer," he says, glaring at me.

"I apologize, but I've always left it up to Central Intelligence to reveal what they see fit."

Commander relaxes, but he's displeased and doesn't appreciate anyone blind-siding him. As a commander, I'm certain he hates surprises. Welcome to my universe. They taught me to only disclose information on a need-to-know basis, with their knowledge and permission, and it's a difficult habit to break. Ten years of keeping everyone's secrets has changed me.

Commander sighs and leans in towards me.

"I'd prefer that you were more forthcoming. If you're planning on staying here, you need to be more transparent. I assure you I have clearance to be aware of ..."

"Again, sir, I apologize. I didn't intend to keep you in the dark, and I was wrong to presume they briefed you. I'll be more careful in the future."

Commander sits back in his chair and grasps the edge of the table.

"You looked surprised to learn Lieutenant Cross is Nadler's son."

"Yes. I'm also kept like a mushroom. In the dark."

Commander chuckles. He leans forward like he's about to tell me a secret.

"I'd have told you," he says, "had you mentioned you worked for Nadler."

Sure, like when you mentioned Michael was your brother?

"Well, lessons learned, I guess," I say, wishing to keep the peace.

"Why is Nadler so interested in you working for him? He has several smart officers under him. What does he have planned for you?"

"I'm not sure. We didn't discuss it, and we wouldn't have unless I agreed to join him."

"He appeared to take a shine to you," Paul says.

"Major Nadler and I worked well together, in perfect harmony, as if we read each other's mind. Of course, that's impossible, but we excelled as a team."

"What did you do as part of his team?" Paul asks.

"Again, sir, they taught me it's the prerogative of Central Intelligence to decide what to disclose. I understand you have clearance, but I don't have permission."

The officers stand. Commander hesitates, like he wants to ask another question, but says nothing and walks away.

As soon as they leave, I switch on my rock-opera music and take my position by the window, eager to listen for the alien communications. The dark cloudy sky threatens rain, and a strong wind bends the trees like a wave.

I watch the morphing clouds drift past the mountains as I slip into my transcendental state and wait for the distant chatter. When the voices come, I sift through them, focusing on a few. As I filter through them, I'm left disappointed and thankful. No word about *Mana-ta-ah*, the Tracker, so I hope no news means good news. I need to be prepared, but I'm relieved to be spared, for now. There's so much to learn. After a long stretch of hearing nothing of value, I abandon my efforts.

The trees stop swaying, the gust that blew the clouds away dies down, and the sun reappears. When I reach out to touch the mountains, my hands meet window glass instead, and I descend into a deeper transcendental state. This time, I relax my muscles and free my mind to conjure up another image of the cabin, after I encountered the Resistance.

§

My prison, a second-floor bedroom in the cabin, was across the hall from the room where I regenerated twenty-five years earlier. They locked my door from the outside and kept the key. Held captive in this barren chamber for three days, I'd grown stir-crazy without even a book to read or music to enjoy. I had curled up on the bed, waiting for someone to bring me dinner. It was the only time I saw my bearded keeper.

The screened, wide-open window allowed warm, fresh summer air to flow in, but escaping was impossible. Forest surrounded the cabin, and the closest trees were out of reach. I'd never attempt to escape that way. I might be brave, but I'm not a daredevil. The exterior siding had nothing to grab onto, so even a monkey couldn't scale down to freedom.

I spent hours lying on the modest bed, staring at a spider hard at work spinning his web in a ceiling corner. They brought me dismal meals twice a day, which I consumed sitting at the only other furniture, a small rectangular table with two mismatched chairs, while my jailor sat across from me, watching. When I finished my meal, he'd start the interrogation. The leader never hurt me and gave up when I refused to speak. Until the next time.

My suitcase leaned against a wall, minus the money the Resistance leader stole. He didn't touch my clothes, most of which were dirty. I wore the same outfit for those three days of captivity, in defiance of these vigilantes. The tiny bathroom only had a toilet and sink, making it difficult to bathe. They supplied me with one washcloth and towel that I seldom used. Instead of offending my keepers, I only offended myself.

The leader didn't appear to mind my ripeness. I had traveled without the benefit of bathing facilities for several days before the fateful day I arrived at the cabin. Most of my garments were dirty, anyway. I couldn't answer their questions, and they had no right to keep me prisoner. No one ever threatened or hurt me, but they treated me like their enemy.

This particular day, my imprisoner unlocked the door and entered, but I didn't recognize him with his trimmed hair and shaved beard until he spoke.

"You need a bath. Grab something clean to wear and come with me."

The leader's beardless face was a vast improvement, but he hadn't brought my tray of food, and I was hungry. A bath sounded appealing, and since my defiance gained me nothing, I grabbed my only clean clothes from my suitcase and followed him to the hall bathroom. He pointed to an old fashion, clawed foot, pink, cast-iron bathtub filled with inviting steaming hot water. A cane back chair with a beige wicker seat sat near the door inside the bathroom, so I set my fresh clothing on it and waited for him to leave.

Instead, he closed the door, planted the chair against it, picked up my clothes, and then sat holding them, waving me toward the tub.

"Are you going to sit there and watch me?"

"Yep, but don't worry yourself. Do as you're told, and no one will harm you. I'm here to make sure you don't escape and make sure no one bothers you while you bathe. My guys haven't enjoyed a woman in a while."

It sounded like a threat. Would he bother me while I bathe?

"I told you my name, so will you tell me yours?" I asked.

"Name's J.D. Abrams, but most call me Jade. Get undressed and climb into the tub while the water's hot. You need a bath. I'll have your dirty things washed."

"All the clothes in my suitcase are dirty. Can you launder them, too? Or I could do it myself if you let me out. I'd rather wash them myself."

Jade shrugged. He sat across from the bathroom window, watching me like I might disappear if he dared look away. Even if I could get past him, escape from the second floor was futile. I'd never fit through the tiny opening. It was too far down and I had no intention of escaping without my meager belongings. I didn't have much, but clothes were hard to acquire, and my faithful suitcase had traveled hundreds of miles with me. He looked comfortable and showed no sign of leaving.

"Can't you wait in the hallway? I can bathe by myself. If you're worried I'll try to escape, sit outside the door. I can't climb out the window."

I crossed my arms over my chest, wondering how long since he's enjoyed a woman. He wouldn't have to wait until I undressed to accost me if that was his intention, but perhaps my pungent odor deterred him.

"Nope. I don't trust you. Get in while the water's hot. Behave yourself and I'll bring your food when you're dressed."

His nonchalant tone convinced me I had no choice. He was staying.

"Can you at least look away? Allow me some dignity?"

"Nope. Need to keep an eye on you. Don't worry yourself."

His unyielding, stern voice lacked malice or irony.

As I undressed, I covered myself as much as possible by holding my removed clothing in front of me. I watched him, guarding, in case he stood and approached me. He appeared bored and indifferent until I stepped into the tub, dropping my dirty clothes to the floor. His eyes twinkled and a faint smile showed appreciation, but he didn't move. Immersed to my shoulders, the clear water hid nothing.

A bottle of shampoo perched on the tub edge, so I washed my weather-soiled hair. Eager to dress and return to my room, I rushed to soap and rinse, but the hot water felt like heaven, tempting me to linger. I could have soaked in the soothing pool for hours. I peeked at Jade.

"All finished. Can you please avert your eyes so I can dry myself?"

Jade sighed and turned to gaze out the window, so I stood and reached for the towel, keeping my eye on him. He remained seated, looking straight ahead, allowing me to dry myself with a modicum of privacy. I wrapped the towel around me and waited.

"I need my clothes."

He stood and handed them to me. I waited until he returned to his seat. He looked away again, smiling to himself. He stayed focused on gazing out the window while I hurried to dress, watching him should he make a move.

I combed my fingers through my tangled, wet hair.

"I'm dressed."

He stood again and moved close to me. I held my breath until it was clear he only wanted to gather my dirty garments and pull the bathtub plug.

§

The music finishes, and in the sudden silence, I snap back to the present. J.D. Abrams, Paul's uncle, the man in the old picture, standing next to his brother, Paul's father. What happened to this man? Why can't I remember him? Or the reason they held me prisoner. The night I spent in Paul's apartment, the night my keycard failed, I had a strange dream which was forgotten by morning. Paul alleged I muttered the word "jade," but he didn't understand its meaning. I'm swamped with more questions now than I ever imagined.

It's easy to translate the once elusive symbols in the Master Plan, open in front of me, but my mind bounces back to Jade and my latest retrieved memory. The Resistance repudiated and worked against the goals of the Overlords. They were soldiers once, in the days before I was reborn to become Caroline. Like me, this group was hiding from the Captors. Young women were scarce, with so many kidnapped, so why were these guys afraid I was a spy? I'd have thought they would have welcomed me with open arms. What happened to these men to make them so distrustful?

Hunger pangs shatter my concentration. The wall clock agrees with my stomach that it's not too early for lunch, so with my work area squared away, I make a beeline for the stairs tempted by delicious aromas rising from the cafeteria. My mouth waters at the hint of garlic and a familiar earthy aroma. Several steam tables overflow with huge stuffed mushrooms. The golden-brown breadcrumb-covered delicacies, with savory filling sprinkled with parsley, pull at me like a bee to a flower.

Mary Jo and her companions watch me stand in line, fill my tray, and settle at my favorite table with my enticing bounty before me. After yesterday's coffee reunion with Commander Nadler, I sense a notable difference in the air. Officers and military women regard me with either a new deference or curiosity. Even the cafeteria staff, who always treated me well, seem to have a newfound reverence and greet me with respect. I hide my enjoyment.

Four oversized stuffed mushroom caps grace my plate. I cut a small piece like I'm slicing a pie. The filling tastes of cream cheese, parmesan, and something else I can't identify yet, but it's wonderful. Halfway through my meal, David approaches and sits across from me.

"So, you knew my father?"

"Good afternoon to you, too, Lieutenant Cross."

He answers with an annoyed sigh.

"He was your handler? It's unusual for commanders to train anyone, let alone civilians. Even more unusual for them to act as their handler."

I take another big bite of a half-eaten treat and take my time chewing, giving me a moment to decide how to answer.

"Your father was a major when I knew him, and most of my handlers were majors. Here at Cavalry, Commander Pierce was my handler, until he assigned that job to Major Abrams. So, maybe it's not so unusual."

I plop the last morsel into my mouth and moan as I savor the flavor.

"He never mentioned his marriage to Elly? Never mentioned his children?" David asks.

"He failed to mention having a grown son, that's for sure. But he hadn't married Miss Elly yet. They must have married after I left."

"So, you've met the infamous Elly Nadler?"

"Did I ever, but we disliked each other. She worked in Major Nadler's office, but I'm not sure what she did, besides getting on my nerves and sometimes on my case. Nadler charged her with ... acclimating me to military life since I had no training and was unprepared. She didn't like me either."

David laughs. He appears to share my disdain for the woman.

"You didn't like her either? I guess she'd be your stepmom, but she's not much older than you. That must have been challenging."

A serious but pained gaze crosses David's face, and he shakes his head.

"I never met her or my siblings."

I skewer another mushroom, mulling over the implications of David's words. Nadler and Elly must have married around the same time David finished his military training and started his service. They're not a very close-knit family.

"You didn't miss anything. At least not with Miss Elly. You should get to know your brothers and sister. Family is so important."

David shrugs and watches me take another bite.

"You should meet my new girl, Cam. Short for Camilla. She's pretty young and might benefit from having an older female friend."

Ouch. Men can be so insensitive. What makes him think I'd want to mentor my replacement? And what does he mean by older? I've kept my youthful appearance.

"Cam can't be that young. Civilian women must be twenty-one to enter domestic service. That's what they told me. She's an adult, and like me, can take care of herself."

"She's twenty-four, but immature, and doesn't have your knowledge."

"Well, she's older than me, and her immaturity sounds like her problem, not mine," I say, glaring at him. "How old do I look, anyway?"

"You look young, but I assumed you were more mature because of your experience. You're not as naïve as my girls. If you served under my father, I figure you must be older."

"Okay ... Do they serve these mushrooms in the Officer's Mess? They are delicious."

I stab one and hold it out to him. He takes a bite, shows his approval, and hands it back.

"No, finish it." I push it back to him. He polishes the forkful off in one chomp, smiles, and licks his lips, then passes my fork back to me.

"These are so delectable. I wish they allowed seconds."

David motions to a cafeteria server refilling coffee cups and she rushes over.

"I want a serving of these tasty mushrooms," he orders.

Pleased to serve him, she disappears but returns a few minutes later with a platter full of the succulent delicacies and sets the plate before David.

"Would you like some coffee with your meal?" she asks.

He declines, and she leaves, but in her haste to please him, she forgets to bring him utensils. I lift my fork and nod at his lack of one. He casts me a conspiratorial wink.

"Give me your plate," he says, motioning to me with two fingers.

I hand David my empty dish and fork. He looks around, shares half of his mushrooms then passes them back and puts his finger to his lips like it's our secret. I offer him the fork first and we share it until we devour every single delightful morsel.

Chapter 5

The sun peeks out for several minutes before hiding again, and morning clouds creep across the sky, morphing into shapes from bunnies to buffalo to old men with bushy white beards. When my daughter Trish was little, she enjoyed finding kittens, turtles, and dinosaurs in the clouds, and when she grew up, she passed on her love to her two girls. Must be in the blood.

Jamie wasn't interested in cloud watching, but my son loved the outdoors as much as any boy, especially catching interesting bugs to show us, much to our disdain. He never minded getting dirty or the scrapes and bruises that were part of playing. He grew into a respectable man, and a decent father, and ... I miss them both.

I relax and let my mind free itself to prepare to listen again for the voices. When they come, I filter through them, and excitement about a new plan dominates the chatter, but I don't catch the details. Still nothing regarding the Tracker, just conversations about events and people unknown to me. More than an hour passes while I'm immersed in deep concentration. I return from my transcendence and notice the clouds have disappeared.

This morning, I reread the final sections of the Master Plan and had no problem understanding every symbol. It's no surprise to learn of their agenda to occupy bases all over the globe with their own kind, to breed extra humans, caged like animals, provided for, kept in prime physical condition, to supply new hosts when their current bodies age out. But they need the Gift. My Gift. I need it, too. Possession is nine-tenths of the law, but I doubt they'd agree.

I'm amazed at their patience and their ability to continue to grow and control. In 2030, when I experienced my first rebirthing, rumors of the Overlords were starting to surface to the outside world. We came to call them the Captors because we learned they were abducting healthy, young people. Life as we knew it was ending.

My music plays as loud as I dare. The apartment door stays open while I'm on duty and I'm not sure if Cassie or anyone else can hear my tunes or me singing when the mood moves me.

I'm so lost in thought, that I don't realize Paul is standing behind me until I turn around, almost smacking into him. He steps back, walks over to the disc player, and turns down the volume.

"How's it going? Need anything? Anything I can find for you?"

"I'm fine. Just taking a much-needed break."

"You're okay. Take breaks whenever you need to. I understand how difficult your work is and you're doing a fantastic job."

"Thank you, Major Abrams."

"Let's talk for a moment," he says, gesturing toward my worktable.

We sit across from each other, and I offer Paul my full attention.

"In our meeting with Commander Nadler, you said you believed we weren't supposed to live here on the bases. Why do you believe that? You expressed reluctance to disclose your theories without more facts, but just between the two of us, what brought you to that conclusion?"

"The Overlords designed our bases to accommodate themselves, not to house military personnel or civilians. We've retrofitted the military bases to suit our purposes. I have no information about the civilian bases, but I believe they also reconfigured them for a purpose different from the original intent."

"So, what does that mean? The Overlords rescued and gave refuge to our parents or grandparents. They provided several of their home bases, so we'd thrive, be protected, and be comfortable. In the outside world, anarchy reigned, with insufficient food sources, oppressive heat, and uncontrolled violence by those who were determined not to join us."

"Uncontrolled violence? How do you know that? There's been no books or magazines written for decades. The most recent magazines I've seen were published in 2035—over sixty-five years ago."

"Weren't you taught these facts in school?" Paul asks.

"No. I'm self-educated. Like Lincoln."

Paul gives me a questioning look. He has no clue who Lincoln was.

"Was your uncle J.D. violent?"

"I doubt it. After my father joined the Peace Force, he never heard from his brother again, until he got word of his death. He spoke well of my uncle. Said he was a smart, brave man. He missed him."

"So, decent folks, like your uncle, lived out there?"

"We never would have survived out there. The Overlords provide everything we need and allow us to govern ourselves, given we follow their core initiatives. The earth responded, cooled, and flourished, thanks to our benefactors, who achieved what we couldn't," he says like a man touting the party line.

"Or wouldn't," I say, remembering how those in power valued profits over human lives.

"Whatever," Paul says. He shrugs and sits back, having made his point.

"People live out there. Blake did. I want to learn how they survived. The Overlords kidnapped young females and sterilized others. But somehow, the outsiders continued to reproduce for generations. No one could endure intolerable heat, so it couldn't have been that dire. And food must have been available."

"What's your point? Are you saying the Overlords didn't need to rescue us?"

"I'm trying to make sense of what I'm reading and everything I've learned. They may have saved the planet. In fact, I don't doubt they accomplished what we refused to do. I'm just saying there's evidence we're not supposed to be here, according to their Master Plan. That's all. I'm curious about their plans for us. Aren't you?"

"There are over fifty thousand citizens, men, women, and children, in our twelve-base cluster, so we're a formidable force in our own right. We, the Peace Force, enforce our laws and rules, not the Overlords. We decide how to raise our offspring, and we define the mores of our culture. Our relationship with the Overlords is excellent, but they manage their bases, and we govern ours."

"And you're not interested in exploring the outside world. Plow your own fields, build your own homes, solve your own problems? We depend on the Overlords for all our needs."

"Do you believe we could do better, Zena, based on our history? We enjoy plenty of privileges, and I'm aware of the world our ancestors lived in. The wars, famine, and injustice. You have no idea what the Overlords saved us from. It fell apart. Everything. Governments collapsed, chaos ruled the day, and violence ruled the night. You're smart for a woman, but you don't have all the facts."

Oh, Paul, if you only knew what I've experienced firsthand.

"Paul, of course, you're right, and that's why I'm hesitant to share my beliefs. Thank you for letting me see the situation through your eyes. I'll consider everything you said. They say it takes a village."

He shoots me a questioning look and I realize my maxims are confusing, especially given our discussion. He shakes his head but seems amused. It seems he's getting used to my oddities.

Paul glances at his watch and shrugs.

"Lunchtime. I'm glad we had this conversation. Whenever you want to discuss something work-related, don't hesitate. If you need anything, ask."

He returns downstairs, and I'm hungry.

§

After finishing lunch, I stare out at nothing, deep in thought. I didn't notice the cafeteria clearing out, and now it's empty and quiet, but I feel no urgency to return to work. Caroline has secrets I must unearth. She carries the key to unlocking my mystery of ending up in the cave as a child with no memory. Now that I've started remembering Caroline's life, it's easier to connect with those memories. By relaxing and focusing on thoughts of sweet breezes and rustling leaves, I become lost somewhere in the past, Caroline's past.

§

Jade brought me a tray of food. This time my lunch included a large piece of dry cornbread smeared with a substance I was certain wasn't butter. He sat across from me, watching me take little bites of something he claimed was stew, but I was afraid to ask about the mystery meat. I was still a prisoner even though I cooperated with the Resistance.

"You eat like a bird," Jade said with a rare smile. He was friendlier that day.

A few crumbs from my cornbread had fallen beside my plate and we both watched a large black ant wander across the table. She hoisted a crumb, bigger than herself, hauled it to the table's edge, and disappeared.

"Man, indeed, does not live by bread alone. Nor does an ant," Jade said with a wink.

"Cornbread is still bread."

"A distinction without a difference?"

I shrugged and flicked another small crumb of dry cornbread from my plate, just in case.

When I returned to the cabin a few days earlier, I assumed it was abandoned. I was wrong. Most people had disappeared, leaving the nearby town almost deserted and a desolate place. I'd heard the Captors had apprehended thousands and moved them to their bases or labor camps. Money was worthless, but some diehards believed it would regain its value, so they hoarded cash whenever they could. Banks had closed along with most businesses.

Roads fell into disrepair and were dangerous. Someone had stolen my Chevy years ago, but gas was almost impossible to find, anyway. I had slept many a night in the back seat, locked in my car. Walking everywhere was excellent exercise, but I missed my car. After it vanished, my travel became a lot slower and riskier, and finding safe shelter after dark proved more difficult. Here, back in the cabin, I had shelter, food, relative safety, and no freedom.

I kept Caroline as my name, although no one would recognize me as Rebecca, and I grew accustomed to that alias. My life, ruled by evading the Captors, kept me on the run for so long, dodging capture, and avoiding the bases. But, by accident, I ended up captured, anyway—by the Resistance. I tried convincing Jade and his band of not-so-merry men that I'd also been trying to remain free, and I hated the Captors, but they refused to believe me.

As I finished eating, Jade grew serious, so I knew the interrogation had started.

"So, ready to confess who you are? Are there more like you? Why did you come here?"

I took my time chewing the last bite of my food.

"Look, they have spies everywhere, so we can't release you. If they find us, we have no defense. We can't be too careful. Our lives depend on it."

"I know how dangerous it is. That's why I'm hiding. Why don't you believe me? I'm telling you the truth. I swear it."

Jade scratched his stubbled chin and stared at me, squinting, seeming to wrestle with a decision.

"There were a lot more of us. We traveled together, trying to stay one step ahead of them. Young men and women kept disappearing, and our job was to protect the farmers and their families. Two young females joined our troop. They were healthy, pretty little things, and we ignored the obvious signs until it was too late. The girls ate with us, slept with us, and one day they betrayed us."

Jade sits in silence for a moment, and his face tells me he's reliving the betrayal.

"They slipped away one night and brought back a small army. The four of us escaped, but they captured the others. We got away with one rifle and the clothes on our backs. We kept going until we found this cabin. Now we spend our time on surveillance and basic survival. I'd prefer not to hurt you, but I can't trust you. It won't happen again. I don't know how you found us."

I stared at him. He would have been a young boy when I regenerated. I hadn't aged in twenty-five years, keeping my youthful appearance, and no one noticed since I never stayed in the same location for long. Few people remained anyway, and I was no doubt their last worry.

"I told you, I'm not a spy. I'm on the run and I want to hide, just like you. The Captors are taking young women like me, and I came here for refuge."

"Where did you come from? What were you doing out there alone?"

"I've been traveling alone for a long time. My family rented this cabin when I was a youngster, and I decided it would be a safe retreat because it's so isolated. Three years ago, the Captors kidnapped my mom and dad, and I watched them handcuff and force them into a van. I had slipped off to the woods and when I returned, soldiers had overrun our camp. They outnumbered us, with several of them against my parents. I could do nothing but hide and watch them cart my folks away. I was helpless and I've traveled alone ever since. The Captors are my enemy too."

My story was at least half true. I witnessed a couple taken, as in my tale.

The only difference was, they weren't my relatives. My devoted mother and absentee father are gone, along with so many people I loved. I hoped Jade would believe my fictional account. I needed their trust.

"We can't let you go. Even if I believed you, which I don't. It's too risky."

"I'm fine with that because I'm tired of surviving on my own, and there's safety in numbers. Plenty of dangerous men exist out there. The Captors aren't my only problem. I'll do whatever you want, and I won't try to leave."

He considered my response.

"If you escape, we'll find you and kill you."

"Deal," I said, with as much confidence as I could muster.

Jade looked surprised but unconvinced.

§

The activity of the cleaning staff wiping down tables in the cafeteria jolts me back to the present. David sits in the seat across from me, staring.

"Where were you? I've been sitting here for an hour."

He's lying. An hour ago, I was engrossed in eating delicious chicken and dumplings, lost in thought, but not that preoccupied.

"That's not true. You know, lying is against the rules."

"Yes, I sure do," he says, squinting, and sounding like he's making a point.

"There aren't any stuffed mushrooms today."

David glares at me. It's obvious he's not amused.

"Something you mentioned the other day makes no sense, and it's been eating at me."

"Cafeterias are the customary venue for eating."

He doesn't laugh and I'm sure he's annoyed, but I'm on a roll.

"Why don't you feed me a clue to chew on?"

He's still not smiling, so I persist.

"Or maybe some food for thought?"

David opens his mouth to speak just as his radio buzzes.

"Yeah, what's goin' on?" David stands, turning his back to me. He walks away a short distance to continue the brief conversation. I can't understand the other voice, but when he returns to the table, he looks annoyed. "Be right there. Out."

David pockets his handheld radio and faces me.

"We're not finished. Catch you later."

And he's gone, and I decide it's not worth stewing over.

The kitchen staff buzzes from table to table, like worker bees flying from flower to flower, wiping tabletops clean, collecting trays and anything left behind. They chatter across tables and chairs, ignoring me, each knowing their task, moving like dancers in a well-rehearsed ballet.

Their scurrying about reminds me of holidays with my husband, Russ, his brother, our relatives, and my two sisters, with their families. After gobbling a huge turkey or ham dinner, including several side dishes and one's choice of various desserts, our men retired to the living room to watch the football game, while the children scampered to the finished basement to play.

Womenfolk cleared the table and filled the dishwasher, put food away, all while gossiping about the current family news, before turning to politics. We shared similar opinions, so our banter always remained friendly, inspired by the latest television newscast or roundtable discussion on *The View*.

Those were the good old days. The norm, long before the pandemic struck, infecting us, and changing the way we lived, loved, and perished. We became isolated while the scourge killed millions all over the planet before it waned and died out.

War in Europe followed on its heels and destroyed millions of lives and homes. Climate change caused droughts, famine, and wildfires that burned down entire forests. Blistering temperatures melted icebergs and glaciers, causing floods. Insurrections toppled governments.

Celebrations happened before the beginning of the end. Then nothing.

Today, on the bases, Thanksgiving is forgotten along with every other holiday, religious or otherwise. If small cheer and great welcome make a merry feast—then its absence leaves a void in the soul.

Chapter 6

A tempting glazed orange bonbon makes my mouth water. Paul notices me coveting the sweet morsel and offers me the saucer with several dainty pastries in assorted colors. I inhale the delightful, citrus-flavored cube in a single bite, relishing it.

I'm reminded of the many birthday cakes I took pleasure in baking for my children, decorated with their favorite themes. Pink flowers, brown dinosaurs, or the yellow Big Bird from Sesame Street for Trish. Anything with trains, trucks, or cars for Jamie, although one year I surprised him with a Kermit the Frog motif. When he saw the emerald amphibian with bulging eyes and lime-colored spiked collar, his huge smile matched the Muppet's. He looked up at me and said, "It's not easy being green."

The children loved their parties as much as I enjoyed planning them. Their celebrations included theme-based paper plates, napkins, cups, and hats with matching paper tablecloths.

Commander walks into the kitchen area, buttoning his shirt. He unzips to tuck in his shirttails as if I'm not sitting right here, then takes his seat and helps himself to a rose-colored confection, his favorite. He stuffs the entire delicacy in his mouth and washes it down with coffee. Jamie loved strawberries, too. I prefer orange and chocolate.

I sip my coffee to cleanse my palate. Paul offers me the last iced sweetmeat, a raspberry delight for someone, but I wrinkle my nose and shake my head. He eats the frosted nugget, stands, and then gathers his cup and empty plate.

"I'll catch up with you," Commander says.

A sentimental tear forms and threatens to escape. I miss my family and my first life so much. My children, my grandbabies. Russ. I wipe away a tear.

"What's wrong with your eye?"

"An eyelash, I guess. It's okay. It's gone," I say, blinking to prove it.

Commander gets up and walks around to my seat.

"Stand up," he says. It sounds like a command, so I obey.

By the light over the sink, he examines my eye. His warm, strawberry vanilla-scented breath mixed with coffee mingles with his aftershave and man scent, and his proximity unnerves me.

"Looks fine to me. Don't rub it. Why is the other one watering?"

"In sympathy, I guess."

Instead of moving away, he pulls me closer and before I can protest, his lips find mine. I had forgotten how much I loved his kisses, and as his hand finds my breast, an old hunger surprises me. It's been weeks since a man kissed me, or I felt the warmth of an embrace or enjoyed a man's touch. Commander's hands move to my backside, down my legs, reach under my skirt, slide up to and under my panties and I know I won't deny him.

"We don't have much time," he says, searching my eyes for permission.

I nod, knowing I shouldn't, but I want nothing more than to feel his hands all over me. With his arm around me, he guides me to the bedroom.

§

Commander lingers in the bathroom while I wait outside the door for my turn. When he exits and spots me standing there, he draws me close for a quick kiss.

"Next time will be slower. I want to see you naked again and I want to pleasure you."

Next time? This wasn't supposed to happen.

The morning drags on and I'm unable to work. Commander punished Zena. Even though Paul administered the punishment, he stood there and ordered it. How could I forget that? How could I forget his cold eyes? Zena would have never allowed this. Would she? His eyes weren't cold this morning. Neither were his hands. What does this mean?

My daily routine of listening to the voices proves fruitless, with meaningless chatter and not a word regarding the Tracker. I'm safe for now. Unable to work and restless, I journey to my second sanctuary, the atrium. Without music, it's quiet until the sprinklers turn on. Then, the smells of water and wet dirt mixed with the floral scents keep me company, and the sensory bouquet assists me in re-entering transcendence.

I concentrate on the cabin, another memory pops up, and I'm propelled into the past, in a familiar but different world.

Jade began allowing me to leave my room whenever he stayed home. They assigned me tasks, helping with meals and cleaning up, but excluded me from their strategy meetings.

I learned their names. They called the tall, dark man Cody. With his clean-shaven face, he was a handsome chap, with deep brown skin and full lips, but a bit too thin. Life was hard in the mountains. Cody was quiet, except when he cracked one-liner jokes, only in the presence of his comrades, but if we were alone in the same room, he became reserved around me. He was uncomfortable and wary, always watching, but when I'd catch him, he'd manage a smile. He appeared unsure of my allegiance to the group, but eager to welcome me into the fold.

Brothers Timothy and Jade had dishwater blonde hair, but Jade's mane was a little darker. They both had azure eyes, and it's clear where Paul gets his features. They got along well, but Jade was the leader. Timothy Abrams admired his older sibling, and I enjoyed watching the two of them, their closeness endearing. Tim was friendly with me but kept his distance at first. His trust in me had limits.

Mica appeared to be the youngest, with light brown skin, dark eyes, and a slight accent that I couldn't place, suggesting he might be of Mexican descent. He was thin with a noticeable limp but tried to hide it around me. He seemed fascinated by my presence. Like Cody, he was skittish whenever we found ourselves alone. He also watched me carefully, and when I gazed his way, I sensed his nervousness. When I read him, I discovered that his uneasiness had more to do with my gender than any threat.

The band of rebels remained respectful to me, and I was never afraid. They were still cautious when speaking in my presence, so I was mindful to be trustworthy and cooperative. One evening, the men gathered in the small kitchen for a game of poker. I had finished cleaning up dishes when Jade invited me to play.

"I've never played before," I said. "Is it difficult to learn?"

"No, I'll teach you," Jade said, grinning. He directed me to sit next to him.

"I'd love to," I said, scanning the other faces. Their friendliness convinced me I was welcome to join them.

Jade explained the rules, noting that the winner often was the best one at bluffing, not always the one with the strongest hand. He divided the poker chips into five even allotments of three stacks of ten each. Cody shuffled the cards and then Jade cut them.

After each round, they showed me their cards and took turns explaining their strategy. They never knew I could sense when they were bluffing, or read their cards if I Paid Attention, but I wasn't interested in cheating. At first, I was on a losing streak, pulling the worst cards, and my chip stack dwindled. But then Mother Luck took pity and dealt me a winning hand. The others folded except Mica, who was practiced at bluffing. I declined to read him, even though it was tempting. It was only a game. He tossed five chips into the pile, and to see his cards, I had to do likewise. My last five chips.

It was my first win, but I raked in a generous pot.

That evening, after retiring to my room, I realized someone had neglected to lock the door. After preparing for bed, I settled in, hoping it meant I succeeded in gaining their trust. If they were testing me, I'd justify their faith by staying put. I didn't want to leave. I felt safe, and a welcomed part of the clan.

While lying awake staring at nothing, unable to sleep, I heard the door open, and then close. Footsteps moved toward my bed. My dark room made it difficult to recognize the figure as he lowered himself next to me, but I recognized his familiar smell and relaxed. I felt his warm body press against my back with his arm draped across me.

"If you want me to leave, I'll go."

I turned to lie on my back, and my silence encouraged him to pull my covers off. In the dark, his hand moved to cup my face and his lips found mine. His passionate kiss had an urgency to it, but he stopped, leaned back, and waited, so I grasped his shoulder and pulled him to me, welcoming his ardent kisses. Jade took me with little foreplay. Neither of us had enjoyed the pleasure of intimacy in a very long while.

§

I had no memory of ever playing poker, understanding the game rules, or knowing how to bluff. What else have I forgotten? It was painful and bittersweet to remember my friend, Tim Abrams. I know he served in the Peace Force, but how he got here remains a mystery. What happened to Cody and Mica? Did they join too? I liked Tim and now I'm working with his son.

Cassie looks up as I return to the office, but avoids eye contact.

"Hello, Cassie, how are you this beautiful morning?"

She gives me an odd look, grunts, and looks away. Is it possible she knows what took place between Commander and me earlier? No, she's never friendly.

"Did I do something to offend you?" I ask, a little sharper than I intended.

Cassie appears taken aback but says nothing and becomes obsessed with tidying the papers on her desk.

"I may be mistaken, but it seems you've disliked me since I arrived at Cavalry. I've tried to be friendly, to no avail. If you have a problem with me, tell me. I don't have female friends here and I'm fine with that, but if I offended you somehow ... I understand military women don't think highly of civilians, but we're both women ..."

Cassie glances at Commander's open door. She squints as if to warn me to shut up.

"You're mistaken," she says in a low voice, displaying an unconvincing fake smile.

I nod, concede defeat, and return upstairs.

§

For the last hour, I've stared at my legal pad in front of me containing my list of mystery questions. The cocoon, the smear on the window, the voices, the dreams, Tommy, and the mystery of me moving from cabin to cave sixty years later. Why I lost my memory. I cross out the word cocoon. I realize now my subconscious tried to remind me of my rebirth. The smear, not a clue, but it led me to the voices. Many of my dreams were memories. There's still a mystery behind my falling asleep in the cabin and waking in the cave, but at least I remember waking up in the cabin and giving myself the name Caroline.

Tommy? Is he a piece of my puzzle? Caroline might know. He talked about her at length. She'd know how I awoke in the cave and the cause of my memory loss. She'll know who might live off base to hide and help me. A coalition? Another Resistance group?

It's past lunchtime, and a growing hunger distracts me from my mystery-solving. I grab my legal pad and head downstairs to discover today's culinary offering.

Most of the lunch crowd has returned to duty, leaving the cafeteria quiet. I eat alone, undisturbed, and after clearing my tray, I position my notes in front of me, staring at the name on the page, and retrace the letters. Tommy. An old man with white hair and ebony skin, rocking and singing hymns, and telling stories I should (but no longer) remember.

With closed eyes, an image appears of a middle-aged Black man in a van passing me on the road, and it's clear he's not Tommy. The driver stopped, greeted me, and offered a ride, assuring me he was a preacher and meant no harm. I read him and determined he was safe before climbing into the vehicle with the handwritten words *Abyssinian Baptist Church* displayed on the side. He inquired where I was headed, and I mentioned I was seeking lodging to rest for a while, hoping to find work. Despite knowing he was a man of the cloth, I concealed the fact my suitcase was full of money. My travels taught me caution.

The preacher asked me when I last had a decent meal. I told him I couldn't remember. He invited me for supper, like in Tommy's story, and when we got to his house, I met his housekeeper, Nana, and his teenage son.

After Pastor Miller said grace, they treated me to a delicious dinner of southern fried chicken, mashed potatoes and gravy, collard greens, and fresh cornbread, hot from the oven. Nana topped off the feast with homemade ice cream sprinkled with strawberry halves. We broke bread in a quaint, cozy kitchen on a red plastic flowers-and-teacups tablecloth and washed the satisfying meal down with sweet tea and fresh-squeezed lemonade. After I helped clean up our dirty dishes, we all retired to the back porch to relax.

Nana mentioned needing help with household chores, and they invited me to stay on in exchange for room and board. Their farmhouse had an extra bedroom, which Nana fixed up for me. The old furniture, handmade quilts, and hardwood floors felt like home. My hosts possessed little but had everything they needed. It was wonderful having a dresser and closet again. I stashed my suitcase under the bed and settled down to a sheltered life with my generous new friends.

Yes, Tommy. I remember. Oh, Tommy, my young friend. We hit it off right away. And I stayed hidden for five years, safe in the bosom of my new family. I'm flooded with memories of living in the old farmhouse, mentoring a teenage Tommy, and helping with household chores.

I was never a believer and going to church didn't make me one, but I attended Sunday services for the fellowship and learned to love the hymns. Old Miss Latisha Johnson's wailing Wurlitzer organ had the power to rattle the rafters and raise the dead. Or at least the sleeping. The full-throated choir, in their black and purple vestments, sang like angels.

I relished hearing Reverend Miller deliver his riveting and hypnotic message, no doubt inspired by the Holy Spirit, more than the sermons themselves. His voice was musical, resonant, and euphonious. Women in white gloves, dressed to the nines, wearing enormous feathered hats, clutched small vials of smelling salts to revive parishioners who fainted from being indwelled by the Holy Ghost, speaking in tongues. Can I have a witness?

Tommy and I spent many evenings outside, studying the night sky together, making up stories, or telling true ones. In the pitch-blackness of the country, stars burned in the heavens above. Tommy had an astronomy book, and by flashlight, we identified as many constellations as we could.

On summer afternoons, we picnicked at the lake, bringing along paper and charcoal pencils. I never revealed my special skills derived from the Gift, so my drawing ability fascinated Tommy. He practiced and became very skillful. I drew insects like butterflies and ladybugs, but he enjoyed sketching frogs, lizards, and serpents. We saw no snakes, so he worked from a library book on reptiles and amphibians. He amazed me with his God-given talent. He created stunning three-dimensional and realistic drawings. The student surpassed the teacher. I could sketch a visualized image, but he made his artwork come alive.

Three years after I joined his family, Tommy enlisted in the Army, what remained of it. They called themselves the Resistance, a stripped-down version of military life, seeking to protect the remaining farmers and villagers, but their numbers dwindled. The Overlords captured many soldiers and others chose to join the new militia. Pops and Nana were getting up in years, and the Captors were uninterested in seizing older folks.

Tommy had been gone for two years when we received news the Overlords were combing the countryside, looking for struggling young people, offering them comfort and food, and then relocating them to the bases or work camps. I had to move on.

After saying final goodbyes, I ran for the hills, a suitable place to hide, planning to return to the isolated cabin one day, doubtful anyone would own it anymore or care. I still had most of my cash, although I left an envelope on the kitchen table to thank my hosts for shelter and kindness. Money was losing its value, replaced by the sharing of community resources, but it was all I had to leave.

I never saw Tommy again.

Why did I hallucinate Tommy as an eighty-year-old man? And what was he seeking to warn me about? Why the Biblical references? I learned the Spirituals from Tommy and his family, but why did he sing them to me? No, it's not Tommy. It's me trying to remind myself of something I need to learn from my life as Caroline.

I scratch Tommy's name off my list.

Freeform doodles fill my pad of paper as I attempt to form connections between the ominous lyrics and the urgent warning delivered with them, without distraction. But fortune is not on my side. A curt David sits down across from me.

"Still no stuffed mushrooms, David."

"What year did you meet my father? And where?"

"Good afternoon to you, too."

He glares at me.

"Good afternoon," he says, obviously perturbed. "So, when did you meet my father?"

A server interrupts, approaching with a pot of coffee.

"Can I get either of you anything?" she asks, focusing on David.

"None for me, but when will y'all serve those amazing stuffed mushrooms again?" I ask.

David folds his arms across his chest and sighs.

"I'm not sure. We'll have to wait for another shipment. You liked them, did you?"

He scowls at me and drums his fingers on the table.

"I loved them. They were incredible. Didn't you love them, Lieutenant?"

His eyes narrow, and he makes a fist like he's trying to control himself, but I suspect he'd enjoy slapping me right about now.

David glares at the server and says, "Sure. Delicious. That's all." He waves her off.

I gather my papers and stand to leave.

"I'm sorry, Lieutenant Cross, but I'm expected for a meeting with Major Abrams, and I dare not be late. Let's pick this up another time."

I walk away.

Chapter 7

Tommy seemed so real when he appeared in the library as a man of advanced years. But he was a hallucination, a figment of my imagination, my unconscious mind trying to break through with an urgent message I needed to hear. He served here at Cavalry two decades ago. My subconscious must have registered his name from the memorial wall while searching for Andrew's plaque.

I'm unaware of anyone on the steps, so it jars me from my concentration when I spot Commander standing across from me. We enjoyed coffee and sweets at my worktable this morning, so I'm surprised he's back so soon.

"How's everything going? You're deep in thought."

"Yes sir. I didn't hear you come upstairs."

His eyes twinkle, a familiar look I remember from last summer.

"I want to see you tonight after I finish working out and shower," he says and waits for my answer.

I'm tempted, but based on previous experience, I know I should decline. It won't pay to encourage him or give him the wrong impression. This man is unhealthy for me, and I haven't forgotten our disastrous, lopsided relationship. I've no interest in his mind games and can't handle more heartache. My focus must stay on completing my mission.

"I'll be here."

He leaves in triumph, and I kick myself.

§

Commander waits for me at his office suite door, wearing a cocky smile like he was certain I'd show. As if I couldn't do otherwise. He's sweaty from his workout and when we're upstairs in the apartment, he sheds his undershirt,

43

gives me a quick kiss, and then disappears into the bathroom. I remove my shoes and set them by the steps. While he showers, I select a favorite disc and unfasten my hair tie, releasing my long ponytail.

The dark view from the enormous windows hides the endless stretch of trees, but the blue-hued moon lights up the mountaintop when it peeks out from behind the clouds. No stars tonight. The expansive room, echoing my soft, relaxing music, becomes a romantic den. What am I doing here?

Fresh and half-naked from his shower, Commander meets me halfway in the middle of the living room and begins his ritual of kissing me with passion and tenderness. I melt into his arms. He scoops me up and carries me into the bedroom, where he kisses me again. His confidence is both presumptuous and exciting.

"Take off your clothes," he says in a husky whisper. "I want to see all of you."

He waits, with his expectant eyes inspecting every inch of me, from my breasts down to my bare feet. Suddenly, I feel self-conscious.

"You take off yours, too," I say, although he's not wearing much.

I remove my garments with care, folding them and placing each item one at a time on a chair, and then lay my lanyard on top. While watching me, he kicks off his slippers and removes his sweatpants, his only clothing. Nude, I stand before him, waiting for him to make the first move, remembering how much he enjoys that. He lifts me with tenderness and sets me on the bed. It takes no time at all for me to forget I'm making a mistake.

§

The music ended a while ago, and I'm swimming in the afterglow of our unhurried lovemaking, feeling content and satisfied. It fades fast. Regrets and concerns bubble to the top of my euphoria. How can making love to Commander be wrong and yet feel so incredible? He's not the smart choice for me, and I can't afford to pretend otherwise. I also don't have the luxury of offending him. He may become a key player in protecting me from the Tracker or getting me to a safer location. But for now, I'm indulging in the sweet pleasure of nestling in his arms, my head on his chest, savoring the moment. This time, he doesn't hint for me to leave.

His eyes are closed, but when I sit up to study him, he opens them, looking pleased.

"What?" he asks.

"Nothing. Just feeling good," I say, brushing his cheek with my fingertips, toying with the idea of reading him. He shuts his eyes.

Instead, with my head on his shoulder, I trace his arm muscles with a light touch. I work my way from his chest, traveling down one side of his stomach and up the other. I make circles with my finger along the edge of his navel like it's a tiny skater. His muscular abs become an ice rink glazed with sweat.

"What are you doing?" he asks, with closed eyes.

"I'm exploring," I say, tracking through his treasure trail. I find a small, round, brown mole, and circle it.

"If you discover anything interesting, let me know."

When I touch his left side near his stomach, he flinches and grabs my hand, bringing it up to his chest, and holding it there.

"Commander's ticklish?" I ask.

"A little bit."

As soon as he releases my hand, I move it back down to the sensitive spot. He pulls me over on top of him with his hands cradling my behind.

"Watch it. You're asking for a spanking."

"I'll be a good girl," I say, feigning innocence.

"That's too bad."

We climb under the covers, and I turn my back to him. When I hear Commander's soft snoring, I slip out of bed, return to the living room, and play my music again, only turned down low, careful not to wake him. Curled up on the couch, satisfied and mellow, listening to the beautiful melodies, I drift off and a blocked memory seeps through the cracks of my subconscious. A forgotten time, another version of myself, a different man in my bed.

§

Jade, Tim, and I were playing cards at the kitchen table when Cody and Mica returned from foraging. They didn't return alone. Two dirty and disheveled young women walked in behind our comrades. Inside the cabin, they huddled together and looked around at each of us. Fear covered their faces.

"Look what we found," said Mica. "They were hiding under some bushes, sound asleep."

"Are you girls all right?" I asked. "Are you hungry?"

They both shook their heads.

"We caught a couple rabbits and cooked them. The girls were starved," Cody said.

We adjourned to the living room, and our guests introduced themselves as Anna and Wendy. They sat close together on the couch to tell their daunting tale.

"After fleeing our farm, we holed up in an abandoned barn outside of Sheffield. We needed to run because we heard the Captors were searching for young women to kidnap, and they were headed for our county," said Wendy, looking from one face to another, wringing her hands.

"But instead, a band of renegades captured us. They made us travel with them," says Anna. "They insisted we ... take care of them since we were the only females."

Anna looked down at her hands, folded in her lap.

Jade fired a cautious look at his comrades. They had been fooled before.

"We saw the rebels heading east. I think they were hunting the girls. We had to convince them we wouldn't force them to come with us," said Mica.

Cody shook his head in agreement.

"I believe their story," he said. "Look at them. These young ladies were scared to death of us. Somebody hurt them." Cody walked over to Wendy, and with two fingers lifted her hair from her face, revealing a fist-sized bruise.

"How did you get away?" I asked.

"For three days, they forced us to travel with them on foot. We ended up miles from anything familiar. Everyone was exhausted, and when we stopped to make camp and the rebels slept, we escaped, fleeing by moonlight, carrying our few belongings. We kept going until sunrise. We couldn't go on. Needed to sleep. So, we came across a safe place to hide ourselves and fell asleep. When they found us," said Wendy, gesturing to Cody and Mica, "we thought we were caught for sure."

"We were so scared," said Anna.

"Found them both conked out near the forest edge this afternoon," said Mica. "They tried to run, but we offered them food and help."

"We promised the girls they'd be safe here," Cody said.

Anna twisted a section of her long, blazing red hair, winding it around her finger. She looked exhausted and worried, and a wayward tear slid down her smudged, freckled face.

I read the young women. They were telling the truth.

"You'll be safe here," I said, hoping to reassure these nervous women. "I've lived here a while and I'm treated quite well. These are good guys."

After cleaning themselves up, the women helped in the kitchen, and we all sat down to a venison meal with boiled potatoes and fresh spinach. They knew their way around a kitchen. We agreed Anna and Wendy could share one bedroom. Jade and I slept in his. The other men took turns sleeping in the remaining bedroom or on the large living room sectional.

Over time, Anna and Wendy became part of our family and the grateful women were glad to pitch in. Once Anna acclimated to our lifestyle, she laughed with ease and cooked the tastiest meals with whatever game the hunters bagged. She had a natural talent for cooking and was a welcome addition. My culinary skills were lacking, especially with the variety of meat the hunters procured. I never minded handing her the reins, and although Wendy and I helped, Anna took rightful charge of the kitchen.

Wendy wore her short curly brown hair in two small pigtails. She was petite, with a generous figure. Rested, she possessed endless energy, more drive than any woman had a right to, always fussing about, picking up after us, cleaning, putting everything in order. Orderliness was never one of my strong suits.

Anna was taller than either Wendy or me, but she reminded me of a Raggedy Anne doll with her round face, longer copper color hair, and freckles. She brightened up the small cabin and added more feminine energy to our male-dominated clan. Both a godsend, we got along like sisters, without the fighting. I welcomed the female companionship. Having more women among us pleased the males, too, and it wasn't long before the women and men paired off, taking turns. But not with Jade. He was mine.

A few weeks later, Cody and Tim discovered Leanna, scared, hungry, and alone, and brought her home, too. She appeared traumatized, so we women set about to get her washed up, fed, and feeling safe again. Leanna brought nothing with her, so we found extra clothes for her. In the beginning, she slept with Anna or Wendy.

Cleaned up, Leanna was beautiful with her dark tanned skin and blonde hair plaited into two long braids. Somewhat standoffish at first, she soon warmed up to the rest of us and was grateful to be part of our family. Our male comrades relished her appealing presence.

All three women were in their twenties, my believed age, and we formed a sisterhood, but our small cabin was getting crowded. Over time, our group split into four pairs, but there were three bedrooms and four couples. They managed the sleeping arrangements by rotating the use of the bedrooms and living room. Everyone took turns using the bathtub in the hall bathroom. My housemates also shared one another, but Jade and I were exclusive, and I wouldn't share him or myself. As the leader's girl, I enjoyed an advantage.

In addition to cooking and cleaning the other women often accompanied the menfolk on hunting or gathering trips. The pursuit of food had become more difficult with more mouths to feed, my money long gone, and signs of winter coming.

Sometimes the men took women with them to "hunt," but I suspected our womenfolk "traded" for whatever they could get in the nearby towns. I never judged because they brought back supplies and it meant we'd have plenty to eat.

With few villages or small towns left, motivated townspeople found ways of acquiring goods. Networks formed of scavengers, thieves, and ordinary people desperate to survive. Barter became the coin of the realm. Our menfolk owned a single rifle and a limited supply of ammo and often ventured out alone to hunt game.

I never imagined my life turning out this way. During the day, our lives were rough, but when the lights went out and I snuggled, safe in Jade's embrace, nothing else existed. Jade was my strength and my companion. Curled in his arms in bed, I felt hopeful, cared for, and could rest easy. Following my rebirth, I hadn't run into any Trackers. Since receiving the Gift, I had made a habit of listening to the alien voices. After years of hearing nothing useful, eventually I abandoned the practice. But the possibility of another Tracker hunting me down never escaped me. I hid my secrets from Jade, and I never sought to be privy to his. It was easier that way.

§

My music finishes again, so I turn off my console player and return to the bedroom where Commander remains fast asleep. I slide in next to him. Jade held great importance in my life. I know he's not out there anymore. Paul said his uncle died when he was a youngster. It was so long ago, a lifetime ago, but my memories feel like it was yesterday. I ache to tell Paul that I knew his father and loved his uncle. But I can't.

Chapter 8

The atrium flowers smell more fragrant tonight, perhaps because I'm more content than I've been in a while. My relationships are improving, I'm recovering more and more memories, and I've had success at building an alliance like I had with Jade and his comrades. David and I remain at odds, but I must set him free, anyway. David. We had our intimate moments. He let down his guard and allowed me to see the real David, the one he hides from everyone. But I'm aware of his dark side and I'll never be what he wants. I fell for his charm when I was innocent, but Grandma knows better. Doesn't she?

Paul and I have forged a civil working relationship. Slow progress is still progress. Knowing who you're dealing with revises the narrative and I need Paul's cooperation. He is Jade's nephew, and my opinion of him has improved. We're connected by fate. He's a very intelligent man, even if we don't always agree, and I understand he was performing his duty when he doled out that punishment swat. It was difficult for Zena to forgive, but I have bigger issues and a different perspective. He has been more than decent to me these past few months.

The cloudless evening sky and the moonshine create enough light. This atrium lacks indoor lighting, and they don't expect visitors after dark, so I always have the place to myself.

Moonlight and starlight filtering through the windows provide a romantic glimmer. I yearn for someone to share my star gazing. Tommy and I spent many long summer nights studying the glowing orbs and dreaming of better days that never came.

It grows dark earlier now, with sure signs of winter. Outside. But inside, it never changes. I'd go stark raving mad if I couldn't gaze out the windows and view the endless forest or witness the never-ending starry black sky that reaches toward infinity. A vast world waits for me just beyond my reach, and somewhere out there lies my destiny. But where?

With my disc player turned on and my headphones covering my ears, I belt out my favorite tunes without concern. It's Thursday, Club night, and I can sing as loud as I wish, drowned out by the noise blasting from Club and its surrounding activity. The partygoers, with their rowdy, noisy laughter, can't hear me. My pad of paper and a pen sit idle next to me. The light is too dim for writing, so I daydream and sing my heart out.

Earlier, when I listened to the voices, the chatter never mentioned the Tracker. Every morning when I pay attention to them, nothing noteworthy emerges from the Jabberwocky. With an entire planet to search, the aliens have no reason to suspect I'm hiding inside one of their bases. Alien communications continue to discuss a colossal event or celebration, but I'm clueless about its meaning. Their culture is foreign to me.

My memories of Caroline living with Jade and the Resistance clan are few, but I've recalled tons of sweet painful reminiscences of my original life, so different from my current existence. For the past decade, I believed I was a young woman, never married, never stepping off base—aside from the day I left the cave. This military culture stands in stark contrast to my former world.

The twenty-first century was a global era. Turn on your TV or computer, or pick up your smartphone, and the news of hurricanes, war, famine, floods, drought, political upheavals, or landings on the moon, streamed right into your living room. Now, it's unknown what became of other countries. I know the Earth rebounded from its catastrophic climate crisis, but what about the world's population? We're so isolated on our remote bases that we know nothing beyond these walls.

Commander has been friendlier since our rendezvous on Monday. This morning he was first to offer me a sweet orange treat but didn't invite me to Club. Whenever I encounter him in the break room, he's pleasant but says little. I need alliances, and the upper echelon would provide protection. This time will be different. I'm not the same and I've abandoned Zena's unreasonable expectations. I'm aware of who he is and won't be drawn off course.

My CD ends. It's late, and I should get some sleep. Clutching my pen, paper, and player, I follow the wall to reach the great floor. It's darker until I'm outside of the atrium, in the illumination of the great floor's dim evening light. My pen tumbles from my hand and I fumble to keep my disc player from meeting the same fate. By accident, my music restarts.

I squat to retrieve my errant pen, readjust my load, and stand to see Commander a few feet away, his arm draped around Mary Jo. As soon as he sees me, he drops his arm from her shoulder. He's speaking to me, but I can't understand him with my headphones on and my loud song playing, so I switch it off and jerk the headset from my ears.

"Where did you come from? Were you in Club?" he asks.

"No sir, I was in the atrium. I visit there sometimes to think or listen to music."

A knife pierces my gut, taking me by surprise. My feelings are illogical. I know better. We're not in a relationship and our two recent sexual encounters were meaningless. He needs Mary Jo for Play. I pretend it doesn't bother me seeing them together, hiding the fact that the knife keeps twisting. I nod to Mary Jo and offer an award-winning fake smile. Commander looks like a little boy caught with his hand in the cookie jar. He wasn't expecting to run into me. Another *déjà vu* moment.

I want to tell them to enjoy themselves, but the words stick in my throat. Instead, I turn away and mutter, "Goodnight. Have a good one." I sense them watching me as I stumble across the rotunda to my miserable tiny room.

Michael's shirt no longer smells like him, and it's irrational, but I wear it to bed for false comfort. It makes no sense, but I do it anyway, slipping it over my nightgown. I hug my pillow and stare at nothing. This shouldn't hurt because he's not mine. It meant nothing. Why does it hurt?

A wave of familiar betrayal washes over me with another memory.

§

I thought I'd go mad, cooped up in the cabin, and needed fresh air, so I joined Cody and Wendy in scouring for wild strawberries or blackberries for most of the morning. I had volunteered to accompany Tim and Mica to help scavenge provisions in a ghost town a mile away, but Jade nixed that idea and asked Anna to take my place. As his girl, he was protective of me. After foraging for meager fruit, I returned to the cabin while Cody and Wendy set off to find wild game. I couldn't be a party to killing an innocent animal. I'd make a lousy hunter.

The quiet cabin appeared empty, and I wondered where Jade and Leanna had ventured off. I didn't trust her, but Jade and I had an understanding. He was mine. I dumped the fruit into the kitchen sink for washing and headed upstairs, looking for Jade. I checked our bedroom. No Jade. The hall bathroom door stood open, and I saw nobody in there.

Laughing and squealing echoed from another bedroom. The door stood ajar, so I peeked in and discovered Jade's whereabouts. And Leanna's. He was on his back, naked, on the bed Leanna shared with Tim. A naked Leanna straddled him.

Anguish started somewhere in the pit of my stomach and erupted in a horrified scream. Jade cursed, pushed Leanna off him, and I turned and ran. I knew the woods well and raced for my favorite spot to be alone to cry in private. Jade found me crumpled on my meditation log, sobbing my heart out. Dressed and contrite, he sat next to me, and when I rose to leave, he pulled me to him.

"Baby, I'm so sorry. I didn't mean to hurt you. It just happened. I love you, babe."

I pushed him away. How could he touch me after what I witnessed? I couldn't blame him for desiring Leanna. She was beautiful and blond, and all the men wanted their turn with her. But he was mine. She could have any of the others.

"Leave me," I cried, choking on my sobs.

"No, listen. She teased me and before I knew what was happening ..."

I screamed, "Liar." A lame excuse. He was lying. It was all over his face. I didn't need to read him to understand his deceit.

"No, baby, come on. I never meant to hurt you. I thought you were with Cody and Wendy."

"That makes it okay? You think what I don't know can't hurt me?"

"Look, you're my girl. But the guys all share the girls. It doesn't mean anything."

"Take your hands off me," I said, pulling away from Jade. Fresh tears filled my eyes.

He forced me back into his arms, holding me so tight I couldn't move.

"I never shared myself with anyone but you. How long have you been fucking those whores behind my back?" I asked, trying to free myself, my anger rising. I fought an intense urge to bite him. Hard.

"I won't lie to you. We're in a war, fighting to stay free, and normal rules don't apply."

"I don't want you to lie. I want you to keep your filthy hands off me. You said you loved me, but it's a lie, a damn lie. How could you ... with her? We're done."

"No, I do love you. Baby, don't say that. I won't lose you. I don't care about Leanna. Not like that. I only care about you. I love you."

"You're too late, Jade. You lost me."

I broke free and ran back to the cabin. For a week, I spoke to no one. Leanna kept her distance. Whenever I saw her, I glared. I hated her. She knew I was Jade's girl. She knew he was mine. They both betrayed me.

Jade tiptoed around me, making sure not to further offend me. He went out of his way to please me and avoid her. At least in my presence. He'd bring me wildflowers and lay them on my pillow and when I discovered them, they flew into the garbage. The next day, he would bring another bundle. Chocolates would have been better received. I couldn't remember when I last tasted the delicious treats.

I couldn't kick him to the couch. Mica and Wendy were sleeping there now. The couples took turns making the living room their bedroom. Everyone except Jade and me. His status as leader had its privileges, but he lost the privilege of my bed when I exiled him to the hard floor.

One night, he ignored my refusal and climbed into bed with me.

"Baby, I love you, only you. I promise from this day forward, I'll never touch another woman. Please forgive me. Give me a chance to show you."

"I'll know if you betray me."

"I'll never betray you. You're the most important person in my life. Don't turn away."

Had I Paid Attention, I'd have discovered his deceit. He wasn't aware of my skills, and I rarely used them. I concealed my special abilities because word travels fast and the Tracker might get wind of my clairvoyant capabilities.

Everyone deserves a second chance.

Chapter 9

It's quiet as I climb the apartment stairs. No male chatter this morning, and I'm grateful to avoid dealing with Commander. I'll miss my sweets, but they're unhealthy for me, too.

I have only myself to blame this time. Maya Angela said that if someone shows you who they are, believe them. I knew who Commander was and ignored it. I want to form a coalition, but I'm afraid I'm still making mistakes because I'm not listening to my head. Another part of my body has hijacked my common sense. Commander should be my ally, not my lover. It causes too much friction and I need a clear head. It's too important.

When I reach the top of the steps, I find the officers sitting at my worktable as if nothing's wrong. Paul rises and moves aside to let me pass. Not eager for a confrontation, I pretend everything's fine, and proceed to set up my workspace. Paul offers me an orange-flavored cake, but a sudden wave of nausea overtakes me, so I frown and shake my head. He shrugs and stands to leave.

"I'll be down in a few minutes," Commander says to Paul.

Paul leaves, and I brace myself for an unpleasant conversation.

"You surprised me on the floor last night," says Commander, watching my reaction.

"It surprised me to see you, too," I say, avoiding his eyes. I try to appear as if nothing's wrong, but I'm dreading this, and I'm sure it shows. After I pull my computer and notepads from the cupboard, I take my time setting up my worktable. I avoid looking at him as I turn on my laptop and shuffle papers.

"You know, sometimes I need to Play."

"Yes sir, I know."

"So, we're good?"

He sounds so nonchalant. I want to lie and tell him everything's fine, but nothing is.

"We've gone down this road before, sir, and I prefer not to repeat it. I blame myself because I walked into this affair with eyes wide open, but I erred in believing I could handle a casual sexual arrangement. It's not who I am. Let's call it a day, say it was fun, and move on."

"Come on, Zena. You can't change the culture here, so you must change. Either accept my time with Mary Jo or Play. It's simple."

"Or I can choose someone who doesn't Play."

Commander rubs his chin. "You don't want anyone else." He leans back with smug conceit. Okay. His confidence was sexy before, but not today.

"I wanted this to work for me. We have amazing sex, but I'm not what you desire most. I'm not interested in an open relationship, nor do I wish to invest in a shipwreck."

He smiles as if he doesn't believe me.

"Seeing you with Mary Jo last night ... it hurt."

His face becomes serious. He's not expecting that.

"I'm confused myself because I understand who you are and that I mean nothing to you. Mary Jo can't matter much either, or you wouldn't have been with me. It makes no sense for me to be jealous. Yet, when I saw you and realized I'm not what you want ... it hurt."

I keep my voice low and soft to avoid sounding like I'm attacking him. I'm showing my belly. It would displease Nadler, but his way failed me. Today's a new day, and I'm different.

"It shouldn't hurt," I say.

He says nothing, waiting for me to finish.

"I promised myself I'd never allow you to touch me after ..." I wave my hand in the air towards the living room, but I'm sure he understands I mean the punishment. "But when you kissed me, I couldn't think. I wanted you and gave in to my desires. You approached me again, and I thought it would be fine to have sex with someone who no longer matters to me, and I should just enjoy myself."

He bites his lower lip and waits.

"But when I saw you with Mary Jo ..." I bite my own lip.

"I won't Play with you because that wouldn't give me pleasure. It bothers me that the idea of hurting me excites you. For me, lovemaking is a beautiful, shared experience, not a one-sided arrangement. If realizing I'm not enough for you is painful for me, then it's an awful deal. I'm not sure why you're interested in me. You know who I am and what I love."

Commander shifts in his seat.

"Zena, I've asked you to Play. You've made it clear you won't even try it. How can you deny me, yet expect me to stay away from someone who is willing to Play ... and enjoys it?"

"I'm not asking you to give up Mary Jo or Lynn. What I'm saying is that I can't engage with you in a sexual relationship. My experience last summer was crazy-making. I won't Play with you. And I don't share."

Commander shakes his head, and his chest falls.

"Look, I want to be on good terms with you. You're the base commander. There's nothing in it for me, and I don't need more pain right now, because I'm swimming in it. Go back to what you love. You will eventually, anyway."

I rest my case.

Chapter 10

This week has flown by, and each day it gets easier to remember Caroline's life. I don't need the transcendental state anymore. My memories are often triggered by phrases I hear, someone's actions, or something unusual noticed. Caroline lived free, and while the Resistance had become her family, living remained hard. The alliance was strong, we each had a stake in it, and our trust and loyalty to the cause eased the hardship. We were all rowing in the same boat.

I'm waiting to meet with Paul later this morning. The Master Plan lays open to the section describing kidnapping Good Actors to use for reproduction and capturing Bad Actors to enslave for building additional bases. My recovered memories of Caroline prove that two and a half decades after my reincarnation, young women still existed in the outer world. Our isolation kept us safe. Or did it?

I'm jolted into recalling an event that occurred several months after the other women joined Jade's Resistance band. This memory hits me hard as if it happened yesterday. The recollection is so vivid I can smell the rabbit stew simmering on the stove and hear the chirping crickets. I opened the screen door to welcome our comrades home on that ill-fated day. Two men and two women set out to secure provisions, but only Cody returned.

§

"They're gone," Cody said, out of breath and frantic.

"What happened? What do you mean, gone?" Jade demanded.

"Uniformed men surrounded us, some type of military detachment. They never spotted me. I was off ... answering the call of nature. When I saw them, I hid out of sight, but they caught Tim and the girls."

Cody slumped into a chair, setting his rifle down on the floor beside him.

"I saw them handcuff Tim and the girls and force them into a truck and I could do nothing but stand there, watching from a distance. I had the rifle, but the Captors had at least twenty armed men," Cody says, his hands shaking. "They outnumbered me, and they had their truck and jeeps, and me, I'm on foot." He flung his arms in the air. "I'm so sorry, man. I don't know what I could've done. They would have killed me before I got them all, and that wouldn't save anyone."

Jade dropped to the couch and leaned back, stunned with disbelief, his eyes wide open, unblinking, staring at Cody. He opened his mouth to speak, but the words never left his lips, just a guttural sound.

I sat next to him and touched his arm, knowing there was nothing I could do to ease this pain. Not even the Gift could relieve the suffering over the loss of his brother. In silence, I watched the two men struggling to deal with the unfathomable.

"Did they hurt them?" asked Jade.

"No. Tim and the girls cooperated and ..."

Cody wept.

"It should have been me they took. Tim should be here telling you this."

Cody shook his head in despair.

"You did all you could, Cody. There were too many. Could happen to any of us."

His shoulders dropped, and Jade closed his eyes. Mica and Wendy stood by Cody's side, unsure of what to say or do. Mica looked to me for answers, but I had none. Wendy put her arm around Cody and wept with him.

That night, in the quiet cabin, no one spoke. Instead, we stared at each other, drowning in the terror we felt. The loss of his brother hit Jade hard, and no amount of comfort lessened his anguish. Anna and Leanna were gone, too. Our missing comrades left unwelcome room for the remaining five of us, and their absence filled the cabin with eerie silence. Another harsh reminder we were casualties of an unwanted war.

§

Sitting at my worktable, staring out at the peaceful mountains, I return to the present. Were Anna and Leanna considered Good Actors? Did they produce children for the Overlords to groom to their liking? Paul mentioned that his father, Timothy, joined the Peace Force. Did he ever see our women again?

I'm glad they didn't send Tim to work camps to build bases, and I'm comforted that Tim seems to have made a decent life for himself. There's a reasonable chance the women also fared well. To my knowledge, the Overlords never send women to the work camps. They might have sent females to cook for the captives or wash their clothes. The Master Plan doesn't cover that.

The Plan states the base builders would enslave healthy, young male criminals and drug dealers, each deemed a harmful element of society. They would abduct them off city streets. Outlaws, thieves, and troublemakers were their prime choices.

Timothy Abrams was a decent person and I'm gratified and relieved the Overlords made the same determination. He was smart to make the most of his detention by joining the Peace Force. If they confined the women to the same base, he would look after them.

Anna and Leanna were young enough to bear children. Base living has more comforts and conveniences than the cabin did. If the Captors sent the women to the Overlords' complex, I believe they would have received fair treatment. If they sent them to ours, the Peace Force might have protected them.

Leanna would have fared well wherever she ended up. She was beautiful, and that would be an advantage. I only wish Jade could have known that Tim was okay, that he married and had a son.

Had the Overlords failed to capture our comrades, my friends' lives would have taken a far different path. Paul wouldn't have been born. Commander's Inner Circle might not exist.

That would have happened decades ago. They might all be dead now. Paul mentioned never knowing his uncle. He was a young child when his uncle died many years ago. I realize if I keep remembering, I'll lose Jade all over again. How many losses can one human being endure?

Paul arrives for our meeting with his arms laden with periodicals. He attempts to set them on the table, and several of them slide off the top, so I grab the errant magazines and canvas their covers to see what he's brought me. The publications are old but in perfect condition as if sealed in plastic containers.

I scan each cover page to learn what Paul chose to show me. The dates center around 2025 and the feature stories reflect the growing chaos that permeated every corner of the world. Hunger drove war to a new high. Fascism destroyed the lives of millions. But behind the scenes, unusual bases were being built. One article called them compounds and there was a great mystery about the groups behind their construction.

Most of the people disappearing were criminals, the disenfranchised, and young females. When white girls vanished, it made the evening news for as long as memory serves. While abductions and sex trafficking explained their disappearances, police found no traces of them.

The end was upon us, and we watched it happen, all while the rich sat on their yachts sipping wine and eating caviar. Instead of the people working together to secure our lives, we divided into factions and fought each other, consistent with the Master Plan's objective to divide and conquer.

Paul and I read through the periodicals and discuss the relevant events or occurrences that coincide with the information I've gleaned from the Book. In my original life as Rebecca, I lived through the chaos, unaware it was part of a planned scheme to conquer the world.

By 2025, I had already received the Gift from the dying alien in the car crash, my husband, Russ, had died, and I was on my own, knowing that extraterrestrials were after me to reclaim my Gift. In 2027, I encountered my first alien Tracker and killed him.

In 2030, I decided to rebirth and reinvent myself with a new identity. It was unclear how long rejuvenation would take, but I was ready. I visited my remaining family one last time before disappearing. I hated leaving them, but fate drafted me into an uncharted destiny, where I would outlive them all, as Caroline.

After two hours, I help Paul gather the magazines and carry them downstairs, past his office space, to a small storeroom. I return upstairs alone, overwhelmed by taking this stroll into the past, remembering how everything changed forever.

I take my post by the window to prepare to listen for the voices while my background meditation music plays, but instead, I sail off to another memory.

§

Everything changed after losing almost half of our group. Even though it had been several months since her betrayal, I'm ashamed to confess I didn't miss Leanna. We had become like sisters before that fateful evening when Leanna latched on to my lover. I never forgave her, but not once did I wish soldiers would abduct our comrades. For a long time, I trusted no one after Leanna's disloyalty. Now she and Anna were gone....

Wendy and I shared the housework, but the men never again invited us on their hunting trips. Jade often took a turn and left us with either Cody or Mica. Often, the men stayed away the entire day, and we worried ourselves sick when it started getting dark—until they returned.

It took forever until we felt safe again, but we continued grieving the loss of our comrades. The mood turned dark, and the tension was thick as pea soup for several months, but when spring arrived it brought a new sense of hope with the dandelions and fresh, warmer air.

It also brought two new fugitives. Shana and Abbey joined us, with a contribution of a considerable amount of stolen food. The former farmers had discovered an abandoned warehouse and had pilfered a large stockpile of canned and boxed goods and other supplies, hoarding them in their makeshift shelter. It took them several trips to amass a large supply of goods before a salvage crew seized the warehouse and interrupted their doomed final trip.

The women escaped capture undetected but encountered Cody and Jade instead. After a short negotiation, the women traded their stash for protection and became willing members of our collective. It took the seven of us several trips to transfer the provisions from their shelter to the cabin, but we all took joy in our efforts. The joint alliance was beneficial to everyone.

Our lives became easier with a surplus of supplies and food, allowing the men to hang around the cabin more. We had more females for Cody and Mica to share, and extra help to prepare meals. Shana and Abbey were tough, coarse sisters, having worked and lived on a farm before their way of life ended, before becoming survivors like us, on the run, embracing a new type of existence.

The dark-skinned, full-figured women, both in their late thirties or early forties, had short black frizzy hair bound in colorful turban headwraps. They were both remarkable cooks and enjoyed fussing about in the kitchen. The overbearing older women took over kitchen duties. After all, it was their pilfered food.

Many mornings, they delighted us with griddlecakes smothered in homemade maple syrup. I watched spellbound as Shana flipped the flapjacks with her spatula and they flew skyward, then tumbled end over end, landing right side up on the griddle to finish cooking. She insisted I try it, and I was game. On my initial disastrous attempt, my pancake took off upward without problem but landed on the floor, gooey side down. Shana laughed. I cleaned up my mess. With much encouragement and appreciated advice, I tried again until I succeeded.

We had never enjoyed pancakes with syrup until Shana and Abbey showed up with a slew of useful skills. Dinners were always amazing no matter what the men brought home, often topped off with sweet potato pie, from tubers harvested from the banks of the nearby river. We had bread from acorns and wild mint tea sweetened with honey. We hadn't eaten that well since we lost Anna and her cooking skills.

The housemothers scolded the rest of us, who had become lax, demanding we pick up after—and take better care of—ourselves, insisting on doing things their way. We all fell in line, knowing it was for our own good.

The men, in particular, got a kick out of being smothered with tough mother love, but Wendy and I enjoyed their supportive attention. It minimized our stress. Wendy and I were happy to step back from kitchen duties. Our depression and fears melted away. Shana and Abbey were decent people, and it was their strength and resilience that got us through the darkest days.

The older women teamed up to create a formidable force, but their gospel singing in the kitchen and laughter were infectious. The cabin bounded back to life. It was never cleaner or more organized and the almost constant activity helped us forget our losses and the direness of our situation.

Their vivid storytelling or soulful singing made even the quiet evenings palatable. I knew many of the hymns, having learned them while living with Tommy's family. Sometimes I sang the old rock tunes I knew, and Wendy belted out her favorite country songs. Cody played his harmonica. We might have been an odd collection of souls, and we weren't blood, but we were family.

In time, Jade took his turn with our new sisters. I Paid Attention, so he couldn't hide it, even though he tried to be discreet. I said nothing. He still mourned the loss of his brother and I suspected he was avoiding becoming too attached to me.

We spent less time together and often quarreled when we did. His brother's capture changed him, and our fears changed us all. My new policy was *whatever gets you through the night* ... I cared for Jade and continued to be faithful because that's my way, but I held no judgment for anyone else. We had all suffered.

§

When I stitch together what I read in the Book with the information the magazines offer, plus my memories as Caroline, it creates a disturbing tapestry of destruction and misery. I remember my tough, desperate life, although in all its darkness we enjoyed a fellowship I never experienced on the bases.

My apprehended comrades no doubt had several advantages when they became subjects of the Overlords, but I can't help believing they lost so much more. Timothy joined the Peace Force, married, and had a son. Base life may be easier, but none of us in the Resistance understood our fate if kidnapped, and protecting our liberty was our ultimate mission. With much more at stake, I'd have chosen freedom over an easier life. But here I am, captured. Again.

My stomach growls, reminding me it's lunchtime. The wall clock agrees, and I need a break. I pass Cassie on the way out. She's head down, absorbed in sorting through documents without looking up. Everyone has a story, and I wonder about hers. She never seems happy, but she looks at Commander like he walks on water. I suspect we'll never be friends, but I understand. She was the queen bee in the office before I arrived. It must be painful for her to share his attention with another younger female. It's disturbing where my thoughts are taking me. Time to shift gears and consider the cafeteria menu.

David waits for me at my usual table. I set my tray down and slide into my seat.

"They don't have stuffed mushrooms today," I say.

"Damn. Guess I'll go." He raises his eyebrows and takes a sip of coffee.

I take a bite of my grilled eggplant and make a face. It doesn't taste as good as it looks, but I'm hungry. The side dish of spaghetti proves tastier.

"How long have you worked for Central Intelligence?" David asks. "What year did you meet my father?"

"Why do you ask?"

David glares at me for a moment, then his face softens.

"You mentioned you worked for my father when he was still a major, and you were unaware of his marriage to Elly, but he married eight years ago. You told me you're younger than twenty-four. That means you were a teenager when you knew my father. Around what, fifteen?"

My eggplant tastes bitter, or maybe it's the panic working its way up from my guts. My delicious stuffed mushrooms preoccupied me when David bombarded me with his questions earlier. Had I paid more attention to our conversation, I would have realized he was interrogating me.

I'm getting careless. A year ago, I'd have never let this happen.

"You're lying about something. They don't allow anyone under eighteen on military bases, and my father isn't sloppy when bringing civilians on base. If I hadn't heard my father myself ...," David says, squinting in disbelief. "And I've never seen my father back down from anyone, especially not a civilian woman. If he decides you're leaving with him ... you're leaving. Had I behaved the way you did at lunch, I'd have paid a steep price. But you ... he didn't react. Why?"

"You wanted me to leave?"

"No, but that's beside the point. He made a special trip here to take you with him."

"What did I do wrong at lunch? I was on my best behavior."

David shakes his head as if he can't believe I don't know.

"First, you don't speak until a commander addresses you. Second, you never refuse to follow a commander's orders. Even a civilian woman wouldn't dare behave as you did."

"No, David, I invited him here for coffee before the luncheon. We discussed my needs, and I presented a strong case for staying here."

"You brought him to the cafeteria?"

David looks as if I just told him I danced naked on the tables.

"Yes, for coffee. I thought Mary Jo and her cronies would enjoy having something to gossip about," I say. I'm not even trying to hide my satisfaction, remembering the pleasure I got from that maneuver.

"Okay, there's much more to this than you're telling me."

"Let it go, David. Some matters are best left alone. You haven't talked about this with anyone, have you? Promise me you didn't."

"Not yet. We need to talk, but not here. Meet me tonight in my office."

"I don't think that's a good idea, David. Just trust me enough to understand I'm looking out for your best interest. Please, just let it go."

David looks at me with suspicion and I fear I've only added fuel to his curiosity.

"Okay, fine. I'll ask Major Matthews what he knows or can find out. I'm sure he'll get to the bottom of this. If he can't, I know Commander can."

He shrugs. He's not bluffing.

"David, please. This has nothing to do with you. It was so long ago, and it needs to stay in the past—where it belongs. I'd tell you anything I thought you should know."

"Why do you think you have to protect me?"

He clenches his teeth and glares at me. He's not giving up and I won't win this one. David's interest in his family affairs is reasonable, but I need to decide how much to tell him.

"Okay, I'll meet you tonight, but you must keep this to yourself."

David nods.

Chapter 11

I approach David's dark office where he waits outside his closed door. "Let's take this to my apartment, where we'll have more privacy."

"I'd rather not go to your apartment. Why can't we talk here?"

He brushes the hair from my eyes.

"I only want to talk. I promise."

He drapes his arm around my shoulders, and I let him guide me to his quarters. Without a word, he heats water in an electric kettle, sets out two cups, and plops a tea bag in each. When the water boils, he pours us each a cup of tea, then sits across from me, drumming his fingers on the table.

"Okay, spill. What's the deal between you and my father? And be honest."

"I've always been honest with you, but I never talk about my earlier life. I can't discuss my service with your father. Not with you, or anyone else. Especially not you. It's not about you. Until I'm ready, I need to hide my past from others for personal reasons. And I will be ready. Before I leave Cavalry, I'll tell the proper people everything they should know."

David watches me, furrowing his brow.

"Believe me, it's important to me to tell them and I want to. But not yet."

"What could you have done that's so terrible you need to hide it?"

"Not what I did. It's what happened to me ... and what I know. Nothing terrible, and my reasons for keeping my business private are personal. It's not what you think. There are parts of my past that I rather not share yet."

"Great. Then there's no problem, so spill the whole truth. I'll keep confidential whatever you tell me, providing you're honest."

"Your father and I have a complicated history and I can't talk about it. You realize anything concerning my work is classified. At least, I'm not authorized to share it. But it's tied to other personal events in my life. The ones I'm reluctant to disclose. I will, I promise, but not until I'm packed and

65

ready to leave Cavalry. You must trust me on this. I have valid reasons for needing it to play out this way."

"How old were you when you started working for my father?"

"Please, David, I beg you. Trust me and let this go."

"Were you involved with Commander Nadler? Were you his girl?"

"He's your father, please."

"Did you lie to me about your age? Did you lie to my father?"

"I've never lied to you. I kept certain things from you, but I never lied. Your father was aware of my age. I care for you, but you aren't mine, and even though you've championed me in the past, you're not my confidant nor my partner. I understand you're concerned, but I promise you needn't be."

"What's goin' on with you and Commander Nadler?"

David no longer refers to Nadler as his father. I read him and sense his discomfort, but not the cause, but I need more time for a deeper reading.

"Nothing. We had a complex work relationship, and it's over, at least for now."

"Were you hoping he'd marry you? Is that why you left? Did he choose Elly over you? Is that why you lie about everything?"

I jump up and glare at him.

"David, I'm not lying about anything. I worked with your father. He was my handler. Marriage was ... the furthest notion from my mind. I was far too young, and it was impossible and unthinkable. Whatever happened with Nadler and Miss Elly, after I left, had nothing to do with me. She was his receptionist, and that's all I knew. I was unaware of their interest in each other. I was wrapped up in learning my craft."

David rubs his chin, staring as if he's trying to read me.

"I'm gonna find out, you know."

"You don't want to. Some things are best left alone."

He sits back, takes a sip of tea, and then stares at me. I can almost see the gears turning in his brain, struggling to forge the next question. One that will pry loose the truth.

"You think I can't handle your secrets?"

"I think you shouldn't have to."

"It's that bad? Come on, Zena. I can handle anything. I've seen things that would curl your hair. What could you know that would devastate me?" he asks with a curdled laugh.

"Let it go. You have a wonderful career, the life you earned. You have a golden future in front of you."

"And knowing what you're hiding would ruin that?"

He throws his hands up and shakes his head.

"It would taint it. Right now, you live in this military worldview where everything works the way it's supposed to. You're proud of the Peace Force and your place in it. I'd hate to take that away from you."

"And you telling me your secret changes that? You underestimate me. I'm aware of much more than you realize."

I weigh my options. Should I reveal nothing and risk him continuing to investigate on his own? Tell him a half-truth and hope he's satisfied? Or spill my entire burden, make him swear to secrecy, and let him deal with the awful truth? Not everything. I must never divulge my knowledge of the aliens and their plans. Not to anyone.

"If I confide in you, what I disclose can't leave this apartment."

He nods and leans closer, his mouth open, like he wants to inhale my answer.

"I was thirteen when your father discovered my ... talents."

David turns pale, gulps, and looks as if he might fall off his chair, but says nothing.

"Major Nadler believed I would be an asset to the Peace Force, so he mentored me. He taught me how to behave in this culture and he trained me for the work ..."

"You were thirteen? What was my father doing with a thirteen-year-old? Were you at Westview or a civilian base? How did he meet you?"

"Yes, David, I was thirteen, and I met your boss, Major Matthews, before I met Nadler. I'm not ready to tell Dan yet. He didn't remember, or at least he didn't recognize me, and I plan to speak with him, just not yet. It's no big deal, I promise. It's personal for me and it has nothing to do with you, your father, or anyone else. Let me do this my way."

"Thirteen? How in hell's name did you pull that off? Where did you meet Major Matthews? If it's not a big deal, why hide your secret from him?"

"Look, Nadler, his commander, and other upper-echelon officers were aware of my age and how they were using me. Everyone else knew how young I was, including Dan. It's not like I could hide it. Major Nadler was my first handler, and I worked with him and Fischer. That's all I'm permitted to say. In fact, I said too much, and if you mention this, I'll face a lot of trouble because I signed an NDA."

I'm aware both the NDA and my contract are invalid since I was underage when I signed. After consulting a lawyer at Cavalry, I confirmed the laws about consent and verified my papers had no merit. I presented my case as hypothetical, and he laughed at the absurdity of giving a child anything to sign. The statutes, in that regard, haven't changed. They tricked me into keeping quiet by frightening me with the prospect of prison, something I feared because of my firsthand experience with prisoners. I would have kept quiet without their threats. They trained me to keep secrets.

"NDA? What's that?"

"Non-Disclosure Agreement. I had to sign one when I left Westview. Everything I did there, anything I witnessed, all of it ... it's classified. I'm sworn to secrecy. You, of all people, should understand my need to keep quiet."

David nods, but I envision wheels churning in his head as he attempts to digest this new disclosure. He understands the importance of discretion. The upper echelon has strict rules concerning confidentiality, and military school instills obedience to those rules. I've always heard that.

"I need you to keep this to yourself. Lieutenant, I'm not one of your playmates. I don't need to remind you, I work for Central Intelligence, and my assignments and involvements are classified. I'm only telling you this because it involves your father and you're so damn curious, but beyond that, I dare not speak."

An unconvinced David smiles. I read him. He doesn't believe me, but he'll comply.

Chapter 12

The Officer's Club vibrates with festivity. I weave through the crowded aisle past familiar faces and the occupied pool tables. The clacking of balls knocking against each other mixes with the men's loud chatter as I make my way to my old spot at the bar. I hadn't attended Club in months, long before the day I remembered my past as Rebecca. Commander and his Inner Circle sit at their privileged table in the back of the Club. Major Paul Abrams and Major Tom Williams, in their usual seats, have their backs to me. Major Dan Matthews sits next to Commander where Mary Jo once perched. They watch me take my seat on the barstool.

Mack sees me and walks over with a welcoming smile. I brought three music discs and hand them to him. I've never asked him why everyone calls him Mack when his real name is Vincent Reed. He has a laid-back, easy-going manner, and it tickles me to remember how we started teasing each other from the first evening we met when I had no clue who he was.

It's charming that someone of his high rank enjoys tending the alcohol-free bar. It's a delicious, out-of-the-ordinary, impractical thing for a First Lieutenant to do, especially in this strict, protocol-driven, unwavering culture. One day, I'll ask him to tell me his story—why he does it and why they call him Mack. I'll bet it's an interesting tale. Perhaps this evening.

"Haven't seen you in a while. Welcome back, girlie," Mack says, leaning on the bar across from me. "Get lost exploring? Couldn't find your way back?"

"I've been busy, Steve, but I decided tonight I'm going to have some fun."

Mack nods, selects a disc, loads it into the player, and returns.

"How's your project coming along?"

"I'm struggling. My progress has slowed, but it's expected, and I'm not worried. It comes in waves. Some days nothing makes sense, and then overnight it falls into place. I think mingling with other people and letting my hair down is the cure for my doldrums. Get my circulation flowing. What do you think?"

"Worth a try. You came to the right place. I'm still interested in how you learned to decipher those symbols. I've heard many have tried. Your report was phenomenal. It takes a lot to amaze me, but I'm amazed."

"I'd love to share my knowledge with you, but I'm afraid you'll need to discuss that with Major Abrams. It's not my decision to make. If he likes the idea, I'm on board."

Mack flips me a sardonic grin, shrugs, and then walks away to fill a drink order and I'm lost in my music. The singer belts out a ballad about love gone wrong, bringing back memories of the song's debut, where I was, and what I was doing. The vocalist croons about unrequited love. He can't make his heart feel what it won't.

I flash back to my early years when I fell head over heels in love with my first sweetheart, Kevin Roberts. I was so young and loved him with a fierce passion, but he never returned my affection. Once he got what he wanted, he lost interest and broke my tender heart. Smashed it and never looked back.

He was my entire world, and when he dumped me, I thought I'd never love anyone again. I'd sing the words to this song every time the radio played it as if it might make him sorry for hurting me. I wonder what happened to him.

It's funny. It devastated me, and I thought the pain of a broken heart would kill me, yet I can't remember what Kevin looked like or why I cared so much for him. He was a jerk, so full of himself, but to me, he was everything. Until Russ came along, and I learned that love isn't all hearts and flowers. It's hard work and commitment. It's mutual respect.

Tom approaches the bar, jarring me from my bygone memories. Instead of motioning to Mack for a drink, he turns to me.

"I'd like you to join me at the table, Zena."

With a naughty boy smirk, he puts his arm around me. Life holds some cruel twists. As Zena, I wanted nothing more than inclusion at Commander's table, to be welcomed, to belong. Now, when it matters least, I receive my long-awaited invitation from the upper echelon. Ironic to the core.

I stand, and with Tom's arm still around my shoulder, I allow him to lead me to Commander's table where he instructs me to sit next to him. I read the officers to discover why I'm now afforded this honor. The officers ignore me while making small talk, so reading them is easier. They have an agenda. They're playing with me.

Paul rises, heads into the cluster of tables, selects a military woman, and escorts her to the privileged table, where she sits next to him. Dan follows suit. The officers continue their small talk and joke-making while their 'dates' sit and wait. Unsure of what's expected of me, I wait and pay attention. I'm not following the banter, all boring shop talk, so I have nothing to add. Paul stands and his woman of choice takes the cue. With Paul's arm around her, they walk out, and I understand.

So, when Tom invited me, it wasn't for me to get better acquainted with them or their chosen women. Nobody speaks to me. When Paul returns alone, Dan leaves with his woman. Still, I'm ignored. I glance back at the bar to see Mack watching me. He's playing my music. I miss talking to him.

Dan returns alone, sits, and the officers turn to look at me.

Tom puts his arm around my shoulder and says, "It's our turn now." He waits for my reaction with a smirk on his face. I read him. He doesn't expect me to accompany him.

"Our turn for what?"

Tom grins as if I'm playing stupid and runs his fingers up and down my arm.

"Well, Princess, you accepted my invitation, so it's time. Let's take a walk."

"When you invited me to the table, I thought it was for conversation. Not for ... sex."

Tom laughs and the others join in. I glance at Commander and realize he has no plans to rescue me, and even though he's grinning, his eyes are hard. He cocks his head with a half-smile as if saying I asked for and deserve it.

"Come on. You're a bright girl. By now, you understand what an invitation to the table means," says Tom. "When women attend Club, they're expected to accompany officers. If someone from this table invites you ... well, you're expected to be a good girl and provide your services."

Message received. I'm no longer welcome at Club unless I service the officers as they expect of military women. Commander couldn't just tell me that, he needed to humiliate me to drive his point home. It's the culture and if I'm not his girl, I shouldn't expect special treatment. I need to conform or avoid Club. Fine.

The officers watch me, waiting for me to make a move. Dan and Commander wear the same goofy expectant smirks. Paul shakes his head but fails to defend me. An impatient Tom grins and strokes my arm. I read them. They expect me to beg off. So, I stand.

"Okay, if those are the rules. I'll get my discs from Mack. It's doubtful I'll be returning."

At the bar, a concerned Mack walks over to me and waits.

"I need my music. I'm leaving now."

"You alright?" Mack asks.

"I'm fine. Just tired. Too much excitement for one day."

He retrieves my CD, slips it into its case, grabs the other two, and hands them to me.

"Take care of yourself."

"Thanks, Mack."

Laughter from the Commander's table stops when they notice me returning to stand next to Tom. I say, "Let's go, Major Tom."

Tom's eyes widen, and he smirks. The others snicker, appearing amused. He stands, drapes his arm around me, and swaggers out of Club with me tucked at his side. I don't look back.

Outside of Club, Tom drops his arm from around my shoulder. A military woman walks towards Club, and he signals her. She nods and heads our way.

"Hey, I'll catch you next time," he says to me and walks away with the other woman.

Is he jilting me or letting me off the hook? I'm not sure if I'm offended or relieved. If it's a game of chicken, maybe Tom's a decent guy after all.

Chapter 13

I must have crossed a line by leaving Club with Tom and spoiling their fun. Every day now, when I show up for work, I'm greeted with an unoccupied kitchen table. I wanted to avoid the morning ritual with them after their treatment last Thursday, but I'll miss my bite-sized orange cakes. Coffee's not the same without them. Commander wasn't in his office when I dropped by the break room, but Cassie was her normal frosty self.

Yesterday, mid-morning, Tom walked into the break room, grabbed his cup of coffee, nodded my way, and left without comment. In the past four days, Paul hasn't stopped upstairs to check on me once, nor have I run into him. It may be meaningless.

The hour I spent this morning listening to the voices yielded nothing of value. I spent the afternoon playing my music and contemplating the meaning of Tommy Miller's warnings. If only I could speak to him one last time. He often haunts my dreams, but the forewarnings are always the same. *I can't stay here by myself.*

While dawdling over dinner, trying to conjure up my buried secrets, I try an exercise in free association, jotting down any thought that comes to mind in my secret shorthand script. The key to my quest lies somewhere in the depths of my unconsciousness. My food grows cold as my scribbles fill my notepad. I reread my notes. Nothing useful, but I have an idea.

I hurry to finish my tepid meat patty and mashed potatoes, clear my dishes, and then stack my tray. With my excitement mounting, I head for my room to drop off my writings and change from my work attire into casual wear. Down two flights, and across the rotunda, I arrive at my sanctuary, the scene of my manifestations of the aged Tommy Miller.

When I walk in, I realize I haven't visited the quiet, deserted library in weeks. Not much has changed. Someone added a couple more bookcases up front, behind the medallion davenport near the entrance. It looks as if the workers no longer shelf the books the way I organized them. The new shelves contain fiction and non-fiction, all mixed in no special order.

The antique couch brings back memories of my initial visit that Friday afternoon when I met David for the first time. It was no accident. He must have known who I was. Commander would have mentioned my arrival at a team meeting. David carried two books, one about tattoos, the other about a dominant and his submissive. He no doubt planned the whole scenario, so he could bring up his interest in Play. I was so engrossed in overcoming my irrational fear of being in a library, after Colonel Wickmore's assaults at Central, that I wasn't Paying Attention. I didn't read him.

It was obvious he was attempting to manipulate me into experimenting with Play, his pseudo-BDSM mind game. I was unaware he already knew about me and my relationship with Michael. It was no chance meeting. It was sport to him, but it matters little now. My season with him gave me a new perspective and led me to the events that woke me up to who I am. I can't harbor any anger about that.

As usual, I don't encounter a single person on my way to the back room. The antiquated chamber, with its somber mood, echoes my visits with Tommy. He seemed so real. I talked to him, touched him, sang with him, and even covered him with an imaginary afghan.

Tommy was warning me, meaning my subconscious was trying to wake me up to something important, yet forgotten, but critical. If Dan hadn't brought me to Westview, I might have ended up where I belong. Was there another resistance faction waiting to protect me? It can't be Jade's band, but perhaps an alliance I came across years later? I remember knowing which direction to go, and my faith was strong that I'd reach my destination. Now, a decade later, I'm nowhere near finding out where I was headed. I'm clueless.

The faded old lavender-colored couch bids me to sit, so I do. I close my eyes, relax my muscles, clear my thoughts, and then allow myself to transcend. I wait for the sounds of Tommy's humming and the squeaking of his rocking chair. Come to me, Tommy. Tell me your secrets.

The chamber door creaks open, and someone enters. Footsteps draw closer.

"So, this is where you're hiding," David says.

I open my eyes, and he sits beside me. I read him to determine his mood. He's not angry, but he still wants answers.

"I'm not hiding."

"I've been thinking about our last conversation, and I have more questions. You said you can't talk about it, but I'm racking my brain trying to imagine what my father wanted from a thirteen-year-old. What sort of *skills* could a child possess that would permit him to ignore military policies? Why would he even bring you on the base? It's against the rules."

"David, that's classified. He didn't bring me on the base, and he had permission to mentor me." I loathe having this conversation.

"You know, kitten, you can confide in me about anything. I need to understand why my father gives you special treatment, different from everyone else. You were a child. What did he expect from you?"

David looks like a light bulb just turned on in his brain. The color drains from his face and I sense a sick panic welling inside him.

"Are you his kid? His daughter?"

"For heaven's sake, no. I'm positive we're not related. I know who my parents were."

David sighs in relief as if a huge weight lifts from him. The thought that I might be his sister would give me the willies, too. It's distressing enough knowing I made love to both father and son, years apart.

"I charmed him. It's said I have a beguiling effect on some. Charmed you, didn't I?"

David grins, shaking his head, although he knows it's true.

"At least I enchanted you for a while," I say.

"Yeah, but I'm easy to charm. My mother couldn't charm a snake, much less my father. What he said was law. She feared him and never looked forward to his visits."

"Some people don't belong together. My parents fought, and I hated it. I wasn't enough to make my dad want to stay."

Memories of the dreadful night Daddy left flash like lightning in my mind. How he hit my mother, reducing us to tears. He disappeared from my life forever. It took a dozen years to understand how his leaving improved our lives. No matter how hard it was.

"You look strange. Are you alright?" David asks.

"I'm fine. Something just reminded me of the magnitude of men's cruelty."

David's ears perk up like a dog hearing the whine of a can opener.

"What's goin' on kitten?"

"Thursday night, I went to Club and learned a painful lesson. I'd been there a few times in the past, as Commander's guest. When officers approached me, I'd turn them down, because I don't service the military men. You know civilian women aren't required. I enjoyed Club for conversations and listening to music. I would talk to Mack and Greg, and we became friends."

David nods. His knowing look tells me he understands what I hadn't.

"I never had a problem until Thursday, and I hate talking about it. That night they informed me, in no uncertain terms, that if I choose to attend Club, I should be prepared to behave like the military women. Service anyone who asks."

He gives me a sympathetic look, scoots over, puts his arm around me, and cradles my chin in his hand.

"Sounds like you learned a rough lesson, but maybe it was time. The Officer's Club has its own rules. Agora has no such requirements."

I glare at him. David should understand how different I am. I push him away. I don't want to hear that.

"Kitten, stay out of the Officer's Club. They don't dance there, anyway. You're always welcome at Agora, and when I'm around, nobody will bother you. No one has to service anyone. I'm here if you need me."

David leans over to kiss me, and I don't stop him. I want my friend, even if we'll never have a relationship. When I hold him tight, for just a moment, I embrace a needed connection and the weight of my challenging week lifts.

"Let's take this to my apartment."

I nod.

§

David's apartment looks the same. Neat, clean, military style, nothing out of order, except for the fluorescent stick-on ceiling stars over his bed. I kick off my shoes and crawl on top of the covers to wait as David undresses. I lie there watching him. All of a sudden, I feel self-conscious. Zena was bolder.

"Those clothes need to come off," David murmurs and slithers naked over to join me. His smell is familiar, and I know his body, the strong shoulders, the narrow hips, and the muscular legs. With a naughty smile, he turns onto his side and lifts his eyebrows.

"Yes, sir."

I slip out of bed. Then I tease him, stripping out of my clothes, and folding them one at a time into a neat pile on the kitchen counter. I remove my lanyard and toss it on the table. David watches with hungry eyes as I slide down naked next to him. Held in his arms, I have a sense of belonging, and all my resolve to exclude him from my life melts like an ice cube on a hot summer day. He kisses me and I forget everything except how familiar his touch is, and how much I miss this man.

§

David rolls over, baring the stunning lifelike snake, winding from his shoulder blades to his waist. I've seen hundreds of tattoos in my previous life, but this creation is extraordinary. Once, I considered getting a small butterfly on my wrist, but Russell talked me out of it. I'm not a fan of pain, so I gave in without debate. It must be agonizing, having your entire back tattooed. I've heard you must suffer to be beautiful, but if that's true, I'll remain plain.

David's colorful, realistic, coiled serpent, with its flicking tongue, looks very familiar. I flash on an image of Tommy's remarkable reptilian illustrations and the similarity in style stuns me. I've seen this viper before.

One lazy summer day, I showed Tommy how to use shading and perspective to make his artwork three-dimensional. After that, I often posed for him to study the figure. Once, while picnicking, I napped as he practiced. He captured the folds of my white sundress, defining my relaxed form, contrasted against the dark blanket, the lush greenery, and the shimmering water of the lake. With his natural talent, it didn't take long for him to surpass my paltry skills.

I calculate the dates. David would have been a youngster when Tommy died in 2080, but he told me he was sixteen when he got his ink.

"David," I say, nudging him. "Where did you get the idea for your tattoo?"

"Why?"

"I'm curious. I think I've seen it before."

"You have. A hundred times," he says, laughing.

"Not *that many*." I deliver a gentle smack to his behind. "No, I mean, somewhere else, like in a magazine."

"Not mine. An old teacher sketched it for me when I was a kid. Tried to teach me how to draw but I was hopeless. He was an excellent instructor, but I had no talent. He was one of the few people I respected. I took no interest in drawing, but we were both fascinated by the stars, and he gave me my first book on constellations."

"Did he do your snake tattoo?"

"No. He was dead by then. When I was sixteen, I asked a friend to try it. He was an amazing artist and was experimenting with a pilfered tattoo kit he swiped from the latest salvage haul. He worked from the drawing, and it took more than a month. I got into deep trouble after they notified my parents."

He chuckles at the memory.

"Thought they would skin me alive to remove the snake," he says with a teasing grin.

I cringe at the idea.

"No. The artwork's too beautiful to destroy. Who would do that?"

David gives me the side eye.

"What was your old teacher's name?"

"Why? You couldn't have known him. He retired from the Peace Force and taught art classes to the young boys. He died when I was still a kid." David looks me over and thinks for a minute. "You would have been a toddler," he says with a chuckle. "I kept the drawing to remember him."

"Humor me."

"My art teacher was an old black fellow. Insisted we call him by his first name, Tommy. I had never met anyone with pitch-black skin—but he was one hell of an interesting guy who loved teaching youngsters about the olden days. Taught me the constellations. He'd allow me to visit the atrium at night to see the stars. Just me."

"What was Tommy's surname?"

"Dunno. Can't remember."

"Was he stationed here?"

"Doubt it. Don't know. Why?"

"There's a plaque of a Major Thomas Miller in the Memorial Room. He died twenty years ago."

"Why were you in the Memorial Room?"

"Someone should pay homage to those who passed before us. I've read that in earlier centuries, they set aside a day for mourning the dead. A lot of cultures paid respects to the deceased and remembered loved ones. We should never forget them."

David looks at me like I lost my mind. He yawns and turns over, away from me. His soft even breaths end our pillow talk. I turn down the light, pull the covers over us, and snuggle next to him. The ceiling comes alive with twinkling stars, and Tommy's spirit gazes at them with me. It feels like a homecoming.

§

Loud knocking jolts me awake. While my sluggish brain is trying to figure out where I am, David scrambles out of bed, pulls on sweatpants, and answers the door. I pray he gets rid of our uninvited company. I want to go back to sleep, but David turns the lights up high. The intruders enter the apartment.

I turn over and peek upward, covering myself with the blanket. Commander and Major Dan Matthews seem in a pleasant mood. They discuss surprise inspections until they spot me in David's bed. Their good moods fade, replaced by obvious displeasure. Dan shakes his head in disapproval and takes a seat across from Commander at the table.

David opens his hands, palms up, indicating he was unaware of this impromptu visit, and throws me an apologetic glance.

"You need to leave, kitten." He heads for the bathroom and shuts the door. Does he think I want to stay and chat?

Thanks, David. My clothing remains in a neat pile on the counter in the kitchenette across the room, David is showering, and I'm naked. Both officers appear amused by my awkward situation. It's all over their faces.

"Could you hand me my clothes, please?"

"Nah, I just got comfortable," Commander says.

I turn to Dan. He cocks his head and shrugs.

I grab the blanket, wrap it tight around me, muster my courage, and shuffle over to the counter to retrieve my garments. The men watch but say nothing.

I return to my side of the bed and struggle to dress while covering myself. They've both seen me naked, although Dan doesn't remember, still....

My shoes lay where I left them, on the floor near Commander's chair. Once they're on my feet, I search for my lanyard. Last night I tossed it onto the table....

Commander dangles my keycard in front of me. Sporting a mischievous grin, he swings it back and forth, offering it to me. He teases, inviting me to approach him to retrieve it. He's loving this, but I'm not. When I'm close enough to grab the lanyard, just as my fingers touch it, he pulls his hand back a little, so I'll have to move closer to him. He smiles, but he stares at me with hard, icy eyes. I grab my keycard again. He keeps a firm grip on it for a moment before letting go.

I'm ready to leave, with my lanyard secured in place. David exits the bathroom and notices I'm dressed, but still here, and slips me a questioning look. He pulls on his pants and an undershirt, and walks over to me, eyeing his superior officers.

"I'll talk to you later, I guess," I say. I turn away from him and leave, taking my humiliation with me, and head upstairs.

§

My coffee cup has been sitting empty all morning, and I'm craving caffeine, but I'm avoiding the break room. Pacing the apartment floor has burned up my energy supply. It's too early for lunch but I could chance going downstairs for a refill. Or stay here and do without. I want to avoid Commander after this morning's fiasco, but I need fuel. If he's doing inspections, he may be gone all day.

I make it past Cassie's desk and into the empty break room where I fill my cup, but as I start back Commander is standing at his door, waiting for me.

"Zena, in my office." He steps aside, allowing room for me to enter, then closes the door behind me.

Commander takes his seat behind his desk and points to one of the visitor chairs. I sit. It's obvious he's enjoying himself. My discomfort is his pleasure. The man is a sadist. I set my cup on his desk and wait for him to speak. He eyes my cup with disapproval.

"So, you're making the rounds now?"

"I'm sorry, sir. I'm not sure what you mean."

"First Williams, now Cross?"

"I didn't have sex with Major Williams. Turns out he's a gentleman. He let me walk. Y'all made your point. You could have warned me I'm not welcome at Club anymore."

Commander laughs. "Oh, you're welcome at Club. We welcome

women—who provide their services. You're not exempt."

"When you change the rules, it would be decent of you to tell me. It's unfair to switch them midstream. I wouldn't have gone to Club."

"That's no fun. Besides, we didn't change the rules. We spoiled you. We allowed you a lot of freedom for too long. But you're a member of Calvary, and you need to fall in line. No more exceptions."

"I understand, but you didn't have to embarrass me this morning in front of Dan ... I mean, Major Matthews. That was unnecessary."

"I didn't have to," he says with a wide grin.

"You're a cruel man."

"You haven't seen anything yet."

"What do you want?"

"You. I want you."

His eyes are cold as he glares at me.

§

This new turn of events leaves me unsettled. I've infuriated Commander without intending to, slept with David after deciding he was wrong for me, and I seem to be on the outs with the Inner Circle. I've spun around in my plans again. Instead of forming a coalition, I'm driving away the people I need most. Nadler was easier to deal with compared to this group. If I'm going to get off the bases, I need allies, not enemies. A growing tightness strangles my guts.

§

The outdoor scenery is serene, helping me slip into another meditative trance. The voices come and their strange exchanges express some excitement, but no mention of the Tracker. I'm safe for now, but for how long?

The cloudless sky leaves little to watch, and even the trees are unmoving. I calm myself with deep breaths, sinking deeper into my altered state, focusing on the cabin and my last day.

§

I sensed the Tracker before he showed up at our cabin. Shana and Abby were busy preparing a late dinner, and we all hoped the men would return home soon. Wendy and I were setting the table, steering clear of the sisters, when I felt an overwhelming eerie feeling of doom, like my first Tracker encounter. I excused myself, hurried upstairs to pack my bags, and prayed to slip away before his arrival. If I could sense him, he might be capable of sensing me, leaving me little time and without a plan, so I had to act fast. My only escape from the second-floor level was the one set of stairs, which ended across from the front entrance, so I needed to hurry.

I made it almost halfway downstairs. The front door opened and before I could see them, I heard Jade and Cody's voices. I scurried upstairs to stow my suitcase in our bedroom and crept down the stairs. From the landing, midway down, I saw the stranger. He looked up and our eyes met. The pleasant, but intent, look on his face surprised me as if it was understood we shared a secret. He didn't want to harm me. He came for the Gift. Just like the first Tracker.

Jade introduced the outsider as Vincent and announced he'd be joining us for dinner. Wendy welcomed the tall, dark-haired visitor and offered to show him where to wash up. I suspected she was excited to gain another male for our alliance, especially one so young and handsome. Her countenance fell when he fabricated a story about meeting up with friends in another Resistance faction, but her face lit up when he smiled at her and said he looked forward to sharing a meal with us. He possessed a subtle darkness that only I could detect. Vincent hesitated to leave the living room, but with the politeness of a gentleman, he followed Wendy to the wash sink.

My dinner was tasteless. I plotted my next moves, debating if I should tell Jade this new arrival was The Enemy, or lure the Tracker away to kill him. Vincent watched me as he told fictional stories about his travels and his plans to meet up with his made-up friends. It wasn't necessary to read him to know he was lying. Everyone else appeared to fall for his deception, but I knew the truth. One of us had reached the end of the line.

I couldn't determine if he had warned his alien brothers that he found his target. He couldn't read me because I'm still human, despite the alien Gift, so I had the advantage. I could read him, but he wasn't communicating at present. He wouldn't dare attempt anything until he got me alone. We outnumbered him seven to one, and he's part human. His alien essence afforded no advantage against us.

Dinner dragged on and everyone asked our handsome guest questions. Everyone but me, although I was curious about what this young human was like before an alien overtook his body. Was he a willing participant in the transfer, brainwashed to believe they chose him to sacrifice for the greater good? Or did he fight to survive? Was the process complete before he knew what happened? The host must come close to death for the extraterrestrial to seize control.

When the alien indwelled me, I survived, but he couldn't overtake me even with his motherlode of Gift. Although I was old, I was very much alive, and its life force expired soon after joining with me, making me the custodian of his entire repository, leaving me and my future forever changed. It gave me an extended but altered and difficult life. In the short time he joined with me, I learned he was trying to locate his own kind to deliver the much-needed abundant Gift, to indwell more dormant aliens into unsuspecting human hosts. Such a waste. I couldn't ask Vincent my questions. It wasn't a subject for polite dinner conversation. Or any other time.

After dinner, I remained in the kitchen to help clean up with Shana and Abbey. Wendy made it her mission to get better acquainted with our guest, and when Jade invited him to spend the night, Wendy was quick to offer to share a room. I was the only one who realized our visitor was dangerous.

That night, when Jade fell asleep, I kissed him goodbye on his cheek in case my plan didn't work. In the darkness, guided by the glow of a small flashlight, I snuck downstairs, out of the cabin, and towards the back, aware Vincent was following me. He was trying to stay quiet while maneuvering unfamiliar ground, with only my flashlight's illumination to guide him. In daylight, I had no problem navigating, but in the pitch-dark night, it was a different story. For him, it must have been challenging.

When I reached the back of the cabin, I sensed his presence close behind me and turned to confront him. I flashed the beam in his face. He covered his eyes with one arm while trying to swat the flashlight away with his free hand.

"I've been searching for you for a long time," he said.

"And you found me. I have what you want, but first, you must promise me something."

I moved the light away from his eyes so he could see my face. He moved closer and reached out to touch my shoulder. I didn't react.

"These people have taken care of me. They're decent and kind, and I'm fond of them, so you must spare them."

"I'm not interested in your friends."

After cradling the flashlight under my arm, I put my hands on the sides of his face, and he prepared himself to receive my Gift.

He stiffened and struggled to free himself, but it was too late. His eyes rolled back, and an anguished moan escaped through clenched teeth as his life force left his body and his allotted Gift merged with mine. His lifeless human remains crumbled to the ground.

"I'm so sorry, Vincent," I said. It was him or me, but I don't enjoy killing.

I slipped back into the cabin, up the stairs to our bedroom, and crawled into bed next to Jade, where I slept hard. When morning came, I told Jade my version of the night's events.

"Vincent was a spy for the Captors and tried to kidnap me again. A few years ago, his unit almost abducted me, and I was afraid he recognized me. He was watching me all evening. After we went to bed, I got up for a drink of water. He startled me, and when I ran outside, he followed. When we reached the back of the cabin, I pushed him hard, and he fell and hit his head. He's dead. I'm sure of it."

"Are you all right?" Jade asked, looking me over, making sure I was uninjured.

"We're not safe here. I need to leave, for everyone's sake."

"I don't understand," he said, searching my eyes for answers.

"They were hunting for me when I returned to the cabin to hide out. I didn't want to tell you about them because I was afraid you wouldn't let me stay. Wouldn't protect me. But now that one of them found me, we're all in grave danger. I hate leaving, but I can't endanger you and the others. If we split up, we'll all have a better chance. I'll draw them away from you and our team. I'll meet up with you once it's safe."

Jade and I spent the past three years together, but now I needed to move on. There will be more Trackers. Jade was reluctant to let me go, but I convinced him I had no choice. I left late that morning after a hearty breakfast, but my comrades stayed behind to bury Vincent's body, salvage what they could from the cabin, and execute new plans.

Chapter 14

Paul arrives for our scheduled mid-morning meeting looking unsettled. This morning, I gathered relevant materials to sort through and considered what to tell him or what not to mention. He's come prepared with a cup of coffee for each of us. Under his arm, he's wedged a notepad and several printouts and almost loses them trying to set down the cups. I jump up to help by grabbing the papers, noting the sheets contain sections of my report.

"Thank you. That was thoughtful," I say. I sip the coffee, craving a couple of sweet orange cakes.

"Sure. I brought part of your report to discuss, but I'm most interested in your progress."

Paul appears agitated, so I read him. He's in a foul mood, but I'm not the cause. He hands me a printout and fills me in on facts he disputes.

"Paul, the Book is a Master Plan, not a documentary, and the Overlords, in all likelihood, improvised or adapted as necessary."

That doesn't satisfy him, but I sense it's not my translation summaries upsetting him.

"Do you want to talk about it?" I ask.

"Nope. I want to discuss your progress."

"I'm still having difficulty translating several symbols, and the work I've been able to pull together is incomplete. Is there an urgency for my next report, or will you allow me the needed time to get it right?"

Paul looks defeated and gives me a look of resignation.

"Take as long as you need," he says, his voice low and soft.

He shakes his head, stands, and departs, leaving his half-finished cup and papers on my worktable.

The rest of the morning, I buckle down and labor over creating a cohesive report for Paul, and by lunchtime, I'm pleased with my documentation. My stack of legal pads containing the entire Master Plan translation, written in my unique scribbles, makes it easy to pull out a section for transcription. Satisfied with my narrative, I pack everything away, give the apartment a once over to ensure everything's in place, and then haul my hunger pains downstairs.

Commander's voice booms as he yells at Cassie.

"Get that done. I want it yesterday."

"Yes, sir."

Cassie jumps when he slams his door.

I'd hate stepping into the middle of that. I've never heard Commander raise his voice to Cassie and when I pass her desk, she looks frazzled. She shakes her head at me. There appears to be trouble in our little paradise.

As I descend the stairs, a whiff of sautéed onions invites me. Serving trays await, full of mouth-watering, onion-smothered pierogies, and a side dish of mixed veggies. The aroma of this luncheon favorite almost camouflages the uneasiness permeating the third-floor cafeteria.

Parked at my solitary table, I search for the cause of the discontent. Everyone appears on edge, both military personnel and kitchen staff alike. No one laughs, and an unusual quiet produces a sense of foreboding.

Lost in my dining enjoyment, I try to ignore the somber cafeteria mood. I glance around between bites of food, hoping to catch David to ask him what's going on, but he's nowhere in sight. Everyone on the base seems jumpy. I hear whispering, but no laughter.

When we expected Nadler and Fischer to visit, there was excitement, loud conversation, and plenty of laughter. Nothing like this. This feels different. I smell trouble in the air.

With my dirty dishes placed in their proper bins, the bleak mood follows me as I take the stairs to the second-floor cafeteria. Even here, the chatter and its usual bustle and noise at this hour is subdued. No one appears to hang out after finishing their meals. There's no laughter and the serving staff dash around like headless chickens.

I descend the ramp and head to David's office, hoping he'll shed light on this phenomenon. He's not in his office, but I find him at the docking area, shouting orders while privates unload a truck. He has officers under his command with authority to manage the troops and supervise the unloading of salvage bounty. It's odd how he's involving himself. I approach him and he waves me off.

"Sorry, kitten. Don't have time right now. I'm busy," he says, turning away. He hurries to join his men, and no one looks happy. They look hurried and tired. His sergeants rush around under David's direction. Something huge looms over the horizon.

The lunch crowd dispersed by the time I return to the third-floor cafeteria. Miss Evans darts about, ordering her workers to perform a better job, inspecting their work as she moves through the empty tables, dishrag in hand. Are we expecting guests again? The staff seems nervous about the cafeteria's cleanliness. I half expect an officer to follow Miss Evans around to conduct a white glove inspection. I dare not bother the busy workforce.

Terry might tell me, but I don't see her anywhere. She might be working in the kitchen. They must be experiencing similar stress.

§

The entire base appears in freefall. Nobody looks happy and everyone seems rushed. Back at the office, I pass by Jen sitting at Cassie's desk, answering the phone. Upstairs, my uneasiness distracts me from proofing my report. I read the words, but my mind is elsewhere, and I process nothing. I listen to music instead, and I'm thankful no one interrupts my peace.

The cafeteria mood hasn't lifted when I stop by for dinner, except now the staff appears haggard and stressed to boot. The officers and specialists eat and return to their duties with little discussion. I consider asking Mary Jo what's going on, but she and her friends whisper to themselves and leave before I finish my meal.

On the second floor, my search for David is unsuccessful, but when I stroll down the ramp to check out the main level, he's busy in his office. I knock and enter.

"Sorry, kitten, can't talk right now," he says, head down in his work.

"Just answer one question and I'll leave. What's going on? Everyone rushes around like it's doomsday. Is something about to happen? Some epic event? Are we expecting visitors again?"

"Naw, babe, Commander wants the departments cleaned up. He's hot on inspections. That's all I can say."

He doesn't even look up.

§

The same air of uneasiness wafts throughout the base for several days. Everybody appears on edge or in a foul mood, but Cavalry glistens. It was clean before, but now it shines.

One evening I wandered down to Mack's office in search of someone to talk to, but I discovered his door closed and lights out. I walked over to Security hoping to run into Lieutenant West or his assistant, Jason, but couldn't locate either officer. I stopped in Agora, wanting to find a sociable crowd, but found cleaning staff instead. They hijacked the club to give it a thorough scrubbing. David's best friend Lieutenant Frank Kelly was nowhere in sight, nor did I encounter anyone else I knew who could explain this downshift in morale.

§

I arrive early at the office. When I pass Cassie's desk, she notifies me I'm expected in a meeting in fifteen minutes. Paul never mentioned having a meeting today, and this one's a lot earlier than usual. Upstairs, I grab my notes, sprint downstairs, and head for the conference room. Perhaps I'll learn what's going on.

I'm on time when I knock and enter. Commander pauses from yelling about something, notices me, and checks his watch, appearing almost disappointed that I'm punctual. He's in an unpleasant mood, and I'd rather not irritate him further, so I slip into my seat, trying not to attract attention.

"Zena, what are you working on? Bring us up to date," Commander says, with a wave of his hand and a challenging glare.

"I'm hammering out my interim report, although progress has been slow. Translating some symbols proved more demanding than I expected."

"I want a detailed status summary on my desk by dinnertime tomorrow. No excuses."

"Yes, sir."

"Dismissed," he says, waving me out.

§

It's a damn good thing I had the foresight to create a brief report and I'm lucky I never submitted it to Paul. Ready to refill my coffee cup, I stop in Paul's office and sit. He turns to me, scowls, and seems flustered.

"Paul. Will you please tell me what's going on?"

He raises his eyebrows.

"You don't know?"

"No, that's why I'm asking."

"It's not for me to say. You should take it up with Commander."

"Did I do something wrong?"

Paul looks at me in amazement.

"Maybe not wrong, but certainly not wise."

Paul shakes his head and waves me off, returning his attention to his computer screen. I'm dismissed. Okay, enough. If I've committed an infraction, I need to understand what I've done, so I can fix it. This can't be about me. In my last conversation with Commander, he stated I hadn't seen anything yet, and that he wanted me. My lord, is he punishing everyone on the base because of me?

§

I make sure everything is in order before leaving for dinner. With my work materials squared away, and my music CDs returned to their storage case, I leave the apartment the way I found it this morning, with nothing out of place.

I stop by Paul's cubicle, hand him my thumb drive, and ask him to print a copy of my report. He acknowledges me with an anxious nod. He makes a copy for himself, and moments later, the printed report is in my hands.

From the break room, I peek to see Commander's empty office. He said he wanted my summary on his desk by dinnertime. I take my printout, and despite Cassie's warning not to enter, I set it in the middle of his desk and leave for the day.

§

If he's maintaining his schedule, Commander will come back from the gym as he does every Monday, Wednesday, and Friday, like clockwork, all sweaty and tired. I pace the deserted great floor between my quarters and the office suite, keeping an eye out for him, hoping his workout will wear him out. I need the advantage. He reaches the top of the stairs, and as he approaches, I move where he can see me, and he meets me halfway.

"Sir, I need to talk to you."

Commander looks fatigued and stressed, his hair wet, and perspiration soaks the neckline of his undershirt and darkens his armpits. A heady odor suggests a brutal workout and I step back. He nods and motions for me to accompany him.

"Can this wait until after I shower?" he asks.

"Of course, sir. Please take your time."

Upstairs, in the apartment, I select soothing music, turn it on low, and sit on the couch to wait, hoping I've made the right decision. The dark view outside the window matches my trepidation. Several minutes pass when Commander enters the living room dressed in sweatpants, slippers, and nothing else. I stand to face him.

"So, what's goin' on?" he asks, frowning.

Inhaling a deep breath, I lock eyes with him and exhale. I'm in no hurry.

"I surrender."

He steps back and cocks his head, smiles with condescension, and rubs his chin as if I made a joke. He doesn't expect this from me and releases a halfhearted laugh.

"I'm yours, if you want me," I say.

He shakes his head and squints.

"Does this mean you'll Play?" he asks. He doesn't trust me, nor does he believe me. I don't have to read him because it's written on his face. He thinks I'm playing with him.

"If that's what you want, sir."

He leers at me like a cat with its prey, ogling me like a slab of raw meat.

"Turn around and bend over," he says, his voice soft. He's testing me.

"There's one condition."

"No belts," he says and shakes his head.

"No, the condition is that you stop punishing everyone, including me."

"Is that what you think I'm doing?"

"I'm not blind."

He considers my offer for a moment.

"Deal. So, let's Play." He's still testing me.

"We don't Play until I'm sure you've stopped punishing everyone. And the ground rules apply. You don't hurt me, and you don't insist on anything I'm not ready for."

"This is your idea of surrendering?"

He laughs, but I read him. He thinks I'm playing with fire.

I shrug. "There must be rules."

"I won't hurt you."

"And I wouldn't allow it. You enjoy women who welcome pain, and you love hurting them, and for me, that's a problem. We'll have to work it out."

"Where did you get that silly idea?" Commander throws his hands up.

"Your girl told me she likes you to hit her hard, and you love that about her."

"You've been talking to Mary Jo?"

"No, not recently. She started a conversation with me that first evening I visited Officer's Club. I didn't ask, but she informed me she and Lynn were your only girls. Seems y'all had a good laugh at my expense, and she wanted to warn me I'm out of your league, that you already have two girls, and that you Play."

"And you went to my playroom, anyway?" he says with a smirk.

"You didn't tell me where you were taking me. I needed a bathroom."

"But you accompanied me after I showed you around and explained what I like."

"I wanted to share myself with you, here in your bed, and I did. We made love. You described what you enjoyed in your playroom, but I knew that some officers who Play also enjoy lovemaking."

"What else did she tell you?"

"She's the best on base at pleasuring men." I shrug.

"Anything else?"

"I don't remember." I shrug again.

Commander nods and I sense rage building in him. Not at me, but at Mary Jo. He clenches his jaw in anger.

"Whatever happens in my Playroom stays there—and Mary Jo knows the rules. We've had a longstanding agreement."

"She was protecting her own interests. I was unaware she wasn't supposed to share. The way the men talk about their sexual experiences, I couldn't imagine anyone expects discretion. Perhaps you'll understand now how I felt when Michael discussed our private moments. At least she omitted details."

Commander nods and I'm unsure if he's agreeing with me or making his mind up about something else. His gaze returns to me, and when he draws me to him to kiss me, I let him. I sense his inner torment as he lifts me and carries me to the bedroom, closing the door behind us. There's urgency in our lovemaking, like medicine for a grieving heart. This time, I sensed he was the one who needed comfort. Grief is an animal I understand.

Chapter 15

It's been just about a week now since I spent the night in Commander's bed. The base returned to normal almost overnight. By noon the following day, I noticed a remarkable difference. The tension evaporated, the cafeterias bustled again, and everyone relaxed, including Paul.

Tom was friendlier when I ran into him in the break room yesterday. He greeted me with an affable nod, asked me how I was, and wished me well. Cassie was her usual chilly self but also appeared less tense. The storm has passed.

I hope I made the right decision and pray it won't backfire on me. Commander remains in a far better mood, which makes everyone else breathe easier. Eventually, he'll want something from me I can't afford to give him.

The light in the atrium fades early with the shorter days. A brief snow flurry left no trace of its swirling flakes, which seemed to melt before they touched the treetops, but watching the first snowfall was exciting. After a long, busy workday, the peaceful sanctuary offers me solace.

This morning, I listened to the alien voices, but I learned nothing of significance. Later in the afternoon, I tried again, but their communications seemed hushed, with sparse, meaningless, irrelevant scientific chatter.

Instead of trying again, I attempt to conjure up another one of Caroline's hidden memories, hoping to discover where I traveled after leaving Jade and my cabin family. I'm only successful in invoking fleeting ruminations of my travels with faces and challenges I'd rather forget. I struggle to focus on the cave, expecting to find answers to my quest hidden there, but I hit a wall. Something prevents me from learning my truth.

Clouds hiding the half-moon and stars leave the landscape dark with nothing to watch, so I work my way to the great floor. The rotunda, usually abandoned at this evening hour, echoes the clicking sounds of Commander and Mary Jo's footsteps walking toward his playroom, mixing with my own.

My disappointment doesn't surprise me. He needs to Play, and better her than me. I've traveled this familiar wretched road too many times before. But this time, he sees me, removes his arm from Mary Jo's shoulder, tells her to wait, and crosses over to me.

"Hold on, Zena."

I stop and stand still until he reaches me.

"It's not what you think."

"No? Seems rather obvious to me."

Commander draws me close and lowers his voice. "I have unfinished business with Mary Jo. She broke my trust, so I must show her what happens since she brags about how hard she likes it. Then I'm ending it with her."

I stare at him in disbelief.

"You're punishing her? And if I disappoint you? You'll punish me?"

Commander steps back.

"No, no, I'll never hurt you. But she must understand ..."

"Drive that point home by telling her she broke your confidence and lost your trust. Allow Mary Jo to explain herself. Tell her you're finished with her. Losing your faith, and the position as your girl is punishment enough."

He shakes his head, and his clenched jaw shows he's set on punishing her.

"Zena, stay out of this and trust me."

I take his hand and plead with my eyes.

"You're angry, and about to make a mistake. The prestige as Commander's girl is crucial to Mary Jo, so take that away if you want retribution. This is a personal matter, and it's wrong to take revenge using corporal punishment. You're better than that. Please."

Commander squints at me and I fear I've redirected his wrath. It wouldn't please him to receive unsolicited advice from a civilian female. I read him. He's torn between vengeance and pleasing me.

"Let me take care of this my way," he says, his tone stern.

I grab his arm and give him my best spanked-puppy look until his anger fades, and he appears mollified.

"If you like, I'll wait near your office, and we can discuss this further."

Calmer now, he considers my offer, nods, and I walk away.

I count the minutes until I see Commander approaching his office. His mood seems lighter, but even though he looks satisfied, I can't determine which path he chose, so I read him. He made the right choice.

We make our way to the apartment in silence. Inside, I cross over to the couch to sit for our discussion, but he has different ideas. He pulls me up, and after a lingering kiss, he leads me to the bedroom, where we undress, and fall into bed.

§

I rest naked in his arms, enjoying the aftermath of our lovemaking. His eyes are closed, but he's not asleep. I'm washed in peaceful and satisfied feelings, and I want to remain like this forever.

Commander opens his eyes and stares at me.

"Why did you stick up for Mary Jo? Is that a sisterhood thing?"

I turn over on my back.

"No, I don't like Mary Jo and she's no sister of mine. But it's wrong for you to abuse your power over someone with so little of her own, no matter who's involved. What's right is right. That's my belief."

Commander sits up and studies me.

"Is that so? You're going to dictate to me how to perform my duties?"

"No, that wasn't your duty. It was your pride. And you wanted to punish her like you punished me because I chose not to share your bed. Maybe in a different way, but still ..."

"Are you suggesting I forced you?"

"You abused your authority to back me into a corner, giving me no choice, and you didn't just go after me. Everyone suffered."

"You don't know what you're talking about."

"All I know is, the entire base was ... unsettled. After I showed up here and we made love, everything got back to normal."

"You think you got it all figured out?"

"It's obvious. That's what I see."

"So, I tell Mary Jo I'm finished with her, and you bring this up now. Does this mean you changed your mind? You have no intention of Playing?"

He glares at me, and I regret bringing up the subject.

"No, it doesn't mean that. I agreed to this, and I keep my word."

Commander's eyes burn with mischief. "Great. Turn over."

"No, not this way. You're angry and you want to hurt me. I'm trying to make the point that you hold all the power and I have none."

A solemn shadow crosses his face, and he leans into me, pressing his cheek against mine.

"You're so wrong. I can't hurt you. Why do you think I had Abrams give you the swat? You were to receive two swats, but when I saw your face ..."

He's silent for a moment. He brushes his lips against my cheek, strokes my hair, and leans back.

"I had to do my duty, and you backed me into a corner. The way you behaved in front of my brother and my team was inexcusable. You say I hold all the power, but you have much more."

I push him away enough to get a clear view.

"You refused to Play but wanted me to be exclusive. When I went to Mary Jo, you got upset, but you wouldn't even consider giving me what I want."

He shakes his head and glares at me.

"When you found out I was Michael's brother, you threw a tantrum, daring me to hit you, knowing I couldn't. Then you brought out the big guns. You stood there, tears running down your face."

The pained look on his face gives me pause.

"Then you stepped aside so I could play poker, but when you walked in on the game and didn't like my behavior, you punished me by withholding yourself. You want to control me, tell me how a man should live, how I should command Cavalry."

His face contorts, and his eyes plead with me.

"When Michael finally showed up ... you chose him, but you didn't go with him. You kissed him in front of me. Your conduct that day was unbelievable, and you don't see how you hurt others."

How I hurt others? I never meant to hurt anyone. He's the one that walked out of Club with Mary Jo, in front of me and everyone else. He's the one that treated me like a whore, left me to play poker, and fondled that woman. I wasn't the only one who misbehaved at lunch, but I was the only one punished. He told everyone I meant nothing to him, and then two weeks later, he made Paul my handler. He wounded me.

No, that isn't true. He told me who he was, but I didn't believe him. And he showed me who he was when he took me to his playroom, but I thought I could change him. I told him to go ahead and play poker because I knew he wasn't enjoying himself. I tricked him into giving up the poker game first, then I let him go. He was never dishonest about himself or his desires. Commander didn't hurt me. I hurt myself.

When he punished me, he was doing his duty. I was disrespectful in front of the Inner Circle, and I broke a cardinal rule. It embarrassed him. I understood it was wrong. He didn't realize how his words hurt me, or how Michael's betrayal upset me.

He was unaware I had just told Michael the awful things Wickmore did to me, revisiting the painful trauma I stuffed down deep inside me, and from which I never finished healing. How Michael didn't react when I told him about the Colonel's repeated assaults but flew into a rage when I admitted to having sex with his brother.

Commander had no idea I was nearing a breakdown, hanging on by a thread. But why should he? I never told him anything. I hid my past, my pain, and all my secrets from everyone.

He didn't understand that I had lost everything, and I wanted to gain control over my life again. I was at the top of my career and respected for my intelligence and my achievements. No one had accomplished what I achieved. Not a female civilian, anyway. I had a wonderful relationship with a man who loved me. I had arrived, and I was successful. And overnight, through no fault of my own, I lost everything.

No, that's not true either. If I gave them what they wanted, if I became who they needed, if I did whatever they asked of me, then I had value. As soon as there was nothing for me to do, I lost it. My belief that I meant something to them was unfounded. I became the good girl Michael desired, convincing myself that his lying and controlling behavior was part of a healthy relationship. I sold myself cheap, to avoid further abandonment. He abandoned me, anyway.

"You're right, and I'm sorry, Commander."

Chapter 16

With my notes spread out in front of me, I'm organized for my mid-morning meeting with Paul. Soft music plays in the background, I'm fortified with a fresh cup of coffee, and I'd rather be somewhere else. The mountain on the horizon catches my attention. I wonder if it has a base built into it, but it's impossible to tell from here.

During my travels as Caroline, I had trekked for months when I witnessed an enormous circular structure several miles ahead. I estimated it could take a week for me to walk around, so to avoid it, I changed directions. I kept my distance, but from my vantage point, the massive construction, embedded in a mountainous landscape, seemed comparable in size to a large city. It was much larger than Westview, which I viewed after leaving the cave when Dan and his men returned there with me as their rescue. Since that day, I've only seen bases from the inside, and the outside world through their windows.

"So, where are you?" Paul asks.

He stands before me, holding several magazines. I didn't hear him come upstairs. He plops the periodicals down in front of me. The top publication shows the date as January 2025.

"Thought these might interest you," he says, then sits next to me.

After an hour of discussing various articles, Paul catches me staring at him and asks, "What?"

"Just thinking."

Paul inherited his handsome features from his father, Tim, but I see a bit of Jade in him, too. When I first arrived at Cavalry, I hoped to make friends with him and Tom. They enjoyed teasing me, but I shied away from them. My primary mission was to prove myself and deal with the aftereffects of the injustice I'd endured at Central Control. I had fears to conquer, and a reputation and self-esteem to repair. I needed their respect, and I longed to fit in, but I made many mistakes.

Had Commander assigned Paul as my handler early on and had he shown this much interest in my assignment, I might have liked him and would have enjoyed working with him. Had that happened, we might have become work friends, as I enjoyed at Central Control. I got along with everyone on my team at Central, but my teammate Mick and I were closer and understood each other. Or so it seemed. He respected my relationship with Michael and my commitment to him, so our friendship was nonsexual and not the least romantic, but we collaborated without difficulty.

"About what? You look a million miles away."

I won't forgive him for hitting me. He was performing his duty and I doubt it was personal, but they had no right or reason to treat me that way. There are more effective, less humiliating, and less painful ways to handle situations. My reaction to punishment was to shut down, stop working, and become more reserved. Nobody won.

I hide my grief from Paul. I mourn what might've been—the coalition I should've created. My plans to make Cavalry my home and these people my own, all fell apart because of my desperate need to remember, to break free of my memory cocoon. I suffered through long months of unraveling to uncover my truth, to escape from my self-made prison. I can't stay here, anyway. Another Tracker hunts for me and time is not on my side. Tommy warned me.

"I'm thinking how different everything would be, had you been my handler straight off."

"It'd be the same, except we might be further along."

I laugh. Does he honestly believe he could contribute more to a project I'm purposely filibustering? He could have been a hindrance to me controlling my pace.

"You think you could have translated the symbols faster?"

He looks contrite.

"You're right. It would have turned out the same."

We gather the materials, and our meeting is over.

"I'll leave you to your work." Paul stands and nods.

"Thanks for the magazines."

I shift my attention to the windows to scan the mountains. A fuzzy picture I can't quite visualize tugs at me, hiding in the depths of my memory, like something I chose to forget. Like a dream I'm sure I dreamed but can't remember the details. Every part of me is desperate to learn my elusive truth.

I change my music selection to rock opera to help me transcend. Outside, autumn has stripped the forest of its foliage, leaving only a spattering of evergreens to color the scenery, and the gray cloudy sky hints at the coming of winter. But a faint memory surfaces—of a hot summer day under a scorching sun, with blue skies, green leaves, and me longing to cool off and wash away the road....

§

My suitcase showed signs of wear and tear, having been my faithful companion for decades. I never crossed paths again with Jade and my temporary family, nor had I ever learned of their fate. My travels took me great distances, but I dodged running into another Tracker. I passed through small towns, often with few remaining residents, many older folks, few younger people, but no children. Some regions evaded the scourge for several years maintaining an adequate living, and a handful managed to generate electric power. Factories and makeshift stores still existed, but they no longer used money. Barter and trade were the norms.

The Captors hadn't yet seized the farms in all the provinces, so citizens pooled their resources and created a new existence. I'd settle in those counties for weeks or months, especially in winter, always reminded of the danger of lingering in a single town. Other settlements weren't as welcoming, and I quickly passed through them. The knowledge that Trackers found me twice already, decades apart, kept me cautious, never knowing how many bounty hunters lurked out there.

I avoided two more enormous bases in my travels, both off in the distance, looking like they could fit a whole metropolitan city in them, but I was clueless about who inhabited them. They built one into a mountain, or perhaps they built the mountain around the base, leaving the top part of the complex poking out. Most of the structure was windowless except for the topmost level, which displayed huge thick windows that caught the sun's glare. There were large sections of windowpanes between wall segments. I've since realized that those casements provided landscape views for apartments, offices, or atriums.

The second base was a massive ground complex with three visible stories, the highest level sporting the standard window sets. I've lived on four different bases, and I'm aware several floors exist underground. Central Control had six levels plus a basement or two, but I never saw it from the outside to my knowledge. The Master Plan describes the bases as well-insulated and constructed to withstand any disaster, like tornadoes, forest fires, floods, and earthquakes. They are designed to cater to the needs of the inhabitants while keeping them confined. Safe from whom? We had no desire to join them.

Living off the land was challenging because I couldn't kill to eat. I had no stomach for it. I'd learned long ago how to build a campfire and find edible plants, but not hunt, because I was unwilling to slaughter and cringed at the thought of skinning animals. If necessary, I could protect myself, but I'm no hunter, so I existed on a vegetarian diet when traveling alone, and the fields of generous farmers afforded adequate sustenance in the summer. Winters were tough. I needed to join a settlement early in the fall to survive the freezing temperatures and scarcity of food. Providence always provided, as old Reverend Miller promised.

My garments, many found along my travels, were few but in decent condition, although some hung on me. The salvage crews weren't the only people who made use of abandoned goods. Wanderers, like me, couldn't be fussy. Sometimes, I'd run across a deserted store and secure packages of new underwear and often clothes that fit. My suitcase didn't hold much, so I was prudent. The heavier my load, the harder my journey.

Everything I owned was soiled, including the clothes I was wearing, as well as those packed in my suitcase. I had been traveling for over three weeks without finding a suitable place to stay, launder my clothing, or take a decent bath. I preferred cleanliness, but my luck seemed to run out for a while. That day, everything changed.

It was late afternoon. I followed a stream that led me to a still lake that reflected the blue sky and fluffy white clouds, a welcome sight for my hot, tired, and dirty body. Without the benefit of laundry soap, I soaked my clothes and my single towel, wrung them out, and hung them on nearby branches to dry in the sun. I hadn't seen a soul for weeks, so after undressing, I felt comfortable laundering my sullied clothing in the nude. While my entire wardrobe dried, I waded into the refreshing lake until it covered my chest, enjoyed the sun-warmed water, and with pure delight washed away the dirt from the road. I splashed and swam like a child, grateful for simple pleasures.

Ready to dry off, I headed for land when I felt someone watching me.

"Mind if I join you?" he asked.

The clean-shaven stranger looked to be in his thirties, with longish brown hair and a deep tan. Not waiting for my answer, he stripped down to his birthday suit and hung his clothes on branches near mine. He waded into the water but kept a decent distance from me. I watched him, unsure if I should stay where I was, or let him see me naked as I got out.

"My name's Joshua, and please don't worry. You're safe here. What's your name?"

"Caroline."

"Well, hello, Caroline."

Joshua swam on his back, took a deep breath, and then submerged. An instant later, two feet stuck out of the water. He surfaced, rocked his head back, and spouted out a stream of water like a whale. I laughed but decided against imitating him. We swam for a while, giving each other a measure of privacy.

"Sure is hot today. The water's a blessing, don't you think?" asked Joshua.

"I'm enjoying it ... and I got my laundry done."

Suddenly, I remembered my underwear hanging on branches. The clear water did little to hide me, but my dangling undies embarrassed me more than my nudity. I had flung them all over the bushes and tree limbs, not expecting company. Josh nodded politely.

"Are you ready to dry off?" he asked.

"Sure."

I watched him head for shore, and I followed, covering my breasts with my arms. Joshua grabbed my dry hanging towel, spread it over a flat boulder, and covered it with his dry shirt. He settled on it, leaving room for me next to him. He patted his shirt, inviting me to join him, then looked away, allowing me some dignity as I parked myself beside him.

Joshua told me how he inherited the land and house from his parents, who settled it years ago. His folks built their house in the woods as a vacation home decades ago, but when the world started changing and chaos ensued, they converted it into a bunker for Josh and his wife to hide from the Captors. The young couple took residence and kept it fully supplied with food and necessities.

"Where's your wife?"

A veil of sadness crossed over him.

"She died last year. Her name was Laura."

His grief and love for her were obvious, but he masked his sorrow with a pained smile.

"I'm sorry."

We talked as the sun dried us. I repeated the same story I told Jade and many others over the past many seasons, that I'd been traveling alone for two years, after separating from my family. I maintained my youthful body, thanks to the Gift's power, so I could hardly reveal I'd been avoiding the Captors for over four decades.

"You're lucky you found this place. I haven't seen the militias that kidnap our young folks since Laura and I moved in a few years ago. I keep watch anyway. We're pretty isolated back here."

"I call them the Captors. I've seen them, but luckily, they've failed to catch me."

"We're a long way from the main road and they tend to stay close to freeways. The Captors have already hit farms along the highway. Everyone left behind is older, making it hard for them to work their land, but they do. And we eat."

Joshua averted his eyes while we dressed. He helped me gather my dry, cleaner clothes and pack my well-worn suitcase. We hiked through the shady aromatic woods to his bunker home, hidden deep in the forest in a small clearing. Joshua gave me the full tour of his impressive homestead. The well-insulated house was quiet and cool, even with ninety-degree temperatures outside. An outdoor thermometer hung near his door, but I didn't need it to tell me it was sweltering out.

With closed windows and no electricity, it amazed me how cozy the house was inside. The kitchen had a vented wood stove and a sink sporting a hand pump. Joshua showed me what I thought was the only bedroom, but in the modest living room, I noticed a comfortable-looking couch. The sparse rooms lacked a woman's influence. Although neat and clean, they were barren of any personal effects. I had decided he must have removed any painful reminder of his loss, something I understood. Then he offered to show me the underground level.

Joshua hit the light switch, and when we reached the well-lit lower level, he explained he had installed solar panels. This floor also had a kitchen, living room, and bedroom, but Laura had decorated it with embroidered pillows and pictures of flowers and gardens. Knick knacks of distinctive figures filled a small curio cabinet, and Laura certainly graced this floor with a woman's touch. Her spirit was everywhere. A rag doll sat on a mini rocking chair in one corner and a vase with pink and blue crepe-paper flowers sat on the fireplace mantel.

Joshua explained they spent winters on this comfy lower level and showed me the huge pantry, stocked with cans, bottles, and boxes of dry goods, along with cleaning and paper products. He proudly showed me another room, a library, with bookcases brimming with books. I had wondered how he survived the wintry season alone, but from the twinkle in his eyes, I knew he loved reading, which must have helped him get through the dark, bitter days.

His most prized possession was an old-fashioned record player in the corner. I noticed a bookcase with one shelf housing a stack of vintage music albums. I rummaged through the stack, recognizing several band names, and numerous familiar songs, but I knew enough to hide my excitement or knowledge of the century-old artists and the outmoded technology. Joshua removed an album, placed it on the record player, and stood back to watch my amazement. I didn't disappoint him.

He explained he inherited his great-grandfather's music collection and player. He proudly spoke of how he always kept them in mint condition and handled them with utmost care. It was his treasure. Powered by solar panels, sometimes when the electrical current wasn't strong enough, on dark days, they had to choose between having lights or music. So, they brought out the candles.

It was dry and comfortable down there, but I was eager to return upstairs to the natural light. The kitchen cabinets upstairs also contained food and plenty of dishes and cookware. Accustomed to camping, my term for living off the grid, I helped put together a decent meal. We enjoyed our dinner and each other's company, sitting at the kitchen table, and it was obvious Joshua relished having a visitor. His gaze rarely left me with his joy reflecting mine the entire time we spent talking. He was interested in learning about my travels and what I'd seen or heard. Joshua told me about his nearest neighbor who lived a good hike away. I was also excited to have a roof over my head out of the oppressive heat, a handsome companion I had deemed safe, and a delicious home-cooked meal.

Joshua said he spent most of the summer outdoors and I guessed he spent a lot of time swimming nude from his lack of tan lines. The first thing I noticed about him was his deeply tanned skin and sun-bleached brown hair. He looked every bit the nature lover he claimed to be. I, too, was tan and weatherworn, but he didn't seem to mind. We talked while we washed the dishes and tidied the kitchen. It was late and the light outside was fading, and I was fading too. The afternoon swim and hike to Joshua's homestead drained me.

"There are two bedrooms. Would you prefer to sleep up here or downstairs?"

When Joshua showed me the lower-level bedroom, I noticed the bare mattress. The upstairs bed was made.

"During the summer I sleep upstairs, but I'm comfortable with either. I'll throw some sheets on the other bed. It's your choice."

"If you don't mind, I'd like to sleep up here with you. I mean, on the sofa, if it's no trouble. I don't want to impose."

"It's no imposition, believe me. Sometimes it gets pretty lonesome, and I welcome company."

"The sofa is fine. I don't need much."

"Your wish is my command," he said with a slight bow. "But don't hesitate if you change your mind. The couch may not be that comfortable."

"I'll be all right. I've had to sleep in some very uncomfortable places. This looks good."

He prepared my provisional bed with sheets, a pillow, and a blanket, and wished me sweet dreams. I slept so soundly that I doubt I moved a muscle till morning.

At breakfast the next day, Joshua invited me to stay. Indefinitely.

§

Joshua. Why is this memory so important? I remove my rock opera CD and tidy up my discs, returning them to their cases and filing them in their holder. My music discs are my treasure and I take good care of them.

Commander's housekeeper will arrive soon, so I'll need to clear out for a couple of hours and it's too early for lunch. I stashed my work materials out of sight. Everything's neatly stored, and my workspace is spotless. Since I have some free time, I can check out the latest book additions in the library. I'm prepared for the footsteps on the stairs, but when I peek out expecting housekeeping, I'm surprised when Commander appears instead.

"I see you're leaving. What say we take a walk to my playroom?"

Okay, he wants to Play. No surprise, but I had hoped to put him off.

"I was planning to visit the library. I'm not ready for Play right now. Could we meet tonight, instead? I need to prepare myself. Especially for the first time. I want it to be special."

My eyes beg for mercy, and I'm pleased when he receives my temporary rejection with grace. Commander walks with me, and when we reach the office door, he turns to me.

"You know, I think I'll head downstairs myself. I need to check on something. I'll give you a ride to the second floor."

We walk across the great floor and as we near his playroom, a moment's uneasiness washes over me until we pass by. We enter the freight elevator and descend, passing the second floor and continuing to the main floor.

"I have a surprise for you."

Commander guides me to an enormous room close to the docking bay near David's office. Inside, salvage bounty, recently brought back from the latest run, fills rows of tables. Stacks of books, clothes, and other miscellaneous items cover one table after another. He leads me to a table lined with over two hundred music CDs arranged in cascading lines. I can easily flip through the jewel cases, all appearing in decent condition.

"Go on and take your pick. I need to attend to a matter, but I'll return."

"Thank you, Commander."

He walks away, with a bounce in his step as I turn to my treasure trove, happy as a child at Christmas finding a load of presents under the tree, all with nametags for her. I search through each disc, reading the labels. Every time I find a CD I want, I stack it in one of three piles: one for music I'm familiar with and love, another for songs or artists that I recognize, and one for unfamiliar music that looks interesting.

A commotion in the back of the immense room catches my attention. I notice David walking towards me. He yells to someone I can't see, and they both laugh. He waves when he sees me. My stomach tenses and my heart hurts. I want him to be happy. With me.

David grabs a small cardboard box on his way over to me. When he reaches my side of the table, he packs all three stacks of CDs.

"I'm not sure how many discs I'm allowed yet. I had them sorted so I can choose those I want most, depending on the number I'm permitted."

"Commander says you can have whatever you want."

David hides his displeasure, but I sense bitterness.

"What did you do?" he asks.

"What?"

"Come on. Don't play games with me. You and Commander?"

"He wanted me, and he promised to stop punishing everyone ..."

"You think that was about you?"

I can't speak. His tone is sarcastic and cruel.

"He gets in a mood this time every year. It's the anniversary of his friend's death. It doesn't last long, and it's not that bad, and he doesn't hurt anyone. Keep this to yourself. No one talks about it."

A punch to the gut would hurt less. Such a stupid mistake. I could have read someone to learn the truth.

"He's gonna want to Play, kitten."

"You pressured me to Play too, but we never did."

"He's not like me. He'll insist on it and he's not patient."

"I won't be here much longer, and I'll figure it out."

David shakes his head, and after a long regretful gaze, turns and leaves.

My music selections are packed, and the storage area is quiet. David and his worker have gone, and Commander hasn't returned, so I wander around to explore the other tables.

As I stroll the massive aisles of salvaged goods, I pass a badly dented metal sphere resting on four spikes that emerge from its dull gray surface, engraved with tiny alien symbols. Well, R2D2, what are you doing here? Nobody alive today would understand my *Star Wars* reference. I check around to ensure I'm still alone and read the pictograms etched into the orb's circumference out loud.

The device suddenly activates, emitting a familiar sweet odor like rotting leaves, humming, with tiny glowing lights, and twitching back and forth like a bird trying to fly away but can't. I place my hand on it, and it stops. David and a private rush into the salvage room.

"What was that? What did you do?" asks David.

"It was nothing. I began humming a tune from one of these old CDs, but something caught in my throat, and I started coughing. That's all."

"It didn't sound like coughing," the private says.

I clear my throat.

They squint at me, then study the alien drone, then look at me again.

"Can you translate the inscription?" asks David.

I study the symbols, then reply, "Made in China." I giggle.

The officers exchange quizzical looks.

"I'm kidding. Nobody can read that," I say, raising my eyebrows at David.

I'm still giddy from my musical windfall and I'm relieved when they laugh at my humor.

"Commander," I say, spotting him as he walks in. I turn away from the sphere and return to the small table covered in music discs. "I selected several promising CDs, and I can't wait to listen to them. Thank you so much."

I grab my box of discs, and with Commander's arm around my shoulder, we head for the exit. The orb spits an ominous last sputter—reminding me of the Tracker.

I search my memory. If I've come across the device before, it eludes me. For now.

§

The housekeeper is gone, and the apartment smells of cleaning products, all environmentally safe, but not odorless. It doesn't look any different. It never does. They do a proper job, but Commander is neat and squeaky clean. Zena acclimated to military-style cleanliness, but my life as Rebecca was much less strict, and "camping" for Caroline was far from this regimented, spotless way of living. I prefer daily showers and access to laundry facilities over bathing and washing clothes in the lake. But Joshua. Another memory floats to the surface of my consciousness....

§

Six weeks passed, and Joshua and I continued playing house together. He took off during the day, sometimes for hours, leaving me alone, so I established a schedule of duties to perform in his absence, including tending to his small garden on the south side of the house. Joshua informed me that his routine was to canvass the area for intruders, and occasionally he visited neighbors a good distance away to trade for fresh food.

He'd return with traded meat or vegetables or other items. Sometimes he surprised me with an unusual stone or pretty flower. And frequently he brought home an interesting story. He often took me scouting with him or to meet the neighbors, but never when he went hunting.

One evening, after dinner, we retired to the living room to relax and read, as was our habit. His collection of books was much to my taste, and we settled in to immerse ourselves in reading. My book, although interesting enough, sat open on my lap while I mulled over a disturbing observation. We frequented the lake weekly, spending our time skinny-dipping, and playing in the water, but Joshua was always respectful and refrained from sexual overtures.

At night, Joshua and I slept apart. I still slept on the couch. He never looked at me with desire or made sexual advances. He was always kind, a perfect gentleman, but he treated me more like his sister than a desirable woman. Since he was married for several years, it was clear he liked women. At least it was obvious he loved Laura, so I considered him to still be in mourning. He had been grieving for over a year, and I understood grief knows no time limit.

"Joshua, can I ask you a ... personal question?"

"Call me Josh if you like," he said, closing his book. "Of course, ask me anything."

"Do you find me at all attractive?"

Josh put down his book, and sadness crossed him. I assumed that meant I was correct. He needed more time to grieve.

"I find you very attractive."

"You've never ..."

"Caroline, unless you have means for birth control, we shouldn't have this conversation."

Josh picked up the book and immediately set it down. He held his breath for a moment and then let out a deep sigh.

"Laura was pregnant, but when she went into labor, there were serious problems. We were alone, with neither of us knowing what to do. Laura and the baby died after she suffered prolonged labor and I can't endure that again, so it's best we ..."

"Josh, there are several ways to enjoy making love. Intercourse is only one way to experience pleasure," I said, bracing myself to reveal my long-kept secret.

"I can't have children. It's something I don't talk about, but you needn't fear. It's not possible. But if you're not ready ..."

Josh stood up, tossed his book aside, pulled me into his arms, and whispered in my ear.

"I wish you had mentioned that about six weeks ago," he said, beaming, and guided me to his bed, where we made up for lost time.

Josh was always truthful with me. He hid nothing. He was upfront about his love for Laura and everything else. So, I hated lying to him, but lying was a necessary component of my mission. I couldn't share my past, the knowledge of the Gift, or the Trackers, and I had to hide my abilities. I longed to tell Josh my truth, my fears, everything, but I didn't dare tell anyone. Josh was unlike men I'd known on my travels, and so different from Jade. He was gentle, kind, even-tempered, honest, and thoughtful, and I loved sharing our lives, but I still had to keep my secrets. If he knew my awful truth, he wouldn't have looked at me the same.

§

I promised to show up at Commander's office just as he's returning from exercising. He wears a naughty, expectant smile as he approaches. Commander escorts me upstairs and excuses himself to shower while I choose music appropriate for the evening.

He exits the bathroom wearing only a towel.

"Should I dress, and we'll visit my playroom, or would you prefer to stay here?"

"Stay here. I have an idea."

I walk over to Commander, take his hand, and lead him into the bedroom.

"You need to lose that towel."

He grins, tosses aside the only thing covering him, and indicates I should undress, too. But I have other plans. I scan the room looking for a makeshift tie, and coming up short, I select a belt from several hanging near his clothes. Commander raises his eyebrows and beams.

"Lie on the bed, sir, on your back, and hold out your arms to me."

"What?"

He squints at me with apprehension but doesn't move.

"I'll bind your wrists, but you'll be able to get free. But don't. It's part of Play."

His smile returns, and he does as I ordered. I wrap the belt around his wrists, slipping one end through the loop until it's snug. There is no way to secure it, and any movement will undo his binding, but he plays along.

"Put your hands above your head."

He obeys, letting me move his arms to the desired position. It's obvious he's curious and excited about my next move. I slip off my shoes, blouse, and skirt, leaving on my black underwear, before climbing onto the bed and straddling his legs. I bend forward and press my lips against his, then inch backward down his chest, softly kissing and massaging everything in my path. When I'm hovering above his knees, I caress his outer thighs, then gently stroke the insides, watching his reaction. I plant kisses below his belly button and nibble my way downward to give him what Zena refused.

"I've never done this before," I say. This time, I know it's a lie. "If I try something you're uncomfortable with, tell me, and if I hurt you, say so. I want to please you."

I savor his expression, one of surprise, excitement, and anticipation.

Chapter 17

The moment I step into the office, Cassie broadsides me with another meeting I'm expected to attend. I rush upstairs to retrieve my notepad and head out to the conference room. Commander and his team are in attendance, so after knocking and entering, I slip into my seat facing Commander across the long table. This time, he's smiling and his eyes twinkle. David's lips form a tight line, and he avoids eye contact with me, but as I scan the other lieutenants, they appear unaware, so I suspect David hasn't mentioned my new standing as Commander's girl.

"So, Zena, do you have anything to share with us?" asks Commander.

"Not at this moment, sir."

Paul would have informed him of any recent developments, and there have been none, so I wonder why Commander invited me to this meeting. Paul keeps him updated, and it would surprise me if Commander had plans to embarrass me after the amazing evening we shared last night.

"That's fine. I have an announcement. Zena has agreed to be my exclusive girl. I'll expect you all to treat her with respect and watch over her. If she needs anything, or anyone gives her a hard time, you'll step in and handle it."

Mack looks at me, first in surprise, then shakes his head. His fake smile is unconvincing. West nods, appearing unhappy about my new standing. Frank appears stunned, then hurt. David must have kept quiet on my behalf, not even telling his best friend. Tom, Dan, and Paul, of course, already in the loop, don't react.

"Okay, that's it. You're all dismissed."

I walk back to the office alone, grateful the others hung back. I need a coalition, but I need Commander's team on board and I'm unconvinced this is the way. Time will tell.

Cassie doesn't look up when I pass by her desk, but I sense she is unaware of the latest developments.

§

A server fills a bowl full of mouthwatering beef stew and hands it to me with a slice of garlic bread, and a teacup filled to the brim with chocolate pudding, topped with a dollop of whipped cream. The cafeteria servers, with unusual deference, regard me with strange stares. The rumors must have reached them, and they stare as if it's inconceivable but remarkable that a civilian woman could snare the Commander. As if they'd love to discover how I did it. Terry is distant, not cold, but she scrutinizes me as if she believes I betrayed her somehow.

Our meeting concluded early this morning, and already the news has spread like wildfire. Officers and military women alike watch me like hawks. Some hide their disapproval, not daring to offend, but I feel it's there, judging me, no doubt deciding I'm a social climber, working my way up the ladder. If I read them, I'd gain a better sense, but frankly, I don't give a damn. I enjoy my meal alone, as usual, ignoring them.

My relationship with Commander was secret, only his Inner Circle had knowledge of it, and they are so closed-mouthed, that not even their First Lieutenants knew. Now everyone does. I feel naked in a new way.

Mary Jo watches me, but when I glance at her, she turns away. Her friends sneak peeks in my direction like a group of teenage girls. I hear whispering chatter from their table, but none of the usual laughter. After I brought Commander Nadler to the cafeteria, I sensed their curiosity, but today it's pure hostility, draped in a cloak of reverence.

I ate my lunch without tasting it, but my hunger was appeased. After setting my tray in the bin, I return to my seat and sit back to relax for a few minutes before returning to work, pondering what effects this latest revelation will have on my remaining days here. I'm sure I've made enemies, which was not my intention, but you can't please everyone.

Just beyond Mary Jo's table, I notice Dan scanning the tables until our eyes meet. He walks over and sits across from me without asking.

"So, it's official. You're Commander's girl now. Welcome to the group."

"He has a group of girls?" I ask, giggling.

Dan purses his lips to avoid smiling and shakes his head.

"No, but we're his brothers, so that makes us your brothers, too."

"I like that. I've never had brothers before. Are there any rules?"

"No," Dan says with a laugh. "As Commander said in our morning meeting, any problems or anything you need, come to us and we'll handle it."

"Thank you. So, what about you? What are your feelings about Commander making me his girl?"

"I'm not sure yet. Make him happy and you and I will get along fine. He likes you."

He stares at me for a moment, looking concerned.

"You remind me of someone, but I can't quite figure out who."

"People have told me that before. I must have a doppelgänger somewhere, but I haven't run into her yet. I'm sure it'll come to you."

"A doppelgänger? What's that?"

"A twin or double. Someone who looks like me."

"I guess that's it."

§

Cassie squints at me when I return to work. All my efforts to win her over have been in vain, but it's too late in the game to make female friends, anyway. I might be moving on within a month. I can't stay here. Tommy's words come back to haunt me.

I fill my cup of coffee and meander over to Paul's office to find him typing away at his computer, so I sit next to him, sip my hot beverage, and wait.

Paul turns to face me.

"What do you need, Zena?"

He eyes me with a warmth I hadn't seen before.

"Nothing. I'm curious about how you feel, now that I'm Commander's girl?"

"Whatever makes Commander happy. Just behave yourself. He's quite fond of you. You hurt him, you'll answer to me."

Paul's not threatening, but he's serious.

"It's more likely he'll hurt me."

He shrugs.

§

My legal pads teeming with my translations wait beside my laptop. I created and formatted a new document, and I'm ready to dive into typing my next report. Central Intelligence will expect periodic interim reports, and I need busy work, but a half hour passes, and the keyboard remains untouched.

My excitement for this project has dwindled to mild interest. The Master Plan's story has played out except for the final act. They built the bases, captured humans, enslaved some, and reprogrammed others. But the ending never manifested. They lost the Gift.

A nagging at the edge of my consciousness draws my attention to the window. It's like a dream you know you were dreaming, but now that you're awake it has faded, leaving you with the sense of it, and nothing more.

I play my favorite meditation music and stand facing the mountains, searching for the source of my agitation. In the distance, a ribbon of smoke rises from a cluster of trees. Is it coming from a cabin, house, or campfire? Joshua. I allow my thoughts to spin freely....

§

In Josh's home, winter was not as dreadful as I had imagined. Josh seldom went out, especially when the snowdrifts were as high as the windows. It was the middle of January, and the snow outside was too deep for easy travel. The temperature had dropped, and we were housebound. We missed our neighbors, their company, and the fresh eggs and meat they provided. The ingredients for our meals came from the pantry, but we were creative and that, along with our carefree banter, made for pleasant dinners.

During the day, the windows reflected the snow's brilliance, providing plenty of light on the main floor. The solar panels Josh had installed on the roof lit the lower level in the evenings. If the lights dimmed on cloudy days, we had an ample supply of candles. They were romantic, but reading was impossible. Instead, we enjoyed wonderful conversations, played games, relaxed in each other's arms, or made love in the dark.

We sailed through the cold snowy days and nights, not just surviving them, but relishing them, playing house, and getting to know each other. I'd never met anyone quite like Josh. Smart, strong, but gentle and patient. He loved nature. He saw beauty in the untouched mountains of snow, braved the freezing temperatures to put crumbs out for the birds, and often expressed worry about our furry friends in miserable, frigid weather.

Ever easygoing, Josh took every challenge in stride. By the end of our first winter, I realized I loved him, and he never had to profess his love for me because he showered me with it. Laura was a lucky woman to have had Josh's love for their brief life together.

To keep track of the passing time and seasons, we created our own calendar. We blocked each month on a large sheet of paper with square boxes for the days, spacious enough to write about significant events that happened each day. If nothing notable occurred, we put an X in the box. That first winter, we plotted out months for the entire coming year, covering both sides of six good-sized sheets.

We circled our birthdays. Mine was the fourth of January, and Josh's was April 10th. We celebrated birthdays and other occasions by giving each other simple handmade gifts, like pancakes decorated with faces made from jam, a drawing, or a massage. It mattered that we set special days aside, giving us something to look forward to, not the quality of the gift.

Once, while rummaging through the art closet, I discovered a box full of Josh's old calendar pages. While he napped that evening, I pulled out a stack of calendars from previous years. It had the months displayed on both sides like the ones we created. I read several of the daily notes.

One page described Laura's progress in befriending a squirrel. By the end of that April, Laura had several squirrels visiting her. Other months noted similar stories about birds, chipmunks, and even a baby opossum. Few date boxes contained an X.

Very few dates mentioned difficult times. I saw the note for the day Laura suspected she was pregnant, reflecting on how overjoyed they were. Someone had drawn a red heart around the news. I stopped reading after that, not because I didn't want to share their joy, but because I knew how their story ended.

Josh and Laura had stored an abundance of art supplies for projects, including various pads of drawing paper. Magic markers and different colored pencils and pens filled a craft box. Many of the markers had dried up, so I tossed them. Laura had a watercolor paint set and multicolored card stock. Had she planned to decorate for the baby? I felt like an intruder trespassing on her privacy, sorting through her art stockpile.

Josh had mentioned how much pleasure Laura got from drawing flowers. He spoke of different craft projects with which she occupied herself to pass the long housebound hours. He had his music and library of books. Our first winter, we had many conversations about Laura's virtues and talents. He needed to talk and grieve.

I ached to express my own grief about my husband, Russ, my children, and my grandchildren. I had a lot more time to live with my grief and my mission overshadowed my sorrow, letting me move on. But grief never dies. You learn how to live with it.

I yearned to divulge my relationship with Jade, how we met, grew close together, and how he was mine. How we fell apart after the Captors took his brother. How I needed to flee after killing Vincent. Those subjects were off the table. I couldn't reveal I was married for fifty years or that I left Jade a decade ago after killing the Tracker. I had to lock my stories away. Instead, I told him sanitized versions of my experiences on the run before meeting Josh. That was safe.

§

My music ends, and silence welcomes me back to the present. The ribbon of smoke is gone. Another hallucination like the cocoon? Like Tommy? People must still exist out there, living free and governing themselves. If I tell Dan the truth about who I am, he might offer information about where he found me, and perhaps provide a map of the area near Westview. It might jar loose important memories. Is Josh waiting for me? He would be older since it's been over a decade since my rebirth, and I know I don't look the same. He wouldn't recognize me, but I believe he'd welcome me. Why did I leave him? Another Tracker? I'm so tired of running.

Chapter 18

The week has flown by, and I've been following the holidays on the handmade calendar that I copied from Paul's original planner. I didn't mark the significant dates, but I'm aware of when Thanksgiving and Christmas passed, even if I'm the only person who notices or pays homage.

I have a secret I can't share and a century of memories, some I experienced during my life as Rebecca, and others in my years as Caroline. Christmas trees with presents under them, and excited children waiting for Santa. Cookies and wreaths, and mistletoe. With Jade, there was no tree or decorations, but I sang hymns with Abbey and Shana, and the rest of our Resistance family. We had delicious food and a sense of homecoming and community. Or celebrations with Josh, just the two of us, making our own special days and celebrating them in our unique way.

Paul expects me to submit another interim report soon, so I've revised, edited, and proofread my next submission, and I'm pleased with my effort. We work well together, and I hate deceiving him, but I doubt anyone is eager to learn what the Overlords actually have planned for them. If I fulfill my mission they'll never need to know.

The view outside the apartment window is a blur of white flurries, and Christmas carols repeat in my head like a broken record, but I dare not sing them out loud. This culture frowns upon religious themes, and I can't explain knowing the songs.

My current calendar for this upcoming year, 2101, is finished. The military bases don't celebrate New Year's Day, and it's doubtful the civilian bases observe the beginning of the coming year either. It's just another day.

I approach Paul's office and voices from his cubicle alert me that the Inner Circle is engaged in a staff meeting. When Paul notices me, he motions me to join them.

"What do you need, Zena?"

"I finished a large section of my report, so whenever you have time, if you like, we can review it. You asked me to keep you informed of my progress, and I'm eager to send it to Central Intelligence."

"Sure, how about in an hour?"

"That's perfect. I'll make sure everything's ready."

"While you're here," Commander says, "my birthday is next week. Every year we throw a party, and you'll accompany me. As my girl."

"Oh, happy birthday, sir. Which day?"

Commander squints at me as if he assumed I already knew.

"January fifth."

I step back in astonishment. My birth date is January 4th, but I'd forgotten that until I started remembering my life with Josh. What surprises me is that January 5th was one of the two days Michael visited Cavalry. He traveled here—for his brother's birthday.

"Is Michael's birthday in June?"

"Sure. The twenty-third. You didn't know?"

"No. Is he coming here for your birthday next week?"

"Yep. That an issue for you?"

"Of course not. I want to prepare myself mentally. Our previous visit didn't go well."

Commander shakes his head.

"I don't foresee a problem. I've only seen him once in the last year, so I'm certain he's moved on."

Commander nods. "I wanted to give you a heads up on what to expect. After dinner, we'll meet in the main conference room. You'll join us, along with seven military women. Each team member selects their own choice before the day of the party, and we'll choose someone for Michael."

Commander watches for my reaction, but I just smile.

"A couple of girls will perform a special show for us, then the couples leave for ... private time. When everyone returns, we'll have cake and mingle and enjoy ourselves. Any of that a problem for you?"

"And I'll leave with you?"

"I never partake in that part of the party. I'm the host and you'll perform hostess duties. You'll sit with me. After the show and cake, the men chat together. That will give the women an opportunity to meet you and get better acquainted. Sometimes we play games or just talk. It's pretty open at that point."

My red flags flare like fireworks on the Fourth of July, but I can't sense why. Tom wears his usual naughty grin, and Dan plays it cool, but Paul turns away and pretends to study his papers. Could their behavior have something to do with Michael's upcoming attendance? He's not bringing a date since they're selecting one for him.

So, this is the secret Michael hid from me. He comes to Cavalry for their birthdays and getting serviced is part of the festivities, part of the fun. Why did he lie? Why wouldn't he tell me? Couldn't he bring me as his "girl," and introduce me to his brother?

A wave of nausea grips me, betraying my effort to be mature about this. It's my own fault. I could have known, but I chose not to read Michael. There must be trust and respect for privacy in a relationship. I withheld my secrets, keeping most of my past to myself, so I believed he was entitled to keep his own confidences.

I sensed he was cheating when he returned from his trips to Cavalry, but I avoided knowing the details. When I asked him, he lied, and I decided not to let it destroy our friendship. I never cheated on Michael or betrayed him and would have saved myself grief had I Paid Attention. Why didn't I read him? Why didn't I want to know? I wanted him to be honest with me, but I wasn't ready to give him up. Not then.

"Zena, you okay?" asks Commander, folding his arms across his chest.

"Sorry ... yes sir ... I'm fine. I just figured out something. I'll let y'all get back to your meeting. Paul ... I mean, Major Abrams ..." I say, to gain his attention, "I'll see you later, sir."

Paul nods and I head upstairs, feeling queasy. Michael and I will be attending the same party, like the ones he concealed from me. And he'll have a date, while I'm with Commander, as his girl? That sounds like a recipe for disaster. This is one party I'm sure I won't enjoy. But this time, when I see Michael, I'll keep my cool. No outbursts from me. Does Michael know? He must have moved on, but still....

My music blankets the sound of Paul coming upstairs and he catches me singing and dancing to a favorite tune. He's early, and my worktable is ready, but I'm not. I turn off my console player and he grins as I settle down in my spot by the sink. He sits next to me so we can share the computer screen. I move the laptop in front of him, give him a quick summary, and show him where to start reading. While he reads, I entertain myself by singing a song in my mind. After a minute, I catch him staring at me. I was unconsciously moving my hands with the tune as if conducting an orchestra.

"What are you doing?" Paul asks with a silly grin.

"I'm listening to music in my head while you read."

"You're quite animated. What are you listening to?" He grins, enjoying his teasing.

"It's called *Zombie*."

"Zombie?"

"Yeah, was I disturbing you?"

"Sing it for me. I want to hear what a Zombie song sounds like."

"It wouldn't sound very good without music. I'd hear the music, but you wouldn't. I have no talent for singing, I'm afraid."

"Ah, go ahead. There's just the two of us. I want to hear the words."

"Okay. But consider yourself forewarned. If your ears fall off, it's on you," I say, winking.

He laughs at that, and I sing, keeping my voice as soft as possible, not wanting Cassie or anyone else besides Paul to hear me. The song lyrics speak of mothers losing their children in wartime. It's a sad but powerful ballad, reflecting the ugliness of war, and describing the suffering and loss of the youngest innocent casualties.

When I get to the Zombie part, Paul squints, not understanding. I give my best rendition of the dated song with passion and conduct with my hands. When I reach an instrumental section, I pretend to beat a drum to the music he can't hear by slapping the surface of the table in rhythm. Immersed in the lyrics and their meanings, I forget my self-consciousness, and for a moment, I'm alone, singing my heart out about a world that no longer exists, and reliving forgotten feelings. I finish, open my eyes, and wait for him to say something, suddenly embarrassed.

"So, what's a Zombie? Sounds like a war song."

"It's a war protest song. I read someone wrote it as a protest during a war in Ireland, but it was during the Russian invasion of Ukraine and the war in the Middle East in the first quarter of the twenty-first century. They bombed civilians instead of soldiers, causing thousands of children's deaths, separating and displacing families."

I can't tell him I remember when it happened. How it dominated the headlines every day for months. How strange it was watching devastating wars brought into our living rooms, and how awful it was knowing the needless death and destruction continued daily. It's risking disclosing information I shouldn't have, but my heart is heavy, and although I'm unsure why it's important, I feel compelled to share.

"A Zombie is a mythical character. Someone who has died and comes back ... the walking dead. I think some ancient stories claim they eat living victims' brains, but I'm clueless why. It's just a fairytale or myth, made up to entertain. In this song, I believe Zombies are metaphors for living people who are dead inside, representing soldiers with guns who kill innocent children, and other civilians, with ease and no remorse or mercy. But it could also apply to the survivors of the devastation who remain without their beloved children, lost in grief, never to hold them again."

Paul's face grew solemn when I started explaining, and by the time I finished, sadness filled his eyes. It must be wonderful to exist in a world where it's hard to imagine the wholesale murder of innocents in the name of war. We sit in silence for a brief minute, then I exhale a long sigh.

"Do you know any cheerful songs?" he asks.

I flip through the music in my head. My favorites are passionate melodies about human suffering, broken hearts, and impassioned love tunes. They produce deep emotions, making me hurt sometimes, but that's when I feel most alive. It's better than feeling numb and pretending the suffering doesn't matter. It has to matter.

I walk over to my console player and thumb through the box of discs I keep in the apartment. I find a CD that features several singers and a variety of music, some light, some beautiful. Once it's inserted into the player, I return to my worktable.

"We should get back to work."

Chapter 19

Michael is due to arrive at Cavalry later this morning. I want to run but that's not an option and nervous energy builds inside me, so I take the stairs down to the library and head to its charming backroom chamber. Curling up on the cozy couch, flashes of Tommy's strange appearances and warnings add to my uneasiness. If only I could conjure him up and he'd dispense his sage advice, reveal his mysterious secret, or at least offer some revelation about Michael's ill-timed visit. But Tommy has no knowledge that I don't already possess, whether or not I realize it.

When Michael was here in July, I assured him I'd return to Central with him after he dealt with Colonel Wickmore, but the Colonel "retired" a while ago and I haven't seen or heard a word from him in over five months. Does he still expect me to honor my promise, or has he moved on, too? We're both invited to the birthday party, and Commander provided him with a date, so perhaps there's no cause for concern.

I trudge upstairs to the office carrying two books I don't need and probably won't read. Cassie frowns when I approach her desk. I'm about to ask her if Michael has arrived when Commander's door opens and Michael walks out. He sees me, and for a second, a wide smile covers his face, before slowly melting away. Commander stands behind him looking smug. Michael's eyes tell me everything I need to know. He understands I'm not returning to Central, and he's disappointed, if not angry.

I remember this man, but as Rebecca, I see him through fresh eyes. He may not love me the way I need or deserve, but he loves me in his own way, so I'm not eager to hurt him. But he has secrets, and connections to the Overlords through his mother, so I couldn't dare take him back. He's too dangerous.

I walk up to him.

"I'm so glad you're here for your brother's birthday party. Family is so important. It sounds like it'll be fun."

Michael says nothing. I feel him watching me as I turn to go upstairs, where it'll be impossible to work. Yesterday, Commander explained the officers would meet for dinner and that the women, including me, will show up at the party room afterward. The last time Michael visited, the luncheon ended with me erupting in an angry confrontation and storming out, so I imagine no one's eager for a repeat performance. That wouldn't happen this time, but I can't blame them for having long memories. Hopefully, the birthday party will be different.

My meditation session this morning was unproductive, and the voices mentioned nothing about the Tracker. I stayed at the window, watching snow floating down like tiny fluffy cotton balls. It's been snowing like this off and on for several days now and it's sticking to the tree limbs. My attempts to recall another memory failed miserably. The excitement of this evening's party kept intruding on my concentration.

I've stored my work materials in their cupboard in the event Michael makes an unannounced visit. I can't concentrate on working, anyway. Rock music keeps me company and helps me pass the time. Michael was my lover, companion, and partner for almost three years. He treated me well and protected me and I won't forget that. I deserve as much blame for our problems as he does, but that's irrelevant. I'll never return to Central or him.

Dinnertime finally rolls around, and when I show up at the cafeteria, everyone stares at me. My presence screams that they didn't invite me to the birthday dinner. Perhaps they never asked Mary Jo either, so I may be wrong. Maybe it's "officers only" to allow them to catch up before the festivities. I didn't want to sit through another uncomfortable meal in the Commander's diner with Michael, anyway.

I absentmindedly pick at my food, trying to look natural, but it appears I'm a curiosity. Mary Jo and her allies watch me and whisper as usual, but today I imagine they're wondering if I'm going to the party. Mary Jo glares at me occasionally, and their table is unusually quiet. She isn't attending this year. I asked. If she's aware I'm invited, she must hate me for replacing her.

Even though yesterday was my actual birthday, my identity papers state otherwise, so it's another secret I keep. Many happy belated returns, Becky. In the previous decade, deprived of my memories, it never occurred to me to celebrate my phony birthday, but Michael secretly celebrated his and his brother's, never asking me about mine. Strange.

The minute I'm done clearing my table after finishing dinner, I rush upstairs to my room. My clothes rack holds several garments, most designed for my professional life, but my casual outfits are unsuitable for the party. I brush my hair, letting it hang free, but I make two small side braids and secure them at the back of my head.

No one mentioned a dress code, and I forgot to ask if there was one, so I choose my low-cut black blouse. I like the way it hangs on me and it's a favorite among my male friends. My black wraparound skirt is sexy, but the overall effect is too dark. I'm not going to a funeral. I hope. A red sash tied around my waist sets it off and adds a splash of color.

I'll look different from the other women, but that's always true. I slip out of my undies and pull on my almost transparent black tights. Commander likes them. So did Michael. So did David.

Earlier, in the apartment, I selected some dance music in anticipation and realize I have no clue what to expect. Will they have dancing? Commander promised entertainment. And cake.

§

Seven military women mingle outside the large conference room, whispering in hushed, excited tones. I don't know any of them by name, but I've seen them in the third-floor cafeteria. Along with everyone else, they keep their distance and stare at me like I'm an alien from Mars.

When they notice me approaching, they stop chattering and turn my way. I nod. They're wearing casual military attire and my worries about being underdressed vanish. By far, I'm the best-dressed female here. If any of them are our entertainers, their costumes must be already inside.

The door opens and we file in. I bring up the rear, soundlessly singing revised lyrics to the tune of an old *Sesame Street* song. *One of us is not like the others; one of us doesn't belong.*

A long table lining one wall displays a covered sheet cake, plates, glasses, and silverware. No plastic utensils or paper dishes, nothing to throw away or recycle. Very eco-friendly.

Three beverage dispensers with spouts, each holding a different flavor, sit next to two dozen glasses. A fourth container holds water. Someone stacked two empty tubs near the table's end, ready for dirty dishes.

A plastic cover hides the cake's design, so I lift the lid slightly and take a little peek. I smell strawberries. Somebody decorated the large sheet cake with piped pink rosettes covering the sides and part of the top, surrounding 'Happy Birthday' written in a pink gel. No candles.

Birthdays must be a huge deal for the brothers since Michael lied about attending every year. The heavily frosted cake looks delicious, but I doubt it's the big draw. The women's purpose isn't just to serve the cake.

Five couches, each large enough to seat four, are arranged like wagons in a circle. The first couch leaves room on each side for foot traffic. Paul and Commander have already taken their seats there. This setup reminds me of the nursery pit, only larger, and no matching ottoman in the middle, but adequate room in the center for performing, depending on the show.

I wonder if they'll sing or dance or tell jokes. Perhaps a sexy dance for the men. I hope it's not a striptease. They haven't dressed appropriately for that. But then, times change. It could work. There's plenty of space for dancing later, but I doubt that will happen. I brought my music discs, one for fast dances, the other for slow ones.

We enter the pit and locate our designated dates. Paul invites one military woman to sit on the end next to him and directs me to take the seat between him and Commander. Not sure of the protocol, I glance at Commander who nods in acknowledgment. I understand the rules governing public behavior, and they frown upon any display of familiarity towards the Commander. This is my first military birthday party and I'm not versed in the etiquette.

To my left, Michael occupies the next couch and appears surprised and embarrassed to see me, but when his date greets him, it's obvious they're well acquainted. She takes her place next to him and David claims the middle of the remaining space. Next to them, Mack waits alone until a military woman joins him, and they have the entire couch to themselves.

One couch over, Frank and West welcome their chosen dates. Mack and West glance at me, looking uncomfortable. I don't belong here. I'll never become accustomed to the casual way military officers treat sex.

On the couch to my right, Dan and Tom are joined by their selected dates. We are all accounted for and paired off, except David, who sits alone. He doesn't appear to have a date. Who would he bring, Cam? He checks his watch and after a few minutes, gets up and leaves.

I'm still holding my music discs, so I excuse myself to search for the CD player. At the far end of the long catering table, I spot it and notice a single disc placed beside it. I slide my dance music under their disc, labeled "disco," and it's good I brought decent dance music, although it's doubtful we will be dancing.

When I return to my seat, Commander, Paul, and Michael lean forward, deep in discussion. Paul scoots back, ending their conversation.

"What are we waiting for, sir?" I ask Commander.

"Cross went to get the performers. Should start soon."

He leans back with a devious look on his face. An uneasiness nags at me, but I can't determine its cause. It seems unlikely they'd put David in charge of the entertainment. He never seemed interested in music or dancing or any art form.

My wait isn't long. David ushers in two of his civilian girls, each clad in short skirts and loose blouses. They each carry a small bundle, which I assume is extra clothes. Or their underwear. One girl walks over to the console player and inserts their disc, adjusts the sound, and they both awkwardly dance into the makeshift pit. I recognize David's Mary, but not the other young woman.

"Allow me to introduce Mary and Jolene, our entertainment for tonight," David says and takes his seat amid woofs and hollers.

The girls look almost like twins, with their shoulder-length brown hair, and short, petite figures. David has a type, and I'm not it. The pair sashay to the disco song, teasing the men, lifting their skirts higher each time until it's obvious they have nothing on underneath. They're not practiced at stripping, and it must be difficult to strip to disco, but the officers don't seem to mind.

The dancers unbutton their tops and tease their bare breasts before finally pulling their blouses off, acutely aware of nearly every male eye glued to them. David, the only unimpressed male, appears more interested in watching the men enjoying the fruit of his handiwork.

Once the dancers are completely naked, Tom encourages the girls to touch each other, so they take turns fondling each other's breasts. Mary smacks Jolene on her bottom and the men howl like animals, egging them on. Jolene then returns the favor. After granting requests from the rowdy male attendees, the women kiss and make up.

I study the men's mixed reactions as they pay attention to this awful, awkward display. Some find it funny, but others are definitely enjoying themselves.

I've seen striptease shows decades ago, but tonight I'm uncomfortable and unimpressed. These military women also have mixed reactions. Some shake their heads, others laugh or grimace, but none appear to care for the risqué production.

The girls continue performing sexual acts on each other, with Tom spurring them on. I glare at him, but he's oblivious to anything except the lewd conduct. Part of me wants to stand up, cover the girls with blankets, and shame the men. Another part of me just cringes. My maternal instinct ignores their pleasure in being the center of attention.

"Hey, how about one of you ladies come sit on my lap?" asks Tom, licking his lips.

Mary walks over and stands before Tom until he slaps his thigh and tells her to sit. She does. I turn my attention to Commander who must have forgotten I was there. He's watching his brother, who calls Jolene over.

She sits sidesaddle on his lap and runs her fingers through his hair. This lascivious behavior lasts far too long. I understand now why birthday parties are so important to Michael.

The girls return to the center without a plan for an encore. They seem lost until David stands, approaches the strippers, and gives them orders. The unpleasant spectacle is thankfully over. Mary and Jolene gather their removed clothing and get dressed.

I stand to stretch. At the same time, Michael rises and gives me a disapproving look as if I was one of the strippers.

"Did you enjoy the show?" Michael asks, his tone sharp and angry, staring at me.

"No, but then, this unfortunate display clearly wasn't intended for the women."

"So, this is who you are now? You want to stay here? Maybe next time you'll join in and dance naked for us," Michael says, his eyes cold.

David laughs. "Well, she certainly has a nice body. She's welcome to join the girls."

"She's not like that," Michael says to David, glaring at me.

"Well, she's not shy about getting naked. And she loves to please."

Michael glares at David and then back at me.

"Tell me you didn't have sex with him," Michael says, nodding in David's direction.

"I won't lie to you. But I'm very private, and I'm not about to strip in front of y'all. I still have a sense of modesty."

"You've changed. You're not the same girl I knew."

"That's true. Did you expect me to be celibate?"

"No, of course not. But Lieutenant Cross? Of all the decent men you could have picked, you chose him? I thought you were better than that."

"Why not Lieutenant Cross? Did you know he has a beautiful snake tattoo adorning his entire back? He also has a cute butt." Touché.

Michael shakes his head. "You see what he does? How he treats women. You Play now?"

"No, I don't Play. And, yes, David preys on young, inexperienced civilian women," I say, waving toward the girls, standing there, dressed now, their mouths hanging open. "And grooms them into sex objects to delight men like you and your buddies."

Michael looks as if I slapped him. The party room becomes quiet except for our voices and everyone stares at us. I'm sure David doesn't appreciate Michael's words, but Michael is higher in rank, and the Commander's brother, so David stands down, clenching his jaw.

"So, you condone this?" Michael asks.

"No, and you and I have had this conversation before, and it's hypocritical of you to judge what Lieutenant Cross does when you certainly benefit from it. Michael, you can't sit on the fence, condemn this behavior, and enjoy it at the same time."

"If you don't condone it, why are you here?"

"Like you, I was invited, but unlike you, I was unaware of the type of show they planned. I'm disgusted by it, and I hurt for these girls, but this is the military culture, and I must accept it. I'm sure I'm the only one who thinks this way."

"So, you accept it. Isn't that a bit hypocritical of you?"

He's pleased, thinking he won a point, and I'm aware of the irony.

"Unlike you, I'm in no position to make changes, but you have the power to do so, yet you ignore it when it suits you. That makes you complicit."

"Stop talking. Let's take this somewhere else."

"No, I've said my piece, and I don't need to explain myself to you. And I'm not going anywhere with you. You talk about my behavior. Take a good look at your own."

"Mind your mouth, Zena."

Michael glares at me, obviously embarrassed I would address him like this in front of his peers, his brother, and subordinates. I was always respectful when we were in public, but even in private, I watched my tone, never raised my voice, and was careful never to challenge him. Not because I was afraid of him. I wasn't. I did it because I wanted our relationship to work. But in those days, he treated me with much more care.

"I'm not your woman, Michael."

"I have half a mind to take you across my knee."

Commander stands and moves to my side and puts his arm around my shoulders. It's probably improper, but I put my hand on his back, to read him deeply in case I've broken a rule again. What I read tells me he set this whole sham in motion, he's pleased as plum pie with how it's unfolding, and I'm curious to know why.

"Sorry, Michael. She won't even let me do that," Commander says, smiling. "Relax. Take your girl for a walk and she'll make you feel better. Come on. It's a party."

"Happy birthday, sir," I say, with a fake smile that would fool anyone.

Commander stands there waiting for his brother to collect his date and leave, and then we find our seats. I watch each couple take turns leaving to make use of the Comfort Rooms, but unlike the practice at the Officer's Club, the men return with their women. David, watching me with a grim expression, doesn't leave with either Mary or Jolene. The women sit together on the couch where Mack and his woman had been sitting.

When Paul returns, he leans over and whispers in my ear. "You okay?"

I nod, but I'm lying. I've always been able to hide my feelings, even in my first lifetime. Nadler taught me to never show my belly, but Zena had already inherited that ability. I don't want to hurt Michael, but he has to let me go. He's not part of my destiny.

Mack and his date return. The civilian girls keep to themselves, sharing their couch, and David ignores them. One by one, each couple wanders back to the pit. When everyone has returned, the two civilian girls disappear into the restrooms. They return wearing their serving uniforms before taking their positions at the catering table. I hope they washed their hands.

I hadn't noticed folding tray tables stacked in a corner until Lieutenant West passes the trays over to Frank, who stands them in front of the couches. The entertainers slice the cake and fill several plates. As acting hostess, I take the lead and grab the first two servings.

"Officers get served first," Mary whispers to me.

"I assumed so. I'll serve the men."

"Then take this," Mary says, handing me a tray large enough to hold six small plates and silverware. She helps me load the tray while Jolene continues to prepare more servings.

I serve Commander first, then Paul, before working my way around to serve the other majors first, including Michael, who glares at me when I offer him a plate and fork.

With one plate remaining, I return to the serving table and Jolene helps me add more plates. I serve the First Lieutenants clockwise, starting with David, who bites his lip and glares at me as he accepts my offering. After serving the First Lieutenants, I offer the last piece of cake on my tray to the military woman sitting with West.

When I revisit the table to refill, both servers are devouring their slices of cake. After handing the last plate and fork to the final military woman, I return the empty tray, grab a glass of water for myself, and lemonade for Commander, and take my seat. Mary and Jolene bring trays of drinks and offer them to officers first.

"Where's your cake?" asks Paul.

"There's none left, but that's okay. A girl needs to watch her figure or no one else will."

Paul lifts a forkful of cake and holds it near my mouth. I receive the offering and take my time tasting it. White cake with Commander's favorite strawberry icing. I lick my lips.

Paul takes a bite and then offers me another, which I accept. His date glares at me while she takes bird-like nibbles of her generous slice of cake. Paul offers me another forkful and his slice is half gone. The icing is too sweet, but I accept his offering with grace.

Commander observes our exchange with curiosity. I read him. He's not jealous of the attention and kindness Paul is paying me. Just curious.

Michael watches with disdain. I don't need to read him. His clenched jaw speaks for him. His scowling date crosses her arms, appearing to resent Michael's undue interest in me.

I don't read David's expression. Perhaps he's remembering how we shared the stuffed mushrooms. It was such an intimate interchange.

I scan each face to gage the mood of the room.

Others also are paying attention.

Mack shakes his head, and I can't tell whether he's jealous or thinks we're ridiculous. He was never attentive toward me.

West and a couple of others seem bewildered, Tom looks envious, and Dan appears displeased.

The servers/strippers bring trays to collect the dirty dishes and silverware, and I jump up to help. I fill my tray and then deposit its contents into one of the tubs.

I return to find Commander and Michael talking, but they both appear guarded. The officers form small chat groups and laugh together, and the military women do likewise.

No one talks to the civilian servers, and I'm ignored too, but I'm too busy reading the room to care. I've stepped on a few toes tonight. Okay, more like stomped.

An hour passes and the women leave in groups of two or three, and David collects his girls and escorts them out. It's my cue to leave, so I walk over to Commander. He wears a smug ear-to-ear grin, so I wish him happy birthday again and bid everyone goodnight.

Chapter 20

Cassie looks up when I enter the front office and watches as I head for the apartment stairs. The residence door is closed and locked, so I retreat and walk past her again. She says nothing, so I check out the break room. The coffeepot is full, and Commander's office is unoccupied. Paul's not in his cubicle, either. At Cassie's desk, I throw her a questioning look.

"Commander and Major Corday are still upstairs. Major Abrams hasn't arrived yet."

"Thank you, Cassie. If anyone asks, please tell them I'm in the library. I'll return later."

She nods, and I head downstairs.

As I pass by the nearly empty third-floor cafeteria, I notice the cleaning staff wiping tables around the few stragglers. I descend another flight to the second-floor cafeteria where several soldiers gather, none of whom I'm friends with, and fortunately, I don't see the officer I want to avoid. I spent a long, wakeful, miserable night trying to understand why David told everyone at the party about our intimacy. It doesn't matter if Michael knows. It may help him let go.

Commander and his Inner Circle are privy to one incident, but hopefully not our two-month affair shortly after I arrived at Cavalry and the few other encounters. My private life is nobody's business, and those gossipy females will have a picnic sharing details of my personal affairs. I never intended to make our lovemaking public. David never permitted his playmates to share his bed, see him without clothes, or see his taboo tattoo. Had he not embarrassed me by inviting me to join his girls, and not revealed to everyone he saw me naked, I wouldn't have retaliated by exposing my intimate knowledge of him. Damn him. I must avoid him until he cools off.

I choose a spot on the edge of the cafeteria where I can maintain a watchful eye and enjoy my cup of coffee. If David shows up, I'll leave.

A salvage unit trickles in, a few troopers at a time, and I recognize them, so it doesn't surprise me to spy another man I'm not eager to encounter. Blake, that civilian scout who busted my lip, swaggers in with three soldiers. I watch them fill their trays and join two other khaki-uniformed men at a large round table, laughing. He notices me and scowls, and I freeze for a second. But I'm safe here, surrounded by the military.

I intended to question Blake about the people living outside, hoping he'd know if my family survived and where I might locate them. That happened before remembering who I am. Now, I need to determine how many Resistance fighters remain and where I'd find them. Westview might be thousands of miles from Cavalry, and I have no idea where his travels have taken him. But, by the dirty looks he lobs at me, I doubt he would tell me the time. Could he have maps of the surrounding terrain? Commander punished Blake for smacking me when I wouldn't kneel for him and likely warned him to steer clear of me. Commander ordered me to avoid Blake. My stomach flutters until he turns away. The library awaits me.

The whole way across the rotunda, as I walk towards my sanctuary, I worry unnecessarily that the scout is watching me. My heart beats faster from a ridiculous fear that he's aware I'm alone and might seek revenge in the library's isolation, but I need to remind myself that I'm protected here. This isn't Central and there's no Colonel Wickmore. Blake's a civilian and therefore the rules apply to him.

Inside the library, I scamper to the backroom. The chamber looks the same, but still no Tommy in his rocking chair, waiting to tell me the stories I need to hear. Caroline knows, but she's hiding from me. After quietly closing the door, I curl up on the timeworn lavender couch and slip off into a transcendental state, welcoming another memory.

§

More than a year had passed since Josh invited me to join his life. The shortened daylight heralded the approaching winter, and I looked forward to spending my homebound days with him on the lower level again. He no longer mentioned his wife and one day, while I walked around downstairs, I wondered if it was too soon to make it my own. I always felt like an intruder, encroaching on Laura's former domain, but I understood letting go of treasured memories of loved ones takes time. To accept the fact that they're never coming back. Her ghost haunted me and understanding his love and grief rendered it more difficult for me. But she was gone, and I lived there now. I took the chance.

When he returned from his scouting expedition, I decided to pose the question.

"Josh, how do you feel about the downstairs decorations?" I asked. "Would you care if I made a few changes?"

He seemed to read my mind and didn't hesitate to say, "If you want to change it—make this house your own—do whatever you wish. This is your home now."

He drew me close for a reassuring hug and I felt a shift in our relationship. I spent the afternoon collecting Laura's personal effects, and then carefully packed them into a memory box for Josh.

"Don't worry, Laura, I'll take good care of him."

I stored Josh's treasure trove out of sight in a closet. I rummaged through the art supplies his wife had brought with her, found the colored pencils, some charcoal sticks, and a pad of paper, and spent my free hours making large nature scene drawings. In no time, depictions of lavish butterflies and flowers covered the walls where Laura's pictures once hung.

Josh smiled in approval. I had no knick-knacks or other personal items to display, so he moved some of his artifacts from his library and filled the slender curio cabinet.

All my belongings from my previous life were long lost, and I never wanted to collect anything I might find, needing to travel light, and realizing I couldn't keep them forever. My ill-fated lifestyle was transient now, and I accepted that.

§

I don't run into any officers when I return to work. Neither Paul nor Commander has returned to their offices, so I assume they're down in the transit bay, seeing Michael off. My dillydallying paid dividends. Upstairs, the door is open, with nothing out of order in the neat apartment, except for the duffle bag that I almost trip over on my way to select my midday soundtrack. Michael is still here.

I need to leave before he shows up. Maybe take an early lunch. Before I can make my escape, someone ascends the stairs, and a flash of Michael's summer visit haunts me. I picture Commander, and Paul with the strap.

Michael stares at me, looking remorseful.

"I'm glad you're here, baby," he says, approaching me.

"Stop," I say, holding up my hand. After last night, how dare he come near me.

"Honey, listen to me. I've done a lot of thinking and I still want you. We'll get past this. Give me another chance. Let's go home, start over, and do it differently this time. I've taken care of my business and I can devote myself to you. I'll never leave you again and if you come back with me, you'll see I'll make everything perfect for you."

He slowly approaches me.

129

"Now that you know the General is my father, I'll properly introduce you, and he'll welcome you into the family. We'll marry, and you'll enjoy all the advantages of being a major's wife. We'll figure this out. You won't need to work, and no officer will dare mess with my wife, no matter their rank. Baby, I missed you so damn much."

"I'm never returning to Central. You're crazy to think I'd marry you now."

Michael closes his eyes for a moment and sighs.

"I've made mistakes, and so have you. We'll put them in the past and focus on the future. Learn from our mistakes."

He steps toward me, and I raise my hand again to stop him.

"Michael, I'm staying here. I'm not the woman you left a year ago. I feel like I've lived a lifetime since then. You don't truly love me, and I can't love you the way you need. I tried, but I'm done pretending to be the good girl you wanted."

He takes another step forward, and I ward him off with my hand again.

"You were happy, provided I did everything your way. When I fell short, when I couldn't give you what you wanted, you chased after your dreams ... with a lie, and without a backward glance. That's not love. You never committed to me the way I did to you."

"I intended to return sooner, but ... it got complicated. I can explain."

"Wickmore told me you weren't coming back anytime soon. He knew. The officers who kicked me out of your apartment knew. Fuck, even your brother wasn't expecting you for a while. It wouldn't surprise me if I was the only fucking person waiting for you."

"Please, watch your language. It's beneath you to use that word."

"You have no idea who I am now."

Michael laughs.

"Babe, I love you no matter who you are now."

"And your empty promise to be faithful to me?"

Michael opens his mouth to speak, but words fail him.

"When I confronted you about having sex with someone here, you denied it. You were unfaithful every time you visited Cavalry."

He bites his lip and looks down.

"Sweetheart, you don't understand."

"You celebrate your birthday—and your brother's—but never asked about mine or invited me to share yours. If birthdays are a big deal for you, why not tell me? No, you celebrated yours by fucking other women. It's obvious why you never brought me to meet your brother and friends."

"Zena, this is our ... tradition. It doesn't mean anything. The girls don't mean anything to me. It's guys getting together for some ... fun, and I didn't want to give it up."

"So, why lie about it? Why not explain it to me? Be truthful. Say it was an important tradition?"

"And you'd be okay with that?"

"Maybe not. But at least I'd have a choice. We'd have an honest relationship. I chose to live with your infidelity and lies, but you lost my trust and respect. I dreaded every January and June knowing you were betraying me and hiding it."

"No, you couldn't have known. You never said a word," Michael says, shaking his head.

"Wrong. When I asked if you betrayed me, after your first return from Cavalry, you denied it, so I waited to see if it happened again. It did, and I chose not to leave you. So, two indiscretions a year. Whoever you fucked didn't mean much to you. And neither did I."

"I love you. I was afraid to lose you."

"Not enough to tell me the truth. And not enough to tell your brother you don't need a date."

Michael sits down on the couch, holding his head, looking defeated.

"Babe, you don't understand. My trips here had nothing to do with you."

He stands and walks towards the stairs, checks the stairway, and turns back to me. He moves close to me and presses his cheek against mine, his lips near my ear.

"You weren't privy to certain matters. I am my father's eyes and ears. By playing the younger brother role, I can learn details others can't. The General likes to keep tabs on all the satellite bases. Reports and conference meetings only tell a fragment of the story."

"Is that why Scott was here?"

Michael turns pale, almost fearful.

"No. My father doesn't know about him. He's part of an effort to help all of us. I can't discuss it yet and you can't repeat anything I say."

I nod. We've talked about changing the culture and becoming one with the Overlords. For most civilians, it would be an improvement, in my opinion, although not everyone would agree. More freedom for women. Less power for the Peace Force. Now that I know the awful truth, the idea sends shivers through me. At least, while the aliens threaten our existence.

"You're playing two sides against the middle?"

"No, I'm doing what I believe is right. I'm unable to confide anything more until you return with me."

"I understand. But I can't do that. Central has too many terrible memories. The officers I trusted and cared about failed to help me. I no longer want to work there. Here, I've made new friends and my assignment keeps me busy. What did you do about the colonel?"

"I gave your statement to the General. He wasn't happy, but he promised to investigate."

"And?"

Michael smiles with mischief in his eyes.

"I copied your testimony and left a copy with Wickmore's receptionist, suggesting she read it, and I passed copies to several other high-ranking officials. My father wasn't pleased."

"So, what happened?"

"They confronted Wickmore with your written allegations and threatened a full investigation. They offered him a way out—the option of early retirement. He swore his innocence, but he took the deal. I did all I could. In fact, I put my career on the line. The embarrassment of your accusations drove the colonel to give up everything he worked for all those years. He retired in disgrace."

"They didn't follow the law. No punishment or imprisonment?"

"Like I said. He denied the charges. Said you enjoyed the game. He swore he never forced you to have sex. Claimed you were willing and enjoyed his attention."

"And you believed him?"

"No. But they'd have been obligated to haul Wickmore before the Peace Council for trial, you would have to tell your side of it in front of everyone, the Overlords would have penalized us, and you'd be ostracized."

Fischer and Nadler said pretty much the same thing.

"After reaching the highest levels, there's no disciplinary action like you think. Only Commanders administer punishment, and only to lower ranks."

"So, that's it? The upper echelon is above the law? They make the rules but don't follow them? Had I not given you my statement, he'd still be there?"

"Rank has its privileges."

I stare at Michael, dumbfounded.

"The General met with all the higher-ranking officers to reiterate the laws and our responsibilities. It trickled down to all levels. Colonel Wickmore's disgraced early retirement serves as a warning to the higher ranks."

"You said Wickmore claimed I consented. Why wasn't I interviewed?"

He nods his head and shrugs.

"They considered the situation handled, and they thought it unnecessary."

"Because I'm a woman. They didn't need to hear my side? My word means nothing?"

"The outcome was in the best interest of everyone involved. I did a little investigating myself. It seems you have a few secrets of your own. You let me believe your uncle was a First Lieutenant. That you came from a respectable, high-level family. Turns out he was your handler."

"You understand I work for Central Intelligence, and I'm not authorized to reveal certain information to anyone without permission. I didn't think it mattered."

"You know I wanted to marry you. I believed you were from a privileged background, not some orphan without family ties. It mattered to me. But I've had time to think about it. I love you and I want you in my life."

A red flag. The General knew about my past. He wouldn't want his son to marry that far below his station.

"Michael, was your father responsible for what Wickmore did to me? They kicked me out of the apartment three days after you left. The colonel started attacking me two weeks later. Work was slow, so they didn't need me. Did the General scheme to get rid of me?"

"No, no baby. The General wouldn't do something like that. Wickmore was a serious problem for him, once he was aware of what happened. It was a huge blot on the Peace Force's reputation."

Michael sighs and his face tells me he hates the thought of my thinking such a thing.

"I spoke often of my love for you, and my father wants me to be happy. He balked when I told him I planned to marry you, but he had no issue with our arrangement. The General sent you here knowing my brother would protect you. He also understands your value to Central Intelligence."

I can't let him go without addressing one final matter.

"When you were here in July, you returned to Central, aware your brother was about to punish me with a strap, yet you didn't warn me. You understood my dread of belts. How traumatic it would be for me. You kissed me goodbye, pretending everything was fine, realizing I'd need someone afterward. I needed you. And you left. How can you say you love me?"

Michael sighs and wipes his mouth.

"I couldn't stop my brother from doing his duty. That's out of my hands. He's the base Commander. I tried to persuade him to let it go, but he was adamant. There are rules. I hated it, but there was nothing I could do. I left— to deal with Wickmore for you. And I have other responsibilities."

"Other responsibilities? You could have warned me they planned to punish me. With a belt. I could have changed my mind and gone with you. In fact, I'm sure I would have."

The color drains from his face.

"Baby, I'm sorry. I needed to make more preparations concerning my new family, and I knew I'd have to make another trip. And I didn't want to leave you with the blowout from your statement, but I wasn't ready to take you with me. It was a tough decision. Turns out I made a mistake. But you're one hell of a strong woman."

"Michael, I'm staying here for now. It's safer than Central. Live out your dreams. I have my own life's work. Your confidences are safe with me. Look, I keep everyone's secrets, including my own. I believe in your mission, but I can't be involved. Marry a suitable woman and raise your sons to be decent men. I'm loyal to you and your cause, but this unmoored orphan has a different path."

I peck him on his cheek.

"What did you name your babies, anyway?"

"Abel and Cain," he says with a mischievous grin. "I'm kidding. Aiden is the oldest by a month. Philip is the youngest. They're both beautiful, healthy, thriving children. I wish they were yours."

He pulls me close for a long hug.

"Hey, Michael, find your duffel?" Commander yells up the stairs.

"Yeah, I'll be right there," he says as Commander reaches the top step.

Michael faces me, and I hold out my hand. He takes it.

"I hope, if we meet again, we'll remember only the good stuff, and be friends," I say.

He hugs me, kisses my forehead, nods to his brother, and walks out of my life.

Chapter 21

I've had enough time to process that dreadful birthday party fiasco, but I must be careful how I respond when I face Commander and Paul. Cassie looks up when I walk into the office. I sense she's disappointed that I didn't leave with Michael yesterday. Someday, I'll read her and find out why she dislikes me. Hopefully, nobody will bring up that disastrous celebration.

My efforts to ingratiate myself with Commander and his Inner Circle have taken an unfortunate turn in the wrong direction. Sometimes it seems I'm my own worst enemy. I've alienated David, and I'm uncertain where I stand with Commander. He can't punish me. I did exactly what he wanted; convincing Michael we're finished, and I'm not returning to Central. At least, I believe Commander planned for the party to play out this way. Luckily for me, it fits in with my agenda, too.

By peeking through the break room window, I discover Commander's not at his desk. I peer around to see Paul's empty office, then sip my coffee until it's half full, before heading upstairs to the apartment. When I cough to let them know I'm on the stairs, the voices fall silent. Paul stands, giving me room to squeeze past him. They quietly watch me pull out my work materials and laptop, then take my seat. I glance up to catch them staring at me, probably trying to gauge my mood. I wish them a pleasant morning and pretend to work.

"Enjoyed my birthday party?" Commander asks.

"It was interesting. I wish you had informed me it was a sex party. I'd have declined."

Commander licks his lips.

"I said the girls would put on a show. You didn't like it?"

I glare at him like he said something stupid, and he grins in return.

"The show was only for the officers. By the expressions on the military

135

women's faces, they didn't care for it, either. Y'all invited the women just to serve or entertain," I say. "Although the cake was delicious."

I nod at Paul.

Commander leans forward.

"So, you and Michael had a spat?"

"You set it up." The words slip out before I can catch them.

Commander sits back, looking shocked, then glances at Paul.

"Come on. When I pay attention, I learn, and that night I paid attention to everything. David is what I call a 'company man.' He's all in. Plus, he knows I'm your girl. He would never advertise the fact we slept together, not to you, not even privately, but especially not to a roomful of his peers and superiors. David had no reason to tell Michael. He's aware of my past relationship with him. Also, Michael is higher in rank, and he's your brother. Lieutenant Cross is smart and disciplined, and he'd never make that mistake. So, I deduce, you put him up to it."

Commander presses his lips tight together.

"Cross told you."

"Oh, no. I've been avoiding him until he calms down. He spoke out of turn against me, and I hit back. As much as I hated him broadcasting our relationship, he certainly never wanted anyone, especially his girls, to know that I'd seen him ... naked. I'm sure his girls are upset since he never showed them his tattoo. He was angry the rest of the evening and I'm smart enough to put distance between us."

Commander nods in agreement.

"But I guess he's collateral damage, too," I say.

"Too?"

"Sure, you obviously didn't care how I felt, as long as you had your fun."

"You have quite an imagination," he says, shaking his head, frowning.

"I believe you invited me to your sex party, so I'd see why Michael never brought me along when he visited Cavalry. You knew Michael loved me, at least in his selfish way. He wanted me to return with him, so you guaranteed he knew I was staying. You knew my presence at the party would spoil his fun. Then you had David drop the bombshell that I slept with him. I have an amazing imagination."

"You're reading too much into this. If you're staying, why do you care about Michael?"

"I care about you using me as a pawn in whatever game you're playing."

"Wrong. There's no game."

"You shouldn't lie. You're inexperienced at it, sir," I say, almost in a whisper.

Commander shakes his head and smirks. Paul looks sympathetically toward both of us.

"Before he left, Michael and I discussed why our relationship failed. I explained every reason I wouldn't return with him, and I'm sure he gets it. I'm not who he thinks I am or what he wants."

"He's crazy about you," says Commander.

"He was crazy about the person who did everything he wanted, his way. When I couldn't give him what he wanted, everything changed."

"What did he want?"

I pause. I may be walking into more trouble, but the truth will come out eventually and it's better to stay ahead of it.

"He wanted a wife to bear him children, someone from a refined family, someone befitting his station. A month before he took leave, he asked me to marry him. He wanted children, so I had to confess I couldn't marry him because I'm unable to conceive."

Both Commander and Paul squint with bafflement.

"Zena, the shots keep you from getting pregnant."

I look at Commander in disbelief. Does he think I'm stupid?

"I don't get them. I've never had a single birth control injection. There's no need because I'm infertile."

Paul finally speaks. "You told Cassie you saw the nurse and took care of your shot. You lied?"

"I told Cassie I saw the nurse, and I did. He asked me if I needed the shot, and I told him I didn't. It wasn't a lie."

"You misled her."

"Okay. Yes."

Commander appears lost in thought.

"Doctors can figure out what's wrong and fix it. If you have fertility problems, we can address them."

"Why would I choose to fix something that's not broken? I don't want children. I'd make a lousy mother and I couldn't protect them. My destiny doesn't include breeding any ... babies."

Commander and Paul both appear about to speak, but neither does.

"Commander, what's going on between you and your brother? Family is so important."

"Family?" He slams his mug on the table, spilling coffee everywhere. "Paul is my brother. Dan and Tom are my brothers ... Andrew was my brother."

Commander jumps up, grabs a dishrag, and mops up his mess.

"Michael is my father's other son. I entertain him twice a year because ... it's expected. We have some fun at his expense occasionally, but he never catches on. He enjoys coming here twice a year to pretend he's one of us. No harm."

"Michael said you didn't get along as teens, but you've both grown up. He told me stories of your younger years when he talked about his brother, Nate. But when he mentioned Commander Pierce, he spoke of him with adoration, never saying a single word against him, always praising him and his Inner Circle."

Commander nods.

"Sure, that's expected. We never talk badly of any high-ranking officer. You're the first person with balls to do that."

He's right. Nadler told me I should never say anything critical about any officer. It would come back to bite me.

"Michael has always been ... competitive. Anytime I fancied a woman, he made it his mission to take her from me. He has the looks and personality, and it was always easy for him."

"He may be more personable, but you have him beat in the looks department ... not that looks are important," I say.

Commander grins and shakes his head.

"When I assumed command here, I picked a disciplined woman who worked hard, and followed the rules, but I wasn't attracted to her. When Michael visited, I couldn't care less if he fucked her. Mary Jo services other officers, so it meant nothing."

He returns to his chair, turns it around, straddles it, and sighs.

"She was my only girl, and she did her duty. She introduced me to Play, and when Lynn transferred here, they became friends, and Mary Jo ... suggested I take a second girl, someone she got along with ... a friend."

Someone Mary Jo found attractive. Does he realize his former girls are bisexual, or is this a case of don't ask, don't tell? If so, my lips are sealed.

Commander finishes what remains of his coffee, glances at Paul, then back at me.

"A few years ago, Michael started bragging about his new girl. She was smart, pretty, and different, coming from an excellent family. Said he was going to marry her. Every visit, he raved about his amazing young woman. He claimed she was crazy about him. And as you know, he had no problem sharing private details. Loved boasting about his good fortune and his successes."

"If you don't have relationships, why did that bother you? And certainly, you're more successful than he."

"It didn't bother me." Commander pauses for a moment, closes his eyes, and shakes his head as if purging a painful memory.

"I busted my ass for everything I've accomplished, sought commandership, and worked damned hard to secure this position, always striving to be the best. All on my own, without my father's help," he says, waving his fist. He stands, turns his chair to face me, and sits.

"But Michael always slid by. Being the General's son was a freaking advantage for him. He moved up in rank despite taking several long furloughs. They promoted him to major only five years ago—and he's taken two months-long leaves already."

"Why does the General favor Michael?"

Commander shrugs, but I sense he knows. I don't believe Commander knows his brother as well as he thinks. Michael is very ambitious, with big aspirations, but his sights aim higher than his brother's.

He leans forward and looks me in the eye.

"Michael informed me he'd be here for my birthday and was leaving with you. He thought he'd show up here and convince you to return with him ... after deserting you. He insisted you loved him and would forgive him. When he arrived, I told him you were my girl now ... but not that you'd be at the party."

It hits me hard. I'm not the pawn. I'm the reason.

"Why embarrass me? Why have David humiliate me in front of everyone?"

"You needed to see Cross for who he is. He's a player and if you mess with him, you end up hurt, or like his girls. Cross is an excellent soldier, but he enjoys messing with women, and he'd never be good for you. And Michael ... I needed you to witness who he really is."

Wow. Knowing you're right and having it proven....

§

My conversation with Commander and Paul leaves me with a very different perspective. Commander wants me to stay, and I need that. But would he choose me over the Peace Force and his duty to the Overlords? I'm running out of time.

At the apartment windows, I prepare to hear the voices. I must keep several steps ahead of the Tracker. Ominous clouds billow across the dark steel-blue sky, and I sense another storm coming.

The glistening snow shrouds the trees like a silky white blanket, and its soft glimmering glow illuminates the otherwise darkened morning. Coin size snowflakes drop from the pregnant purple angry sky as the wind picks up, flinging them against the windowpane where they stick. The squall's wrath obscures the mountains and I see nothing but its frosty fury.

I close my eyes and slip into my transcendental state. Alien voices ring out all at once until I filter them. The excited buzz is disturbing, and after a few moments, I hear the dreaded news. The Tracker, known as *Mana-ta-ah* has arrived at the Overlords' complex. He'll visit each of our twelve bases to search ... for me. They mention Central Control by name, and it sounds like that's their starting point. It's only an hour away by transit so I'll need lead time and someone at Central to give me a heads up.

Tommy cautioned I couldn't stay here alone. I believed he meant I had to leave, but his message may mean I need a coalition, people willing to help me. I'll need permission to travel to other bases. Nadler will help me, I'm sure of that. But he'll want me to stay. I need answers now.

I slip deeper into my meditative state to summon another one of Caroline's memories....

§

Josh and I had been living together going on four years when he brought home a surprise. I was sitting at the kitchen table when he walked in with a young couple.

"Caroline, I want you to meet Brandon and Kyra."

He turned to the strangers and said, "And this is my lovely companion, Caroline."

"Glad to meet you," said the tall, deeply tanned, brown-haired, smiling woman.

I immediately liked her. She was friendly and soft-spoken, and it was clear she and her partner appreciated us welcoming them into our sanctuary.

"Likewise," said her tall companion with a huge grin. "We've been on the run, avoiding the Captors, for longer than we care to remember."

"Josh offered us refuge, and we're so grateful to sleep under a roof for a change," Kyra said. "We haven't had a decent meal or a place to stay since we left our farm weeks ago. We had to leave my parents and uncles. The Captors aren't taking older folks, so they'll be safe."

Josh showed our guests where to wash up and I pointed out where to stow their belongings. Kyra and Brandon helped in the kitchen while I put clean sheets on the bed they would share. During our meal, Kyra talked about their life on the farm and how scared they were when the uniformed men started canvassing the countryside, searching for children and young adults. And taking them God knows where. There was nowhere to hide, so they left before the Captors reached them. That happened three weeks earlier, and they kept one step ahead of the Captors, but life on the run was hard. I know. Josh welcomed them to stay indefinitely until it was safe to return to their farm. It was our moral duty, and in our self-interest, to watch out for one another.

Brandon and Kyra shared the upstairs bedroom, and we moved downstairs. Kyra and I shared the housework and gardening, and the menfolk handled hunting and other responsibilities. But we didn't share each other. Josh was mine.

What Josh and I lost in privacy we made up for in other ways. Brandon accompanied Josh on patrol, giving me peace of mind. There's safety in numbers, but it also gave Josh some "man" time, and I enjoyed having another female to talk to and keep me company in their absence. The solitude hadn't bothered me before Kyra's arrival, but now I rested easier when Josh went patrolling or hunting.

I allowed my body to age normally, expecting to remain here for years, because I never wanted to leave. Josh was my lover, protector, and companion. Sharing our home with decent folks was a bonus. Kyra and I got along better than sisters, sharing our stories, fears, and dreams.

On one of their treks, Josh and Brandon encountered an older couple living in a small farmhouse, a two-hour walk away. The pair owned several farm animals and tended crops in their fields. Walt and Milly, possibly in their fifties, were hardy farmers used to a rough life. Once a week we either traveled there to visit, or they came to us. They brought eggs and fresh vegetables and we offered whatever we could.

Milly was a tough, country woman with a brash way of speaking, but she was all heart, and we enjoyed her stories and opinions—when asked. Even though she never bore children of her own, she was like a mother to their four cows, twenty or more chickens, a lazy dog, a black feline mouser, and several pigs. They also boarded Fury, a gentle old horse with big soulful eyes but little fury left. But Milly loved her animals as if they were family.

She reminded me of my grandmother, full of advice and wisdom, but she never meddled in our affairs. Milly was a God-fearing woman, but experience taught her to allow others to find their own path. She would say "God is Love," when we sat down to eat at her table. That's all. We finished with "Amen," and dug into whatever amazing dishes she had prepared. Her round middle was evidence of her cooking and baking skills.

Milly also reminded me of Shana and Abbey. Devoutly religious, and religiously compassionate and welcoming. We spent hours listening to her childhood stories. "When I was your age ...," she'd begin, peering over the rims of her glasses. Her stories came from an era of communities desperately hanging on to the old ways—county fairs, church socials, barn raising, kids running wild, and neighbors knowing everything about you and willing to help in a second. She wanted children, but it was auspicious that she had never conceived. The Captors slowly decimated the communities, and young men, women, and youngsters started disappearing.

Walt was quiet, never saying much. I was never comfortable with the way he'd steal glances at me. He liked to remind Josh what a lucky man he was. Too often. I never allowed myself to be alone with him.

This was our extended family and our new life.

§

The morning blizzard rages, leaving a ton of newly fallen snow. I watch the white swirls spread layers of sleet, covering the acres of trees, and obscuring the distant mountain with the heavy snowfall. Safe and warm in the apartment, I return to my worktable, but working remains impossible. Footsteps coming up the stairs alert me, and when I peek through the cabinet opening, I see Commander. He sits across from me, and I wait for him to speak.

"I need to know where we stand. Are you still my girl?" he asks, looking worried. "I messed up. But I couldn't just let you leave. This is who I am, and how I do things. When I want something, I go after it, full force."

I nod. I needed to convince Michael our relationship was over, but I'm not crazy about the way Commander handled matters.

"Do you manipulate your Inner Circle to get what you want?"

He squints, then shakes his head, answering, "No."

"Why not?"

"It's different."

"Because you care about them. You care about their feelings, and you need their respect and friendship. You don't worry about David or anyone else because they're not in your Inner Circle. They must obey and honor your bidding."

Commander wets his lips but says nothing.

"You didn't consider my feelings either."

He nods and sits back.

"If you wanted me to stay, you should have told me so. If I'm going to be your girl, you can't play games with me. Talk to me. And listen to me."

He looks hopeful and rubs his clean-shaven chin.

"I've never tried having a relationship with a woman. This is new."

"Do you want one with me?"

He thinks for a moment.

"I want something with you. Some form of relationship."

"I didn't get any sweets this morning," I say, as a less-than-subtle hint.

Commander looks relieved, stands, nods, and leaves.

§

The Book is splayed open in front of me, but my concentration left the building. The Master Plan is irrelevant now. It describes their intentions that lead to an unfortunate ending for us. One I must prevent.

In my life as Caroline, I always formed a coalition to help safeguard myself with friends and lovers to make my wretched life on the run palatable. My time with Tommy and his family, Jade and his Resistance clan, and Joshua and our collection of rebels all kept me safe for several years. I remember these alliances and their importance to my survival and sanity. Tommy warned me I can't stay here alone, but he never said I can't stay. Even without my memories and knowledge of my mission, I realized the significance of finding an alliance, knowing I needed protection.

Footsteps on the stairs break my train of thought. Commander appears bearing a plate with four orange-flavored miniature cakes. I slide the Book to the side as he sets his olive branch down and sits across from me.

"I can't promise I won't make mistakes, but I'll voice any concerns with you in the future," Commander says.

He shakes his head and offers me a promising smile.

"I'll probably make mistakes, too," I say.

Commander stands, walks around the table, and pulls me close. His peace offering will keep. I ache for his warmth, to wrap myself in his embrace, so I melt into his arms and surrender. He brushes my lips with his own, but I turn away and hold him tight, pressing my head against his chest, listening to his beating heart.

Chapter 22

This morning, I'm gazing out the apartment window, mesmerized by the constant snowfall. It's been snowing for three days straight. I can't judge the snow's depth from this height. Yesterday, the sleeting hadn't stopped when I quit work for the day.

The officers consumed their sweets and coffee, made small talk, and left, and my concentration followed them. I'm hypnotized by the swirling blizzard spraying the forest with coatings of snowy frosting. I imagine the wind whistling through the trees. It must be freezing outside. The climate-controlled base keeps me safe and toasty warm inside, and if you never looked outside, you'd be oblivious to the winter weather. January brought a ton of snow with it, and today it's twirling around like a pure white whirlwind.

Paul mentioned wanting to meet with me later this morning and I welcome the distraction. I've read the Master Plan in its entirety at least twice in the past month, and the remainder of my report is ready for translation from my unique script. Without the time-intensive necessity of translating symbols, I'm left with an abundance of free time for listening to the voices, working on creating an escape plan, and concentrating on recovering more of Caroline's memories. She'll know where I'm supposed to be and what I should do.

Lost in thought focusing on the outdoor scenery, another snowstorm from over a century ago comes to mind—a freezing winter day. Before everyone started talking about global warming, some winters were particularly savage. Schools closed, snowplows worked long hours, and snow piled up like miniature mountains on tree lawns and parking lots.

It was the mid-1980s, and we were experiencing heavy snowstorms. The snowdrifts covered the lower part of our windows from the strong snowy gusts of wind, and outside, it was white everywhere you looked. We couldn't open the garage door, driving was hazardous, and it was too dangerous for the children to play outdoors.

Schools were closed, and my husband, Russ, was stuck at home. By early afternoon, we were all getting on one another's nerves. The children were horsing around and teasing each other. The television blared weather reports, and all I wanted was peace and quiet.

I found refuge by hiding in my upstairs bedroom, away from the kids' fussing and fighting, and Russ's begging them to stop. From the window I marveled at the clean, untouched snow piling up on the driveway, my mood alternating between a feeling of impending doom and reverence for the frozen beauty.

The snowstorm was fraught with potential danger. What if the electricity went out? Would we freeze to death? What if we ran out of food? Worse than anything, we'd be stuck for several days without television. Russ and I certainly would go mad, trapped in the house with two bored, whining children fighting over everything and nothing.

The view outside showed a cold, white desert, but we were safe, snuggled in our noisy but warm home with plenty of food, and the lights stayed on. Of course, by the next day, the snowstorm had stopped, and the sun appeared. The temperatures climbed. Everyone bundled up and ventured out to shovel snow or play in it, building snowmen, snow fortresses, and snow angels. We finished with snowball fights, all with the engine sounds and scraping of the snowplows humming in the background, and life continued....

§

Paul bolts upstairs two steps at a time and settles beside me at my worktable, ready to work, yanking me back to the present.

"Paul, I've been thinking. I'm far enough along now that it makes sense to share what I've learned. Mack is interested in learning how I decipher the symbols and the Central team would be excited to get involved. I propose we invite one or more of my old colleagues to join Mack's team to learn from me. If we did, could we provide rooms for the visitors?"

"Lieutenant Reed also expressed interest in your project to me. I'll bring it to Commander, and if he's on board, we'll take it up in the next meeting. We have guest quarters for visiting officers."

"Great. I was thinking my friend Mick would be a suitable choice. We worked well together. But I'll leave that up to y'all. I could use some extra eyes on this because I've been struggling with several symbols. I'm afraid I'm not making much headway and fresh ideas might hasten my progress."

Paul settles at the table in the chair next to me.

"You're doing a great job. Sometimes projects hit a wall, and then everything falls into place. Keep doing your best and don't worry about anything. Commander's pleased with your effort, and Central Intelligence is delighted."

"Thank you."

He reads my rough draft and typed notes while I stare out at the snow flurries. All I can see from my worktable is the whiteout blizzard. He doesn't comment about my skimpy work product, and when he stands, preparing to leave, I stand too.

"By the way, Paul, when I slipped on my left shoe this morning, I noticed the strap was tearing and it felt looser than usual. These are my only decent shoes. I'd order another pair, but they're custom-made for civilians and they'll take forever to get here. When I arrived this morning, I intended to ask Cassie who to contact for repairs, but she was on the phone. By the time I got settled upstairs, I forgot."

Paul nods and holds up his index finger. He chats on his handheld radio with someone for a few minutes.

"Major Williams is in his office, and he'll take care of you. He's on the second floor between the Radio Room and Infirmary. Ask anyone and they'll direct you. Meanwhile, I'll have Cassie submit a shoe requisition for you. They'll have your size on file."

Paul takes my arm as if I might trip and escorts me downstairs. He stops in front of Cassie's desk.

"Wait. We'll take the elevator. Fewer steps with your broken strap. Too dangerous, especially on the stairs."

He instructs Cassie to order two pairs of shoes for me.

"My sandals are custom-made at Melbourne Ridge, and they know my size," I say.

"Oh, Melbourne. I'll submit a request today, sir."

As we walk across the rotunda, my shoe feels looser. Riding in the elevator was a smart idea. On the second floor, Paul guides me to Tom's office, where we pass his receptionist and go right in. Tom looks up.

"I'm leaving you in excellent hands," Paul says, and he's gone.

"Allow me to inspect your glass slipper, my princess."

I giggle, genuflect, and sit to remove my left shoe and present it to Tom. After he examines it, he pages someone, and a minute later, a young private appears. Tom hands the private my defective shoe.

"This poor damsel in distress has a torn shoe strap," Tom says in a chivalrous tone.

"No problem, sir," the private says as he examines the strap. With a smile, he absconds with my shoe.

We sit in uncomfortable silence for a moment. Electronic parts mixed in with papers clutter his desk. The office is small but busy with shelves and bookcases filled with manuals and more electronics. It looks more like a workshop than an office.

"So, how's everything going for you?" Tom asks.

"Fine. What do you do down here?"

"Fix broken items and rebuild usable ones. We handle anything mechanical or electrical. We also build cabinets or repair broken items the salvage crew brings in. Pretty much anything. Even broken shoes."

"Can you mend a broken heart?" I ask, teasing.

"Nah, you need a doctor for that."

"So, your office is on the second floor ... but I've never seen you on this floor."

"I'm hands-on, so I'm all over the base, wherever there's a problem. I prefer to make sure the job's done right. It's fun to get my hands dirty on occasion." He nods and examines his fingernails.

After another uncomfortable silence, I say, "How do you feel now that I'm Commander's girl?"

He bites his lip with a crooked smile, pausing before he speaks.

"A little disappointed," he says with a wink, "but I'm happy for Nate. He likes you a lot."

This time I nod. Tom appears out of his element, talking with me alone in his office. The bravado has vanished. Or perhaps my new status as Commander's girl constrains him.

"Did you enjoy the party?" I ask.

Tom blushes and looks away.

"Do you always have live entertainment?"

Still avoiding my eyes, Tom shakes his head.

"No, this was new. Sometimes we show a porn movie on a big screen television."

He peers over at me.

"I've never had a birthday party, but I don't think I've missed much," I say. "I'd prefer male strippers. And a bigger cake."

Tom laughs, and the tension evaporates.

"When's your birthday, Zena?"

"January fourth, but no one knows that. Until now ... you know."

"Happy birthday. How old are you?"

"Thank you. I guess I'm twenty-four."

"You guess? So, your birthday is the day before Nate's. Why didn't you tell anyone?"

"I don't talk about it, and I never celebrate."

My identity papers list my birthday as April 10, 2077, but because it's fabricated, I never mentioned my phony birth date to anyone, nor did I celebrate it, not even in private. Before I regained my memories, birthdays had no meaning.

Three lipstick-sized crystalline cylinders line up together on Tom's desk. I learned about them at Westview. They're our universal energy source, but I never chanced to see one. They sparkle like diamonds, clear and reflective, with a thin, blue filament running through its center like a threaded bead.

"Tom, are those the crystals I've heard about?"

"Sure, these babies run the base. Miniature ones like these power your door lock. The larger versions handle everything from the base lights to the heavy-duty kitchen appliances to the elevator ..."

He waves his arms to encompass everything on the base.

"The crystals driving the central operations are super-sized," he says, holding his hands up about three feet apart. "Larger systems require two or more power units."

Tom glances around his small office.

"The smallest crystals drive the smaller devices, like your portable disc player or our handhelds. We retrofit the salvaged appliances with these bad boys. Television sets, music systems, movie players, and even coffee makers. Everything."

He reaches over to the bookcase and pulls a container off the shelf. It looks like a small toolbox, and when he opens it, I see four rows of different-sized gems. The top row has lipstick-sized crystals, and each row below has smaller ones. The last row displays diamond-sized crystals.

"In the old days, appliances and lights ran on electrical currents that were harmful to the environment, but we've improved that. Some devices we recover don't work, no matter what we do. The television sets don't work unless you hook them up to a movie player. But you wouldn't know what I'm talking about."

I do. No radio, no T.V. signals, no internet, no satellite transmissions. I shrug and nod.

"If you have any problems with your disc player, come see me. We can fix anything," he says, with pride in his voice.

"Can you build more rooms for women?"

Tom cocks his head and squints, and then rubs his chin and stares at the ceiling as if he's reading imaginary blueprints.

"Regulations state women's quarters must be in their own area separate from the men. We can't construct new rooms because there's no access to plumbing. We could build the shelter and install locks, but we can't install lavatory fixtures, and you'd need access to a bathroom. It's possible to enlarge one of the comfort rooms. They have toilets, but ... well, they're an important part of military culture. We expected you to leave before it was necessary to get that done. We understood your stay to be temporary."

"What about that spacious storage room off the ramp to the main floor? The one with the circular pit. It was once a nursery, according to the symbols. It has a washroom."

"How did you discover that room?"

I shrug.

"It's used for storing surplus goods and ... has other uses," says Tom.

I nod, and Tom gives me a strange look.

"Lieutenant Cross?" he asks, shaking his head.

The private returns with my repaired shoe just in time to dodge his query. I try it on and it's nice and snug, almost like new. He did an excellent job.

I click my heels three times, and whisper, "There's no place like home," but nothing happens.

Chapter 23

As usual, no one joins me at my table in the crowded cafeteria. I set down my tray holding a plate filled with mouthwatering chicken pieces paired with fried potato dumplings. As soon as I sit, I notice Dan walking towards me.

"Miss Roberts," he says with a nod.

"Major Matthews."

"I'm headed upstairs, but I want to meet with you in my office after you finish your lunch. In an hour. If I'm not there, wait for me. I need to discuss a serious matter with you."

"Where is your office?"

"See that suite of offices?" he says, pointing across the rotunda. "Ask anyone and they'll direct you."

"Can you give me a hint of what this is about?"

"No. See you in about an hour."

Dan turns and heads to the stairs, leaving me curious as a cat.

My food lost its appeal. This serious matter hangs like the sword of Damocles over my head. He didn't look angry, just resolute, but an eerie feeling creeps over me. What does Dan need to discuss? Perhaps something I let slip to Tom. I mull over my conversation with Tom and can't think of what I might have unwittingly disclosed. This morning, neither Commander nor Paul mentioned anything concerning. Dan claimed it was a serious matter.

I arrived early for lunch, not planning to hang around, hoping to avoid David should he decide to confront me. With each bite, my apprehension increases as my appetite diminishes. Did David say something to Major Matthews? I trusted him. Would he betray me over that silly exchange at the birthday party? He started it.

I finish my meal and my stomach is full of food I didn't enjoy and don't remember eating. My curiosity, soaring to an all-time high, makes me restless, so I stroll over to the suite of offices. A lieutenant escorts me to Dan's receptionist who appears to be expecting me. She asks me to take a seat across from her desk. I return her fake smile, sit, and thank the gentleman who ushered me. And wait.

I'd love to check out Dan's office to get a sense of the man he's become, but that's not allowed.

"I'm Zena Roberts. Major Matthews asked me to meet him here," I say, trying to start a conversation.

"Yes, ma'am," she says, and shuffles papers on her desk, attempting to look busy, I suppose, or perhaps to avoid talking to me. It's a long, silent, forty-five minutes before Dan strolls in. He motions for me to follow him and closes the door behind me. I sit in one of the visitor chairs and glance around while he moves papers on his desk aside. He sits back and sighs.

"I had a very interesting conversation with Lieutenant Cross. He tells me you're hiding something. Something you'll tell me before you leave."

Damn you, David. You promised. Dan's tone isn't menacing, just suspicious and official.

I say nothing.

"How well do you know Cross's father, Commander Nadler?"

"I worked with him a long time ago. He was my handler."

"Sure, that came up at the meeting. How long ago?"

"Years."

Dan wears a dubious smile. I'm not making this easy, but I'm not ready for this conversation.

"How old are you?"

It's clear where he's headed, and perhaps it's time because I'm tired of secrets and of pretending. I've had a dozen fantasies visualizing the moment when I finally revealed my secret to Dan, and none of them looked like this. I glance around his immaculate office. Everything in it is work-related. No personal or frivolous items that I can see. Even his waste basket is empty. A bookshelf in the corner displays a few books, several binders, and manuals. The walls are bare, and his desk holds a computer and a few papers.

"Well, Dan ... may I call you Dan?"

He bristles for a moment, then nods and shrugs. It's part of the game. He needs to yield a little first if he wants information from me. It's Interrogation 101. At least at my school.

"I'm twenty-four."

"That's strange. You told Commander you've served ten years working for the military. Did he hear that right?"

"He did."

"So, you lied to Commander?"

"No, sir. I told him the truth."

"Ten years ago, you would have been fourteen. They wouldn't have allowed you on a military base, much less permitted you to work. See the problem here?"

"There's no problem. In fact, I was thirteen when Major Nadler discovered my skills and trained me to work under him. So, it's closer to eleven years. I just turned twenty-four."

Dan frowns and stiffens.

"You were thirteen ... at Westview? How is that? They don't permit children on military bases, not even children of the upper echelon. No exceptions. The rules are strict."

"Well, they made an exception. They always make exceptions for me because I bring value to the table. They make exceptions whenever it suits them."

Dan stares at me in disbelief.

"What skills could a child possess that would warrant them bringing you onto a base ... and expect you to work?"

"I'm afraid that's classified. I signed an NDA, and if I disclose classified information, they'll throw me in prison. You don't want me to end up in prison, do you, Dan? You should take your questions to Commander Nadler. I don't have permission to discuss that period of my life."

Dan glares at me and says nothing. His silence unsettles me.

"I already explained this to David. It happened a long time ago. It's been eight years since my tour of Westview, that part of my life is over, and I don't talk about it."

"Your uncle allowed this?"

I'm not going to win.

"Lieutenant Bennett was my handler, not my uncle."

Dan appears perplexed.

"Does Michael know?"

"He does now. He recently found out and told me before he left. But that was my cover, and I couldn't tell him the truth at Central. I stuck with that story because it's not for me to say otherwise. I do as I'm instructed."

"Who the hell are you?"

"Someone who once thought you hung the moon." The words tumble out unchecked.

"What?"

A bewildered expression crosses Dan's face. He's not remembering.

"Cross says you met me years ago, but I have no memory of you."

"You brought me to Westview over a decade ago. I was on the road when Andrew crashed his jeep, and I used my dress belt as a tourniquet. Before I could stop the hemorrhage, Andrew's blood covered half of my white dress. You cleaned me up in a stream and gave me your shirt to replace my ruined clothes. I keep your shirt tucked away in my treasure box."

Dan turns white as a sheet and stares at me for several minutes. He's remembering.

"I stayed with Andrew for six months until he went to rehab. I slept in his hospital room on a cot and was his companion and helper. We became very close."

"Angel?"

I nod as tears well up.

Dan stares at me like I'm a ghost. His mouth hangs open.

"This summer, I discovered Andrew was stationed here, and he's gone. I often visit the Memorial Room to talk to him. News of his death crushed me because ... I loved him. Before he left for rehab, he promised he'd find me and take care of me, and I always believed he'd search for me. Andrew loaned me his cross necklace to hold until he found me, so I guess it belongs to you now. I planned to tell you everything and give you the necklace along with your shirt before I leave Cavalry."

I take a deep breath and slowly exhale.

Dan sits in silence for a moment, then clears his throat and says, "Return it to Commander. The necklaces were a gift from him to symbolize our brotherhood."

"I longed to tell you, but the timing was always wrong. You didn't recognize me, and I've seen so little of you."

Dan shakes his head, studying me as if he's trying to see Angel.

"Do you remember anything? Where you're from? What you were doing alone in the middle of nowhere? Damn, I assumed they sent you to one of the civilian bases."

"Some memories are coming back. I remember my birthday."

"What happened to you? How did you end up working for Nadler?"

"After you and Andrew left, Nadler took me under his wing and the rest is history."

Dan sits back, his face etched with a pained expression.

"I'd like you to keep this to yourself. I'm not ready for anyone else to know this."

"Princess ... Angel ... I'm sorry, I can't do that, but I can assure you, it won't go past the Inner Circle."

I nod. I understand, but I need more time. Everything's moving too fast.

Dan stands and I follow suit. Suddenly, he turns white again and sits.

"Zena, you told us someone molested you when you were thirteen. At Westview?"

"Dan, please, I don't want to talk about that."

"Please tell me it wasn't Andrew."

"Oh, Dan, don't even think that. Andrew was my Buddy. I took care of him, and he always respected my innocence. What a horrible thought. He was in such pain, and I was scared and alone. We were good for each other. Never say that again."

"Then who, Zena?"

"It was so long ago. It doesn't matter anymore. No one investigated Wickmore. What makes you think they'd bother with something that happened over a decade ago? I'm over it."

"Why do you protect men who hurt you? You tried to cover for Blake. Why do you do that? Damn, if I had known ..."

"If you had known? You know about Wickmore. Everyone does, yet nothing changes."

Dan looks pale like he's getting sick.

"Look, Dan, it's military culture. Y'all talk out of both sides of your mouth. I don't blame you. Colonel Wickmore was a predator and a senior officer, accountable for his own misdeeds, and you're not responsible for what happened when I was thirteen. You had a job and responsibility. You and Andrew were the only men who respected my virtue and took care of me even when it wasn't practical. I'll never forget how safe and secure I felt with you in the scary, foreign world you brought me to."

"What about Nadler? He was supposed to find out where you belonged."

"Nadler decided I belonged with him. He and Miss Elly were my guardians. Let it go."

Damn, this isn't how I imagined telling Dan. None of my rehearsed scenarios played out like this. I walk around the desk, Dan stands, and I fall into his arms. He holds me tight and kisses the top of my head.

Chapter 24

I'm expecting and dreading the unavoidable conversation with Commander and Paul. Dan must have told them my long-kept secret by now. Both officers sit at my worktable sipping coffee as usual, but they're quieter and more reserved this morning than usual. Paul stands to let me squeeze into my spot by the sink. I pull out my materials and busy myself with setting up my work area while waiting for someone to speak.

"You've been holding out on us. Major Matthews shared an interesting story about you," says Commander.

He's hiding his feelings, and I can't gauge his mood. Sometimes he's very hard to read.

"What did Dan tell you?"

"It's Dan now?" he asks, with a surprised grin.

"He told me his name was Dan, and I called him that during the short time we spent together, sharing the same Comfort Room for two weeks."

Both officers raise their eyebrows, fear behind their eyes.

"Nothing improper happened. Dan was a perfect gentleman and treated me like a father would. We slept in separate cots, and he protected me like the child I was. He took excellent care of me and made me feel safe. Then he left me with Andrew."

Both men wince at the mention of Andrew's name. An uncomfortable veil of sorrow drapes like a blanket over them. It's painful for me too, but it's time I unburden this heavy cross. I've held this sadness inside me for far too long and I'm ready to share.

"After Dan rejoined his unit and they moved out, I slept in Andrew's hospital room. I stayed with him for several months, to comfort him, to keep him company, and to help him deal with his pain. We became very close and before he left for rehab, he gave me his cross necklace."

155

I dig inside my bra, pull the cross necklace out from its hiding place, and then kiss it one last time.

"He called it a loan and proposed I return it to him when we meet again. He promised to take care of me when he found me. Said it was his turn. I'm able to care for myself now, but whenever life got too messy or sad, I'd bring out the necklace and hold it. It was my connection to him. I've kept it in my treasure box, along with Dan's shirt ... and Michael's."

Unexpected tears come out of nowhere, streaming down my face, despite my repeated rehearsals of this moment. I'll never see Andrew again. It's final. It's over.

I place the necklace on the table in front of Commander.

"Dan says it belongs to you now."

Paul pulls out a handkerchief and offers it to me while Commander gently picks up the cross necklace and reads the engraving. He shows it to Paul, then stands and leaves the table, and I suspect he's headed for his bedroom.

"Andrew said he lost the necklace," Paul says in a quiet voice.

There are no orange sweets today. Nothing to celebrate.

Paul covers his mouth with his hand, and I ache for men who believe they can't cry. He takes several deep breaths and nods as if he's made a deal with the gods. Commander returns after several minutes, sits, and then studies me for a while.

"I assume you all have identical necklaces, except for the engravings. I saw Dan's cross necklace years ago, but I've seen no one wearing theirs here."

Paul says, "We stopped wearing them after Andrew..."

"I understand. Someday we can trade stories about him. I've been wondering what he was like when he was here. It seems he still suffered bouts of darkness. I helped him through his depression ... a few times. Did he ever mention me?"

Paul and Commander shake their heads in sympathy and my heart breaks. Why should Andrew share our precious moments with his brothers? Perhaps he forgot about me. I guess I mattered less to him than he did to me.

That's unfair. He may have feared they'd misunderstand his relationship with a child. I never spoke about him, not even to Nadler. We both moved on, living our lives. He was my secret. Maybe I was his.

"Why didn't you say something? You recognized Dan, so why didn't you tell him? You had lots of opportunities," Commander asks.

"Dan was on leave when I transferred here. In your office, I noticed the faded photo showing Dan and Andrew, but it was so old. I intended to ask you about it, but I was negotiating for more freedom. Months later, I learned Andrew was here but ... passed. Then I discovered Dan was stationed here and is part of your Inner Circle, but was on furlough."

"What about when Dan returned to Cavalry?"

"He didn't recognize me, and my life had turned upside down. It wasn't the right time. I was grieving for Andrew, everything spiraled out of control, and I kept making stupid mistakes. I wanted a special reunion, but he didn't seem to like me the few times I ran into him. Then Michael showed up..."

Commander closes his eyes and shakes his head. Paul sighs and looks away.

"I was hurting and angry with everyone. Then something extraordinary happened, and my memories began coming back. I understood and viewed everything in a different light. It still wasn't the right moment. I needed to figure out how to move forward."

"I don't understand," says Commander. "What happened? What do you remember?"

"My mind started unlocking suppressed memories, and now they filter in one at a time. I can't explain it yet. It doesn't make a lot of sense."

I can't tell them the truth, but I'd love to share it with someone. My burden gets heavier by the day.

Chapter 25

My luck runs out at lunchtime. I'm finished eating, but I failed to make my getaway fast enough. David plops down across from me, and I stand up.

"Sit. I want to talk to you."

It sounds like an order, so I sit.

"I don't want to talk to you."

"Fine. Then just listen."

He bears the same angry expression he wore when he discovered I spoke with three of his former girls. I read him and I'm wrong. He's much angrier.

"It wasn't smart, what you did at the party. Mary and Jolene are avoiding me. Most of the girls are avoiding me. Cam won't Play anymore. Word travels fast around here."

"David, you embarrassed me in front of the entire party. Our affair is nobody's business. Was it necessary to advertise that you've ... seen me naked? I certainly didn't appreciate your broadcasting our private business to those military women. I don't discuss my personal sex life with anyone unless I'm involved with them. You ruined that."

"Then you should have kept your mouth shut. You're the one flaunting the fact you saw my tattoo."

"And your cute butt."

He's not amused.

"What gave you the right to put down my girls in front of everyone? We invited them to entertain us, and you shamed them."

"Sure, you brought them to debase themselves. To strip and perform lewd acts to excite the officers, who then left with the military women. Not one man talked to the girls after they ogled them and treated them like animals. The military women ignored them, too. No one spoke to me either. We're

158

good enough to entertain and serve y'all, but not enough for conversation."

"It was the Commander's birthday party. That's what we do. Well, you really messed things up. You gonna take my girls' place? You gonna take care of me?"

"No, of course not. I'm with Commander now."

David glares at me, pursing his lips together.

"Talk to Major Matthews yet?" he asks with a cocky grin.

"Yeah, thanks for that," I say, glaring back at him. "Is that your way of punishing me for something you started?"

"It's my duty to inform my ..."

"Bullshit."

"Come on, you were going to tell him, anyway."

"I'm relieved it's out in the open, though I'd have preferred to tell Dan myself. But thank you. It's good to know who I can trust and who I can't."

"You don't want to pit against me, kitten. I'm no match for you."

"Don't be so sure."

David gives me a wicked grin like he deems me ridiculous.

"You promised not to say anything if I told you the truth. You betrayed me. I don't want to do battle with you, David. But don't underestimate me. That would be a mistake."

David laughs. "You think you're tough?"

"I have information that would hurt you far worse than having your little girls upset with you for a while. I'm not threatening you, but don't push me. You started this and you can end it."

David smirks. We're both angry, but I hate every second of this.

Please, David, stop this and go away. I don't want to fight with you, and I can't tell you what you want to know.

"You're a smart girl. What makes you think a little ... fluff like you can best me? You need to mind your station, girl."

Ouch. His words stab me like a knife. Colonel Wickmore uttered the same ugly words before he assaulted me.

"I learned from the toughest officer in the Peace Force."

He blanches.

"Be careful who you step on. I'm sure Commander Nadler taught you that much. You think spending a little time with my father makes you tough?"

"I learned what was necessary."

"Sure, you did."

"Come on, David. Do you believe your father let me stay here because he's a nice guy?"

David stares, and I see wheels turning in his head, trying to decipher my meaning.

"Who are you?"

"I work for Central Intelligence."

I stand up and glare at him with as much confidence as I can muster. What I'm suggesting isn't altogether true, but I pray he believes it and backs down.

"You know nothing about me that could hurt me."

"Okay." I shrug my shoulders with a nonchalance I don't possess.

He cocks his head, opens his mouth to speak, then closes it. With a nod, he stands, and when he leaves, it feels like he's walking out of my life, too.

Chapter 26

The snow hasn't eased up for several days, although the wind died down, and the view outside the apartment window has become a white sea. This morning, the men treated me with my own little saucer of sweets, the orange-flavored ones I love. I don't even pretend to work.

"The snow's falling nonstop out there. Wonder if it'll get so high it covers the window," Paul says with a teasing grin.

"I'm sure we're too high up, but will we have trouble getting food and supplies from the Overlords? The roads must be impassable."

"We've stored plenty of food, and snow grounded the salvage units on other bases, so we have fewer mouths to feed. Besides, the Overlords prepare for winter by giving bases extra supplies in the fall, should the weather cause a problem for travel. Weather doesn't affect the underground transit system, and we share if necessary. Our basement is stocked full of extra supplies, but food choices might suffer. No fresh produce. We store frozen food, and our cafeteria staff does a great job using staples on hand," says Commander.

There's another option. The large columns in the center of each base encompass large elevators. The Overlords could land their spacecraft on the base roof and use the elevator to bring in supplies. They haven't done this in decades, to my knowledge, and I expect they don't want to reveal that capability. The Master Plan describes the elevators in notable detail, but I left that information out of my reports. I didn't understand their significance. They're no longer in use and everyone believes the Overlords are our benefactors. Not an invasion threat.

When I visited the atrium once, I thought I was dreaming when I saw an aircraft moving away from the base overhead. I've never heard of the elevators on our bases used for any reason. I wonder if we could hear the elevator moving through the middle column. No one seems to be aware of the column's true function. Perhaps the Overlords use their spacecraft to travel between the bases in their complex to ferry supplies or people.

"Well, let's get moving," says Commander.

"Oh, we're meeting to discuss your proposal to create a team to learn how you translate the symbols. In an hour or so. I'll come up to get you and walk you over," says Paul.

I nod. Commander grabs my empty saucer and winks. I watch them leave and marvel at their changed attitudes since learning about my past. Cassie still looks at me like I stole something, but everything else is different. Maybe it's the nature of life, to remain always in balance. Like a teeter-totter. One side dips as the other rises. Yin and Yang.

I take my philosophical thoughts to the window to listen for the voices, which come as soon as I slip into my trance. The voices chatter about the accumulation of snow and the impassable roads. The Tracker has postponed his scheduled visit to the bases until the weather improves and they can clear the roads. It sounds like we expected him, but no one here has mentioned receiving Overlord visitors. Not to me, anyway.

Despite watching the snow-covered scenery, a memory springs to mind of a hot summer day, eons ago. I had lived with Josh for several years and we settled into predictable habits. Life with him was easy, and we were isolated from the roads the salvage troops traveled. We didn't know much about them and believed they belonged to the Captors. Now it's clear they were special salvage units working under the Peace Force. We had a lot of freedom outdoors and I enjoyed nature with Josh as my companion.

§

Josh and I marked our fifth year together with a small celebration. Josh promised me a surprise and refused to reveal anything until we arrived at our destination. He would have blindfolded me, but the terrain was too dangerous for such foolishness. Save that for the bedroom.

This time, we didn't head in the direction of our favorite swimming spot. Josh carried a forest green blanket and a backpack stuffed with items he secretly packed. After a half-hour trek from the house, we ended up near the foot of a small mountain. Josh moved the foliage away from a hidden cave, uncovering its gaping mouth.

He withdrew two flashlights from his backpack, handing me one, and we entered the cave. We spent the next few hours exploring the cool, damp refuge, a welcome treat, away from the hot sun. Tired, Josh threw the old blanket over a large flat rock, and we rested. He pulled some cornbread Kyra had baked that morning from the backpack, along with fresh strawberries. It was a weird combination, but it was the best meal I ever ate, sitting next to this man who loved and treasured me.

Josh confessed that he often visited the cave to think and reflect on whatever was bothering him, but hadn't come here since Brandon and Kyra joined our family.

"You came here after I moved in?" I asked.

"Sure, at first it was necessary because I was afraid to touch you," he said, smiling. "I had to ... meditate a lot."

"And after? After we made love? You needed to spend time away from me to ... think?"

"Sure, Caroline. I was falling in love with you. I felt guilty and scared. At first. After a while, I'd return to offer prayers of thanks. Everyone needs a special spot to reflect."

How had I not known this?

"And now?" I asked, unsure I wanted to know.

"Now I want to share it with you."

We talked for a long time, with him reminiscing about his early days, and his childhood and young adult life. Josh believed I was almost two decades younger than him, so I pretended ignorance about that period. I had to hide my own experiences, especially those that happened before he was born. They would have made interesting stories.

We never talked about the future. There was too much uncertainty. I blocked out of my mind any thought of the Tracker finding me, forcing me to leave. I couldn't bear the thought. We understood we lived on borrowed time and every day was a blessing. So, we played. When we went to the cave, we played like children. We laughed, made-up stories, and imagined a world reigned by peace and love. That was my first cave visit, but not my last. Josh and I visited the cave many more times. I remember.

As I return to the present, I realize I visited our cave once on my own, to be reborn. The rock we rested on, ate our picnic lunches on, and sometimes made love on, was the same rock where I awoke. On April 10. Josh's birthday. And that day, he was forgotten.

§

Paul arrives at the apartment to escort me to the meeting. As we cross the rotunda to the conference room, Paul informs me they're on a break. Their meeting started a lot earlier, and as usual, they finished their business first.

We reach the conference room and I take my place across from Commander who beams when he sees me. Paul sits at my side next to Mack. Everything has changed. I'm finally an important part of the group and accepted by almost everyone. David doesn't frown but hides the animosity I'm reading from him. I'm receiving different vibes from the Inner Circle now. Tom gives me a respectful nod. Dan gives me an approving look, and Paul is much friendlier. When I was Zena, I dreamed of earning this. By accident, I accomplished what Zena failed to achieve because she needed to change to succeed.

Commander clears his throat and addresses everyone.

"We've been talking about building a special team to work with you, Zena, to learn your procedures for translating the symbols. Lieutenant Reed has chosen two people to join the special unit and has expressed a desire to share the lead with Major Abrams."

I look at Mack with warm approval. I'll enjoy working with him and his team. If they're as smart as Mack, it'll be interesting to watch them put the pieces together. Or at least try.

"We've also sent an inquiry to Central with a proposal to combine forces. They selected two people interested in coming here to learn and return to share the knowledge with the lab members. In fact, I think the entire team wanted to come, but they settled on two," Commander says with a smile.

Commander turns his attention to me.

"Lieutenants Micky Sanders and Keith Stellman from Central Control will join us for three days next week. Lieutenant Reed will meet with you and Major Abrams, you'll liaise with his designees, and you'll plan how to proceed. Questions?"

"No, sir. I'm looking forward to being part of this effort. I'm excited to see Mick again and catch up on the lab gossip, and I'm eager to pass on my knowledge."

Commander seems pleased with the plans to infodump what I've learned, and so am I because Mick may be privy to future Overlord visits.

"Great. That's all for now."

With that, we're dismissed, and everyone stands to leave.

"Zena, hang back a minute," Commander says.

He finishes last-minute details with Paul and Tom. While I wait, Mack joins me.

"I'm looking forward to learning more about the translation process," says Mack. "I think you'll like the team I selected."

"This should be fun. I can't wait to meet them."

Mack nods and heads out with the other lieutenants. Commander motions me to him.

"Join us for lunch."

"Thank you, sir."

§

Commander's dining room evokes unpleasant memories of Michael's visit and the problematic luncheon with Nadler that could have gone south. This time I feel like I belong. Paul sits next to me, smiling. Tom flips me a furtive wink, and Dan has warmed up to me now that he knows I'm Angel. When I was Zena, I craved this.

The large windows behind us show a calm but glaring white landscape. I can't see much unless I turn around.

"The snow stopped. When will the Overlords resume delivering our supplies?" I ask.

"We suspended above-ground travel for supply convoys and salvage units alike. It's a perfect time for our salvage troops to visit family and friends since underground transits are unaffected by weather. We still have plenty of provisions. We won't begin eating the weaklings for a while," Commander says. He licks his lips.

"Don't worry. We'll spare the civilian women. Too much fat and not enough meat," Tom says, contributing to the nonsense.

There are no "fat" women on any base I've been on. I doubt they've seen overweight women, except perhaps in movies. The military females are too fit, and the civilians stay too active to gain unnecessary weight. The food managers control our diets and portions.

"I'm not worried," I say. "You would miss the women. They cook the food."

"We have male cooks up here in the Officer's Mess. We'd be okay," Paul says, giving me a mischievous look.

Dan says, "We have enough food for months if required, but now that it's stopped snowing, roads should reopen in a few weeks. Worst case, we're well versed in survival tactics."

I turn my attention to the servers, bringing in plates of juicy steak, sides of thick-cut home fries, and steamed asparagus topped with Hollandaise sauce. The food looks scrumptious and smells delicious. We never get fancy cuisine like this in either cafeteria. It's good to be king.

I toggle between feeling like a fraud and belonging to the group. The meals Josh and I shared were far simpler, but sharing each other's company made our dinners memorable. I gaze from one face to another, wondering if I'll ever experience that same sense of harmony, of family. I wonder if I'll have time.

"Have you ever had steak before?" Paul asks.

I nod. I must finish chewing my thick, tender, and juicy mouthful before speaking.

"Yes, but this is very tasty."

Paul looks surprised.

"Where did they serve you steak?"

I can't tell him Russ charcoal grilled T-bones a few times every summer or that I sometimes cooked a Ribeye indoors, but they weren't as good as his. Russ and I would share a bottle of red wine with a tender flame-broiled Porterhouse on special occasions. Sometimes, on date nights, we'd go out for surf and turf. That happened before we started a family, and then again when our nest was empty. We were far from wealthy, but we enjoyed a rich family life. And good food.

But in my early years on the military bases, I also got a taste of privileged dining.

"Sometimes Major Nadler and Miss Elly would invite me to dinner in the Officer's Mess. And at Mountainview, my handler invited me a few times. I mean, they served *filet mignon* a few times, and that was quite enjoyable. But we shared a meal every Sunday."

"Miss Elly? Military woman?" Commander asks.

"Specialist Elly Baskins. Commander Baskin's favorite daughter ... so she had the privilege. She often took meals with her father but never invited me. Major Nadler and Miss Elly took me to the Officer's Mess, more to teach me military table manners than for breaking bread."

I finish the last bite of steak and spear my asparagus.

"Michael never took you to the Officer's Mess?" asks Tom.

"No."

Tom cocks his head and nods.

"He joined me for most of my meals in the cafeteria."

Tom grins.

"So, you were never invited to Central's Officer's Mess?" Dan asks.

"Well, Colonel Wickmore invited me, but I declined."

"He invited you to the Officer's Mess?" Tom asks. "Why did you turn him down?"

"I wouldn't go anywhere with him. The way he looked at me made me uncomfortable. The Colonel is more than twice my age, and I wasn't attracted to him. Plus, I explained I was in a relationship and I'm faithful."

"What's wrong with sharing a meal with him? I don't understand. He's quite a few notches above your station. One might think you'd be honored," says Tom.

"I didn't want him to get the wrong idea."

"Did he request sexual favors?" Dan asks.

"Not then, but I disliked him. He was ... crude. Besides, I expected Michael to return soon, and he'd disapprove of me accompanying another man, even just for dinner."

Dan squints like he doesn't understand.

"Accompanying the Colonel might have been a strategic move and I'm certain Michael would approve. If you're lucky enough to get the attention of a colonel ..." Dan says.

"I don't understand. How could accompanying a lecherous old goat be beneficial to me?"

"He could do a lot for you," Tom says.

"How?"

"He holds a lot of power. Come on, you know that," Tom replies.

"Oh, I understand his power."

Commander says, "The Colonel assaulted Zena several times, and she feels Central failed to do enough about it."

I stare into Dan's eyes.

"Besides, what could he do for me? I worked on the fifth floor of Central with the best and brightest officers. I'd reached the pinnacle of my career, even though I'm a civilian, and a woman, having earned my reputation by working—not sleeping—my way to the top. He took it all away from me. If you're suggesting I need to 'be nice' to any officer to keep him from breaking the law, then I'm appalled. That's a problem."

Dan seems taken aback.

"Most women would jump at a chance to accompany a colonel," Tom says, shaking his head. "To dinner or anywhere else. They'd consider it an honor."

"I'm not like other women."

A server knocks and enters the dining room, pushing a cart filled with an assortment of elegant desserts. This time, when the tray comes around to me, I choose a generous slice of white three-layer cake with fluffy orange frosting. Commander knows it's my favorite. My face lights up in appreciation, and he winks in return. A few months ago, I'd have balked at the offer of dessert, but I'd have loved the gesture.

Coffee washes down the creamy sweet cake. Small talk becomes shop talk, and I sit back to marvel at the comradery. Full and satisfied, I regard each face again, watching them chatter about work, sometimes laughing—then it hits me. Now I understand why I blocked all memories of my life as Caroline or Rebecca. Russ and my entire family are dead. All my friends from my early days—long gone. I never saw Jade again, and Paul told me he died years ago.

Josh might be dead. I can't believe I would have left him, like I left Jade, except, perhaps, to save his life. I loved Josh and the easy, loving way we lived our lives. It would have broken my heart to leave him.

Was I on my way to rejoin him after my rebirth in the cave? Our cave. Did I choose to regenerate to throw off the Overlords? Was I headed back to Josh's house? As a child? That makes no sense. No, I wouldn't have erased those precious memories. It wasn't necessary. I needed ... to remember.

These officers, in their prime, perhaps at the peak of their careers, will age as I did. Their hair will turn gray, their skin will wrinkle and sag, their joints will hurt, and they'll slow down until ... until I lose them, one by one. Like I've lost everyone I ever cared for, everyone I loved.

David. He'll grow old too. But I can't stay here so I'll lose them, anyway. I won't be around to watch them grow old ... and die.

How many times can a heart break? How many people can one person love and lose? Can a heart hold that much sorrow without giving up? It's understandable why I'd hide the memories of my loves and losses, but I needed to remember my mission and where to find my Resistance coalition out there. My rebirth was indeed like a death ... and a brand-new beginning.

"Zena?"

Commander touches my hand, and I snap back to the present.

"Where did you go? I asked you a question."

"Sorry, sir. I got lost in thought, miles away. What was your question?"

"Are you excited about working with your former teammates again?"

"Yes, sir."

I'm eager to see Mick and Keith again. Mick, most of all. We'll work well together, and I want to share my expertise and pass on my knowledge. I'm glad we have teams from Cavalry and Central. The officers will claim credit for my success.

Once, I'd have felt slighted, but I see the world through different eyes. If several experts receive the glory and recognition for the successful translation of the Book, it will deflect from me and my special skills. I won't stand out so much or attract the Overlords' attention, and with luck, it'll free me from the responsibility of finishing the work myself. I promised to complete my assignment and I intend to honor that commitment if I have enough time.

My top priority is to save humanity from extinction, even if they never realize what I've done for them. It's my cross to bear, knowing what the aliens have planned for us. I can't trust anyone with this knowledge, and they'll fare better, left in the dark.

Especially if I fail....

We finish our meal and conversation, and file out of the Commander's dining room, through the Officer's Mess to the exit. David and Frank watch me from a table they share with two other officers near the far wall. I glance their way, but I hide the heaviness in my chest, and I turn away to leave.

Chapter 27

The third-floor cafeteria clears out as the lunch crowd returns to their duties. My meal finished; I prepare to leave, but I stiffen when David plunks himself down across from me. I'm not expecting to see him again so soon after spotting him in the Officer's Mess yesterday. Although he's smiling, I read him and determine he has unfinished business.

"Hey, kitten."

"Hello, David," I say with care, not interested in another fight.

"I was especially rough on you the other day. In a rotten mood, and overreacted. You were right. It's my fault for embarrassing you," he says, wearing his spanked puppy look.

"I should have paid attention to my words, too. Michael unnerved me, I guess. I didn't want to hurt you or your girls. When I'm attacked, sometimes I fight back."

David nods, flashing an insincere smile.

"I don't want to talk here. Too many nosey people around," he says as one of the kitchen staff approaches and asks if we'd like anything else. We both shake our heads, and she turns away. She clutches a dishrag, a cue for us to leave so the staff can clean.

I nod.

"Meet me in my office tonight after dinner. I want to fix this and ... I don't want us to be enemies. Let's work it out."

"I don't want to fight either. We'll talk, but not in your apartment. I'm with Commander now and I'm faithful. I'll meet you in your office."

With a grin, David walks away, leaving me with a sour stomach.

§

169

David and another officer huddle, steeped in conversation in his office, so I stroll from the ramp to allow them additional time to finish their business. It delights me David intends to mend our broken friendship. I want that, too. I wait in the shadows until the officer leaves before approaching the office. David notices me before I open the door and grins as I enter. He walks past me to lock the door.

"I don't want us to be disturbed."

He opens the playroom door and turns on the light, and alarm bells start blaring in my head. He turns off the office light, grabs my arm, and pushes me into the playroom, slamming and locking the door behind him.

"What are you doing? You said you wanted to talk ..."

"That's exactly what we're going to do. I don't want any interruptions."

My heart pounds. David pushes me against the padded table, pressing hard against me. I'm trapped, unable to move. A whimper escapes my lips. I calculate the probability of leaving here in one piece, and the odds aren't in my favor.

"No one knows you're here, and no one can hear if you scream. You'll tell me what I want to know."

"I thought you wanted to talk? Make things better between us?"

Pressed up against me, I feel his hot breath on my face, and although he keeps his voice low, it's menacing.

"Yep, we're talking ... What do you think you have on me? What's going on between you and my father?"

"David, I told you I won't come between a father and son. Family ..."

"Look to your left, at the wall."

His intimidating black leather straps and paddles hang like threats on the wall.

"I don't want to hurt you ..."

"And you won't," I say, pushing him away, hard. "because you're military, and the law is the law. Don't try those scare tactics on me. I know who you are, and you won't hurt me."

He looks down for a moment, bites his lip, then looks about to speak.

"And you know what else, David? You care about me, whether or not you admit it. You'd never hurt me like that. And I don't want to hurt you. Stop pressuring me like this."

"You're driving me up a wall. How could you hurt me? You know nothing about me. Stop playing games. I want answers and I'm gonna get them."

"You're not as insensitive as you pretend. You idolize your father, and you believe the military ..."

"I hate my father," he yells, spitting as he speaks.

David's face contorts in a wild scowl I don't understand.

"I watched the way he was with you, how he treated you, how he let you talk that way to him. When I was a child, I never dared speak to him like that or I'd get my ass whipped. I wasn't afraid of getting whipped ... I was afraid I'd never measure up to his standards. He's perfect, never makes mistakes, and everyone dances around him and fears him. No matter how hard I work, it's never enough. He's disappointed, no matter how successful I am. I'll never meet his impossible standards."

He tosses his head like a wet dog like he's trying to rid himself of some affliction.

"Are you jealous of me?" I ask, unnerved by his uncontrolled anger.

"No, kitten. I want to understand the power you have over him. You're a civilian woman and you get away with behavior he'd never tolerate from anyone else. I'll never be half the man he is, and he'll never let me forget it."

"You're twice the man your father is."

David shakes his head.

"You're not perfect, and neither is he. I'm not perfect. You abuse your girls, but at least they're all of age."

David swallows hard. He grabs me and his wild-eyed stare drills into mine.

"Did he ... hurt you?"

"Yes, in more ways than you'd imagine."

"But ..."

"He'll lose everything if anyone finds out. He crossed the line. But David, it provides me a tactical advantage and if I keep quiet, I maintain leverage."

David steps back, staring in disbelief.

"I love you. But I need his protection. I've made mistakes too, and I wish to God I could tell you everything. I wish I could tell someone, anyone, because my secrets are eating me alive. It's not over and I must be careful. You betrayed me once, so I can't trust you with this."

David shuts his eyes tight, wincing as if I smacked him with an openhanded slap. When he opens his eyes, he pulls me to him and kisses me gently, and I read his torment. He holds me close to him and I want to read more. But I don't.

Chapter 28

The snowstorms died down, leaving the landscape an endless frosty layer of white. It's been decades since I've seen so much snow at one time. From my vantage point, it looks like the snow buried the trees, but that can't be true. No clouds, so the blinding sunshine reflects off the snow. It almost looks warm outside, but that can't be true either.

This morning, the voices have decreased in number when I listen, and the scant chatter offers no valuable information, so I hope this means I have more time. I'll try again later. While staring at the distant white-covered mountains, I recall another memory, from a life in an earlier century, a different mountain, and much warmer weather.

§

Every summer Josh and I hiked to the same cave. This year, our tenth anniversary, was no exception. The oppressive heat drove us to the cooler cavern. We packed a picnic lunch, spread out on our favorite rock, and indulged in our favorite pastime, telling stories, and reliving our happy memories together. We spent several hours enjoying ourselves before hiking back to the house.

On our trek home, we took a detour to the lake for a quick swim to cool off. Storm clouds threatened, the sky turned dark, and the air suddenly turned chilly. We cut our swimming short and headed home, but even using the blanket as an umbrella, our dry clothes became drenched with fresh rainwater. Soaked to the bone, we laughed the rest of the way. Our shoes got saturated and muddy, and the downpour didn't spare the backpack holding our flashlights, even though we tried to shield it.

As we neared our home, Brandon stood in the doorway laughing with us,

172

and Kyra greeted us with dry towels.

That evening, we listened to the howling winds and watched out the windows as the storm picked up. The four of us gathered in the safety of the upstairs living room. Kyra and I jumped and screeched a little whenever the thunder boomed and shook the house, despite Josh assuring us they built the house to withstand the storm. We shivered, but not from the cold. It was toasty warm, huddled on the sofa with our men. We finally retreated to the quieter lower-level living room. While sipping hot tea, we told stories about storms we each had experienced in the past.

Brandon talked about surviving a hurricane that swept through the countryside when he was a young boy. It demolished one house or barn, sparing the next, as it zigzagged past their pardoned farmhouse. The landscape became scattered with the litter left by the torturous winds, homes of neighboring families, shredded, tossed, and spread without mercy. Nature had the last word.

Kyra recalled when she was six and hid under her bed with her older sister, Kathy, during a super violent storm. The deafening thunder followed a terrifying lightning display. I asked her if she knew her sister's fate and she grew quiet for a moment before telling us how the Captors caught Kathy almost twenty years earlier and Kyra never saw her again. She was fourteen when they kidnapped her.

We hadn't seen signs of the Captors for years and it was easier living out in the open. Other small groups or couples were finding our spread-out community and building their lives on farmland a short distance away. We had more neighbors and worked together, sharing crops and skills or talents.

We were no longer survivors, but pioneers, creating a new self-sustaining existence. There were still few children or women who could produce offspring, so it was imperative to keep vigil over the sacred youth in our small community, especially the young girls. Families with young women or children founded homesteads off the beaten path.

The Captors no longer seemed intent on sending troops to find and kidnap young females or healthy young men. Some farmers occasionally observed other troops from the bases, but they seemed more interested in finding abandoned cities and collecting forsaken items. They raided deserted towns for undamaged furniture, serviceable electronic equipment that no longer worked without cable or satellite signals, and other useful artifacts.

They traveled past some farmhouses, with empty trucks. Days later, they would pass by again to return to their base, their trucks no longer empty. These soldiers differed from the troops the Captors deployed. They wore different uniforms, and although they carried guns, they were much friendlier.

Their trucks and jeeps were quiet, powered by a strange new technology. Gasoline was no longer available anywhere, as far as we knew. The soldiers sometimes waved to anyone outdoors, and I'd heard that some soldiers made friends with the locals, and sometimes they made trades. I made it my mission to stay away from the soldiers. Just in case....

The members of my community felt safer but remained cautious. Feeling safe was a luxury I couldn't afford. It had been years since I dealt with a Tracker, but for me, the danger was always within arm's reach. My relationship with Josh and my new family lessened the sting of the threat.

§

This morning, Paul advised me of our afternoon meeting with Mack's team. I spent most of my morning preparing and sorting through my papers but then decided not to share them, just the Book. I listened for the voices but again heard nothing of value.

Mack and two of his team members are already seated at the conference table. All three officers stand and wait for us to take our seats. At first, I assume they're showing proper manners because I'm a lady and an expert, and I'm tickled, but I soon realize they're showing respect to Major Abrams, not me. I don't recognize the two lieutenants with Mack.

Mack introduces Lieutenants Robert Ashland and Brian Cambrey. No Specialists. I guess they don't believe military women could handle this project. It doesn't matter. I've always been the only female.

"And this is our Special Consultant, Zena Roberts," Mack says to his comrades.

"Good afternoon, gentlemen. I'm excited to meet y'all."

When I hand the Book to Mack, he passes it to Lieutenant Cambrey.

"I've been working with this Book for several months now and I'm far enough along to share what I learned. I've discovered that this text, created by the Overlords in their symbolic language, reveals a Master Plan. It outlines and describes their plans to build the bases with slave labor and fill them with chosen citizens. It details their design and construction specifications for all bases."

Both men wear blank expressions.

"I'm sure you're aware that two of my former colleagues from Central, Lieutenants Mick Sanders and Keith Stellman, will join us in a few days. I enjoyed working with them for over two years. Do you have questions for me?"

"How were you able to translate the symbols?" asks Brian. "Lieutenant Reed said the Book has passed through several hands, but nobody could fathom how to even begin translating these strange markings. How did *you* manage?" He opens the Master Plan in front of him and studies the alien patterns, tracing his finger over them.

"Well, Lieutenant Cambrey, I taught myself, several years ago, by studying symbols I found on the different bases where I've worked. I seem to have a natural talent for it."

"How are you sure your translations are accurate?" asks Robert.

"I've spent an immense amount of time making sure I'm as accurate as possible. I cross-check and verify everything, which is why I've delayed releasing anything sooner."

Robert appears hesitant to trust me. I look at Paul.

Paul hands out a copy of my preliminary report to each lieutenant. Brian flips through several pages and reads a portion to himself. Robert starts reading the first page and peers up at me, looking impressed.

"These reports are for your eyes only. Central Intelligence elected to assign this project with a third-level classification, but we're limiting the number of eyes on it until we understand the complete text. Only members of the immediate team, Commander's team, and Major Morgan have privileged access to anything involving this project."

"And me," I say.

Paul smiles. "That was a given," he says. "We supplied the officers from Central with Zena's preliminary report. You can study it and judge for yourself. You'll leave your copies with me between meetings, and you'll have ample time to read the report before we adjourn this afternoon. Today, we want to discuss plans going forward. How often you'll meet and how we'll proceed," Paul says.

"I've known Zena for a while now, read her reports, and I trust she knows what she's doing," Mack says to Robert.

Thank you, Mack.

Chapter 29

Commander, Paul, and Tom wait for me outside the office. We stroll across the great floor and make our entrance into the raucous Officer's Club. Mingling officers and military women move out of our way, the rowdy laughter diminishes, and everyone watches us make our way to the VIP table.

This morning, when Commander invited me to join them, he reassured me with a wink that this time would be different. By now, it's common knowledge I'm his girl, and when I take my coveted seat next to him at the privileged table, the Club settles down except for low murmuring.

From my seat, between Commander and Dan, I have the advantage of viewing the entire room. Mary Jo walks in and takes her seat, joining Sergeants Greg Wolf and Eric Jackson, and their Player friends. Lynn sits with a group of military women and appears engrossed in muted conversation, her back to us, but the other women glance my way, and whatever they're thinking never makes it to their faces.

Mack occasionally peers over at me. If he's concerned, he also hides his feelings. I left my music behind, foregoing any need to approach the bar or speak with him. I miss our conversations, but I'll see him at our team meetings and our Book translation sessions. Greg and Eric glance over with disapproving looks, so it's clear whatever friendship I developed with them has eroded. Teeter-totter. Everything remains in balance.

None of the Inner Circle officers have invited women to the table yet. Dan turns to me.

"Zena, how did you get your name? And when? Why did you change it?"

"I had amnesia, so when Andrew called me his Angel, it stuck, for lack of a better name. When I left Westview, I needed a proper handle and title, so they allowed me to choose, and I picked *Zena Roberts*. They provided me with official identity papers, classifying me as a Special Consultant."

"Why Zena? Who was Roberts? Where did you get your surname?"

"I chose *Zena* after reading stories about the fictional female warrior because it sounded strong. The meaning in Russian is *guest* or *belonging to Zeus*, a mythical god. I'm not sure where *Roberts* came from, but I guess it fits. That was a long time ago."

I'm uncomfortable lying to Dan, but I can't tell him Kevin Roberts was my first love. I had forgotten Kevin when I chose it, so it's not a fib. Technically.

"So, you see yourself as a warrior?" asks Tom with a teasing grin.

"No, but I was fifteen, and it was romantic."

"Ahh, a warrior princess," Dan says with a mocking smile.

"No, I'm sure I'm not. I'm more of a lover than a fighter."

"Why does Cross call you kitten?" asks Tom.

I feel my face turning red. I asked David once why he called me "kitten" and he said it was because I purred like one when he pleasured me. When I asked him if he ever saw any kittens, he gave me a squirrely look and questioned whether they allowed young girls to visit the petting zoo.

I knew they schooled girls and boys in separate classrooms until age sixteen, although children had supervised co-ed playtime. I covered by saying that I didn't think they allowed boys around baby animals, that it was for little girls only, because girls were caring and nurturing, and little boys were monsters. He laughed and pretended to be a monster and play-attacked me until I begged for mercy. Then we made love again. That was before he broke my heart.

"I'm not sure. Just a nickname, I guess. Maybe he calls all women that."

"Did you ever remember your birth name?" Paul asks.

"No, but I believe it should be the law for everyone to choose their name at maturity. At least the first," I say. "But y'all have suitable names, so no need to change them. They're all Biblical, you know. Paul, Thomas, Daniel, and Nathanial."

"It's Nathan. Nate, for short," says Commander.

"That counts. Paul means *small or humble*."

Paul grimaces like he tastes something bitter. The others laugh.

"Ask any of my girls. They'd disagree with you," Paul says.

"I don't think it means penis size, and I'll take your word for it. I'll see if I can find more information. Thomas means *twin*."

"No, there's only one of me," Tom says with a grin.

"Daniel means *God is my judge*. Nathanial or Nathan means *gift of God*. The name Michael also has the same meaning."

"How did you learn about Biblical names? The Overlords outlawed Bibles, along with any form of religious manuscripts, and all manners of spiritual cult ideas. We learned about these forbidden beliefs in the Academy. Where did you learn about Bibles?" Commander asks.

"I found a book in the library with a list of names and their original meanings. I read a lot. It's odd how a culture opposed to religion has so many people with Biblical names. James means *something that replaces*. Paul, I mean, Major Abrams, you mentioned your father's name is Timothy. *One who honors God*. That's what it means."

Paul glances from face to face with uneasiness.

"What is the General's full name, Commander?" I ask.

"General Joseph Cameron."

"There you go. Joseph means *God will give*. David means *beloved* or *favorite*. Mary has several meanings, like *beloved* or *bitterness*. All from the Bible."

"What do you think it means?" asks Tom. "My father's given name is Peter."

"From the Bible," I say. "It means *rock* or *stone*."

Dan says, "Waylen is my father's name, and my mother was Ruth."

"I doubt Waylen is Biblical, but Ruth is, and means *friend*. I'm unsure where Waylen originated."

"Wow, I've learned something new today," Tom says.

"So, Paul, you told me your father's name. What was your mother's?"

"Leanna. Leanna Abrams."

If I hadn't been sitting, I might have wound up on the floor. I take a couple of minutes to recover. They captured Tim and Leanna together, along with Anna, but....

"When did your parents marry?"

"They joined the Peace Force and married three years later. I was born the next year."

Paul studies me. "Are you alright? You look flushed."

"I'm fine. Leanna is an uncommon name, isn't it?"

"No idea. Outsiders had unusual names. In earlier days, they rescued countless outsiders and transported them to our bases. And of course, many citizens were born on base. They intermarried, and some named their children from the Preferred Name List, and some after their kin."

"How was the Preferred Name List created?"

"Not sure," Paul says, giving his fellow officers a questioning glance.

The officers either shake their heads or shrug.

"How did you get started working for Central Intelligence? What could an inexperienced child do better than a trained, experienced adult? What did Commander Nadler rope you into?" Dan asks.

"He was Major Nadler back then. Because I was a child, making me overlooked, I could gather information and report back to Nadler. No one suspected or paid attention to me. When I got older, Nadler discovered my ability to be innovative and see patterns others couldn't, which led to learning how to decipher the symbols."

I hated lying because they were starting to trust me. Nadler and Fischer are the only ones with knowledge of my special skills, and they protect me.

"So, you were a spy?" asks Paul.

"Yes, but for the good guys."

"They sent you here to spy?" Tom asks with caution, biting his lower lip. Everyone stares at me.

"No, and you know better. I'm assigned to study and translate the Book, which I'm doing. They made a spur-of-the-moment decision to send me to Cavalry because I quit. When they failed to protect me, I had to safeguard myself. But with the Book's arrival, they were determined that I take this assignment and transferred me here for protection. What happens on Cavalry stays on Cavalry unless somebody else blabs. My policy is to be loyal and faithful to my handlers and their superiors."

I turn my attention to Dan.

"I'd never do anything to hurt you or yours, Dan. You were the only one who cared for me, treating me like an innocent child instead of using or abusing me. In my mind, you were my hero, because others weren't so considerate. The older I got, the more I appreciated those two weeks when you protected me, without exploiting me."

Dan swells with pride. I'm relieved to say the words I've longed to say to him, to express how much it meant to me he was respectful of my younger self. To lay bare my long pent-up feelings. Dan had loomed large in my mind as my hero, my prince, my dragon-slayer, all because he behaved as every man should. All because he placed my innocent needs above his own and didn't hurt me like others did. The way Nadler did.

Chapter 30

The dim light in my tiny room casts eerie shadows, and my blanket swaddles me like a shroud. I've taken to wearing a nightgown now that I'm Rebecca, no longer enjoying the freedom of sleeping naked, except on nights when I share Commander's bed. But now, tucked in my quarters, I feel more vulnerable. The first night, after my breakdown, or breakthrough, I pulled out one of my never worn nighties, part of my clothing allowance, and I've been wearing one since.

The wall clock reminds me I've been lying here for over an hour, but sleep won't come. I've cycled through memories of all the notable loves of my life. Some treated me very well. Others broke my heart. Some killed the love I had for them, and some I will love until my dying breath. But the love I hold dearest is my love for Josh. The lost memory of a pivotal day in our lives slips into my consciousness.

§

Josh never raised his voice to me, or his hand. I adored my gentle, patient, and always kind lover. He impressed me so much that I always agreed with him and afforded him whatever he wanted, and he made it easy because he was a decent man. I don't believe we ever argued, although I haven't recalled all my memories yet. Maybe I'm remembering only the best and leaving bad times forgotten, holding on to the peace and love we shared.

One chilly day in early fall, we packed a picnic lunch and headed to the stream, not to swim, but to spend time alone and enjoy the outdoors before winter showed its frosty face. I needed to discuss an important matter with Josh, and I wanted us to be swathed in the bosom of nature when I brought up the subject. I was unsure how he would react.

We sat on a heavy blanket draped over our favorite flat rock. We wrapped ourselves in sweaters and each other, discussing our winter plans, while I worked up the courage to bring up an unwelcome subject.

Kyra had confided her suspicion she was pregnant, and I requested she let me tell Josh. I told her about Laura and her ill-fated pregnancy, and his terrible loss. Josh never talked about his wife anymore and I wasn't sure he wanted to share, but the circumstances demanded it. I explained how traumatized he was after losing her and their newborn, and I knew it still haunted him.

I reassured Kyra that women have babies all the time with rare complications. She didn't need to fret for the next few months, so I prayed I spoke the truth. In her late thirties, Kyra was pregnant with her first child. We avoided discussing the dangers of late pregnancy, especially with no hospital, no doctor, or a midwife. I placed my hand on her stomach and sensed life and Kyra's fear.

She'd bring forth new life into a hard existence and uncertain environment. But hadn't danger always existed? I considered the life I left behind. Political upheaval, race riots, widespread school violence, daily mass shootings, and rescinded women's health rights. Marginalized citizens' rights—overturned. Hate and lies. Power and land grabs. Conspiracy Theorists—the new high priests of a dying earth.

But in this New Age, we formed a coalition of neighbors working together to survive and thrive. Kyra's child might experience a healthier world than mine did. No Internet, no television, but perhaps no hate or war. I needed to believe that, to fulfill my purpose.

"I had a chat with Kyra yesterday," I said, easing my way into the uncomfortable conversation.

A puzzled Josh studied my face and waited.

"She believes she might be pregnant. She's three weeks late. Kyra is probably breaking the news to Brandon as we speak."

Blood drained from Josh's face, and for the first time in my memory, he appeared close to panic. He stared out at nothing for a while, and I sensed him struggling. I touched his arm and held on to him, to read him clearly and to be his comfort.

"Josh, no matter what happens, we'll get through it together. I understand this will be difficult for you if Kyra is indeed pregnant, but we'll band together, all of us, and figure it out. Kyra and I discussed her staying with Milly towards the end. Milly has helped birth many animals on their farm and she'll know what to do. Of course, we'll need to speak with Milly. Right now, it's all just speculation, but we should mentally prepare ourselves. I love you, Josh, and we're going to be fine. We can weather anything together."

Josh's eyes betrayed his apprehension, but I sensed him calming himself. We hugged, and when we released, I felt closer than ever to him. I wanted to share this awful moment, fraught with anxiety, with him. It was a cloudy, dismal afternoon, but the air smelled so sweet, and we were together, safe, and deeply in love. Our life was hard, but I had grown to love these people.

When we returned to our home, Kyra nodded to me, and I understood she told Brandon the news. Brandon was quiet. He smiled, but his eyes registered fear. Josh walked over to Kyra and gave her a gentle hug, then offered Brandon a congratulatory handshake.

§

I've traded one family for another. Life on this base differs from surviving outside its walls. I spent decades avoiding capture, but because of my own stupidity, I ended up trapped in enemy territory with no means of escape. Before, I had an entire planet to roam and hide in. Now I'm stuck in this cage, and I don't want to leave.

Chapter 31

Paul shows up for our weekly meeting at the scheduled time, but I'm more interested in learning about his mother than in discussing the Book. He brings a couple of magazines with him and settles next to me at my worktable. I pretend to scour the magazine for useful information.

"Paul, tell me about your mother. What was she like? Did your father meet her on a military base?"

"No, they knew each other before they both joined the Peace Force. They enlisted rather late in life. Today, most people join at eighteen. They're sure they want to enlist. Especially if at least one parent is military. Mine were in their early thirties."

"So, the Overlords captured them and brought them to a base?"

"Not sure. They never talked about it. My parents only said they were older when they joined the Peace Force and later married."

"They never mentioned how they met?"

"Never asked. Why?"

"I'm curious. Tell me about your mom."

Paul shrugs his shoulders.

"Leanna was beautiful in her younger days. Her blonde hair was military short for as far back as I can remember. She told me that before joining the Peace Force, her hair was long, down to her waist, worn in braids. My father told me my mother got a lot of male attention, but she only had eyes for him."

"So, you got your looks from your father?"

Paul laughs, shaking his head.

"Guess so."

"Is Leanna still alive?"

"Sure, they both live on Coventry Hill after retiring a few years ago."

"Coventry Hill?"

"You haven't heard of Coventry Hill? That's where you end up when you retire. You live out your life there. No work, just relaxing, with all your needs taken care of."

"Is Wickmore there?"

"He should be."

"So, you stop being productive. Then die?"

"That's the nature of life, babe."

"Do you visit your parents?"

"Haven't in a while. It takes over four hours each way and involves four transit trips. First to Central, then to Melbourne, next to Silver Plains, and on to Coventry. You can't stay long. It's not like visiting family at Valleyview where you can visit for months if you wish."

"So, what was your mother like? When you were young."

"She took care of my needs. That was her job."

"I see," I say, but I can't imagine Leanna as the motherly type. "No sweet memories of mother love?"

Paul gives me a wry grin.

"Your father? I'll bet he was an interesting guy."

"He was a great man. A powerful influence on me. One of the few fathers who visited Valleyview often. He was stationed there at one point and spent plenty of time with me when I was young. When I got older, he prepared me for service. My father adored my mother and spent as much time with us as allowed. What about you? What were your parents like?"

"I lost both of them at an early age, and I don't remember much, and never talk about it. When did you, Dan, Tom, and Andrew become friends? I saw the old picture on Commander's desk of the five of you. You were so young I almost didn't recognize you."

"The four of us hung out as kids. We enrolled in the same classes, joined the Peace Force together, and ended up in the same training class with our instructor, Corporal Pierce," Paul says with a wink. "All four of us could select the officer's track since our fathers were officers. We moved up in the ranks together and transferred here after Nate, uh ... Commander, became Cavalry's base commander. He's three years our senior."

Paul becomes quiet. I read him and realize he's remembering Andrew.

"So, why did you bring me these particular magazines?"

Chapter 32

The transit announces its arrival with a low rumble before it pulls into the station. It slows to a grinding halt, reminding me of my first day at Cavalry. Little did I realize that my unraveling had begun. The stranger traveling here with me wasn't real, but the first of many hallucinations. The hopes and dreams I brought with me shattered into pieces, pummeled by my rollercoaster experiences here, and from learning who I am.

They say what you don't know can't hurt you, but I beg to disagree. My buried secrets hung like a millstone around my neck, undermining my awakening. Now it's far worse. When I arrived, I had a plan and knew exactly what I wanted. Now that I understand my purpose, I'm trapped without a plan until my memories return. All of them.

This morning, Paul explained the procedures. We wait with two privates for my former teammates to exit the shuttle. Mick and Keith will receive temporary lanyards. The privates will escort my old colleagues to their guest quarters in the officer's section on the third floor. My comrades will visit for three days on this trip.

Lieutenants Mick Sanders and Keith Stellman descend the transit steps and when they catch sight of me, their faces light up, but they maintain military decorum.

"Mick, Keith, this is my handler, Major Paul Abrams."

I want to greet my friend Mick with a welcoming hug but refrain from doing so. Protocol reigns. Mick's eyes tell me he feels the same.

"Major Abrams, allow me to introduce my former teammates, Lieutenants Mick Sanders," I say, gesturing to Mick. "And Keith Stellman."

"You'll get settled first, then Zena and I will meet with you in an hour," Paul says.

Both officers know the drill. The privates grab the duffel bags and escort my comrades to their quarters.

§

Mack and his two team members, having taken their seats in the conference room, stand when Paul and I arrive with the Master Plan and writing materials. Mick and Keith arrive minutes later. After I introduce Mick and Keith to Mack and his lieutenants, Robert Ashland and Brian Cambrey, we sit, and I open the Book to its first page.

The officers come prepared with spiral notebooks. Mick always uses pencils, and like me, he enjoys doodling while listening. Keith's habit was to pen extensive notes in his indecipherable cursive, and I often wondered if he could read them. It looks similar to my illegible script. Mick is always quiet but never misses a beat. Like me, he watches everyone but keeps his opinions to himself. At Central, he'd share them with me later, when we worked alone.

I like Mick. A couple of years back, with utmost discretion, he disclosed suspicions about Michael to me. He trusted me to keep his confidence. One day, he pulled me aside and showed me a pen he found near my workspace. The gold and black pen belonged to Michael. It bore his initials, *MC*, and I'd often see Michael use it. I'd never noticed anyone with a similar pen. We lock the lab at night unless someone works late, and the night before we all left together.

Even though Michael, in his position as a major, has access and rights to enter the lab anytime, he had no official business there. I inspected my desk area and found nothing unusual or out of place. I assured Mick that Michael must have dropped the pen when he picked me up—although I remembered Michael waited at the door to escort me to dinner the previous evening, and later, he left the apartment for over an hour.

That following day, in the apartment, I asked Michael if he was missing his pen, and then handed it to him. He studied me for a moment, then thanked me. It would have been improper for me to ask Michael about his presence in the lab. His snooping around my workspace after hours was irregular, but I learned early on that although I should always pay attention to my surroundings, I should also make sure I'm not stepping on toes. I'm not privy to everything. I like Mick and would keep his secrets, without a doubt, but I was faithful and loyal to Michael.

Other minor details about Michael concerned Mick, but we found no evidence of anything verifiable. We never discussed the timing of the terminated radio messages soon after Michael left. Mick and I exchanged disquieting looks, but never voiced our apprehension. I read him and understood his suspicions, but I kept my concerns to myself.

Since every officer received a copy of my preliminary report, they've had ample opportunity to read and study it beforehand. I turn to the first page of the Book.

"I've been trying to decide how best to teach my methods, and I plan to first show you what some symbols mean. If you'll notice these markings," I say, pointing to five glyphs, "these are enumerations. In studying them, you'll notice they have a similar pattern, followed by a squiggle symbol. This compares to an ordered list with numbers followed by a period. I encountered the same markings at the rightmost corner of each page, and the beginning of sections, following matching patterns in the same order."

"How can you be sure of your conclusions based on similar patterns? That seems quite a leap," asks Brian.

"I may make it sound oversimplified, but this comes from years of deciphering symbols around the bases, and months of working with these texts. I'm bringing y'all in late in the game and I promise this wasn't an impulsive observation."

"Is this text in some sort of outline form?" asks Robert.

"No, but they enumerate lists of actions."

"I've never seen anything like this," says Brian.

"Well, the ancient Egyptians had hieroglyphics and the Chinese had their *Hanzi* characters. It's not a new concept. The lack of a dictionary or documentation creates a major challenge for us."

Brian shrugs.

§

We break for lunch and I'm ready. Brian challenged me on every other point I made.

"Zena, join your team in the Officer's Mess. You'll have a lot to talk about," says Paul.

Every officer, including Mack, looks surprised. At Central, they never invited me to the Officer's Mess. Although I had earned a reputation for my expertise and worked beside these officers as an equal contributor, a clear distinction existed between my accomplishments and my lowly female civilian status.

Mack leads the way and Paul hangs back to secure our work materials. The Officer's Mess is a short walk from the conference room, and Mack directs us to a table large enough for our team. Minutes later, Paul walks in and heads to Commander's dining room. Halfway through our meal, David and Frank enter and seat themselves at a table near the wall, a few feet away from our party. David glances over and catches my eye.

"So, you enjoy living and working here?" Keith asks.

"It's different, but I've grown used to it."

"The lab's not the same without you."

Mick and I exchange looks.

"Thank you, Keith, but I won't be returning to Central. But I'm glad y'all agreed to work with our team. It's great working with you again."

Keith understands what I'm not saying.

§

For the past three days, I've dined with my new team in the Officer's Mess, but each day after we finish our session, they go their way and I go mine. Today, their last day for this trip, I take Mick aside and ask to meet with him in private, insisting I want to show him the atrium. I escort Mick to my second sanctuary, where we'll be alone and undisturbed.

After commenting on the beautiful view and how it contrasts with the mountainous landscape on the opposite side, I invite Mick to sit. I note how different this scenery is from the enormous atrium at Central and its magnificent panoramic view. We make small talk about the lab gossip while I determine the best way to approach the subject.

"Mick, I need to ask you a favor, but I can't tell you why."

"Ask me anything. I'll always keep your confidence. What do you need?"

"I've reason to believe we're expecting a visit from the Overlords. Please don't ask me where I got this information. It was unintended for my ears."

Mick nods, squinting.

"I've heard nothing at all. Why is this an issue? Something to do with Michael?"

"Why would you ask that?"

"Just a hunch."

"I doubt it involves him. Is Michael still at Central? I haven't heard a word about him. I'm just curious."

"Sure, he's back, but we don't see much of him. Since you're not working in the lab, he never visits. You two finished?"

"Yes, we talked and parted ways when he visited in January."

"You might be unaware Michael's getting married in two months. They're adopting two boys. Babies. I haven't met her."

Mick scrutinizes me, observing my reaction.

"Great. That's what he wanted, and I'm pleased he's making his dreams come true."

I don't have to pretend. I'm glad Michael is moving on with his planned family, and that at least that part of his secret is out.

"Do you know anything about her? Military or civilian?"

"Sorry, I'm out of the loop. But if I hear anything, I'll pass it on."

"Commander hasn't mentioned anything. I wonder if he knows and if he's invited to the ceremony. I can ask Paul ... I mean Major Abrams."

Mick appears surprised at the mention of Commander and starts to speak but stops before a word slips out.

188

"Commander and I ... I'm his girl now. I've made friends here and I'm staying. I have no idea what my future holds, but for now, this is it."

Mick seems agitated, so I read him. He's taken aback by my disclosure. Like many others, it appears he believes I'm treading in deep waters where I don't belong. I feel him withdrawing and I fear he won't help me now. I wanted to be honest, but it seems I've made a mistake.

"If there's any mention of Overlords visiting, will you send me a heads up? I've never seen a high-level Overlord and if he plans to visit Cavalry, I'd like advance notice. I don't understand why that should be a secret, anyway. Do you?"

"No. I'll let you know what I can. You do realize Commander Pierce will intercept any communication between us before you chance to see it? We must play it close to the vest."

"Understood."

He suggests sending a coded message that would elude detection by curious eyes. We work out the details and I feel reassured he understands my alliance with Commander is superficial at best. In our three years working together, we developed an unspoken understanding, as if we could read each other's minds. Well, I certainly could read his....

Chapter 33

When I walk into the break room, I recognize Tom's voice coming from Paul's office. I dump my lukewarm coffee into the sink, refill the cup with freshly brewed coffee, and walk around to his cube. They both look my way. Paul removes papers from the spare chair and waves me to sit.

Mick and Keith returned to Central four days ago, and our team get-togethers are in a holding pattern until they return in two weeks. I haven't spoken to Mack since. Our paths don't cross unless I attend Club and then I take my place at the VIP table next to Commander.

"Hey, there's our girl," says Tom.

"Hey, yourself."

"Going to Club tonight for some R & R?" Tom asks.

"What?"

"Rest and recreation."

"Sure, I could use some. Although nobody dances at Club, at least there's conversation."

"How do you think the team sessions are going?" asks Paul.

"I'm happy with them. I can't teach anyone how to do the translations, but the more symbols we recognize, the easier it is to piece the meanings together. Passing along everything I've learned is easy. I believe we've accomplished a lot."

Paul nods and says, "I'm impressed with our progress myself. We have a great team. How many more sessions do you expect we'll need?"

"I'm not sure. We still have a mountain of symbols to translate."

Commander and Dan walk into Paul's office, so I stand to surrender my seat. Dan grabs his chair from under the table.

"Hey, princess, what's going on?" he asks.

"Nothing much," I say.

As I pass by, Commander pulls me aside.

"I want to see you tonight," he says, whispering close to my cheek. His lips brush my ear, causing a tingle to ripple down to my nether regions.

"Aren't we going to Club?"

"Sure, we can go. We'll stay for a while, then leave together."

With a naughty grin, Commander pats my shoulder and takes his seat. I head upstairs. He hasn't mentioned Play since learning about my past.

§

We enter the crowded and noisy Club, make our way to the private table, and take our usual seats, with me next to Commander. This time, Paul leaves to select his girl for this evening, and Tom follows suit a few minutes later. The two military women join our group, but the conversation among the officers wanes, and it isn't long before the couples take their walk. In their absence, Dan invites a woman to sit with him. He doesn't introduce her, and she doesn't speak to me. Instead, she eyes me with suspicion, so I offer a fake smile, and she turns away.

Paul and Tom return alone. Dan stands, followed by his woman, and they leave. Paul and Tom head for the pool tables.

"It's time for us to disappear," Commander says.

He guides me out, with his arm draped around my shoulder, and when we're near his playroom I peek at him, but he continues steering me towards his apartment. We walk with his arm around my shoulder the entire way, and when we reach the offices, he stops to plant a sweet kiss on my lips, out in the open, and I relax.

Upstairs, I kick off my shoes, remove my lanyard, and unbutton my blouse on the way to his bedroom. He removes his shoes and shirt, so I unbuckle his belt and unzip his pants.

"You're sure in a hurry tonight," he says, pulling off his undershirt in one swift move and tossing it on the dresser. I kiss him.

"We can take our time," I say, removing my blouse and skirt.

He slips his fingers beneath my panties and pulls them down to where I can step out of them. He reaches around to unhook my bra. Commander removes his pants and socks, his gaze never leaving mine. We fall across the bed.

"I surrender," I say.

He laughs before grabbing me and turning me over, face down. I tense for a moment until I feel him caressing my shoulders. His gentle hands move down my back to massage my behind and then my legs. He pauses for a moment, then turns me over on my back, and kisses me full on my lips before drifting down to my breasts, kissing me every inch of the way. With his mouth on my nipple, he teases me with his tongue. He slides his hand down to spread my legs. Right now, I'd do whatever he asked of me.

§

Commander lies on his back, eyes closed, spent. Exhausted, I lie with my head on his chest and soak in the peaceful satisfaction. His faint smile fades away, replaced by soft snoring. I watch his chest rise and fall with each breath, and the rhythm makes me drowsy. I don't intend to fall asleep....

§

Colorful flowers border a red brick winding path leading to a small cottage. The scented air wafts with a sweet flowery perfume, and the gentle wind caresses my hair like invisible fingers. A monarch butterfly floats among the blossoms, circles me, and then flies away. This scene is familiar. As I approach the tiny house, I catch sight of an elderly man with a shovel, and to my horror, he's digging up the beautiful plants.

"Stop," I yell to him. He looks up, surprised to see me, and grins.

"Caroline, you're late. It's about time you showed up," the toothless old gentleman says.

"Why are you destroying the garden?"

"You can't stay here, you know."

As I move towards him, he morphs from an ancient man to a much younger one. A lover I haven't seen in decades but recognize nevertheless.

"Jade, what are you doing? The lilies are so lovely. Why are you killing them?"

"You can't stay here, babe."

He walks away and enters the cottage, leaving the door wide open. I enter the modest lodge to find someone sitting at a table, his back to me, and I instinctively realize he is no longer Jade. As the morphed figure turns to face me, my heart leaps and weeps at the sight of him.

"Josh, sweetheart, you're alive. I was looking for you."

I run closer to him, but when I reach him, he morphs again, and I jump back. He stands, and it's Vincent, the Tracker I killed, standing before me.

I scream.

§

"Zena, wake up, You're dreaming."

I tremble in the dim light. I'm safe in his bed, wrapped in Commander's arms. He holds me close to him, his arm around my waist, my back pressed against him.

"What were you dreaming?" he asks. He kisses the back of my head and strokes my arm.

"I can't remember," I say, but I can't forget. What is my subconscious trying to tell me?

§

Commander wakes me with a kiss. He's dressed and clean-shaven, smelling of soap and aftershave. He sits on the bed and pulls the covers off, exposing my bare body.

"Morning, sleepyhead. Paul will be here soon, and he doesn't need another show."

My face warms at the memory of my first sleepover with Commander when he disappeared downstairs to take a phone call without waking me. Unaware Paul was upstairs, I surprised him when I made a naked bathroom run. Once is enough.

I grab my clothes, wash up, and dress, finishing just in time to sit down for our morning ritual. Paul brings in a tray with three cups of hot coffee and the usual plate of sweets. He and Commander wait for me to take my seat. Paul hands me the saucer of miniature cakes and I select my favorite orange cube.

"After we finish here, we have a surprise for you," says Commander.

Paul wears his Cheshire cat smile and I'm intrigued. I study their faces, hurry to finish my coffee, and wish they'd do the same. Commander keeps glancing at his watch. I could read them, but that would ruin the surprise.

"I need to run to my room to get clean clothes, shower, and change."

"You can do that later. The surprise won't wait," Commander says with a huge smile.

After a few minutes which feels like hours, Commander checks his watch and decides it's time. The three of us walk across the rotunda. I alternate between searching their faces for clues and scanning ahead to see where they're taking me. Tom stands near Commander's playroom and my curiosity soars. Dan appears at the top of the stairs and heads in our direction and the mystery intensifies. By the time we reach the playroom, Dan has joined us. Commander hands me his keycard and motions for me to open the door. I look at him, not understanding what's happening.

"Open the door. Go on. We're waiting," Paul says, nudging me.

I swipe the keycard, it unlocks with a click, and I ease the door open. The lights are on. I don't recognize the playroom. The bench and hanging rings are gone, replaced by a double bed, dresser, desk, and chair—and a rack filled with my clothes. Someone stored my boxes on the lower shelves, but I'll have lots of cabinet space for my clothes and accessories. A music disc player sits on an end table. Someone fastened my digital clock to the wall across from the bed.

Tears run down my face, and I turn to Commander.

"I love you."

Commander looks uncomfortable in front of his brothers, but I hug him anyway. I know what this means.

"You'll have a long walk to the showers in the morning," Commander says. "There's not enough space in the bathroom to install a shower."

"Unless you'd rather use mine," Tom offers.

I slip Tom a playful stink eye, followed by a teasing smile.

"What do you think?" asks Commander.

"I don't know what to say. Y'all painted the gray walls. This creamy beige wall color and the burgundy carpet complement each other. The warm undertones give the room a harmonious feeling. Very cozy. Your men even gave the white cabinets a fresh coat of paint. They glisten like new. Thank you so much."

"I thought it's time since you're staying."

I pull Commander aside and whisper.

"There are four men in my room, so I guess I'm breaking a rule."

Commander's face lights up and he gives me a playful swat. "I'll address that later."

Chapter 34

I didn't sleep well in my new quarters, even with my generous-sized bed. It's not as comfortable as Commander's bed, but an immense improvement over my tiny old cot. Before I turned in for the night, I squared away my belongings, either in my dresser drawers or the cabinets. Most of the storage space remains empty, yet there's no place to hang my clothes other than my rack. It'll take days before I feel comfortable in these quarters, but no amount of time will help me forget its former purpose. Yet I'll never forget Commander's sacrifice.

As I turn the light up to cast out the shadows, I know I should get ready for work, but in my quiet hour, my mind snaps back to my strange dream. I want to see Josh again, and last night I hoped he'd visit me in my dreams again, but he never appeared. Tucked under my covers, I enter my transcendental state and sail off to another buried memory.

§

The weeks after learning of Kyra's pregnancy were difficult for all of us. Brandon wasn't excited about his impending fatherhood and hid his feelings from Kyra. I know this because he confided in Josh about his fears. Our lives were difficult and unpredictable, never knowing when the Overlords would show up. We had all felt safer these last several months, but bringing forth a new life complicated our struggle and renewed our fears as if the Overlords could smell young blood. Our lives would change, and I didn't welcome it, even though I believed our people needed to reproduce, grow, and strengthen our communities, to reclaim what was ours. I just didn't want it to alter my life or Josh's.

Kyra was worried and often scared at the prospect of giving birth without a doctor or midwife, and Josh shared her concerns. We both were apprehensive about having a baby living with us, for similar reasons. I understood it was hard on Josh, but he concealed his thoughts and feelings from Brandon and Kyra. On the surface, he was Brandon's greatest support, reassuring him that everything would work out. In private, he didn't need to share his fears with me. I knew.

In her third month, Kyra lost her baby.

I stayed close to Kyra for the next few weeks, listening when she needed to talk, holding her when she needed to cry, and sitting in silence when it was required. Soon Kyra regained her emotional strength, and our lives became normal again. Normal for us. When we were alone, Josh and I discussed Kyra's loss and the meaning behind it. We both felt guilty for our selfishness. While relieved the problem resolved itself, we felt guilty for that too.

I couldn't reveal my past, the family I left behind so long ago, and how bitterness for my losses remained. Had I stayed, the day would come when I'd have to bury the children I bore, raised, and watched grow old. I would never conceive again. It's too dangerous for me. If I allowed myself to get pregnant, the Gift may transfer itself to the new host. That's something I'd never chance. I wouldn't put that burden on any child. Josh was my strength, and my purpose kept me staying the course.

Chapter 35

The aroma of roast beef lures me, making my mouth water as I approach the cafeteria line and grab a tray. The server heaps a generous helping of meat with mashed potatoes and gravy onto my plate, but when she starts to scoop the peas, I tell her I'll pass on them. She offers me candied carrots instead. The next server fills my coffee cup and offers dessert, a sliver of apple pie with a dollop of whipped cream, which I accept, and I make my way to my favorite solitary seat.

I take my time eating lunch, scanning the cafeteria, and for the first time since remembering my past, I long for someone to join me. Everyone realizes I'm Commander's girl by now, but they still avoid me, no doubt for that reason.

Mary Jo looks my way, and I wonder if she's aware the Commander's playroom is my new residence, fixed up special for me. She lives on the third floor in the women's quarters, the same floor where she works. I doubt she ever visits the fourth floor except on Thursdays for Club night now that she can't rendezvous with Commander.

David parks himself across from me.

"I hear you have new quarters."

"How did you know that?"

David gives me a knowing smile and shakes his head.

"Not too much gets past me. My men moved Commander's playroom furniture to the basement. How did you convince him to sacrifice his playroom?"

"I didn't. He surprised me, and he even had all my belongings moved in before he showed me the room. They painted the walls and cabinets, and it looks nice. I have more storage than I need to hold my few possessions. They brought in a double bed and a dresser that is bigger than my needs. I'll need more clothes."

David smiles at my joke.

"Also, I have a writing desk. It's been tough getting used to, after living in my tiny, cramped coffin-like room. I can almost hear the ghostly screams of women being whipped ..."

David laughs.

"Only one or two women. And I doubt they screamed. So, Commander hasn't taught you the joys of Play yet?"

"Joys?"

"I'm telling you; Play isn't what you think. You're the most stubborn woman I've ever met. Try it. You just might enjoy it."

"No, thank you."

David looks around before turning back to me.

"So, how are you? Haven't seen much of you of late."

"I'm okay. The Inner Circle treats me better now that they've learned about my past. I should have told them long ago. It might have saved me some grief."

"So, you forgive me?"

"I shouldn't forgive you. I do, but I'll never trust you."

David winces.

"Saw you with your teammates in the Officer's Mess. How's that going?"

"It's very productive. I'm transferring my knowledge to them. They're all very intelligent and our sessions are proceeding well. They're returning for another three-day session next week and I'm looking forward to it. How's everything on your side of town?"

"What?"

"I mean, on the main floor."

"Couldn't be better. Agora is rather dull without you shaking up the dance floor. Tim often asks about you. Commander lets you have fun?"

"He's never denied me personal time."

"Then come to Agora tonight. Sit with me, like old times. Get to know Cam. She won't bite."

The mention of her name cuts like a knife piercing my heart. I try not to cringe. This makes little sense since I'm with Commander now. Still, it hurts watching David from across the table, knowing I must let him go. He'll never be mine, and I deserve better. My appetite shrivels up, and I fight to hide my pain, so I smile instead.

"I'll think about it. I'd love to dance. Tell Tim I said 'hi' and I miss dancing with him, too. My plans for tonight are up in the air."

I won't read David because it doesn't matter whether he's over me or hurting, too. Is he playing a new game? Doesn't matter. I don't understand my love for him. I love two men immensely, in different ways. This one, I can't have.

§

Cassie's not at her desk, but I hear a woman's voice coming from Paul's office, and it doesn't sound like Cassie. I stop to refill my coffee cup in the break room and then walk around and see Jen standing next to Tom. They stop talking when I walk in. The phone rings and Jen sprints past me to answer it. I sip my coffee until I realize they're busy with work.

"Need something, Zena?" asks Paul.

"No, well, I'm wondering if y'all are playing poker tonight?"

Tom smirks. "You want to play, too? We weren't planning on having girls tonight ..."

"No, of course not. I'll let you resume your meeting."

Commander's door is open when I pass the break room, so I walk to the doorway and peer in. Jen acts like she wants to warn me not to enter without an invitation, then changes her mind, but watches me.

Commander waves me in.

"What's going on?"

"I wondered if you're playing poker tonight."

"Yeah, it's Tuesday. No girls, I promise. Did you want to ..."

"Maybe tomorrow night. I thought I'd go to the Agora tonight and kick up my heels."

Commander tilts his head, puzzled.

"Dance."

"Sure, go ahead and have fun. You don't need to ask me."

"No, no, I'm not asking. I want to be transparent."

"Great. I appreciate that."

Jen still mans the front desk and watches me head upstairs. I turn and wink at her.

§

The Agora teems with young privates, civilian women, and a few officers. No one dances yet, although the music blares. I hand my music discs to the private tending to the disc player and look around until I spot Tim sitting and talking with a small group of other privates. He spots me and his face lights up. He waves me over and introduces me to his friends. After some small talk, Tim pulls me to the dance floor, and we move to the music like we're made for it. After two more dances, he wraps his arm around me and ushers me to his table.

"Can I get you a drink?" asks one private.

"Water with lemon, please."

"Where did you learn to dance like that?" asks another, staring at my breasts.

A slow blush warms my face.

Tim and I make an impressive pair. A skillful dance partner makes dancing effortless and fun, and Tim is without a doubt a gifted dancer. He anticipates my moves and his enjoyment is contagious.

The private who asked me what I'd like to drink whispers to the one undressing me with his eyes. The second private straightens and bows his head with a nervous but respectful nod.

"Does Commander know you're here?" he asks with a sheepish grin.

"Yes, of course, I'm entitled to a private life, as is he."

Tim disappears for a few moments, leaving me with his friends in uncomfortable silence, but when he reappears, he whispers for me to follow him, so I do.

David and Cam sit at our booth, but there's at least a foot of space between them. He looks relaxed, as always, but Cam looks like a scared rabbit. David motions for us both to sit. Tim slides over first, leaving me ample room. I set my water glass on the table and slip in beside Tim, across from David.

"Zena, this is Cam. Cam, Zena."

"Hello, Cam."

I smile to reassure her I don't bite. She blinks and purses her lips but says nothing.

"Having a good time?" asks David.

"Yes, it's been a while, but it's wonderful getting out on the dance floor. And Tim is the best dance partner I could hope for."

I look at Tim, who beams and nods in agreement.

"I didn't think you'd show."

"My evening plans fell through, so I decided to show up and have some fun. It felt good to dance again."

"You and Cam should get better acquainted."

Cam looks horrified, lowers her head, and crosses her arms around herself. David appears to enjoy her discomfort. What is he up to?

"I don't think Cam and I run in the same circles."

"She likes to Play," he says.

"I don't Play."

David bites his lip as if he's biting his next words.

"You will."

I laugh. "And you think I'm stubborn."

"Tim, why don't you take Cam and show her how to dance?" David asks, but it's more like an order.

Cam glares at David like it isn't the first time he's sideswiped her with this move. I've traveled this road before; but on this trip, I need to stop and turn around.

"Tim, why don't we show Cam how well we dance together?"

I get up and wait for Tim. He looks at David, who sighs before nodding. Tim slides out of the booth and a minute later, we're dancing again.

We dance another fast number and then two slow ones. I want to ask Tim what David's thinking, but I'm sure he wouldn't tell me, even if he knows. I dance with two officers and another private by evening's end.

Chapter 36

This morning, over coffee and sweets, Major Abrams mentioned wanting to show me some stored magazines and documents and promised to stop by to fetch me. He needed to notify security and make proper arrangements, so I'm not surprised when we approach the storage room where they caught me last summer after my corridor adventure. That miserable evening when Commander left Club with Mary Jo right in front of me. The same storage room where Lieutenant West held a gun on me as Jason searched me.

A familiar security officer guards the unlocked, open storage room door. Jason, my old poker partner, smiles when he sees me and steps aside. The lights are on, and the room looms larger than I remembered.

Like a deer caught in headlights, I stand in the middle of the storage room, paralyzed for a moment, because this time I realize it's the Gift that slides open wall panels that reveal concealed doors leading to the corridor. It would be unfortunate if I triggered the wall to open. I'm unsure which wall I should avoid or how close I need to be.

Without my memory, I was unaware I had the Gift, but the corridors are a different story. I now understand why the hidden walls and locked doors opened for me and no one else. The Master Plan describes the hidden passageway, the corridor, with access reserved for the selected few. But the Book never explained that they're extraterrestrials and that the modicum of Gift indwelling inside each of them makes it possible. I assumed they had a special access key to trigger the corridor.

I was even more confused about the doors opening for me, but I accepted my ability along with the other "skills" I'm accustomed to using. But now it's crystal clear how they accomplished the feat and the alien nature of the selected few.

I'm afraid of triggering the hidden wall by accident, so I stay frozen in place, glancing about, trying to figure out where I entered last summer. The room becomes blurred in my mind's eye, and I easily locate the entry point. In this state, I understand how to control triggering the device. And how to avoid doing so.

"Zena, are you alright?" Paul asks, approaching me.

He was selecting packed boxes, opening them, and sifting through the contents, but now pauses his activity and studies me.

"Sorry, yes, I was recalling my first experience in this room. It looks so much larger, yet there seems like a lot less floor space."

"Sure, we've filled it with several more boxes since then. Come with me. I want to show you something. We received an enormous collection of books and magazines plus a few documents and haven't had time to vet them. I figure your security level allows you access."

"Why do you vet the books?" I ask. At Westview and Mountainview, I had access to reading material before they shelved it but was unaware it was inspected or scrutinized before distribution to libraries.

"We ban books deemed too controversial or unhealthy for most readers to have access to. No one told you that?"

"No, do you have access to them?"

"Sure, we charge several officers with reviewing and cataloging the contents of the books before they're released. We destroy some materials. Others get packed up and stored until we dispose of them."

"What determines if a book is unsuitable for adults to read? I mean, we're all adults here, aren't we?"

"The Overlords instructed us to destroy all religious material or books that teach adversarial doctrines. They've turned a blind eye to our salvage activity provided we follow a few simple rules. This is one of them."

"So, you destroy Bibles?"

"Or store them," Paul says, pointing to boxes in the corner with the initials "RM" stamped on their side. "Religious Materials."

"Why do you keep them?"

Paul shrugs, and says, "It's a process to destroy them. We'll get around to it. Meanwhile, they're locked up in here—out of sight, out of mind."

"Who gets to decide if an adult's allowed to read certain books or materials? What are the guidelines? Is there a list?"

"Yes. We have a standards list. Four officers, versed in the standards, form a Censor Board. They spend time each month reviewing the material."

"So porn is okay, but Bibles, they forbid? Interesting."

"Well, although it's on the list, some porn slips through. It's an open secret. There'd be a revolt if we banned it outright. All adult entertainment passes through the censors. Certain types of porn never make the shelves. Violent pornography, for example. Same for books and magazines. Why are you anti-porn … and why are you pro-Bible?"

"I'm neither. I oppose censorship. Educated adults should decide for themselves what's worth reading or not. A larger group should judge something as irredeemable. Not four *male* officers. But the violent smut could end up in the trash bin with my blessing."

"Some materials give readers harmful ideas. Our prime responsibility is to keep the peace. The Overlords taught us that subversive ideas are harmful to the harmony and peace of the public. If you give citizens false information or destructive notions, the result is chaos. Our history's full of examples."

"What happens if you give them some uncomfortable Truth?"

Paul glares at me with impatience. By now, he should realize how much I love to debate.

"Truth, like beauty, is in the eye of the beholder," he says.

"Belief, like beauty, might be subjective to the individual, but Truth is absolute. You can believe a lie and it becomes your truth, but it remains a falsehood, no matter how you spin it. You must gather as much accurate information as you're able. Investigate. Question everything. Pay attention with an unbiased mind. The Truth is out there awaiting discovery. Some truths may be unknowable, but if you don't seek with an open mind, then you'll never learn, and you'll live in the dark."

"Zena, the Overlords know best. Who are you to question our benefactors? They saved the planet and everyone on it. We trust they have our best interests at heart. The system works, and it's worked for decades. Everyone knows the rules, where they fit in, what's expected of them, and the consequences of breaking the rules. Besides, if everyone's unaware of something, no one can demand it."

Paul hands me a stack of magazines.

We sit on boxes and scan the contraband, but I'm more interested in learning something I can't glean from old *verboten* publications.

"Are periodicals or books that promote women's rights on the list?"

Paul flips me his *you ask too many questions* look.

"Women accept their role and function. We take care of our women, protect them, and ensure their needs are met. Why put foolish notions in their heads?"

"So, that's a yes? Foolish notions?" I ask.

"Zena, you should sit down and talk to some of the women. I can't promise they're all happy, but if you make the most of your station in life, you'll be content. If you fight everything, you won't. The system isn't perfect, and I acknowledge there are problems, but it works."

"It didn't work for Andrew."

I regret the words as soon as they slip out.

Paul flinches and sits back as if I hit him.

"I'm sorry. I shouldn't have said that. You knew him much longer, but I loved him, too."

I scoot over closer and put my hand on his arm.

"Paul, I am so sorry. I know I don't understand what drove him to take his life. He suffered from depression. I've no right to say anything. Please forgive me."

Paul nods his answer and pats my knee.

Chapter 37

Snow still blankets the treetops and mountains. I can't view any roads from here, but no salvage units have checked in for days now, meaning the roads are impassable, signifying we won't get our supplies or unwanted Trackers.

I slip into my transcendental trance and listen for news about weather conditions and the mention of undesired visitors. After an hour and a half of useless information, I abandon my undertaking. I'll try again later.

During lunch yesterday, I overheard cafeteria chatter about this winter's hazardous snowdrifts and brutal cold. The treacherous snow drifts grounded all salvage units until further notice, and no one shows concern. Rightfully so, due to the surplus of supplies.

The seasons don't change inside the bases, except for the availability of seasonal food. Without celebrations, except for the birthday party in January, and with controlled temperature and the full-spectrum lighting, you wouldn't know it's a new year, much less winter.

I miss holidays even if I never believed. With Russ, it always meant relatives forgetting their disagreements and sitting at the table together in peace. Our families were far from perfect, but on holidays we buried our quarrels in bowls and platters of home-cooked cuisine, put aside differences, and remembered we were family.

With Josh, it was different. We made our own traditions, but we always celebrated with friends. Even with Jade, our group joined for song and kinship. Here, it's a social desert devoid of holiday festivities.

Muscular arms grab me from behind, and someone nuzzles my neck. I spin around, sensing it isn't Commander. I push Paul away.

"Oh, Paul. Behave yourself. It's dangerous to sneak up on a girl like that."

Paul grins and feigns innocence.

206

"Wanted to make sure you remembered our meeting this afternoon. Your teammates from Central will arrive soon."

"Thank you."

We met again for three days last week, and my teammates are returning for another session. With my collected materials, Paul and I take the elevator down to the main floor. I'm eager to hear from Mick to find out if he learned of any plans for the Overlords' visit. During his previous stay, he reported no word of unwelcome visitors.

The perilous weather continues, and the voices haven't mentioned progress, but someone should be aware of his plans, and which base he'll hit first. Will he travel alone? What is the pretext for visiting our bases? So many questions and I can't ask anyone here without needing to explain how I obtained my information.

$$\S$$

We greet Mick and Keith at the transit station, and Paul hands them their temporary lanyards, which they always surrender before returning to Central. It's almost lunchtime, so after the lieutenants settle in their temporary quarters, the four of us meet in the Officer's Mess. Paul sits with us but doesn't order food. He'll join Commander and his team when they arrive.

While my comrades and I are catching up, Commander, Tom, and Dan enter the Officer's Mess. They walk over to greet our guests and make small talk before proceeding to Commander's dining room. Paul excuses himself to join them.

I watch Mick, waiting for some sort of signal that he has news for me. He plays it cool but the first chance he gets, when he sees I'm the only one looking, he shakes his head. Okay, maybe that's not troubling news, but I hoped for advance notice.

There's only one transit out of Cavalry and it culminates at Central. From Central, there are four transit options to other bases, but if I can't discover the Tracker's agenda, I can't stay one step ahead of him. I need to invent an excuse to travel and somehow obtain permission. No one travels without the coordination of upper-level authority. I need to stay two steps ahead to pass through Central without detection. Then there is the problem of knowing when it's safe to return. I need an alliance, someone in the know, someone I can trust.

We finish lunch and discuss the project until Paul rejoins us. We head for the conference room to start this week's session. Mack and his team have already arrived, and we spend the entire afternoon together. We discuss building a database with the symbols and their possible meanings.

Mick and Keith relate their experiences of sharing their new knowledge with the rest of their team. They brought me questions and suggestions which we discuss before starting with new translations. I'm omitting the ominous information concerning the Overlords' plan to take possession of our human bodies. My people won't need to learn that awful truth if I'm successful. If I'm not successful, it might be better if they're ignorant. Or would it? At least they could fight. But it might be too late. It would help if I had a crystal ball to guide me.

Chapter 38

Mary Jo watches me, but every time I turn her way, she avoids my gaze. She appears very interested in me today. I'm halfway through lunch when David pulls the chair out across from me and takes a seat. He appears upset, but I won't read him. I need to let David go.

"Hey, kitten. How's it going?"

His disingenuous smile betrays his affable greeting.

"I'm fine, but you appear somewhat frazzled."

He nods, biting his lip, like he needs to tell me something, but would rather not.

"Seems like you and Cam are back together, but she doesn't seem pleased about it."

"I didn't come here to discuss Cam. We need to talk."

"What about?"

"Not here."

"Why not?"

What is David up to this time?

"A disturbing matter has come to my attention. Things could get ugly."

"I think you're exaggerating. Nothing disturbing has happened in a while," I say and laugh. What game is he playing now?

"Zena. Listen to me. You made a huge mistake ..."

Not this again.

"I told you Commander doesn't insist I Play, and he's been good to me. Now that he's aware of my past, and I've agreed to be his girl, he's changed. I doubt he'll ever love me, but he treats me well. Let it go."

"I'm not talking about that. You must be careful what you share. Word gets around fast. Commander will explode when he finds out. I'm required to tell him. It's my duty."

"What are you talking about? I haven't heard anything. Not that I would. Nobody talks to me. What happened?"

David looks confused.

"Meet me in my office in ten minutes."

"David ..."

"Don't fight me on this."

He gets up, looks around, nods, and walks away.

I finish my last bite, put my tray away, and glance around the cafeteria. Mary Jo snickers when she notices me looking their way, and I hear giggling coming from her cohorts. No one else pays me any unusual attention.

I descend the stairs to the second floor and then follow the ramp to the main level. David paces in his office but looks relieved when I enter. He orders me to sit across from him and takes his seat at his desk.

"Look. I'm not sure how you learned about the promotions, but you must keep your mouth shut about them. They haven't made it public yet."

"Wait. What? What promotions?"

"Come on, let's not play games. I don't have time for this."

"Neither do I. Nobody told me anything about any promotions."

David stares in disbelief.

"Look, Zena. It's you and me. Kitten, I've got your back. I know you've told others."

"I still don't get what you're talking about. If I overheard anything about promotions, I'd never tell anyone. Not even you, much less anyone else. I'm not stupid, David. Central Intelligence trained me to keep everyone's secrets. Full stop."

"Story is you're spreading the word about something you shouldn't even know. Tell me where you learned this information. We can deal with your source. It's my duty to go to Commander and disclose ... this situation."

"Do that. Tell him. I'm telling you the truth. I don't know what you're talking about. If it's something I shouldn't be privy to, then please don't tell me."

"I don't want to make trouble for you. Tell me how you found out, and I'll do whatever I can. Let me help you. I can quash this before it goes any further."

"I don't need help because I didn't do what you allege. And I'm not afraid of trouble. I'm innocent. I can't confess to something when I'm not guilty."

David shakes his head.

"I must report this."

"Please do. You should do your duty."

I stand, pivot, and then leave without a word.

I've wasted the entire afternoon replaying my conversation with David. He was honest, and I knew that without reading him, even if his accusations were baseless. Did he believe his own words, or was he testing me, tricking me to find out if I knew anything? I was often party to that kind of grilling. People will often tell you more if they believe you already possess incriminating evidence.

I can't concentrate on the Book and its ominous finale. I suppose Commander will want a word with me soon.

§

Commander pops upstairs to invite me to dinner. I wonder if David has already spoken with him or if he even intends to. If Commander knows something, he's an expert at hiding it.

When we arrive for dinner, I notice David and Frank aren't in their usual seats. We join the Inner Circle in the private diner and make small talk until the servers bring our plates.

"Are you enjoying your new quarters?" asks Tom.

"Yes sir, there's plenty of room to move around, and I love the writing desk and the cabinet space, although I don't have much to fill it. There's even enough space to dance. My new bed is a vast improvement over the cot, and my quarters are starting to feel like home."

That's not true. No amount of paint or different furniture can disguise the room's former use. I appreciate what Commander gave up, but in my mind, it remains a former playroom.

I study Commander to sense any regret, but his genuine, pleasant manner eases my fears and I reason it's safe to ask for a little more.

"There's something else I'd like," I say.

"Ask," says Commander.

"I need another art pad and maybe more charcoal or colored pencils."

"Are you still drawing? I'd like to see your work sometime."

"I enjoy doodling when I'm problem-solving. One day, I'll show you some of my drawings."

"I'll talk to Cross. When something comes in, he'll set it aside for you. In the meantime, I'll tell him to have someone check inventory," says Dan.

"Thank you, Major Matthews."

I should have figured David would be involved in securing my art supplies, but I wasn't thinking. I've grown sloppy since regaining my memories. As Zena, I was far more careful.

Dan smiles. "I think it's all right if you call me Dan ... in private."

He raises his eyebrows at Paul and Tom. They turn to Commander, receive affirmation, and nod in agreement.

"Sure, in private ... call me Tom."

"You can call me Paul," says Paul, and I wink at him. I already call him by his given name in our private meetings, and he hasn't admonished me yet.

Commander doesn't speak. He touches my hand under the table, and I sense he's pleased when he nods in approval.

I'm blessed with an abundance of good fortune. Zena wanted this so much. Now I have everything I wanted, and I'll have to leave. Sometimes you get what you want.

Chapter 39

Breakfast comprises oatmeal, maple syrup, and two thin slices of toast with a scant touch of butter, for the third day in a row. Word has it the staff is conserving eggs and other items until the snow lets up. I'm happy with oatmeal. And no Tracker.

When I arrive at the office, Cassie appears in a pleasant mood for a change. With uncharacteristic glee, she informs me I'm to report to the meeting room as soon as I come in. She says I won't need to bring anything. Just show up.

I walk in after knocking, finding the meeting in full swing. Everyone stops talking to stare, except for David, who avoids looking at me. It's obvious he fulfilled his promise to report to Commander. The usual welcoming faces have turned serious. I sit and wait for the show to begin.

"Zena," Commander says, shakes his head, and taps his finger on the table. "I've received some troubling information. As you're aware, promotions are coming up ..."

"I didn't know."

"You didn't know," Commander says if he doesn't believe me. "It's come to my attention that you told a couple of people that ..."

"I told no one because I knew nothing, and I still don't. I have no idea who's being promoted, so I couldn't have spread any rumors."

"Look, I'm not concerned with you passing on a bit of gossip. I'm only interested in where you got your information. Did you overhear something, or did someone tell you? I appreciate honesty over everything. How did you find out?"

"Find out what?"

Commander lets out an irritated sigh.

"Come on, Zena. I'm not angry yet," he says, like a warning.

"I was unaware of any promotions until Lieutenant Cross accused me yesterday of leaking privileged information. And as I told him, I know better. I'm trained to keep my eyes and ears open, and my mouth shut."

I fold my arms across my chest and take a deep breath.

"Most of the people I talk to are present at this meeting. And none of them spilled any secrets. I eat my meals alone unless you invite me to join you. The military people in the cafeteria ignore me. And even if I overheard someone, which I didn't, who would I tell? And why would I?"

Commander stares at me, bewildered. I turn my attention to David. I read him and he's not happy.

"Lieutenant Cross, who informed you I told him this secret?" I ask.

David wets his lips but doesn't answer.

"Come on, David. Help me figure out what's going on."

David looks to Commander who nods.

"Sergeant Wolf congratulated me. I questioned him about where he got his information, and he alleged a woman overheard some girls in the shower room talking about how you were spreading confidential information. She reported to him her concern that you had ... loose lips."

"And she is?"

"He didn't say. She's not in trouble. She did the right thing, bringing it to Sergeant Wolf's attention. We rely on personnel coming forward to report such leaks."

"I see. Well then, I'll find out who's spreading malicious lies about me."

I get up and walk out.

It took me an hour to walk off my anger. This is a job for Supersleuth. Or Zena the Warrior. Boxing gloves are off.

The quiet cafeteria is almost dead until several officers trail in for lunch. Lucky for me, Greg is an early bird and I have just the worm for him. Before he can get in line, I approach him.

"Hey Greg, how are you?" I say in my sweetest voice.

He eyes me with suspicion. I snuggle up to him and whisper in his ear.

"I'm really hungry. But not for food. Want to take a walk? I think we're well enough acquainted now."

Greg's face breaks out in a wide grin, but he steps back.

"I thought you were Commander's girl now."

"Well, he never minded sharing Mary Jo with you. He doesn't keep me in a cage."

His smile widens.

"You Play now?"

"Hmm, something better. I can't promise to Play but I promise to blow your ... mind."

I lick my lips as he glances around.

"Let's go."

He doesn't put his arm around my shoulders as he guides me to the closest Comfort room. He looks around again and opens the door, and I forget my fear of Comfort Rooms. I'm too angry. In the middle of the small room, I pull him close and kiss him. Hard. He pulls back in surprise.

"Kissing really gets my motor started. Come here, soldier. I won't hurt you. Get me in high gear. I've been wondering what those lips taste like since the moment I met you."

Greg moves in close and lets me teach him the joys of kissing. I join with him. He's unaware of me or time passing, but now his secret about who spread the rumor is mine. I let him go.

I push him away.

"Why did you lie to Lieutenant Cross? I thought we were friends."

"What?"

"You know what. You told him I was spreading rumors."

"That's what I heard."

"Fuck you."

I storm out of the Comfort Room, leaving a dumbfounded Greg to pleasure himself.

§

Military staff continue to trickle into the cafeteria, and I get in line right behind a very nervous Mary Jo. She turns around and I give her a warning glare. I'm close enough to read her and discover the name of her accomplice. This was easier than I expected. The list is short.

I study Mary Jo while I eat. Greg returns to the cafeteria and stops by her table to chat. They both look over, frowning. I wave but keep a straight face. I'm finished with my meal and this part of my investigation, so I head upstairs.

Cassie watches me march right up to her desk and stand there.

"Let's take a walk, Cassie," I say.

"I can't leave my desk."

I raise my voice and say, "Well, fine. We can talk right here."

She blanches and makes the wise decision to get up and walk around. We move into the rotunda just outside the office. It's deserted at the moment and if we keep our voices low, we'll have privacy.

"I asked you once what you have against me. It's clear why Mary Jo dislikes me. Maybe it's time you enlightened me."

"Why do you need a reason? Can't I just dislike you?" she says in a snippy tone.

"Oh, I don't care how you feel about me. That's your business. But when you spread lies about me, you've crossed a line."

"I didn't spread any lies."

"No, you gave Mary Jo the ammunition she needed. She fired the gun."

Cassie glares at me.

"Prove it."

"We will."

Cassie steps back.

Commander stands in the doorway. "What are you two hens clucking about?"

Cassie returns to her desk, and Commander asks me to come into his office. I sit and watch him take his seat. I read him and he's not angry that I walked out of the meeting.

"How's your investigation going?" he asks.

"I'm making progress."

"I understand you took Sergeant Wolf into a Comfort Room."

"Yes, I started my investigation with him. I wanted to have a private conversation."

"How'd that go?"

"I'm not sure. But I got a lead. I'd rather keep that to myself until I verify."

"I believe you're innocent, but I can't play favorites in these matters. Optics are important. We'll get to the bottom of this."

§

I still can't concentrate on my report. The Master Plan doesn't interest me. I don't need any enemies. I have enough problems.

Paul comes upstairs even though we haven't planned to meet. He sits down next to me.

"You walked out of the meeting."

"Yes, I need to find out who wants to hurt me and stop them."

"Any ideas?"

"Sure, but I wish I had someone to confide in and advise me. Someone who understands this culture better."

Paul appears hurt so I touch his arm.

"I appreciate I can talk to you, but you're too close to the situation. If I'm right, it will be difficult for all of us, and if I'm wrong, it'll be worse for me. When I figure it out, I will come to you first, I promise."

"Why would it be bad for you? How are you involved? Tell me. I can help you."

"As I see it, I have two major problems. One, someone wants to hurt me. Sully my name. Get me thrown out or punished. Make y'all mistrust me. I'm not sure of their end goal. They were certain to attach my name to this rumor. By the way, is there truth to this rumor? I don't want you to disclose anything confidential. Just whether or not it's true, because that makes a difference."

"It's true. But why would someone want to hurt you?"

216

"A couple of people here really dislike me, one with fair reason, but I'm clueless why the other has a problem with me. As Commander's girl, there's a downside. I imagine every woman on this base wants to be Commander's girl. For a civilian like me, not even one of their own, chosen ..."

"So, you think it's a woman spreading the rumor?"

"I'm sure of it. I'd like to think some officers are upset I'm no longer available," I say with a presumptuous smile, "but they'd never pull crap like this. Their careers and reputations are more important than one little woman like me. They have far too much to lose. A woman, on the other hand ..."

I squint at Paul with that knowing look.

"A jealous or scorned woman is a dangerous creature," I say. "I'd rather tackle a grizzly bear. Women fight dirty. I prefer not to fight at all. Not over a man."

Paul laughs and then becomes serious again.

"You said there were two problems."

"Yes, someone knows something they either shouldn't be privy to or shouldn't speak about. If David is up for promotion, as he suggested, he would never tell anyone. He's too smart for that. But someone talked and someone heard and used it to their advantage against me. I've identified the culprits, but I have no hard evidence."

"Tell me anyway. I'll keep it between the two of us. We'll investigate."

"No, you don't understand. Without proof, I can't breathe a word. I'm grateful you believe in me, and that's enough. My concern is that they haven't finished with me. I have no desire to try to keep one step ahead of them."

"Again, anything you confide stays between us."

"I have a question. When you discussed promotions, did you only do so in a closed session? Do you ever discuss confidential matters in your staff meetings? I've come into the break room, and I've heard voices coming from your cubicle. Usually, the talk is about sex," I say with a wink.

Paul laughs.

"Occasionally, I've walked by your office to the supply cabinet while you're in conference with others, and although I don't pay attention, I overhear some of your work-related conversations. I spend most of my time upstairs, so I'm unaware of who comes into the office during the daytime. I'm only aware of three women. Cassie, Jen, and me. But again, I don't see everything."

Paul cocks his head and squints.

"You think it was Cassie or Jen?"

"I'm not saying. I need proof. Without it, they win."

§

By dinnertime, there's a sullen mood in the cafeteria. Mary Jo's absence is noticeable. Greg sits alone at a table that seats four. When I glance at him, he looks away. Jen, Lynn, and another woman avoid looking in my direction. There's no laughter or giggling at their table now.

Chapter 40

I eat breakfast alone, as usual, with the cafeteria almost to myself. My oatmeal soon disappears. Last night, I tossed and turned, and when I fell asleep, my dreams were full of doom and gloom. I need my new alliance, but it's tricky going against these women who have established themselves in the trenches of Commander's high-level faction. They have years of devoted service. I'm a newcomer.

When I arrived at work yesterday, Cassie had a smug look on her face. By lunchtime, her self-assured manner had shattered, and she looked miserable. Perhaps Commander had questioned her, and she was worried, but her face gave no clue of the outcome. At lunch, Mary Jo was still a no-show. Greg still ate alone with his back to me. By the end of the workday, Cassie's desk was cleared off. She was gone. And Mary Jo never showed up at dinnertime.

As I walk toward the office, I notice a Specialist I've never seen before sitting in Cassie's chair behind her desk. She looks up at me and her pleasant smile is like sunshine on a rainy day. I stand before her desk, ready to show my badge to this unfamiliar cheerful woman with short-cropped red hair framing a freckled face.

"Miss Roberts, I presume."

"Yes. I work upstairs."

"I know. My name's Helen. I arrived at Cavalry yesterday. This is my first day, and I'm excited to meet you. You're a legend at Central. I worked on the fourth floor, but news of the civilian woman who made it to a top position in the labs traveled to our offices. You're a great inspiration to all of us."

"Well, Helen, I'm pleased to meet you, too. I'll try to live up to my name."

I grab a cup of coffee and, from the break room window, I see Commander is not at his desk. Excellent. He must be upstairs.

I bound the apartment steps as fast as I can without spilling. Commander and Paul are scarfing up the sweet little cakes, but they've left two orange cubes for me. I stuff one in my mouth and wash it down with my hot coffee. The orange tangy flavor is a welcome treat after the bland oatmeal.

"I met Helen. She seems very nice," I say, settling into my spot by the sink.

"Yes, she had a lot of praise for you. It seems you had quite a reputation at Central."

I wait for one of them to tell me what's happening, but they both sit there smiling and enjoying their treats.

"Okay. I've noticed a few changes around here."

"A couple," Paul says.

Commander nods and flashes a mischievous grin.

"You're going to make me work for answers?"

The men exchange amused expressions.

"You're good at figuring things out," Commander says.

"So, Helen is our new receptionist, and I haven't seen Mary Jo in the cafeteria for a couple of days. Sergeant Wolf doesn't look happy."

"Mary Jo and Cassie have transferred out. I demand honesty and loyalty from my troops," Commander says in a serious tone. "I won't tolerate less."

"How did you discover it was them?"

"We followed your lead. You talked to Wolf. So did we. We noticed a rift between you and Mary Jo and questioned her. You had a chat with Cassie that looked serious."

"So, you interrogated them. Did they tell the truth?"

"Not at first."

That sounds ominous. I let his words sink in for a minute.

"I realize Cassie and Mary Jo were special to you," I say to Commander. "They served you for a long time, so I hated implicating them. I knew, but I had no proof. It was a sticky situation."

"I'm disappointed in Cassie. She was good at her job. I sensed she didn't like you, but that's fair. Nobody is required to like everyone they work with. But plotting to hurt someone like that is unconscionable. Especially conspiring to hurt somebody I care about."

I gulp.

"We have no idea how she learned about the promotions. She wouldn't say. It appears few people were in on their conspiracy. If I find out different, I'll deal with them."

Commander rubs his chin.

"You may as well be advised. In a couple of months, we'll be announcing several promotions. Our First Lieutenants will move up. They've been part of our meetings for a while now. They've been training their replacements for over a year. Cavalry is growing. We have more men joining us each year than retiring. Without Andrew, we've had to shoulder more responsibility, and with the growth, it makes sense to expand at the top."

I nod in agreement.

"It was important to keep this quiet. It's not a big secret *per se*, but we didn't want the candidates for First Lieutenant to know we were testing them. No real harm. But I need to trust those closest to me."

"Yes, sir, you do. Thank you for trusting me with the truth. My lips are sealed," I say, running my finger across my lips like I'm zipping them shut.

The officers leave, and I stand at the window to connect with the voices. If my luck holds, there won't be any scary news this morning. The voices' chatter is meaningless until one mentions the progress being made in clearing the roads with the improved weather. Bad news, but they'll have twelve bases to search and hopefully it will take forever. It affords me time to create a plan, although I've had difficulty doing that so far. I pray providence doesn't desert me.

Chapter 41

An uneasy feeling shadows me all morning. I arrive for work and find Commander and Paul in a cheerful mood, but the nagging gloom persists. My orange cakes are too sweet, the coffee too strong, and inside I want to scream. But on the outside, I play the part until they leave.

Now, alone in the apartment, I turn on my meditation music and hasten to the windows to slip into my transcendental state, trusting my intuition. I muster all my gumption and tune into the voices. After an hour of listening, I return from my transcendence empty-handed, but the specter of doom remains ever present despite this sunshiny morning.

The melting of the snow is gradual, but the landscape retains its glistening white covering. I see tiny patches of blueish evergreens poking through the top layer. The sliver of snow clinging to the windowsills shrinks, leaving puddles of water.

The foreboding lingers and a disturbing memory creeps into my mind. I catch my breath as I sink into the flood of images and feelings, flashing back to a quiet summer day in my life as Caroline, which began like most. A gripping dread foreshadows a turning point, and I sense my life twisted upside down....

§

Brandon and Josh headed out that morning after an early breakfast. I kissed him goodbye as usual, and Kyra and I set upon our chores. We cleaned the kitchen and planned the menu for the day, then made our respective beds.

Finished with our tasks, we took a break before starting lunch. We hoped the men would return in time to eat with us. We sat sipping hot tea at the upstairs kitchen table. From the window, we watched a bird tend to its nest.

Brandon returned alone.

The panic on his face screamed trouble. Before I could ask where Josh was, he blurted out the horrible news.

"Caroline, we need to hurry. Someone shot Josh. I left him at Walt's place and it's a two-hour trek. They're treating him best they can, but there's no doctor or medicine."

The three of us made the journey to Walt and Milly's farmhouse in a little over an hour, half running, half walking fast. When we arrived, Milly was standing outside, and her face told me what I didn't want to hear.

"I'm sorry, honey. We did all we could. He was hurt real bad."

Milly tried to hug me, but I pushed past her. Maybe I could have saved him if I had arrived sooner. I never attempted to use the Gift to heal someone else and wasn't sure it was possible, but I'd have tried. I would have done anything.

Inside, Josh's body lay on the couch, and I ran to him, desperate to find some sign of life. He appeared different in death. Not like in the movies. He no longer looked like my Josh, and I knew it was too late.

I screamed. It wasn't fair. It was too soon. He was only fifty-one. We had plenty of time left and I loved him so much I couldn't stand living a single hour without him.

They told me I collapsed on the floor next to his body and the rest remains a blur. I must have spent the night there. That day was foggy. I half remember a service where everyone said something kind about Josh. I couldn't speak. Walt and Brandon buried my lover, my best friend, near a flower garden out back.

The following day, Brandon, Kyra, and I returned home. Brandon told me it was an accident. A hunter shot Josh, and he doubted the man knew what he'd done. It didn't matter.

The house hadn't changed, but it felt different and empty. I walked around, looking for Josh, knowing he was forever gone, but refusing to accept it. He had to come back. What about his books, his music treasures, and everything we shared? What about me?

I took to my bed, our bed, where I slept alone for the first time in thirteen years. Kyra made me eat food I didn't want and couldn't taste, and I spent the rest of my time in bed, hugging Josh's pillow, and praying to a god I didn't believe in, for this to be a dream. No, a horrible nightmare, but I'd wake up soon, and tell Josh how awful it was and how thankful I was he's still here.

I kept looking for Josh. My memories haunted me day and night. The couch where we read our books together, the kitchen table where we shared thousands of meals and conversations. Our bed where we made sweet love.

The house was so empty and quiet. I waited and watched for him to appear, even though I knew his body was buried on Walt and Milly's farm.

His side of the bed stayed cold and his empty chair at the table stuck out like a swollen red sore thumb. I listened for his voice, but he was silent. He'll never hear me tell him how much I loved him and how much he meant to me, and I never got to say goodbye. I'll never see him again. I told the walls, the furniture he sat on, and the bed we slept in, how much I missed him. And how much it hurt.

That happened fifteen years ago, and I now remember it as if it was yesterday. The dark days turned into darker months. Every morning when I woke, the nightmare defied the sunshine, and my world remained soaked in miserable darkness. The house was silent.

Kyra and Brandon suffered, too. We were a family, and we understood one another's grief, but I held nothing but emptiness and blackness inside me. Even the Gift couldn't heal this. I couldn't offer them comfort, but they had each other.

Months passed, and I made a gradual return to my empty shell of a life. My sorrow, my constant companion, never left my side. I removed my artwork from the downstairs level and packed Josh's clothes and belongings. I stored them in the closet with Laura's effects. If I believed in the afterlife, I'd see the irony of them ending up together once more.

Angry at the world, I cursed the Gift, but deep down, I realized it was necessary to continue living because of my vital purpose. I came this far and understood my obligation to keep the Gift from the aliens until they're all dead. If I died, what would happen to the Gift? Would it transfer itself to Brandon or Kyra? Or would it die too and complete my mission? I didn't know. I couldn't risk taking a chance. This was my responsibility, not theirs, and I'd never inflict my burden upon anyone else. Humanity depended on me, but I was so tired.

My body started aging faster. My hair turned white. It was safer because the Captors ignored older folks. I hadn't encountered another Tracker in many years. After two years, I gathered my belongings, packed my stored suitcase, and left. The memories and familiar surroundings kept me despondent. Kyra and Brandon understood and although they begged me to stay, I knew it was time. We had one last dinner together. Josh's home was theirs now.

I hoped a change of scenery would snap me back to life. It didn't. I traveled for three more years, weary and afraid to love. On some bitter days, I was ready to walk to the Captors' base to give myself up. Those were the bleakest periods in my life, and fate kept me from finding the Overlord home bases. I felt every bit of my hundred and forty years.

It was time to make a grave decision. It made no sense to continue wandering, and I had lost my will to live. Traveling was difficult, with no reward. I had stopped taking care of myself and took too many risks. Perhaps I was daring fate to do what I lacked the courage to carry out.

My first destination was the cemetery where my whole family was buried and I spent an entire afternoon reliving memories and saying my goodbyes, apologizing for deserting them, and never checking on how the great-grandchildren fared. The skies turned as dark as my mood and rain poured down on my tears, washing them away.

I returned to Milly and Walt's farm to say my final farewell to Josh. Milly hardly recognized me at first. I looked older than she did. They invited me to eat with them and I enjoyed my first decent meal in so long. We talked about Josh. She chided me for letting myself go, insisting Josh wouldn't approve. He loved me and would want me to live well. I had already made my decision. I hugged Milly for the last time and said goodbye to Walt.

In a deserted town, I salvaged an old but sturdy backpack and several pieces of clothing someone left behind. Then I chose a white dress with a matching tie, folded it with care, and stored it in my backpack. I packed some fruit I had picked, crackers I found sealed in a tin box, stale, but edible, and a pack of matches that I slipped into an inside pocket.

I chose another white dress for my rebirthing pilgrimage. After shedding my travel garments, I dressed in the soft white dress and returned to our cave, carrying my backpack and a discarded old navy blue blanket. I moved the brush aside and entered the cave. The memories of our explorations brought tears to my eyes. I felt Josh's spirit in the familiar surroundings. This was our getaway, our playground, our special place. Soon it would be Josh's birthday. Happy birthday, babe.

I knew this once magical place. But the magic died. Without my lover, the cave felt cold, damp, and hostile. A suitable place to die.

I went straight to our flat rock, where we shared many picnics. Where we made love. I spread the old blanket over our love rock and prepared myself. I wiped away my tears, removed my dress, draped it across the blanket, and curled up on the covered rock in a fetal position.

This time, I chose to be reborn with a child's body. The Tracker wouldn't be searching for a child. The Gift allowed me to bury all my memories, beyond the knowledge that the Captors were my enemy. They were dangerous, and I needed to stay far away from them. I'd be unconcerned but would realize I had a mission and I'd have faith that I'd understand my purpose when it was time. I'd be aware of my Gift and have Knowing when I needed it to protect me, to help me fit in, and establish a new life without remembering my past.

It was risky, but I couldn't continue, losing the ones I love, having to leave each new family, and having to live with my sorrow. My depression was choking me, and I was existing on the fumes of knowing that humanity was counting on me to fulfill my destiny. Even if they would never know. I may not have chosen this, but I committed to seeing it through. I had to stay hidden and complete my mission. Nothing else mattered. Saving humanity was paramount.

I was wrong all along. Caroline didn't have anyone out there to help her. No one was waiting for me. I am alone.

§

Commander bounds upstairs and finds me sitting by the window with streams of tears trailing down my cheeks. I look up at him, unable to mask the deep sorrow I feel. He squats next to me and studies my face.

"Something happened?"

"No, no ... well, it happened long ago. I'm remembering."

He nods in sympathy, stands, and motions for me to get up, offering an arm to help me. He pulls me to him for a long hug. I put my hand between my face and his shirt, not wanting to mess up his uniform with my tears and runny nose. I suspect he believes I'm grieving for Andrew, and I can't say otherwise. If Andrew's agony was anything this awful, then I forgive him. He chose his way out, but that's not an option for me. I must live to complete my mission.

Before Russ died, we had discussed aging. He insisted he had no regrets in his life and accepted the fact that the remainder of our time together might be short. He believed in God and the afterlife and said he was ready, but I wasn't, so I lied, knowing I had the Gift and might live much longer.

I never told Russ about the accident, the alien entering me, giving me the Gift, or what I intended to do. I had wondered if it was possible to save him if he succumbed to disease or accident, and I didn't know if I could give him part of the Gift.

It kept me alive and healthy and allowed me to heal myself, but I never had the chance to test it on anyone else. I needed to carry on, because I had an important responsibility, and I planned to join him when I completed my mission.

I always believed I could save Andrew by bringing him out of his darkness, so word of his death was devastating. Someday he'd find me, and I'd be his strength when life became too painful to keep going. I had so many childish fantasies about our reunion. Like Andrew surprising me at Mountainview, Central, or even here. He'd walk in and tell me how much he missed me, and I'd run into his arms and tell him I missed him, too. We'd be best friends and ... that will never happen. Death is final.

Commander walks me to the couch and orders me to sit with him. He cups my face and looks deep into my eyes.

"Honey, Andrew had serious problems that he hid from most people, but we believed he had a handle on it. It was the worst day of my life when we discovered what he'd done. Dan found him and we all witnessed what he did to himself. We held each other together. The five of us were close friends for almost twenty years. Losing him took its toll. Every year around the anniversary of Andrew's death, we suffer our own ... what you call darkness. We mourn our old friend, but we pull each other through. Whenever you're hurting and need to talk about Andrew, come to any of us, and we'll listen. It's been over five years for us, and it still hurts like hell, but you only recently learned of his death."

I crawl into his arms, pressing myself against him.

"I read to him and sometimes sang or danced. We had long talks, having plenty of time between meals and naps," I say, smiling and remembering. "Andrew would slip into dark moods sometimes, not wanting to eat or talk. He was in a lot of pain. I'd lie with him in his hospital bed and stay with him until his storm passed. As his pain lessened, so it seemed, did his mood swings. I begged to go to rehab with him, to help him, but he insisted I couldn't, and he'd have plenty of help there. I loved him so much."

Commander brushes the hair from my wet face.

"I'm glad he had you to care for him. Andrew recovered from his injuries, but he was a changed man. We tried to pull him along with us because we all dreamed of working together. When I won commandership here at Cavalry, I brought my friends in. They all worked hard and moved up, but Andrew lost a year recovering from his significant injuries. That threw a wrench into our long-term plan. We were very close and sailed through several difficult times together. We thought we were unbreakable."

Sadness hangs like a shroud over Commander, and I swear I see a glistening in his own eyes, but I doubt he'd permit himself to cry.

"In my position here, I had no difficulty bringing Andrew to Cavalry and making him a part of my team. At first, everything went well, and we were a strong team. Everything was falling into place just like we planned."

Commander closes his eyes as if to block out an unwanted memory.

"At first, Andrew suffered from spells of depression and refused to see the doctor. He said he knew the way out. It was difficult for him to get up to speed with his responsibilities, but he was determined, and he succeeded. Then he met Jessica, shortly after she transferred here. She was military, but the most beautiful woman he'd ever laid eyes on. He was sweet on her for over a year. She was the joy of his life. It was the happiest I'd ever seen him. Then they started fighting, and his depression returned. Jesse asked me for a transfer, so I granted it."

Commander shakes his head like he's trying to jettison the past.

"We decided, all of us, that women were never to intrude on our lives, take more than we wanted to give, play with our friendship, or our wellbeing. Hell, fuck with our minds."

He clenches his jaw and stares at the wall with familiar cold eyes. But they soften again when he looks at me.

"Andrew seemed fine at first, but soon his depression worsened even though he tried to hide it. He couldn't fool us. But he powered through it before, so we ..."

"He should have sought help, Commander. There are treatments for depression. He took the coward's way out and we all suffer for it. I loved him and now I'll never see him again."

Fresh tears trickle down my cheeks.

Commander pulls me to him again and holds me. I've never seen this Commander before. Maybe I'm seeing Nate for the first time. I like this Nate.

Chapter 42

The past two weeks have been peaceful, inside the base and out. The snow has melted, the sun has shone every day, and I sense the forest waking. With Mary Jo and Cassie gone, I don't need to watch my back. Helen is a gift, so pleasant and accommodating. Every morning, she greets me with her sunshiny smile and wishes me well. She's already learned her way around, and we've had several interesting and enjoyable conversations, but I'm still careful about what I disclose. I have trust issues.

Helen worked as a secretary for a lawyer at Central. She jumped at the chance to transfer to Cavalry to work the front desk for the base commander. It was a huge deal for her, and Paul assured me she came highly recommended. He said she's a quick study, loyal to a fault, and young. An excellent combination. Sounds familiar, like how they used to describe me.

When I listen to the voices this morning, the excited chatter reveals the success of the Tracker.

He's here.

The tide is turning, and it's about to become a tsunami. He's been in our base complex for a while, but they don't mention which base by name. I continue to listen for as long as possible. I gather no further useful information. It's only a matter of time, and time's running out. I need to locate my enemy before he finds me. But how?

I'll need to leave soon. I've spun a thorny web, trying to serve my wants, along with meeting my needs. But I don't want to hurt Commander or David. And I'm tired of hurting. There must be a better way. It's not safe here, but I want to stay. I can't leave yet because I need more information. I solved the mystery of how I ended up in the cave, but I'm still lost.

Caroline had no destination in mind when she erased my memories. I'm no better off trying to survive outside than I am staying here, like a sitting duck, in my enemy's lair. I hated my life when I was on the run, always in transit, making friends, only to keep moving. There's no one out there waiting for me. No Resistance alliance. No Josh.

Caroline knew I had to keep moving, keep living, and finish the mission. She understood I couldn't continue, depressed and carrying the weight of all my losses. She also recognized that if I was unsuccessful, the fear of being compromised would be devastating. I'd die and take humanity with me. Should I fail, she wanted to die without fear. Apprehension, maybe, but not the burning fear of defeat. This is what I wanted.

I pass by Helen on my way to the break room.

"Commander wants to see you," she says in her cheery voice.

She taps on Commander's closed door. She opens it and waves me in, easing it shut behind me.

"Sit down. I need to discuss something with you. Relax, you're fine," he says, sitting back, with a faint smile. "I wanted to inform you we're having a visitor later today. We're expecting him around noon. He's an inspector sent by the Overlords."

My stomach tightens, and vomit threatens to erupt. *Mana-ta-ah*. The Tracker. He's here, and it's too late to escape. I thought I had more time. I'll never find a way to the outside and I can't leave Cavalry by transit ahead of his arrival.

"He's conducting an inspection. He wants to speak with all the women, both military and civilian, to ensure we're following the rules. We received short notice, but we're spreading the word. Military women understand the drill, but we want to make sure all civilians comport themselves according to protocol. I need to be sure you appreciate the gravity of this matter."

Oh, I do.

"It's not the time to air grievances. I realize you're still upset about your ordeal at Central with Colonel Wickmore. But that case is closed."

Commander sighs and seems to search for the right words.

"I understand. We can't reveal what really happens on the bases," I say. "How the laws don't apply to the upper ranks."

Commander looks distressed and shakes his head.

"Zena, I'm aware Central didn't handle the case very well. Bringing this to the Overlords' attention will only make it tougher for you, as well as the people you care about. They will install their own authority here and nobody wants that. Everyone suffers."

Commander pleads with his eyes.

"Zena, you have friends here. People you care about and those who care about you. I care about you. We all do."

"I care about you, too. I won't do anything to hurt you or my comrades."

Commander sighs with relief.

"There's something else, and I probably don't need to tell you. He must not learn about your project. Or that we have the Book in our possession."

"That's a given. How long is he staying?"

"I'm hoping he'll only be here a few hours. He has several other bases to visit, so I hope he'll be gone by evening."

"Can I stay in the apartment until he leaves?"

He holds his chin and taps his finger.

"You don't want to meet an Overlord member?" he asks, teasing.

"I'm not interested in this person even knowing I'm here. Does he know I'm here?"

"Probably not. I'm not inviting him to my apartment, so you can stay here. I'll bring you some food. What are you afraid of?"

"When Dan found me, I knew the Overlords were my enemy and my family was dead. I can't remember why, but I feel a strong sense of danger."

"The Overlords couldn't have killed your family. They are against any kind of killing except in self-defense. Perhaps they took your family, and you assumed they were dead. You were a child. You don't remember anything?"

"No, just that I fear them. I always have. I don't have any reason to talk to him, anyway."

"Okay, you don't have to meet with him. I understand. Stay here. Someone will bring you food and I'll check in with you. I'm not looking forward to this."

My thoughts go to Terry. Commander punished her for refusing to peel potatoes. Will she say something?

Chapter 43

The visitor, aka the Tracker, will arrive soon and the game of hide and seek will begin. I consumed a hearty early lunch and Paul promised to bring me more coffee later. I don't want to chance even sneaking downstairs to the break room. According to Paul, the inspector spent six days at Central, but this is a much smaller base, with far fewer women. I received no warnings from Mick. The Tracker is only interviewing women, so it's possible Mick was never informed, but that's improbable. My former team members made it a priority to stay in the loop. It's C.I.'s job to keep tabs on Overlord activity.

If everything progresses as planned, my nemesis will finish by late afternoon and move on. If he never realizes I'm here, I'll have dodged a bullet, giving me much more time to decide my future path. Perhaps there's a slim chance I may never have to leave at all. Once they are sure I'm not in this complex, they may move on. There's an immense world out there. They couldn't have searched the entire planet already, could they?

I've spent most of the day paying attention to both the voices and sensing his presence. So far, nothing on either front. I also meditated to determine if I could cloak my Gift's energy, so the Tracker has no clue I'm here. If I can, I'm not aware how.

Paul doesn't bring me coffee, but I assume he's busy with our guest. I need the Tracker's visit to go down without a wrinkle, so he's satisfied I'm not here. I've considered sneaking into the corridor and hiding on the lowest level. The thick walls might add protection, but if he follows me there, I won't be able to explain his absence after I kill him. And how would I handle the body? No, my best bet is to stay hidden until he's gone. He'll be talking to military and civilian domestic workers, not special consultants. I'm a unicorn, there's none other like me, so he won't be expecting me unless somebody blabs. If he finds me....

At last, Paul brings coffee. I've paced all afternoon and my nervous stomach craves caffeine. He sets the cup on the table and sits next to me. I've cleared my table and hid the Book, just in case. But it's not the Book the Tracker's interested in.

"Have you met him?" I ask.

"Yeah, he's young but very polite. His name is Taylor. Didn't give a last name. The Overlords have a different culture, that's for certain. He spoke for a long time with the third-floor cafeteria girls, meeting with individual staff members, which went well, and he's expected to interview the second-floor staff next. Seems more interested in the civilians, but he plans to meet with our women next. Seems like a decent sort. Has a diplomatic air about him."

I want to ask him why the cafeteria workers aren't their women, but I'm not in the mood for debate. Instead, I unwrap my food and dig in. A few months ago, I'd have needed to employ different tactics to avoid my enemy, but Commander and Paul are bucking Peace Force protocol to protect me.

"How long do you expect him to stay?"

"Bad news. He's asked for visitor quarters. Claims he wants to rest before traveling to his next destination. We invited him to the Officer's Mess, but he wanted to eat dinner in the third-floor cafeteria."

The Officer's mess generally caters to all male diners. He's looking for a female. The game moves to the next level.

"And? Are you accommodating him? To visitor quarters."

"I believe so, but you can remain here until he turns in. All night, in fact," he says with a wink. "He'll be on the third floor, so you're fine. Commander mentioned you're afraid of him, but you know we'll protect you. Relax."

"Thank you."

§

Commander brings me dinner and sits across from me while I eat.

"Looks like our visitor will stay overnight and leave in the morning. He's finished with his inspections and hasn't asked about you by name, so don't worry. It's almost over and soon he'll be gone."

I nod, but I won't rest easy until I receive news that my hunter left the complex.

"You can spend the night pleasing me," he says with a grin.

I give him a peck on his cheek.

"I'll take you up on that, but I need clean clothes. Later, when the base is quiet, I'll run to my room and get a fresh outfit and a nightgown."

"You won't need the nightgown," he says, while his bedroom eyes undress me.

"Stop. I'm eating," I say, with a playful, stern look.

"Our visitor is quite friendly, but he doesn't understand military

233

protocols. I suppose it's expected."

I wince. They'd make an exception for an Overlords member. He would expect special treatment and his wishes to be followed. And they would be.

"I'm going for a run, then I'll shower, and we can ..."

"Could you escort me to my quarters to grab some clothes? Stop by for me when you return from the gym? We can kill ... accomplish two goals at once."

"Sounds like a deal."

Commander disappears into his bedroom and several minutes later he reappears wearing his sweatpants, undershirt, and running shoes. I've finished eating, rinsed and dried the plate and silverware. He grabs the dishes.

"I'll drop them off on the way to the gym."

We walk across the rotunda to my room, and I keep careful watch. I expect the Tracker to stay on the third floor, but that doesn't mean he will. Commander waits for me to unlock my door. I scan the fourth floor one last time, making sure no monsters lurk nearby, before kissing Commander and promising to see him later.

Inside my room, after washing up, brushing, and selecting clean clothes, I realize I have an hour-long wait, so I curl up to relax on my bed, staring up at the ceiling. Two fixtures remain on the ceiling overhead that once suspended two rings. Why didn't they remove them?

I'm drifting off to sleep when I jerk awake, alerted to his presence. He's nearby, and he knows I'm here. He can't read my mind, but he senses me. I could read his mind, but tonight, he hides his thoughts. He's focusing all his awareness on locating me. It's too late.

I slip out of my quarters and head for a nearby hallway with corridor access. If I descend to the main floor, I'll be safer there.

"Hello, we finally meet."

I turn around fast, and I'm face to face with the stranger. He was closer than I thought. Game change.

"You have something we need. It doesn't belong to you. You've killed two of us already, but I won't be so easy to kill. And why would you do that? We only want what's ours. Please give me what I want or I'm taking you back with me."

"Commander, he wants to hurt me," I squeal.

He turns around to face an empty rotunda, and I run, heading for the elevators. He's close behind me, so I find a dark alcove and hide out of sight. I watch him walk to the elevators searching for me and I follow. The freight elevator is docked on the first floor. I get as close as I can without being seen, and with everything I possess, I join with his mind.

He sees me on the elevator, my back to him, the closed elevator gate between us. I can't see his face from here, but I can feel his delight in cornering me with nowhere to run and no escape. He opens the gate, watching me turn around in slow motion to face him. He steps into the elevator, but it isn't there and neither am I. His screams follow him down the elevator shaft to the main floor, and I return to my room unseen.

§

The numbers on the wall clock change so slowly, it seems time has almost stopped. No sound passes through the playroom walls. No sounds of frantic activity. Silence. I suppose pandemonium will occur on the main floor when they find his body. Maybe I can't hear it from here. I take deep breaths to steady myself. Commander will be on his way to collect me soon and spirit me back to his apartment. The hunter can't hurt me now, but I hate dealing with the aftermath alone. This never gets easier.

After gathering my clothes and toiletries, I wait for his knock. When Commander finally knocks, I tousle my hair like I've been napping, open my door, and yawn. We proceed to the office in silence. He unlocks the office suite door, and we head upstairs.

"How was your workout?"

"Great. What did you do while you were waiting for me?"

"I laid down to rest, not intending to nod off, and fell fast asleep," I say, "and woke up just before you knocked. I must have sensed your presence."

"Well, after my shower, you can take another nap. Much after ..."

He kisses me, then heads for the shower.

I select calming music, turn it low, and then collapse on the couch to wait for the bombs to go off. As Commander walks out of the bathroom wearing only a towel, his hand radio buzzes.

"What? How did that happen? Give me a few minutes. Just got out of the shower. I'll be right there."

"Poker game?" I ask, teasing.

"No, our visitor broke his neck. He's dead."

"What? Are you sure? How's that even possible? People don't just break their necks."

"They found him in the elevator shaft on the main floor. They think he may have fallen from the third floor, but no one knows why he wouldn't notice the elevator wasn't on that floor. I need to go. Something doesn't add up."

"Can I stay here until you return?"

"Yeah, sure."

Commander dashes to his bedroom while I curl up on the couch and take a deep breath to calm my nerves. The music doesn't help. Did anyone see me? Sean is usually out patrolling in the evening. But if it's quiet, like tonight, he stays in his MP office. I never saw a soul, so I hope he didn't either.

I wonder what happens to the alien when it leaves the body and can't enter another host. Does it go where human souls go when we die? Do humans have souls and are they similar to the alien consciousness?

Commander hurries into the living room dressed. He looks anxious but takes the time to give me a quick kiss.

"I might be gone a while."

"I understand. Go. I'll be fine. Wake me up when you get back if it's late."

He leaves and I return to the couch. I'm too unnerved to sleep, so I listen for the voices. I need to find out if the Tracker notified his home base before he died. If they know I'm here. If they realize he's not. Even if they're in the dark, it's going to be difficult to explain that their agent fell down an elevator shaft and broke his neck. I had no choice, but if they suspect I'm here and I killed him, then we're not safe. None of us. Game over.

Chapter 44

I crawled into bed alone, during the night. Commander hadn't returned, and sleep eluded me, so I slipped on my nightgown and slid under the sheets. I left the living room lights on low. I finally fell asleep after midnight. Alone.

Commander nudges me awake. I squint from sunlight streaming into the bedroom through the open door. He's dressed. Has he even been to bed? He looks haggard like he's been up all night.

"Did you get any sleep?" I ask.

"Not much. You were asleep when I got in. It was late, and I didn't want to wake you."

I yawn and stretch. "What happened to Taylor?"

Commander cocks his head.

"How did you know his name?"

"Paul mentioned it yesterday. He said Taylor introduced himself by his given name and no last name. He thought it was odd."

"We're doing an investigation, and I'm sure there will be an inquest. I'll contact Central later this morning. They'll inform the Overlords of the situation, and they'll send orders on how to proceed. Our doctor will conduct a preliminary examination, but I imagine the Overlords will have their coroners perform an autopsy. I can't understand how this happened."

Commander appears stressed. He's always in control, but now he seems like he's unraveling. No one wants the Overlords to descend upon the bases and take control. I didn't think this through. But what else could I have done? Taylor knew I was here. He came up to the fourth floor and sought me out.

"Get dressed, sweetheart. Today will be a long, difficult day."

After I wash up and dress, I meet Commander in the kitchen. A pot of coffee and three cups wait next to a saucer of sweets. An exhausted-looking

Paul already took his seat at the table, and someone poured me coffee.

"Aren't there lights by the elevator shaft on every floor? I mean, how could he not know the elevator wasn't there?" I ask, with convincing innocence.

"The lights were fine, but we found the fourth-floor gate open," says Commander.

Why didn't I close the damn gate?

"What was he doing on the fourth floor? I thought you said they gave him guest quarters on the third?" I ask.

"No idea. But the Overlords will soon swarm Cavalry demanding answers, so we must come up with a …" says Commander.

"Logical explanation," Paul says. He shakes his head in dismay.

"Right," Commander says. "Nothing like this has ever happened here. On any base. Ever."

Neither man touches the sweets.

§

Helen grasps the gravity of the situation. It's written all over her face. She informs me the officers are in an early morning meeting and I must join them as soon as possible. I thank her and head to the conference room.

Lieutenant West's assistant, Jason, has joined the meeting along with the night shift MP. Sean looks surprised when I walk in. I read him to find out if he spotted me last evening, and then sigh in relief.

"We're interviewing everyone who might have witnessed something yesterday on the fourth floor. The offices and Officer's Mess are closed at night. Club was closed, so no reason for any traffic on the floor," says Commander.

"We interviewed the women residing in the women's quarters and no one noticed anything. Commander vouched for you," West says to me. "When Sean made his last rounds, he saw no one and heard nothing. We also questioned everyone on the third floor. No one witnessed Taylor leave his quarters or knows how he ended up on the fourth. If he fell from there. You're good at thinking outside the box, as you say. Any clue how Taylor ended up dead in the elevator on the main floor?"

I've done nothing else but try to come up with a believable scenario. Something the Overlords would accept as true.

"He had no business on the fourth floor. How could he leave his room with no one noticing?" I ask.

"He was settled in for the night. We weren't guarding him, and no one noticed him leave," West offers.

"Nobody here has reason to harm the inspector, hence no motive. I haven't heard mention of any weapon like a gun or knife, and I assume he wasn't shot or stabbed, so we have no means. Since nobody engaged with him, where's the opportunity? Add it up and there's no evidence of a crime. So, my guess is it's an unfortunate accident," I say.

"The Overlords have a dead inspector, so that's not going to fly," says Jason. His bloodshot eyes suggest he pulled an all-nighter. West also appears to suffer from a lack of sleep.

"Perhaps he boarded the elevator from another floor, went up, exited thinking it was the third floor, accidentally sent the elevator down, and slipped and fell. It seems implausible to me, but I'm curious why he used the elevator in the first place. I would think he understands how they work since all our bases have elevators. I'd investigate his whereabouts earlier that night. Whether anyone on any floor observed him where he shouldn't be, unescorted," I say.

"We've done that," says West. "He had no business roaming around on his own. However, the Overlords won't see it that way. We're preparing the body for transport tomorrow. After they secure his remains, they'll do an autopsy and determine the cause of death. We'll be on lockdown until they decide their next course of action."

"And lockdown means?" I ask.

"No one leaves the base until further notice. Anyone planning to take leave will need to cancel. No transit trips and no salvage runs," Paul says.

"How will they retrieve the body?"

"We'll build a makeshift casket, and an honor guard will transport it to the tunnel's entrance to rendezvous with the Overlords," Dan says.

§

Back at the apartment, I encourage Commander to take a nap. Nothing more can be done today. I offer to join him, and he accepts. Once we remove our clothes and slide under the covers, I crawl into his arms. I want to make love in case it's the last time, but he's exhausted. Soon his soft snoring fills the bedroom.

I lie awake staring at the ceiling. What happens now?

An hour passes and I start to nod off. Commander reaches for me, folds me in his arms, and his mouth finds mine.

§

Everyone on Cavalry looks nervous and fearful. Word of Taylor's death must have traveled to every corner of the base. Commander had another meeting, so I eat dinner alone in the subdued cafeteria.

I walk down to the second floor to take one last look in case it all goes sour, smile at the friends I've made, and secretly say goodbye before taking the ramp to the main floor. David stands in his office talking to two officers. I hide and watch him, not wanting to talk to him, just to see him.

Cavalry often felt like a prison, and I felt alone, like I didn't belong. Now the familiar walls and faces feel like home.

I drink in every sight I can. When they take me, if they do, I won't have time to collect these memories.

Back on the fourth floor, I make one last visit to Cavalry Memorial. In the plaque room, I trace Tommy's name with my finger and pray a wordless prayer. He knows my heart. I do the same with Andrew's name.

I'm always saying goodbye.

Chapter 45

I learned the privates are constructing a makeshift casket in a small wood shop near the immense salvage drop-off room next to the loading dock on the first floor. When I sneak into the room, two privates are putting the finishing touches on the coffin. I hang back against the wall, and I watch.

Two uniformed men enter the chamber, each grasping an end of a zippered, black body bag. They walk to the makeshift coffin, and with care, they lower the deceased into his resting place. The black bag hides his death mask and his broken bones, and I fight the urge to take one last look, knowing I don't dare. They wouldn't allow it, nor would they understand. I'm not sure I understand.

The privates let me stay provided I keep out of their way, so I stand back, lost in silent thought, riveted by them performing their last duties. They position the top panel, and one worker secures the coffin lid in place while his partner wields the hammer. I make the sign of the cross, although I'm not sure I'm doing it right.

I count.

It takes nine strikes to drive the first nail flush into the improvised casket.

Eight nails await their turn, lined up in a row on the nearby stool.

A nail rolls off the stool, hitting the floor with a clink, leaving seven nails.

The first private grabs another nail and passes it with the hammer to his coworker to secure the opposing corner. Six whacks set the second nail.

The remaining nails require only five minutes to sink their four-inch lengths deep into the soft pine wood.

Three more young privates arrive, load the box onto a cart, and leave.

Two workers remain behind to clean up.

One looks my way and says, "It's finished."

Is it?

ABOUT THE AUTHORS

Gerry Conrad is an outsider artist from Cleveland, Ohio. To cope with the isolation of the COVID-19 pandemic, she envisioned a dystopian adventure of a young woman set in the future. At night, Gerry would relate the next installment of her story to her husband, writer Sam Conrad, who encouraged her to write it down as a novel. Together, they spun the tale into *The Awful Truth* series as a parable for our time.